Dauntless Protector

Book 1 in the Fierce Protectors Series

Jade Dollston

Copyright © 2022 by Jade Dollston

All rights reserved.

No portion of this book may be reproduced in any form without written permission from the publisher or author, except as permitted by U.S. copyright law. Short quotes for book reviews are acceptable. For permissions, contact: jdollston@gmail.com

Cover Design by Sammi Bee Designs

Cover Photo by Emma Jane Photos

Cover Model: Sterling Snedigar

Editing and proofreading by Chrisandra's Corrections.

Chrisandra, Master of the English Language, Commander of Commas, Princess of Punctuation, Goddess of Editing. That's actually on her birth certificate. True story.

This is a work of fiction. Names, characters, businesses and locations are either products of the writer's imagination or used in a fictitious manner. Any resemblance to actual persons, living or dead, is purely coincidental.

WARNING: THIS BOOK CONTAINS GRAPHIC SEXUAL CONTENT AND PROFANITY. READERS 18+ ONLY.

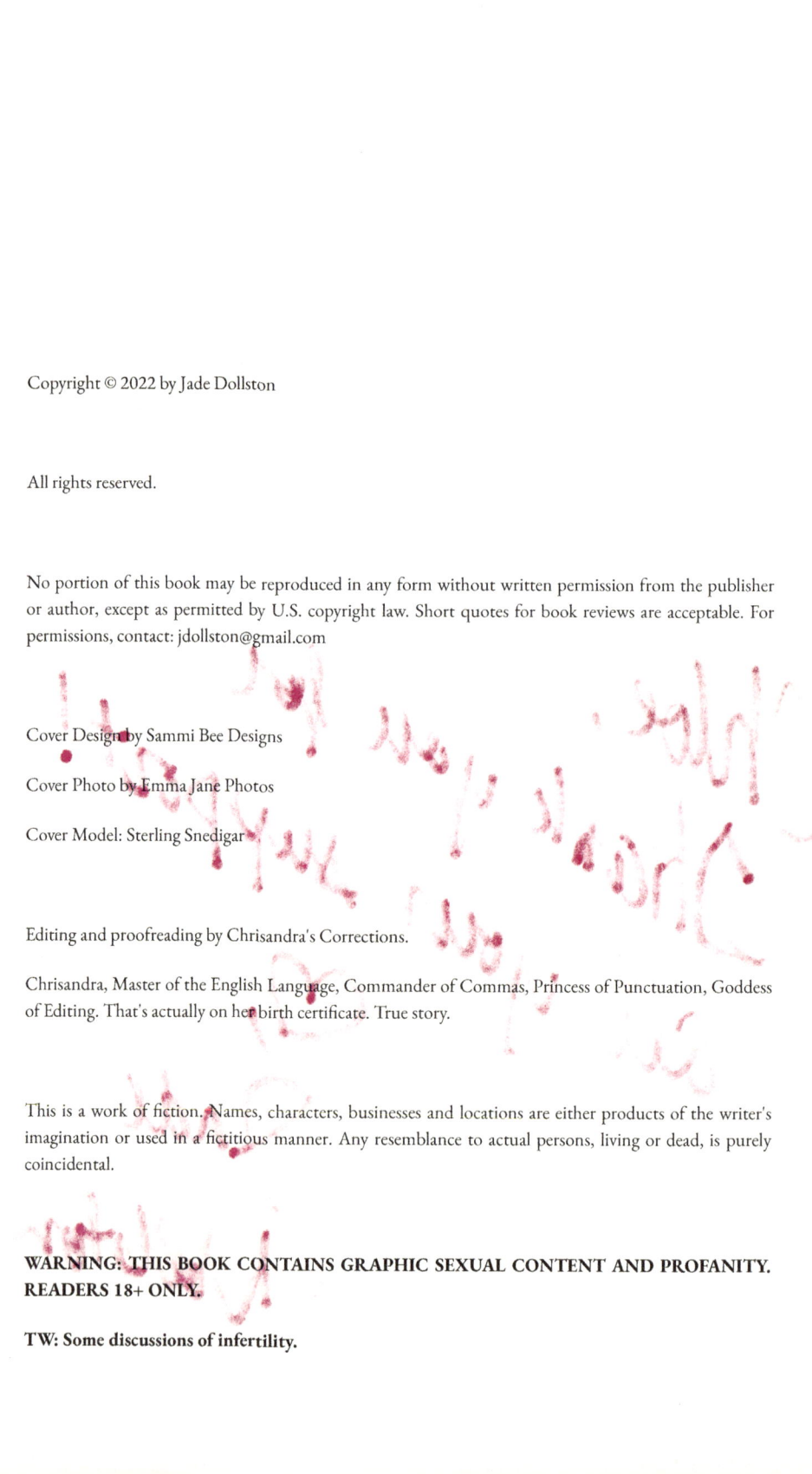

TW: Some discussions of infertility.

Contents

		VI
1.	Beau	1
2.	Beau	13
3.	Beau	19
4.	Charli	23
5.	Beau	27
6.	Charli	31
7.	Beau	35
8.	Beau	43
9.	Charli	51
10.	Beau	59
11.	Charli	65
12.	Charli	73
13.	Beau	79
14.	Charli	84
15.	Beau	88
16.	Charli	99
17.	Beau	105
18.	Charli	114
19.	Beau	127

20.	Charli	132
21.	Beau	140
22.	Beau	150
23.	Charli	157
24.	Beau	165
25.	Charli	171
26.	Charli	175
27.	Charli	184
28.	Charli	192
29.	Beau	199
30.	Charli	204
31.	Charli	210
32.	Beau	214
33.	Charli	223
34.	Beau	229
35.	Beau	235
36.	Charli	240
37.	Beau	245
38.	Charli	248
39.	Beau	258
40.	Charli	262
41.	Beau	267
42.	Charli	269
43.	Beau	276
44.	Charli	281

45. Beau	287
46. Beau	291
47. Charli	299
48. Beau	305
49. Beau	309
50. Charli	312
51. Beau	317
52. Charli	322
53. Beau	328
54. Charli	330
55. Charli	335
56. Charli	339
57. Beau	350
58. Charli	353
59. Beau	357
60. Beau	366
61. Charli	372
62. Two Years Later	376
Also By Jade	389
Playlist	391
Acknowledgments	392
About Author	395

"Those that go searching for love, only manifest their own lovelessness. And the loveless never find love, only the loving find love. And they never have to seek for it."

—Mark Twain

BEAU

"Happy *thirtieth* birthday, sis," I said a bit smugly, walking into my sister's house and kissing her on the cheek as I dropped my bag of groceries on the gray marble foyer table.

Blaire tossed her auburn hair over her shoulder, green eyes flashing with annoyance. "Do *not* mention that number to me ever again, jerkface."

I laughed, poking her in the ribs until she swatted my hand away. "You're gonna be as old as me pretty soon. Now, give me my niece." I took six-week-old Danica from my sister and kissed her sweet little head as we walked into the vast, high-ceilinged living room, dotted with soft, comfortable brown furniture. My sister and brother-in-law had more money than God himself, but their house was markedly... homey. "Hello, darlin'. Have you missed your uncle Beau?"

"She has. She was just telling me this morning," Blaire said with a grin. "Hi, Cam," she said, hugging my buddy who had walked into the living room behind me.

Camden Fitz and I lived together. We were former Navy SEALS, and I had opened my own security firm in my hometown of Dallas, Texas, a few years ago and hired Cam and four other members of our former team.

"Happy birthday, gorgeous. Where's Axel?" Cam asked, grabbing Blaire around the waist. "No, wait. Don't tell me. You've kicked his loser ass out so you can marry me, right?"

Loser ass. Yeah, right. My sister's husband was the top paid tight end in the NFL.

I heard Cam clear his throat and realized he was standing right beside me, staring at the young nanny. "I'm so fucking jealous of your nephews right now. She could check my muscles anytime. I have one in particular I think she would really enjoy," he said lasciviously.

"Cut that shit out," I grunted. "She's the kids' nanny."

"Well, she ain't my nanny," Cam retorted. Then his lip curled up on one side. "Actually, that's not such a bad idea. Do you think she would spank me if I misbehaved?"

"Shut the fuck up, Cam," I growled before I could stop myself.

"Why? What's the—" he started, but then stopped short and laughed in my face. "Oooh, you like her."

I shot him a withering glare. "No, I don't. I don't even know her, and you know she's not my type." This chick was way too... delicate. I needed any woman I was with to be able to handle me. I would break Charli in half with one hard thrust.

Jesus, why did the thought of that make my cock so fucking hard?

"Uh-huh. So, you wouldn't mind if I took her home and made her scream all night so you could hear it?" he asked, chewing one corner of his lip in an attempt to control his smile.

I did my best to tamp down the unexplainable rage I felt at his words. I had no interest in this woman... this *girl*. "Do what you want," I said, aiming for nonchalance, but failing miserably. "She's probably not even old enough to drink."

"Bet she's old enough to drink my..." I couldn't hear the rest of his sentence over the blood rushing through my ears, but I could fill in the blanks as I turned on my heel and stalked toward the house, throwing my shoulder roughly into Cam's for good measure. Once inside, I angrily—*why the fuck was I angry?*—snatched the bag of groceries from the foyer before heading into the kitchen.

I looked around the expansive kitchen filled with appliances that probably cost more than my truck, thinking that my little sister had done well for herself. She was fucking brilliant and had rocked her way through medical school and become an orthopedic surgeon. Axel played for the Fort Worth Wranglers and was well on his way to becoming a football legend.

I found a huge bowl and started to empty the hamburger meat into it. Tossing the empty packages in the trash can, I washed my hands before kneeling beside the cabinet where Blaire and Ax kept their spices. But there were no spices here.

There were just a bunch of plastic bowls and plates. I stuck my head a little farther into the opening, thinking that maybe Blaire had...

"Are you Beau?"

The voice from behind me startled me, and I jerked my head up, banging it on the cabinet. I said every curse word known to man, and I think I even invented a few new ones as I turned and sat on my ass on the Carrara tile floor. *Holy shit, that hurt!*

"Oh my gosh! I'm so, so sorry! Are you okay?" Through a rush of dizziness, I saw tan legs running toward me, and then someone knelt beside me. "Let me feel your head," a sweet voice said. I vaguely thought that if a peach could talk, this would be what it sounded like.

I must have hit my head harder than I thought.

A gentle hand felt along the back of my head, and I tried not to wince when it came across a knot. *Don't stop touching me.*

"You've got quite a bump, but it doesn't feel like it broke the skin. Lean forward and let me look." I tilted my head forward and smelled the sweetest, happiest scent I had ever experienced.

"You smell like rainbows," I heard myself utter. *What in the holy hell am I saying?* Apparently, traumatic brain injuries made me goofy as fuck.

A soft, tinkling laugh met my ears, and I smiled stupidly at the enticing sound, my chin pinned to my chest to encourage those soft hands to continue their exploration of my head.

"I smell like rainbows?" the peachy voice asked, and I nodded languidly. "Let me look at your eyes and make sure your pupils aren't dilated."

I lifted my eyes to meet hers, and... *Holy shit.*

Those eyes brought back memories from a lifetime ago.

Memories of my first day of Pre-K.

"Mommy," *I yelled, spotting her by the gate to my school, exactly where she'd said she would be. I waved and ran to her, and she squatted down, her arms wide to welcome me as I leapt at her.* "Hi, Mommy!"

"Hi, baby. How was your first day?" She kissed all over my face, and I didn't even care if anyone saw, not even stupid Kip Norris. I had the prettiest mommy in the whole world, and she could kiss me as much as she wanted.

"It was good, Mommy. I made a new friend named Camden, and I got to be the line leader when we went to the bathroom."

Her eyes got big like she was really excited. "Are you serious? That's fantastic, Beau." She rubbed her hand through my messy brown hair as she stood. "First day of school, and you're already a leader. I'm so proud of you."

I liked it when my mommy was proud of me. I wondered if my sister would be proud of me, too—well, when she was old enough to understand stuff like being proud. She was just a little baby now. I stood on my tiptoes to peer into the stroller beside Mommy.

"Hi, Blaire. You look so pretty today. I like your pink dress." My little sister laughed, her mouth open wide with her little pink gums showing. She always laughed when I talked to her, because I was her most favoritest person in the world. That's what Daddy told me, anyway. Daddy said it was my 'sponsibility to always take care of Blaire, 'cuz I was the big brother.

"You want to push the stroller?" Mommy asked, and I nodded eagerly, reaching up and putting my hands on the soft handle. "So, tell me all about your first day," she said as we started walking toward our house.

"We had snack time, and I ate all my apples."

Mommy smiled down at me. She had the nicest smile... pink lipstick and shiny, white teeth. "My precious little boy is always a good eater. You're going to grow up big and strong, just like your daddy." I felt my cheeks squishing up in a happy smile.

There's nothing I wanted more than to be big and brave like Daddy. He took care of everybody. Not just me and Mommy and Blaire. He took care of the WHOLE country because he was in the navy. I was going to be in the navy, too. But I had to eat all my food—even the gross broccoli—if I was going to be strong when I grew up.

"We got to play outside, and Kip Norris acted like a fartface."

"Beau Atwood! Watch your mouth!"

Uh-oh. I was in trouble now.

"But Mommmm, he pushed Maria Gonzalez down and made her cry. Her knee was bleeding and everything." I frowned at the thought. "I was going to punch him, but the teacher ran over there before I could get to him."

Mommy's hand rested on the back of my neck, her soft fingers playing with the new haircut I had gotten since I was starting big boy school. "Beau, honey. You can't go around punching people. What Kip did was wrong, but it's not your job to punish him."

I'd wanted to, though. I'd wanted to punch him until he fell down and scraped his knee, too. Just like Maria. Maybe that would teach him not to be such a stupid fartface.

"You let the teachers handle it, okay? I don't want to be getting phone calls from the school about you fighting. Do you understand me?"

She was using that Mom Voice that told me she wasn't messing around, so I nodded. "Yes, ma'am," I told her.

"Good boy," she said, her Mom Voice gone and her Nice Voice back in action. "What did you do after that?"

"The teacher let me walk to the nurse's office with Maria. The nurse was nice and put a Scooby Doo Band-Aid on Maria's knee, and then she gave us both a peppermint. And after we got back to our classroom, we had coloring time, and I colored a flower for you."

"Oh, my goodness! I can't wait to see it."

A few more blocks and we were at our house, and while Mommy unlocked the door, I pulled off my Captain America backpack and rummaged through it until I found my picture. For some reason, I felt shy as I handed it to her. "I got out of the lines a little bit," I said sadly, unsure if she would like it since I had messed it up.

Mommy took the picture and looked at it, and her big smile made me feel like I had sunshine in my belly. "I didn't even notice. I think it's perfect. Thank you, Beau. Let's go put it on the refrigerator so I can look at it every day."

"You really like it?" I asked. Oh, this was exciting! Maybe she would want me to color some more stuff. With my favoritest new crayon.

She squatted down so that her face was the same height as mine. She always did that when she had to tell me something important. Her pretty eyes were sparkling like green diamonds. I had green eyes too, and so did Blaire, but mine were darker green than theirs. "Beau, I love it so much. It's the best picture I've ever seen."

She pulled me into her hug, and I wrapped my arms around her neck and squeezed. Mommy's hugs made my chest feel warm. Her bronze hair tickled my nose, but I didn't care. She always smelled like red raspberries, so I snuggled my nose into her soft hair and sniffed. "I love you, Mommy."

Her eyes were all shiny when she kissed me on the nose. "I love you, too, son. You and Blaire are the most important people in my life."

"And Daddy?"

Mommy's pink lips curved up on the sides, and her cheeks got fatter and prettier. "Oh, I guess he's okay, too," she said, but I knew she was teasing. Her and Daddy smooched all the time when they thought I wasn't looking. And Daddy was always squeezing her and whispering stuff in her ear that made her giggle. Grownups were weird.

My mom put the flower picture right in the middle of the refrigerator with a letter B magnet—B for Beau. Then she fixed me a snack and set it on the round table by the kitchen. "Be right back!" I yelled over my shoulder. "I'm going to color some more since you liked my picture so much." I dug through my messy bookshelf until I found the coloring book I was looking for. It had lots of dragons and stuff in it, but I had seen a princess on one of the pages.

I bounced back into the kitchen and opened the page up to the princess with the big, floaty dress. "If I color this for Blaire, do you think we could put it in her room?"

"Of course, we can, sweet boy. Now, you color and eat your snack while I get dinner ready."

I dug my hand into my backpack and pulled out my box of crayons. I had been so excited when Mommy had let me get the ginormous pack of colors because there was a sharpener on the back. I opened the box, and all the colors made my eyeballs happy. Especially the blue one in the second row. The one I had used to color the flower picture.

I pulled it out verrrrrry carefully, so I didn't break it. "Mommy, what does this say? It's something blue." I could read a few words like 'blue,' but the first word was really long.

She came over and took the crayon from me. "It says 'cornflower blue.' It's really pretty, huh?"

I nodded my head so hard, my brain hurt. "It's the prettiest color in the whole wide world."

I started on Blaire's princess picture while Mommy cooked chicken sketti—the most delicious food ever invented. I made the princess's eyes green, but everything else, I colored with my cornflower blue crayon. Dress, hair, shoes, and even that crown thingy on her head. Honestly, it was some of my best work.

I smiled as I ran my finger over the poofy dress. Cornflower blue. I loved it so much.

I shook my head to dispel the bittersweet memory and looked directly into a set of blue eyes. Cornflower blue. *The prettiest color in the whole wide world.* Those beautiful eyes were set in a face so sweet, I was certain I could feel cavities forming in my molars.

Then I was damn near blinded when Charli shined a light from her phone into my eyes. "Your pupils are reacting fine. Do you want me to go get your sister?"

"No, Peach. I'm alright."

"Oh, um. My name is Charli. I'm the new nanny," she said, holding out her hand to shake mine.

As soon as I took her tiny, soft hand in my rough one, I felt a bolt of lightning shoot up my arm, and her eyes widened. *Did she feel it, too?* Not wanting to lose the feel of her, I slid my hand up her arm to her elbow and back down. I felt goosebumps pebbling her skin and found myself wanting to make that happen again.

But first, I needed to get off this floor and stop thinking about goddamn rainbows and peaches and cornflowers and shit. What the fucking hell was wrong with me? I was a former Navy SEAL for Christ's sake, and here I was sitting on the floor because of a little bump on the head and some mesmerizing blue eyes.

Cornflower blue eyes.

I motioned for her to move back, and when she did, I pushed myself to my feet. "I'm good," I said, rising to my full height over her. Damn, she looked even tinier when she was standing right next to me. I felt my body responding to her, wanting to hold her and protect her from... what? I had no fucking clue.

Her brow furrowed slightly as she looked up at me. "Are you sure? I can get you an ice pack." *Jesus, that voice.* Her little hand came up to rest sweetly on my cheek, and my eyes closed at the immediate connection I felt. Turning into her touch until my mouth was resting against her palm, I pressed my lips forward and kissed her there, just briefly. Her eyelids lifted and I heard her sharp intake of breath before she sunk her perfect white teeth into her luscious bottom lip.

That fucking lip bite combined with the smell and feel of her skin had my cock swelling in my shorts, so I stepped back before I did something colossally stupid. "I'm good," I repeated.

"I'm really sorry I startled you. Were you looking for the seasonings?" At my nod, she pushed around me, her face flushed a lovely shade of pink, and said, "We had to move them up higher. My mom walked in one day to find Dex emptying the whole bottle of paprika on the floor, and Max was trying to dump cinnamon into Rox's mouth." She laughed as she stretched one arm up into a high cabinet. "What do you need? Salt and pepper?"

I pulled my eyes away from her butt, which was rounder than I would have expected for such a petite girl. *Don't go there, dude. No ass thoughts right now. Your goddamn penis is already out of control.* "Yeah, and garlic salt and Worcestershire." She pulled down the dry seasonings and then stood on her tiptoes to try to reach the Worcestershire sauce on the top of the spice carousel, her fingers still several inches away from their target.

Without thinking, I stood behind her, pressing my front against her back and pinning her to the counter as I effortlessly plucked the brown bottle off the shelf. Instead of backing away as soon as the sauce was in my hand like a normal person, I lingered there, enjoying the way my erection fit perfectly into the curve of her spine. Did I imagine that she pressed back against me just slightly, or was that wishful thinking?

Yes, baby. That's for you. Every hard inch.

"Thanks, Peach," I said low in her ear, eliciting a shiver from her that made things south of my waist quite happy before finally backing away and giving her space. I found it was almost painful for me to do so. I didn't want to give her space. I wanted to give her whatever the *opposite* of space was.

She turned with a smirk on her pretty little mouth. "Why are you calling me Peach?"

Because I'm thinking of a soft, juicy, sun-warmed fruit saying my name with your voice.

I couldn't say that shit out loud. She would probably yell for my sister, and then there would be talk of hospitals and neurologists and nice men in white coats. Hell, maybe I had a concussion and needed an MRI or CT-scan or something. I'd never had weird ass thoughts like this before.

I needed to get my shit under control. Like now. "It fits," I said gruffly, turning to the big bowl of hamburger meat I had left on the marble-topped island. Charli asked if she could help me, but I needed her intoxicating scent and honeyed voice far away from me, so I huffed out a short, "No." The wounded look on her face at my swift conversion from hot to cold made me feel like an asshole, so I softened it with a mumbled, "Thank you, though."

Bode and Cam burst into the kitchen then, and Bode threw his arms out and said, "My brother! We have arrived to assist in the formation of the burger patties." *Fucking Bode.* He turned to Charli, grabbing her hand and kissing the back of it. "And who are you, lovely lady?" I had the urge to pull her protectively behind me and rip Bode's goddamn lips off.

But why? He was certainly more suited to a girl like Charli than I was. He was a few years younger than me, and he could actually hold a conversation that consisted of more than grunts and commands.

She laughed that high, sweet laugh again, and I found myself feeling disappointed that someone else had drawn that beautiful sound from her mouth. "I'm Charli. I'm a nanny for the Broxtons."

"Taking on the Broxton children? Ah! I do love a brave woman," Bode said, lifting an eyebrow and making Charli giggle again. I looked down and realized I was dumping entirely too much salt into the meat. *Christ, Atwood. Get yourself together.* I took the metal bowl to the sink and dumped out the extra salt before turning back and finishing my seasoning. As Bode and Cam introduced themselves to Charli, I dug my hands violently into the meat to mix everything together.

"Dude, you're abusing your meat," Cam said, and I tossed him a middle finger coated with raw hamburger.

I glanced at Charli and saw her lips pressed together as she fought a smile. "Beau, it looks like you have plenty of help here, so I'm going to get changed and see if I can help Axel and Blaire with the boys in the pool."

Cam and Bode said goodbye, and I grunted in my usual asshole fashion. "She seems nice," Cam said, his eyes on her ass as she left the room, and I shot him a warning glare.

"*Very* nice," I said pointedly. *Too nice for you assholes.*

The thought of Bode, Cam, or anyone else for that matter, touching my little Peach made my head hurt. *She's not* your *little anything, dumbass. You've known her for all of ten minutes, and then you rubbed your dick in her back.* Yeah, that didn't exactly scream committed relationship. Plus, I've never had a real relationship with a woman. I had gone directly into the military after high school; after that, I was busy with my sister and Carrie. I didn't have time for dating and drama and shit.

My sister had her own life now, but I had never given a thought to settling down and having a family of my own. Shit, Cam and I would probably end up rooming together in a nursing home when we were eighty-year-old bachelors, trying to get nurses to sneak into our room for a little fun in the sack.

"What are you smiling at, Shark?" Cam asked me, his voice taking on a cajoling tone. "Would you happen to be thinking about a certain pretty little nanny?" I looked down to see that we were almost done with the hamburger patties, and I washed my hands and grabbed the foil while Bode and Cam finished up.

"Nope," I snapped.

"Yeah, bro. Keep telling yourself that," my roommate said with a chuckle.

BEAU

Cam, Bode, and I changed into our swim trunks and walked out to the pool. "Nice trunks, dude," Woody said as soon as I dove into the pool. All of my SEAL buddies and I had nicknames, and since mine was 'Shark,' my sister had bought me a pair of black trunks with a repeating shark print all over them. They were ridiculous, but Carrie had picked them out, so I tried to wear them whenever I came over to swim at their house.

"I like 'em, Uncle Beau," my darling niece said, swimming up to me as soon as I surfaced.

"Thank you, sweetheart. You have excellent taste," I said, pulling her to me for a quick snuggle. We batted a beach ball back and forth for a while until Rox started whining for her, and she swam off to appease her little brother.

"Let's grab a beer, man," Cam said to me, and we climbed out and snagged a couple cans from the cooler on the deck.

I heard the back gate open, but I didn't turn around until Cam spewed an entire mouthful of beer on me and coughed a couple times. "What the hell, asswipe?" I asked, swiping at my chest and stomach.

"Holy fucking shit," he muttered, gesturing with his head. I turned around and saw Charli standing beside the patio table. She was wearing a sheer white thing with an open zipper all the way down the front. I saw a sleek, red, one-piece swimsuit peeking out from the slender gap before she slid the cover-up down her shoulders and off her arms, revealing the front of her body.

Her breasts were round and full—but not overly so—and perfect for her slim body, making her tiny waist even more appealing. I took a long swig of my beer, wondering if I could wrap both of my hands around her waist.

As she rode my cock.

Naked and panting my name.

Atwood! Stop it!

Then she turned to lay her cover-up on the chair, and I got a glimpse of a rounded, heart-shaped ass. *Dear God in heaven.* I could just imagine my hands gripping those fantastic cheeks as I pounded into her. "Shit," I mumbled, and Cam elbowed me.

"Seriously, Shark. If you're not going to hit that, let me know. I'm all over it," Cam said under his breath.

"No one is *hitting that*, dammit. Stay the fuck away from her," I growled, turning my back to the pool because I suddenly had a very severe erection issue in my trunks. I grabbed a towel from the outdoor rack and went to sit on one of the thickly cushioned turquoise lounge chairs, wadding the towel up in my lap to disguise my obvious excitement.

I glared at Cam's back when he walked over to Charli and took her hand. "Come on, Charli. Let me introduce you to the other guys."

Swear to God, if my eyes could shoot bullets, Cam's body would look like Swiss cheese right now. There was nothing I could do at this point because my dick showed no signs of going down any time soon. Maybe if I kept my filthy-ass mind off Charli's body, I might have a chance of getting off this chair before Christmas. It was October.

I watched as Charli met all the guys, who greeted her warmly, because *of course they did.* Woody started calling her Charles, and the nickname caught on. *Yeah, really fucking cute, guys.* I glowered at them all for flirting with her, not that they would have fucking noticed because all their attention was on her. They really should leave her alone so she could do her damned job.

Thirty minutes later, all the kids were inside for naptime, and the activity in the pool got a bit more raucous.

I grabbed a beer and flopped down onto a lounge chair beside my sister.

"I'm not sure what to do with myself," she said. "I don't think all five of my kids have been asleep at the same time since Danica was born."

"Just enjoy the peace and quiet," I said, popping open my beer.

"Let's have chicken fights," Cam yelled from the pool.

"So much for peace and quiet," Blaire muttered.

"I challenge Woody," Charli said with a mocking grin.

"Oh yeah? You're going down, shorty," Woody retorted. "Pick your partner, Charles." *Seriously, enough with the cutesy nicknames, asshole.*

Charli swam over to our side of the pool, resting her forearms on the stone edge, and asked sweetly, "You playing, Beau?"

Charli on my shoulders? Her little cunt pressed against my neck. Fuck yes! I mean, no! Definitely not.

"No," I grunted and pulled my sunglasses down, effectively shutting her out, though my eyes stayed locked on her face like they were physically incapable of looking away. I needed to stay far, far away from that tempting morsel.

"Oh. Okay." she said, her chin dipping and her smile fading a little as she turned away. *Jesus, why am I such a fucking jackass?* Charli swam back to the other guys and stood for a few seconds before saying, "I choose Cam." *Dammit all to hell.* Cam's look of triumph almost had me coming out of my chair.

"Hell yes," he crowed. "We've got this, babe." *Babe?* I wanted to throat punch my friend.

Woody climbed up on Hawk's shoulders, and much to my displeasure, Charli mounted Cam's. *Fuck, fuck, fuck, fuck, fuck.* Why had I refused to play? That could have been me with Peach on *my* shoulders, her legs wrapped under *my* arms. Instead, she was sitting on my best friend, his arms wrapped around her legs as he held her slender thighs with his dirty, rotten hands.

Woody tugged her by one arm, and she shrieked, "Don't let me fall, Cam!"

Cam tightened his hold on Charli, her calves held firmly between his sides and his biceps, while his large hands gripped her thighs. "I won't, sugar."

How. Fucking. Dare. He. I thought I had made it clear she was off-limits, but the prick just...

"Something wrong, Beau?" Blaire asked, breaking into my thoughts of maiming and murder.

I looked down and noticed that I was crushing my beer can in my fist, the foamy liquid bubbling out over my hand and onto the polished black tile. "Fine," I snapped. "I'm going to get started on the burgers." I shotgunned the rest of the beer before tossing the crumpled can into the trash on my way into the house.

I snatched the two trays of burgers out of the refrigerator and stomped back outside. Firing up the grill, I snuck a look at the pool. My eyes were immediately drawn to Charli, who was having a sword fight with Bode using pool noodles. She seemed to fit right in with our group, laughing and playing like she had known us all her life. I couldn't help but like that about her.

When I was ready to flip the patties, Charli walked up to the grill holding packages of cheese. "You need some help?" she asked.

"Sure," I answered, but I wasn't sure why. I didn't actually need any help. "You can hand me the cheese." She started separating the slices and handing them to me as I slapped a piece on each patty. When I got to the last one, I looked at her expectantly.

"Oh, no cheese for me. Those burgers are big enough. I don't need any more calories," she said with a little laugh, her hand fluttering over her flat stomach. *What the hell is she talking about?*

My eyes traced up and down Charli's body. "You don't need to worry about that," I said gruffly. "You look... nice." *Nice?* Had I just said that? She looked a helluva lot better than *nice*. Her body was pretty fucking perfect in my eyes. But her face brightened at the compliment, and I found myself wondering what kind of man she liked. Probably the kind who wore a suit every day and called her 'darling.' You know... pretty much the opposite of me.

"So, what do you do, Beau?"

"I own a private security firm. We do P.I. work, security, stuff like that."

"Wow. That's awesome that you have your own business. Do the rest of the guys work with you?"

"Yeah, those five nimrods are my security experts," I said, jerking my chin back toward the pool where said nimrods were attempting to drown each other. "We're all former military, so our backgrounds help with pretty much everything we do." I glanced down at her, curious to know more about her. "What about you?"

"Well, of course I'm working as a nanny right now, but that will help with what I really want to do." She hesitated.

"And what do you want to do, Peach?"

She shrugged her slim shoulders like she wasn't sure it was worth mentioning. "I want to open a daycare. But not just any daycare... more like a school. I want to develop my students' minds while they are still in early childhood. Just look at Carrie. Now, I know she's exceptionally intelligent, but part of her aptitude is due to Blaire working with her so much when she was little."

"Yeah," I said, smiling like I always did when discussing my niece, "she's pretty extraordinary. And Blaire read to her constantly when she was a baby."

Charli snapped her fingers and pointed at me. "That's exactly what I want to do. *Every* child has the aptitude for learning at an early age. Reading, foreign languages, even simple math. There are so many constrictive learning plans pushed by the powers that be about when children should learn certain things, but I want to break down those barriers. Children's brains are like giant sponges from birth to five years old. Their capacity to learn is amazing, so why should we be told, for example, that reading shouldn't be taught until kindergarten or first grade?" Passion for her subject infused every syllable she uttered and listening to her talk made her even more attractive.

I was pleasantly surprised by this woman. She was so young, and yet she showed remarkable insight and intelligence for her age. "I think it's an excellent idea," I said.

"You do?" she asked, astonishment sparking through those hypnotizing eyes of hers.

"Of course," I said with a little laugh. "If I had a kid, I would definitely send him or her to your school. Who wouldn't think that was a great idea?"

"You'd be surprised," she said vaguely, her bottom lip trembling just slightly before she trapped it between her teeth and walked away to throw an empty cheese package in the garbage can. My eyes followed her and noticed the slump of her shoulders as she walked back toward the house. Seeing that defeated posture pissed me off, and I motioned for Woody to come cover the grill as I marched into the house on a mission.

I found Charli in the kitchen cutting up tomatoes. I put my hands on her shoulders and quietly commanded, "Turn around." She slowly did as I asked but didn't meet my eyes. "Why did you walk away from me?"

"Not much more to say. It's probably a silly dream anyway." Her shoulders hunched up in another self-conscious shrug.

"Who told you that?" I demanded.

"It... it's not important," she stammered, her eyes wary now.

"It's important to me," I said softly and realized that I was feeling very protective of this woman I barely knew. I put my hands on the counter behind her, effectively caging her in, our bodies close but not touching. "Tell me who."

"Just a... someone," she said, and my blood burned with the thought of another man with her.

"Boyfriend?" I asked more harshly than I intended.

She started to nod her head but then shook it instead. "Ex."

Relief flooded my system as I lifted her chin with my thumb, letting my fingers rest on her cheek. "Good. Because any man that doesn't support you and your dreams is a fucking idiot," I growled. Her eyes searched my face as mine did the same to hers. "Tell me you understand, Peach."

"I understand, Beau." The way she said my name did things to my insides—not to mention the way those luminous eyes locked onto mine with an inherent trust that I wasn't sure I deserved—and I found myself leaning toward her until only an inch separated our faces. I felt her soft breath brush across my lips as her cool hands slid around my waist to rest on my back. It felt like an invitation.

This is a bad idea, Atwood. I closed my eyes and rubbed my nose against hers, my lips wanting to taste this sweet little peach more than they had ever wanted to taste anything.

A split second after my lips brushed against hers, a door slammed at the back of the house, and we both jerked apart before we could even complete the kiss. As Charli quickly turned and placed another tomato on the cutting board, I felt a mixture of relief and disappointment seep underneath my skin. Relief because I knew I shouldn't be kissing this young woman, but disappointment because I *really* fucking wanted to.

I whirled away when I heard footsteps and yanked open the refrigerator door. Blaire breezed into the kitchen, chirping, "Whatcha looking for, big brother?"

"Oh, um, the lettuce," I said, making up something on the fly. She pointed to the two green bundles directly in front of my face, and I gave her a chagrined look as I pulled them off the shelf and closed the fridge. She leaned back against the counter with her arms crossed and looked speculatively back and forth between me and Charli. She smiled and waggled her eyebrows at me, and I gave her a hard stare that would wither most grown men. Not my darling sister though; it just made her grin wider.

Thankfully, Charli was blissfully unaware of this silent eyeball feud going on right behind her back. "I'm just gonna go outside and check on the, uh, the… stuff," Blaire said with a mischievous smirk as she turned to saunter back out of the kitchen. *Well, that wasn't fucking awkward at all.*

BEAU

AFTER DINNER AND CAKE, most of the guys went home, leaving only me and Cam. I was sitting on the couch holding Dani when Charli came into the room and asked if she could keep the baby in her room for the night.

I saw Axel squeeze Blaire's leg, and they shared a longing look before my sister said, "Okay, Charli. I'll get Axel to bring the little cradle downstairs to your room."

"I'll do it," I volunteered. Heading upstairs, I got the portable cradle from Danica's room and brought it downstairs. I knew there was only one bedroom down here, so I carried the thing to the room and knocked on the open door frame.

"I've got the baby in the tub. You can just leave the cradle beside my bed," she called out, her sweet voice echoing from inside.

I set it down where she asked and then looked at her bed. It suited her, decorated with light pink and ivory covers that made me think about creamy ice cream. I resisted the urge to lift her pillow and smell it. That's all the fuck I needed... Blaire walking in and catching me sniffing her nanny's pillow. My nosy-ass sister already seemed suspicious.

Across the room, a door hung half-open, and I angled myself so that I could see inside. Yeah. Big mistake. Charli was on her knees, leaned over the bathtub. She was wearing short denim cutoffs, and the frayed edges were riding high, exposing the bottom cups of her ass. *Fuck me.*

I couldn't help myself. I crossed the room and pushed the door open, croaking out a husky, "Hey."

Charli looked over her shoulder at me and smiled, oblivious to the filthy thoughts that were swirling through my head. Thoughts of running my tongue along the crease where her leg met her ass. Thoughts of biting those round globes hard—hard enough to leave my mark on the perfect skin there. *See?* That's why this was so fucked up. What kind of perv wanted to leave marks on such beautiful flesh?

Me.

"Come look at this little angel, Beau." I entered the room and knelt beside Charli on the bathmat, resting my thick forearms on the edge of the tub. She had put Dani in a baby bathtub inside the big tub. The kid was splashing and kicking happily, grinning like she was in heaven. *I don't blame you, sweet Dani. I would be happy too, if Charli had me naked in a bathtub.*

I ran my index finger down my little niece's face, and she cooed and smiled at me. "She really is a sweetheart," I said.

"Yes, she is," Charli said. "I've already bathed her and washed her hair; we're just having playtime now."

"Playtime in the bathtub can be really fun," I said with a dark smirk, and Charli looked over at me and bumped me with her shoulder.

"Stop it," she said with a laugh. "Hey, watch this." She fashioned Danica's wet hair into a mohawk and said, "Now she's a little punk rocker."

"She just needs some ink," I said with a grin. Then Charli made two horns on the top of the baby's head and giggled at her handiwork. "Uh, don't you think devil horns would be more appropriate for the triplets?" I asked.

Charli flashed me that perfect smile and said, "Oh, I've already done that. Keep your hand on her and let me get my phone." I placed my hand on Dani's slippery belly while Charli turned and grabbed her phone. "Look. Isn't that hilarious?" She asked, showing me a picture of my little nephews in the bathtub, each sporting devil horns and cheesing for the camera.

"Very," I said, laughing at the adorable little hellions. *When was the last time I had laughed this much?* Probably the day before... never.

"Okay, the water is getting cool. We'd better get this precious girl out of the tub and get her warm. Can you hand me that towel?"

I stood and grabbed the pink baby towel and turned to wrap it around Dani, who Charli had picked up and cuddled against her chest. When she was all bundled up, I noticed that the baby's wet body had soaked through Charli's thin tank top, allowing me to see the darkness of her nipples through the fabric. Damn, I wanted to wrap my lips around those peaks and suck until she screamed my name.

Christ almighty, Atwood. Cool your jets.

Charli took Dani from me and carried her to the queen-sized bed, laying her down before expertly putting on a diaper and footie pajamas. She grabbed a soft brush and combed the baby's auburn hair before picking her up and kissing her head. "I love how babies smell," she said, nuzzling her nose against Dani's cheek.

"Can I say goodbye to her before I go?" I asked, and she handed my niece over to me. I cradled her in my arms and looked down into her sweet face before kissing her on the nose. "Good night, darling. Uncle Beau loves you." I gave her back to Charli, who was looking at me with a warm softness in her eyes.

"Okay, I should get her to sleep," she said, settling on the bed with the baby and picking up a copy of *Goodnight Moon*.

I went to the doorway and turned back for one more look. "Sweet dreams, Peach."

"Sweet dreams, Beau."

I'm sure they will be, baby.

By the time I got to the living room, I was already mentally kicking my own ass. I was thinking of Charli and babies and hard nipples and soft lips and frigging peaches, for God's sake. What the hell was I doing? This was *not* going to happen. I wasn't right for Charli. She deserved someone who would give her kids and a home with a white picket fence, and that man was absolutely not me.

I shot off a quick text before elbowing Cam and grunting, "We need to go. I've got company coming over." He raised his eyebrows at me but nodded. I was just horny, I decided. I needed to fuck someone hard and get rid of all these stupid ideas in my head.

We made it home in time for me to grab a quick shower before I heard a knock on the front door. I swung it open to find tits and ass by the name of Miranda standing on our porch. "Hey. Come on in," I said, closing the door and leading her directly back to the bedroom. This was what I needed. No wining. No dining. Just a woman willing to come to my house, go directly to my bedroom, and let me fuck her nine ways from Sunday.

I closed my bedroom door and pushed Miranda roughly against it as I grabbed either side of her shirt and ripped it open, scattering buttons everywhere. "Damn, baby. You did need me," she said, slipping off the shirt and taking her bra off. I went straight for her giant fake tits, squeezing them tightly and reveling in the way they overflowed my hands. I leaned my head down and bit one of her nipples. "Ow, Shark! Ease up."

I pulled her short skirt up and found her pantiless—*thank Christ*. I spanked her bare ass and said sharply, "Don't give me any shit tonight, Miranda. I'm not in the mood."

I bit the underside of her other breast, but this time she leaned her head back against the door and sighed, "Okay, baby. Whatever you need."

Releasing her, I stepped back and began unbuttoning my shorts.

"On your fucking knees."

CHARLI

I WAS UP EARLY the next morning with Danica. Blaire liked to breastfeed her and spend some quiet time with the newest Broxton before the other kids woke up. She looked up at me from the rocking chair in Dani's room and spoke softly. "Charli, I hate to ask this, but I really need a favor. Carrie left one of her library books at Beau's house Friday. I meant to have him bring it last night, but I totally forgot about it, and she needs it for school today."

"No problem. I can run over and get it before the kids get up, if you think Beau will be awake." Even saying Beau's name sent a little shiver through my body. That man was hot as hell.

"He and Cam are always up early. Just grab my phone and look under 'Annoying Brother' for the number. You can text him to let him know you're on the way over."

I got Blaire's phone and laughed when I saw that she wasn't kidding about the 'Annoying Brother' thing. I plugged Beau's number into my phone and headed out to Blaire's car. I texted to let him know I was leaving to come pick up Carrie's book before tapping his saved address on Blaire's GPS.

I thought about him the entire drive to his house. Everyone talked about what a grouch he was, but he'd been really sweet to me yesterday. Hell, he'd almost kissed me. He had me so wet before his mouth even got close to mine. Just his gruff, demanding voice when he said, "Tell me you understand, Peach." *Dear God, that man was sex on legs.* I had no idea why he was calling me Peach, but I liked it. A lot. It made me feel... special.

And when I had walked out to the pool and seen him with his shirt off, I almost peed my pants. All of his friends were hot, but looking at Beau Atwood did things to my body that I had never experienced before. The man was a supreme male specimen.

I pulled up to his house and parked on the street before walking up to the door and knocking. I knew Beau and Cam lived together, but for some reason, I was surprised when Cam answered the door. He seemed equally surprised to see me. He glanced behind him before walking out onto the porch and closing the door. "Hi, Charli. Uh, what brings you by this early?"

It was chilly outside this early in the morning, but the shirtless Cam seemed unaffected by the temperature. "Hey, Blaire sent me over to pick up a book Carrie left here. She needs it for school today."

"Oh, um. I'll just grab it for you." He looked down at my bare arms because I hadn't taken time to grab a jacket. Cam let out a long sigh and said, "It's cool out here. Why don't you come inside and wait?" He said it like I was imposing, but when he held the door open for me, I took a few steps inside.

I heard a loud banging from the back of the house and started to ask, "Is everything—" but he cut me off.

"I'll be right back. Just... uhh... stay right there." He jogged down a hallway toward where the noise was coming from. Then I noticed a squeaking noise. *Oh God. Was that... bedsprings?*

A high-pitched voice screamed, "Oh, God! Shark! I'm coming *again*." I had heard the guys calling Beau 'Shark' yesterday, and it dawned on me. *Beau had a woman here, and they were...* "You fuck me so good with that big dick, baby," the woman cried. I stood there listening in horror for what seemed like an hour as the woman had a screaming orgasm. I was simultaneously pissed and hurt. *And a little bit jealous.* But mostly pissed.

Beau Atwood had been hitting on me just last night. He almost kissed me! And all the while, he had a girlfriend? What a bastard! I tried to tune out the noises, but Miss Screams-A-Lot was a little hard to ignore. I heard a couple deep grunts, and the squeaking and banging slowed and then finally stopped.

Where. The. Hell. Is. Cam?

He finally dashed back down the hallway, looking nervous, his eyes searching my face. "Hey, uh, I don't see the book. I'm so sorry, Charli." I wasn't sure if he was apologizing for not finding the book or for his roommate's behavior.

"Did you check under her pillow? Sometimes Carrie sticks her books under her pillow before she goes to sleep," I said, forcing my voice to remain neutral even though I was feeling... some other kind of way. I thought we'd shared a connection yesterday. But it was only a few minutes and obviously one-sided, so it was none of my business. Beau Atwood was nothing to me. Just because... *Don't even go there, Charli.*

Cam went back down the hall, slowing his pace this time since Beau's playtime seemed to be over. No wonder he had been so reluctant for me to come inside. Almost as soon as he disappeared, a woman came sashaying down the hallway wearing the t-shirt Beau had been wearing last night. She stopped short when she saw me, her eyes raking me up and down. She was blonde like me, but that's where the similarities ended. This chick looked like a stripper with her long legs and oversized boobs.

"Hey, honey. You a friend of Cam's?" I couldn't help but notice that she had great 'just fucked' hair, whereas I always looked like a family of beavers had nested in my hair after sex. How the hell could I have thought Beau would ever be interested in me when *this* was the kind of woman he liked?

"Y-yes," I stammered. "I'm Cam's friend."

She grinned at me, giving me a little finger wave and saying, "Have fun, girl-friend!" before sauntering out the front door.

Thankfully, Cam returned a few seconds later holding Carrie's book. "I found it," he said breathlessly, approaching me cautiously. "Hey, you okay, babe?"

"I'm fine. Why wouldn't I be?" My voice sounded strained, even to my own ears. *Goddammit.*

"That was nothing, Charli. He was just blowing off some steam. Beau likes you."

I gave him a sarcastic smile. "Obviously not as much as he likes her," I said, jerking my head toward the front door.

Cam reached up and tucked a stray piece of hair behind my ear. "Charli, just—"

We were interrupted by Beau walking into the living room bare-chested, looking down and adjusting the waistband of his gray sweats. As embarrassed and disgusted as I was by this whole situation, I couldn't help but gawk at him. Beau Atwood was one gorgeous hunk of man. His torso looked like it had been carved from a block of granite, and his chiseled jaw, full lips, and evergreen eyes put him smack dab into the category of stunning. His brown hair was cut short on the sides, but the top was mussed to sexual aftermath perfection.

"Cam, remind me to buy more rubbers this week. I'm down to five and…" His voice drifted off when he saw me, and his eyes narrowed as he looked at Cam's hand on my hair. "What's going on?" When neither of us answered, his gaze fell on me, and I saw something akin to worry there. "Peach, uh, how long have you been here?" he asked, his voice raising about an octave.

"Long enough," I snapped, pulling the book from Cam's hand before storming toward the door, tossing a "Thanks, Cam" over my shoulder.

I made it to the car on pure anger alone, and then the ache hit me. I drove down the block and stopped in the parking lot of a fast-food restaurant and let my tears fall, which just made me angrier. Why the hell was I wasting tears on that prick? He had absolutely no regard for anyone, and I guessed that was why it hurt so much. I barely knew him, but I felt like he really *saw me* yesterday. Not to mention the flirting and the almost-kiss. And God, I had wanted that kiss. It was embarrassing how much I had wanted to feel his lips on mine.

You know what? Fuck Mr. "How Will I Make It Through The Day With Only Five Condoms." I wasn't going to waste another second of my time on him. I pulled a pack of wet wipes from the console of Blaire's SUV and cleaned up my face before heading home.

BEAU

"What the fuck was that?" I asked Cam angrily. "Why were you touching Charli when I came in here?"

He looked at me incredulously. "Seriously, dude? You and Miranda were practically fucking the house down, and you want to know why I was touching Charli's hair? Because honestly, I don't think it's any of your damned business."

"I'm making it my business," I growled, getting in his face until we were nose-to-nose.

"What's it to you, Shark?" he yelled in my face. "It seems like you don't want Charli, but you don't want anyone else to have her either."

"I didn't say I didn't want her." *Shit!* "I mean, I *don't* want her. I just don't want her to get hurt," I said, quieting my voice a little and taking a step back.

"Well, too fucking late. You should have seen the look on her face when she figured out what was going on, man. What's the deal with you two anyway?"

Well, that was a loaded fucking question if I ever heard one. I tried to answer as honestly as possible as we both sat on the couch. "I don't have the first fucking clue. Yesterday was the first time I'd met her, but I started having strange thoughts." At Cam's questioning look, I clarified. "Just... stupid stuff. Like about her eyes and how she smelled and how she talked and shit."

God, I can't believe I'm telling him this.

Cam closed his eyes dreamily and said, "Mmmm, I know what you mean. That voice of hers hits me right in the damn dick."

I guessed he could feel the weight of my laser-focused glare because he opened his eyes and looked at me for a moment before pressing his lips together and then pretending to zip them and throw away the key. He circled his hand in the space between us to indicate that I should continue.

"Anyway, I had bumped my head on a cabinet because she startled me, and then she was just being so fucking sweet, and it made me feel... good. I thought maybe that knock on the head had given me a concussion or a freakin' brain tumor or something because of the stupid thoughts in my head."

I looked at Cam and expected him to be smirking at me, but he wasn't. He was just listening, so I continued. "I barely even know this girl, but when you all started laughing and flirting with her, I wanted to beat the hell out of all you."

Cam lifted a challenging eyebrow at me. He was the best hand-to-hand fighter I had ever met, an expert in several forms of martial arts. Needless to say, picking a fight with Camden Fitz wasn't the wisest thing to do.

I stood and linked my hands on top of my head as I paced. Cam pointed to his mouth as if to ask for permission to speak. I gave him a wry look and nodded. "You're a protector, Shark. You always have been. Look at how you are with Blaire and her kids."

"Yeah, so?"

"Sooooo," he said, drawing out the word, "maybe that's what you're feeling for Charli. Maybe you see her as a surrogate little sister."

"Trust me. The thoughts I had about Charli were far from brotherly." Cam tilted his head curiously. "I, uh, I started to kiss her."

My friend shook his head back and forth several times as if trying to clear it. "Wait, wait. Hold the fucking phone. *You kissed Charli?*"

"No," I said through gritted teeth, "I said I *started* to kiss her. We got interrupted." I frowned at the thought. "What's fucking with me is that I really wanted to, though, and I never just want to kiss a woman for the hell of it."

A slow smile spread across Cam's face. "You *do* like her," he said, looking pleased. I started to protest, but he held up his hand.

Cam rested his elbows on his knees as he looked down at his hands. "Trust me, I recognize the signs. I wasn't always like this, you know? So fucked up," he said so quietly, I had to sit in the chair adjacent to him to hear what he was saying. "I had a girl back in high school. Her name was Shiloh, and she was the sweetest girl in town." He glanced up at me and then back down at his hands clasped between his knees. "I fell in love with her."

I had never heard Cam talk like this. We had been friends since elementary school, but his family moved to Denton before high school, and we hadn't seen each other much until we reconnected in the navy. My quiet tone matched his. "What happened, Cam?"

His lips tightened before he spoke again. "I joined the navy, and she went to college. We talked when we could, wrote letters when we couldn't. I went to see her one weekend when I was on leave, and she just wasn't the same."

"You had drifted apart?"

"No, she had changed, though. She was thinner, *a lot* thinner, and she was no longer the funny, happy girl I had left behind. She cried a lot and had dark circles around her eyes like she wasn't sleeping. It was obvious that me being away was hurting her, so... I broke it off."

"You didn't love her anymore?"

"No, I broke up with her because I *did* love her. I hated seeing her so miserable, and I couldn't stand that I was doing that to her. Losing Shiloh was probably the biggest regret of my life." He finally looked at me and gave me a sad half-grin. "You probably think I sound like a fucking sap."

"No, man. I don't. And I'm really sorry about Shiloh. But why did you tell me all that now? You've never mentioned it before."

"Because I don't want you to fuck up like I did. I know you just met Charli, but I can tell you like her, man. She might be a really good thing for you, and I think you should go for it."

My jaw dropped to the floor. "You think I should go for it?" Cam nodded. "But she's too young for me."

He shrugged casually. "You've heard that term, 'Age is just a number,' right? And besides, I was with her most of the day yesterday while you were pouting and nursing your blue balls. She didn't act any more like a kid than the rest of us. In fact, she fit right in with our group."

"But I'm no good for her," I argued. Cam huffed out a loud breath of exasperation. "Really, man. Look how I am with women. I can't be what she would need."

"You're just making excuses, Shark. Either be with her or don't. You know *how* to treat women, even if you don't put it into practice. Just treat her like you would want someone to treat Blaire."

I scrubbed a hand over my face. "What about this morning? How obvious was it that Miranda and I were fucking?"

He visibly winced. "Bro. It was *so bad*. The headboard banging against the wall, the bed squeaking. And let's not forget about Miranda screaming about your big dick inside her. It actually made me cringe, and you know I like listening."

"Perv," I muttered. I felt my face reddening with embarrassment that Charli had heard all that. "Do you think there's any chance for us after she heard…" I waved my hand toward my bedroom.

"No clue," he said, looking a little dejected on my behalf. "I mean, you flirted with her and almost kissed her yesterday, and then this morning she finds you trying to fuck Miranda through the bed… I just don't know, man." He raised his hands, palm up, and let them fall.

I sighed. "Maybe I should just forget about the whole thing."

"Yeah, maybe you should," he said, rising from the couch and walking toward the hallway. "But just a warning. She's only been in town a few weeks. Pretty soon men are going to come sniffing around a girl like her like wolves. Just ask yourself if you're prepared to see her with someone else."

I leaned my head against the back of the chair. I didn't have to think about it. The answer to that was a big fat "*Fuck no*."

CHARLI

"So, let me get this straight," my friend Bristol said around a mouthful of Blue Bell ice cream, Buttered Pecan, to be specific. "This Beau guy almost kissed you, and then you went to his house the next morning and he was knocking boots with some other girl?"

"They were knocking more than boots, by the sound of it," I said, dipping my spoon into the pint of Chocolate Chip Cookie Dough ice cream. "Seriously, Bris. It sounded like a porno with all the screaming."

"So he knows what he's doing," she said with an eyebrow wiggle. She held out her pint and said, "Switch." We exchanged ice creams and dug in. "But Beau is a hottie?"

"Christ on a crutch, Bris. He's the hottest guy I've ever seen. His damned muscles have muscles. And his abs... he's got that sexy V thing."

"Oh, hell. He has sex lines? You need to get on that, girl. That makes for some good fucking."

I giggled at her. "You're so bad, Bristol."

"Hey, I'm not the one having porno fantasies." She ate another bite of ice cream and grinned at me with cookie dough in her teeth.

"Oh, and he's a former Navy SEAL, and every damned thing he said to me sounded like a command. I think he could say, 'pass the potatoes,' and my panties would get wet."

"Mmmm, there's nothing like being bossed around in bed," Bristol said with a dreamy look in her eyes.

"I've never been with someone, you know, dominant. My first was Nick in high school, and neither of us really knew what the hell we were doing. And then there was Hayden…"

"Hayden didn't melt your butter in the bedroom?"

"Hardly," I said scoffing. "We did it in the ever-respectable missionary position twice a week, and he thought he was quite the stud for managing that."

"Seriously?"

"Yep, like clockwork every single time. He would diddle between my legs for sixty seconds, managing to hit everything except the good parts. Then he would crawl on top of me and pump for two minutes before he finished. Acted like he was king of the world when he was done. I kept thinking it would get better, but it never did."

"If you have enough functioning brain cells to actually time him, he's doing it wrong."

I giggled. "You're telling me."

"I never liked that jackass," she said fiercely.

"He wasn't so bad at first," I said, taking another bite of the creamy delight on the end of my spoon. "When he became CEO of Harrison Hotels, the pressure got to him, and he started drinking. Just a little at first, but then it got worse. He was such an ugly drunk, but at least he couldn't get it up when he was sloshed, so I didn't have to lie there and fake it."

Bristol's jaw dropped almost into her tub of ice cream. "Jesus, Charli. That sounds like a fucking nightmare," Bris said, reaching over to squeeze my knee. "What made you finally leave?"

Oh, let's see. Where should I start? Maybe having my daily caloric intake monitored for the last two-and-a-half years because Hayden wouldn't "tolerate" me getting fat. Or perhaps having our joint bank account scoured every night and getting yelled at for spending four dollars at the convenience store.

"I guess I just finally wised up," I muttered, too embarrassed to tell her about *the incident*. The one that made me pack my shit and get the hell out as soon as Hayden left the house for work the next morning.

"You are a strong, independent woman, Charli Casper," she said forcefully, jabbing her spoon so close to my face, I feared she was going to take an eye out. "You were smart to get out before it escalated."

"Yeah, I guess," I said, swatting her hand away. I sighed and scraped up the last bite of ice cream out of the container, barely tasting the sweet cream on my tongue as I thought about how bad it could have been.

I put the container down on my nightstand and picked at some non-existent lint on my soft, pink bedspread.

Bristol reached across and hugged me tightly. "I've missed you, Charli."

"I've missed you, too, Bris," I said, returning her embrace. "Luckily, the Broxtons hired me as soon as I got here, so I have a place to live and a steady paycheck."

"And you're doing what you love. Teaching and taking care of little ones."

"I'm super lucky. They're a great family."

"Speaking of family, let's get back to Blaire's brother. Did you check out his package?"

I laughed at her segue back into all things dirty. "Yeah, I may have *glanced* down south of the border."

"And?" she asked, leaning toward me, her gorgeous violet eyes sparkling.

"There was a bulge, and it was... substantial." I said, raising my eyebrows.

"Oooh, substantial is good. So, you gonna hop on and take him on a ride to Fucksville, U.S.A.?"

I laughed at my crazy friend. "You forgot something. He has a girlfriend."

Bristol crossed her arms over her chest and pouted. "It was probably just a booty call. Any man who looks like you say he looks, who has a big dick, and fucks like a porn star is probably not tied down to one woman."

"I don't know, Bris. Oh, did I tell you about the condoms?"

"Were they XXL?" she asked excitedly. Nothing made Bristol's eyes sparkle more than the thought of an extra, *extra* large penis.

"No clue, but when he came out from his room, before he realized I was there, he told Cam to remind him to get more condoms this week because he only had five left."

"Jesus, how much does he fuck in one week?"

"I don't know, but I don't want to be with someone who is sleeping with half of the DFW area. I'm not looking for anything serious after just getting out of a bad relationship, but I would like to have someone I could date monogamously. You know, a nice man to go out to dinner with or hang out and watch TV with." Bristol feigned falling asleep, and I rolled my eyes at her. "I'm not really a one-night stand kind of girl. No offense."

"None taken," she said with a grin.

"After this morning, I'm pretty sure Beau Atwood is not that man," I said sadly.

"I'll tell you what. Forget Mr. Porno. I'm taking you out this weekend. You pick the night."

"Well, I have to help get the kids ready for bed," I said hesitantly.

"Shit doesn't get cranked up until at least ten o'clock anyway. Get the kids to bed, put on something sexy, and we'll hit some clubs. Saturday?"

I grinned. "Okay, that sounds really fun. It'll be just like old times." It had been years since I'd been clubbing.

"Hell yes, bitch!" she said, high fiving me. "We're gonna find you a man!"

"No, no! Bad Bristol!" I practically shouted, shaking my finger at her like she was an errant puppy. "I'm not on some kind of manhunt. We're just going out to have a little fun."

"We'll see," she said, smirking at me.

Jesus, help me.

7

BEAU

I CALLED MY SISTER a little before noon on Tuesday. "Hey, Blaire. How is the most beautiful sister on the planet today?" I was in my office downtown, and I swung my chair around to look out the window at the Dallas skyline as we talked.

"Confused as to why her brother is calling and trying to butter her up."

I chuckled. "No reason. I was just seeing what you were doing for lunch. I haven't seen you since this weekend."

"I'm sorry, Beau. I can't today. I'm taking Dani to the pediatrician, and then I'm swinging by the hospital to look over a couple surgical cases I'll be doing when I get back to work in two weeks."

"So, the boys are with Ms. Casper today? I thought I might swing by and see them for a little bit."

And maybe catch a glimpse of your young nanny. I had decided not to pursue things with Charli; she was too young for me, but I wanted to apologize for... what? Leading her on with the near-kiss? Fucking Miranda? I wasn't sure, but I just felt like I needed to man up and say I was sorry.

"Actually, Ms. Casper is in Waco visiting her sister today. Charli is with the triplets."

"By herself? Yikes! Poor girl," I uttered.

I heard my sister's laugh on the other end of the phone. "I can assure you, she's perfectly capable of handling my wild boys, but you're welcome to go by and see for yourself."

"I might," I mused. I knew the boys napped in the afternoon. That would give me time to talk to Peach. "Would you mind if I came over for dinner tonight too, so I can see Carrie?" I missed my precocious niece. She'd been a huge part of my life since she was born.

I had grown incredibly close to Carrie during the almost five years she and Blaire had lived near me in California, and I was accustomed to seeing her practically every day. She was the sunshine in my sometimes-dark life, and I missed the kid when I went days without seeing her.

"Of course, you can. You know you're always welcome. Will you be bringing the crew? I need to know how many pizzas to get."

"I think I'll just come by myself tonight, so you don't have to take out a second mortgage on your house."

"Ha! I appreciate that."

"You know I'll always look out for you, baby sister."

"I love you, ya big goofball."

"I love you, too, ya little brat."

We disconnected with plans for me to come over at 6:30 that evening for dinner. I stared out of my office window for a while. I had paperwork to do, but I couldn't bring myself to concentrate on it. I finally rose and left my office, going into Cam's next door.

"Hey, I'm going to lunch. I'll probably take an extra hour. Got a couple things to take care of."

"That's cool. You're the boss. Anything I can help with?" Cam asked.

"No. I was just going to run by Blaire's house and check in on the boys."

Cam's smirk irritated the shit out of me. "And their nanny, who you're not interested in *at all*?"

"Shut up, smartass," I said, but my dick chimed in with a resounding *hell yes. Well, fuck.*

I stopped by a local deli and picked up a couple sandwiches. I didn't know what Charli liked, but I figured a turkey club was a safe bet. When I arrived at Blaire and Axel's, I knocked on the front door, and Charli answered with a confused look and a slight blush on her face.

"Beau, hi. Um, Blaire's not here."

"I know. I just talked to her. I thought I would come by and see how the boys were."

She crossed her arms defiantly over her chest, making her boobs swell up over her forearms. Not that I noticed…

I did, my dick said, and I resisted the urge to slap him.

"So, you were concerned that I was unable to do my job," she said, narrowing her eyes at me.

"No, not at all," I said quickly, holding up the bag of food. "I just thought I would bring some adult people food since you might not have time to cook lunch for yourself with the trips running around." I gave her my most winning smile and wondered what the fuck I was doing here.

"Oh, um, okay," she said cautiously. "I'm feeding them lunch now, and we're working on some stuff while they eat." Instead of turning toward the dining room where I would have assumed they'd be having lunch, Charli led me toward the living room.

I grinned when I saw the boys sitting on the floor underneath blankets stretched out across some chairs. I glanced back at Charli. "A blanket fort?"

She shrugged. "Everything is more fun in a blanket fort."

I lowered my voice and let my eyes sweep down her body before returning to her impassive gaze. "Everything, Peach?"

"My name is Charli," she said coolly, sitting cross-legged in front of the boys. "Sit with your nephews. You might learn something." I squeezed into the blanket fort and was greeted by the toddlers, who each had a cheese sandwich on a plate in front of them. I noticed that Charli had a stack of large, wooden letters beside her with stuff painted on them.

She held up a B with bananas all over it. "What's this one, Max?"

"B for 'nana!" he said.

"It is a B," she said delightedly. "But can you say banana?" Max repeated the word, and Charli said, "Good boy. You're so smart." He leaned forward in anticipation, and she gave him a soft kiss on the cheek. I watched fascinated as these two-year-olds went through their letters, getting a smooch from their nanny every single time. I was inordinately enthralled by her reward system.

"I would have been a genius if I had had a teacher like you, Peach," I said with a grin.

"Charli," she corrected. "Finish your sandwiches, guys. Let's see if Uncle Beau can get this one."

She held up the letter C with kitten faces painted on it, and I proudly said, "C for cat." Then I leaned forward with my lips pursed and my eyes closed, hoping for the same reward she gave my nephews. A split second later, I felt something cold and moist hit my lips and chin. I jerked my eyes open to find a slice of cheese plastered to my face, much to the amusement of my nephews, who were giggling like mad men. She had hit me in the mouth with a fucking piece of cheese!

"Unca Beau, you got cheese on your face," Rox said.

I peeled the cheese off and took a bite of it. "Thanks, buddy. I'm aware," I said dryly, shooting Charli a mirthful look. She was smirking back at me playfully. The little minx.

Max climbed up in her lap and started sucking his index finger, his tell that he was ready for a nap. Charli smoothed his dark hair from his forehead and kissed him there before tucking his head under her chin and rocking from side-to-side. "Is my little sweetheart sleepy?" He nodded and sighed contentedly. I don't blame you, bud. I wish she would hold me all pressed up against her chest like that.

When Max's eyes fluttered closed, she said to the other two, "Okay, guys. It's naptime."

"Don't wanna take a nap," Dex said stubbornly.

I was about to reprimand him for talking back, when Charli fixed him with a no-nonsense stare and said sternly, "Or you can clean your room."

Dex frowned and shook his head. "Okay, nap," he conceded.

Wow, this girl is good.

"Let me put Maxie down, and I'll come back for you two." She rose gracefully, hefting Max's weight up in her arms.

"I'll get them," I offered, scooping the other two up, one in each arm, and following her to the stairs. "You don't want to take the elevator?" I asked quietly.

"Nah. This is good exercise. I don't really have time to go to the gym." My eyes stayed trained on her perfectly rounded ass as she walked up the stairs ahead of me. Walking the stairs obviously worked for her as far as a glute workout went. That shit was *tight!*

She laid Max down and pulled his finger from his mouth. He reached his tiny hand out, looking for one of his brothers even in sleep, and I laid Dex down beside him. Max's hand rested on his face, and when I put Rox down, he curled against Dex's back. Charli stroked her fingers through their hair, and they were snoozing within minutes. She smiled affectionately down at them before covering them with a light blanket and motioning me toward the door.

As we descended the stairs, I told her, "You're really good with them." I couldn't hide the awe in my voice as I continued, "I can't believe you can get them to sit still long enough to learn their letters."

She shrugged. "Food serves as a good distraction. They're already sitting down to eat, so we might as well learn some stuff while they're still." Then she laughed her tinkling little laugh. "Plus, we ran around in the yard playing football for two hours before lunch, so that usually wipes them out pretty good."

"Hey, do you want to eat lunch in the fort? Some really amazing woman once told me that everything is more fun in a blanket fort."

Charli eyed me warily but then grinned and crawled under the tent of blankets. I handed her the container holding the turkey sandwich and crawled in behind her with my roast beef. "She sounds freaking brilliant," she said.

"Oh, she is," I said, quirking an eyebrow at her before getting down to business. "Peach, I wanted to apologize about Monday morning. I, uh, didn't know you were coming over, and I'm sorry if I put you in an awkward position."

"It's none of my business what you do in your free time, Beau," she said smoothly, but her eyes didn't quite meet mine. I took a bite of my sandwich, but she hadn't even opened hers.

"I just wanted you to know that Miranda's not my girlfriend or anything. I wouldn't have, you know, flirted with you if I had a girlfriend. I don't do relationships, but if I did, I would never cheat on a woman," I told her sincerely.

"I guess that's good. It honestly didn't sit well that you almost kissed me and then went home to a girlfriend." She opened her container and peered at her sandwich. "So, she was just like a one-night stand or something?" she asked, curiosity threaded through her voice.

Now I was the one having trouble meeting her eye. "No, we see each other from time to time, but we both like to keep it casual. I really didn't mean to make you feel bad," I told her honestly. "And what happened in the kitchen with us... I promise it won't happen again."

"Hmmm," she hummed noncommittally as she meticulously picked the bacon and cheese from her sandwich. Then she shyly asked, "Why not?"

"Why won't it happen again?" She nodded but wouldn't look at me, her face flushing a pretty pink. "I just... we wouldn't work," I said lamely.

"Oh," she said, her head down.

"You deserve a relationship kind of guy." I polished off half of my sandwich quickly while she sat in silence and stared at hers.

"So, it's the old 'it's not you, it's me' thing? Gotcha," she said, raising her eyes to mine with a humorless smile.

"Well, it's definitely not you, Peach. I think you're great."

"But you're not attracted to me." She said it as a statement, not a question, and took a small bite of her sandwich. A bite so small, I was surprised she even had to chew it.

How the hell was I supposed to answer that? I took a deep breath and decided to go with honesty. "I'm insanely attracted to you, but I can't give you what you need, Charli."

A furrow appeared between her eyes. "And you're an expert in what I need, Beau?"

"Well, I'm too old for you." She took another tiny bite of her lunch and looked at me speculatively.

"How old are you?"

"I'm thirty-four," I told her, thinking she would understand, but she tilted her head as her mouth tipped up on one side.

"And how old do you think I am, Beau?"

I laughed. "Oh, no. My mother taught me better than to guess a lady's age." I continued eating.

"I don't mind. Tell me what you think."

I hesitated as I chewed. "Twenty?" She started laughing then, and I panicked. "Oh, God. Tell me you're not nineteen." *Please tell me I didn't almost kiss a teenager.*

She gasped through her laughter. "I'm twenty-seven, Beau." I stopped mid-chew and stared at her, my mouth finally clamping shut as a piece of roast beef tried to escape.

"You're shitting me," I said bluntly.

"I am not. Almost twenty-eight, in fact. You want to see my driver's license?" she asked with amusement as she closed up her container without finishing even half of her lunch.

"No, I believe you." She had just cut our estimated age difference in half. What did that mean? My mind was spinning as some of my protective walls began lowering. "You don't like bacon and cheese?" I asked, purposely changing the subject.

"It's fine," she said curtly.

"You didn't even eat half your sandwich. That's not enough to keep a bird alive."

Her eyes flared with anger and something else I couldn't define. "Look, Beau," she snapped. "I don't need another man counting every bite I eat."

She snatched up both of our containers and rose, walking swiftly into the kitchen, leaving me sitting there in a blanket fort with my mouth hanging open. Her words finally sunk in, and I stood and hurried after her, my stomach in knots. "What did you mean by that?" I barked.

She was stuffing the containers into the trash can when I approached her from behind. "Nothing," she said, closing the lid but not turning around.

I put my hand on her shoulder. "Peach…"

"Charli," she corrected quietly.

"Peach," I said firmly, "has someone been telling you what you can and can't eat?"

"Not anymore," she said, finally turning around and looking at me, her chin raised, and her arms crossed defiantly over her chest. She was so tiny, but she looked as fierce as a tiger right at that moment. And I'll be fucked if it didn't turn me on.

"Who?" I demanded.

"Nobody important," she mumbled, her brow creasing. I didn't like it when she frowned, so I reached up and ran my thumb across the wrinkles marring her perfect skin. Her face relaxed as she looked up at me. "It doesn't matter."

"It matters to me," I said softly. "Tell me. Please."

Those gorgeous blue eyes filled with pain, and it almost broke me. "I really don't want to talk about it, Beau."

A red haze started seeping into my vision from the periphery until it covered every inch of my sight. Whoever the man was who had made her feel like that needed his ass whipped, but I tamped down my anger.

This woman needed to know how extraordinarily *beautiful* she was, so I lifted her by the waist easily and set her on the counter. I held her face in my hands, my thumbs under her chin so I could raise her face to mine. "Look at me, Peach. No one has the right to talk to you or treat you like that. There is absolutely nothing wrong with your body."

She tried to drop her chin again, but I held firm. "Do you want to know why I sat over on that lounge chair for so long at Blaire's party?" She didn't answer, instead squeezing her eyebrows together in confusion. "It was because when I saw you in that red swimsuit, I had a, um, very embarrassing situation arise."

"What kind of situation?"

I moved one of my hands to cup the back of her head and slid my lips against her ear as I whispered, "My dick was so fucking hard I could barely stand up, baby." She gasped, and when I took her earlobe between my lips, her body melted against mine. "You have the most gorgeous body, Peach. I've never been that turned on by a woman in my life."

"Beau..." The way my name fell from her lips on a soft moan almost brought me to my knees. I needed to lighten the mood before I did something I would regret.

"I'm serious, Charli. I had to keep a towel in my lap to cover up my hard-on. That thing was enormous, and I was afraid it was going to scare the kids or poke someone's eye out." She giggled then, and I pulled my face back so that I could see her smile.

"Stop it, Beau." Her smile faded, and her face turned serious. "I don't know what's going on here, but I don't do casual hook-ups." She blinked a couple times. "But we could be friends," she said, attempting to keep her tone light, but sounding as regretful as I felt.

Shit. I was being fucking friend-zoned, and for reasons I couldn't explain, I didn't like it one bit.

BEAU

I RETURNED TO BLAIRE'S house for dinner that evening and was greeted at the door by a grinning Carrie. "Uncle Beau! What are you doing here?"

I lifted her over my head until she squealed and then settled her on my hip. "I came to eat dinner with my favorite girl," I told her, kissing her on the cheek.

"Will you sit by me? We're having pizza."

"I guess I could do that. As long as you don't try to steal my mushrooms."

"No promises," she said tartly as I carried her into the kitchen. My eyes immediately zoomed in on Charli putting paper plates down on the table. She looked up at me and gave me a soft smile, which I returned. I looked over to see Blaire watching us, shifting her focus between me and Charli. *Fuck.* That's the last damn thing I needed... my nosy-ass sister poking around in my business.

Axel walked in a couple minutes later with three large pizza boxes. "I come bearing food for my family," he proclaimed, and the triplets jumped happily around him until he put down the pizzas and picked each boy up to greet them. "And how is my baby girl?" he asked, kissing Carrie's cheek.

"I'm good, Daddy. I got an A on my math quiz today."

"I'm glad you got your brains from me," he teased. He turned to me and slapped me on the shoulder. "Hey, Beau. Glad you could join us tonight."

"Yeah. Thanks for letting me crash the pizza party."

Axel strolled over to the island where Blaire was pouring drinks for everyone. He grabbed her from behind and whispered something in her ear that had her turning around and wrapping her arms around his neck. It reminded me a little of how our parents used to be together, which made me happy and sad at the same time. Blaire giggled at something Ax said, and then they put on quite a disgusting display of affection that had Carrie rolling her eyes and shaking her head. "They're so gross sometimes," she muttered to me.

I normally agreed, but tonight I found myself wondering what that would be like. How would it feel to walk in the door and know that someone was so happy to see you, she couldn't help but wrap herself around you? I glanced over at Charli, who had taken the seat across the table from me, and saw her smiling wistfully at the couple. I wondered if she was having the same thoughts as me.

Axel sat at the head of the table with Blaire on one side and the kids spread out between the adults. Throughout the meal, I noticed that Blaire often reached over and touched Axel's hand or arm, and they would share a smile like they knew a secret no one else did.

I had no idea where it was coming from, but I found myself envious of their easy, loving relationship. The touches, the smiles, the fucking secretive looks they gave each other, like they couldn't wait to be alone. I looked at Peach and was pleased to see that she was chowing down on her piece of pizza. She raised her eyes to me and smiled when I winked at her.

I slid a box toward her and asked, "You want another slice, Charli?"

"Umm, sure," she said, grabbing another piece and taking a bite, her eyes locked on mine. I didn't hear any of the chatter from the kids for a couple moments as I watched her eat. Why did watching my *friend* eat pizza fill me with a sense of elation? Then I realized that we were sharing our own special secret look right in the middle of the chaos that was dinner time at the Broxton household. And I fucking liked it.

Toward the end of dinner, Dani started to get fussy. "Is my sweet girl hungry? Maybe Uncle Beau wants to feed you," Blaire said, smiling over at me.

"Of course," I said, reaching for my tiny niece.

"I'll get her a bottle. Take her in the living room," she said. I talked to Dani as I carried her in the living room and sank into the plush couch. Blaire came in a few minutes later with a warmed bottle and handed it to me.

"Here you go. One bottle of boob juice."

"Ugh, Blaire. Why you gotta say shit like that?" I asked, scrunching up my face. "Why can't your mommy act right?" I asked Danica, and she grinned at me.

I popped the bottle into her mouth, and Blaire stroked a finger through Dani's wispy hair before sitting next to me on the couch. "Ax and Charli are getting the kids ready for bed. I thought maybe we could talk."

Oh, hell. Not talking. Anything but that.

"M'kay," I said warily.

Her gaze sharpened on me. "Is something going on between you and Charli?"

"We're just friends," I said quickly, sounding defensive as hell.

"Do you like her?" my sister probed.

"Sure. She's very nice, and she's great with the kids," I answered evasively.

"But do you *like her* like her?"

"I'm not answering that on the grounds that I'm not a thirteen-year-old girl," I retorted.

"Cut the shit, Beau. Are you attracted to Charli?"

God, she was going to be so pissed at me. "Yes, but I swear to God, Blaire. I'm not going to act on it. I know I'm not good for her." My sister closed her eyes and shook her head. Here it comes. At least she wouldn't hit me because I was holding the baby. Probably.

"You're the biggest fucking idiot I've—"

"I know, I know. I'm sorry," I broke in. "I'll just stay away for a while, and maybe it will all blow over."

"That's not what I'm saying, idiot. Why do you think you're not good for her?"

I stared at her like she had just shot champagne out of her ass. Wasn't it obvious? Shrugging one shoulder, I said, "She's all sweet and good, and… I'm just me."

"I happen to like 'just you,' Beau."

"You're obligated. You're my sister," I said with a smirk.

"Tell me specifically why you think you wouldn't be good for her." I just stared at her, unable to give voice to my thoughts. It didn't sound at all like she was *against* me and Charli getting together.

"Why don't I tell you some reasons why I think you *would* be good for her?" She started ticking them off on her fingers. "You're successful, you have your own business, and you work hard. You're sweet and protective, especially with females. And you're kinda good-looking, I guess, if you like handsome, strong, muscular guys," she finished with a crooked grin.

"Okay, let's take these one-by-one. Yes, I'm successful, but having my own business takes up a lot of my time."

Blaire rolled her eyes. "Oh, give me a fucking break. Millions of people run businesses and have relationships. I'm a freaking surgeon, which is one of the most demanding jobs in the world, and I still managed to get married and have an entire brood. So, I don't accept that as an excuse. Next." She raised her eyebrows and flicked her hand dismissively at me.

Huh.

"I'm protective of my family, but I'm not sweet," I growled.

"Don't tell me you can't be sweet. I know you like to pretend like you're this big growly jerk, but I've seen you with my kids. And hell, you're even sweet to me sometimes."

"Don't let that get out. You'll spoil my asshole reputation," I said, trying to conceal my smile. "But I'll concede on the good-looking point. I've been told I'm quite the hotty."

"And so modest," she said mockingly.

I sighed dramatically. "Well, it's my burden to bear, little sister."

She rolled her eyes. "So, what's the problem?"

"Charli... she's so sweet, and I'm rough. We wouldn't be compatible. Plus, I don't know how to do relationships, Blaire. Hell, I don't even date."

"Look at me and Ax. He's big and rough and hot-tempered, and we work. And I'm the sweetest angel in the world," she said, batting her eyelashes at me as I scoffed. Her head tilted as she regarded me, her soft green eyes clashing with my darker ones. "Why don't you date, Beau?"

"I've just never had time."

Her face softened. "I'll tell you exactly why. It's because you've felt responsible for *me* for so long." *Nailed it, little sister.* "But I'm good, Beau. You took wonderful care of me and Carrie when we needed you. You've put in your time. But who takes care of you?"

"I take care of myself," I said, gruffly.

"If that's a masturbation reference, I'm going to throat punch you," she said flatly, making me laugh. "I think you care about Charli. I've seen the way you two look at each other." She shifted, curling one foot under her butt as she craned her face closer to mine and lowered her voice. "And what the hell was that at dinner? In the entire time she's been here, I've never seen Charli eat more than a half a piece of pizza, and you got her to eat two. I was beginning to get concerned that maybe she had an eating disorder."

I felt my temperature rising just thinking about Charli's ex and the things he must have said to her to make her feel like she couldn't eat when she wanted to. "I dunno, Blaire. Maybe she just needs reassurance that she looks, you know, good." *Very good. Fucking amazing.*

A knowing smile crossed my sister's lips for a second before slipping away. "Ms. Casper told us that Charli had just gotten out of a bad relationship, and that she left Georgia because of some kind of incident with the boyfriend."

Anger and fear and panic melded together to form a hard ball in my gut. "Incident? Did he lay a hand on her? Because I will fucking end him."

"Protective much?" Blaire uttered with a cocked eyebrow as I proved her point. I did care about Charli. "Would it really be so horrible to take a nice woman out to dinner? I mean, you seem to get along with each other. I've never seen you talk to a woman as much as you've talked to her in the few times you've seen her. Usually, you just grunt and point to the bedroom."

"Hey!" I said, feigning offense. "I don't just grunt. I make rude hand gestures as well."

My sister pinched the bridge of her nose and closed her eyes. "Jesus, give me strength."

"Women find it very charming," I said in explanation.

She turned serious again. "Don't you want to get married someday, Beau? I'm not necessarily saying to Charli, because if you steal my nanny, I will cut your ass. But you need to grow the hell up and start dating like a real man. You act like some twenty-year-old frat boy bringing home a different bimbo every night."

That really hit home. I was a very responsible man in every way except my dating life. In that, I had to admit that I was remarkably immature. I knew exactly what to do with a woman in bed, but on a date? That scared the shit out of me to even contemplate.

"I guess."

"So, you'll ask her out?" Blaire pressed, and I shrugged. "Beauuuu," she whined.

"I don't know how to act on a date," I admitted, looking down at the sleeping baby in my arms before lifting my gaze back to my sister. She looked like she wanted to smack me.

"Oh, for Pete's sake, Beau. Mama raised you to be a gentleman. Just use your manners. Open doors for her. Oh, and when you're walking with her, put your hand right here," she said, indicating the small of her back. "Women find that hot as hell. Unless you're walking on a beach or something. Then hold her hand."

There were rules about what I was supposed to do with my hands? "This sounds complicated. Can you make me a study guide or something?" I asked, only halfway teasing. Blaire took the sleeping baby from my arms and gently laid her in the little bassinet beside the couch as I rubbed my forehead in frustration. I felt like an idiot.

"Here's a good rule of thumb. If she's wearing a dress or a nice outfit, put your hand on her back. If she's wearing shorts and a t-shirt, that's more casual, so just hold her hand."

I made a little grunting noise to let her know I understood.

"And make sure you compliment her."

I grunted again, though internally, I was in a near panic. *How was I supposed to know what to say?* I was soooo out of my comfort zone. Was I really thinking about doing this?

"There's no set rule on what to say," Blaire said, as if reading my mind. "Just whatever you like, tell her you like it. Her dress, her hair, if she smells good, whatever. And be nice about it. Don't just tell her she's making your weenie hard." I snorted at that.

I pretended to take notes on my hand. "Do. Not. Discuss. Hard. Weenie. Got it." Blaire gave me a flat look, and I gave her an apologetic smile. I knew she was trying to help me, but I was struggling hard with this.

Undeterred by my lack of enthusiasm, my sister rattled on with her recitation of *Dating for Dummies*. "Let's see... what else? Oh, sexting." I slid my eyes toward her and lifted one brow. "First rule of sexting is no dick pics and no asking for nudes," she said, her eyebrows creeping together and her mouth in a firm, stern line.

"Blaire. I work in security. I know what kind of place the world is, and I know better than to send nude pictures out into the ether."

"Okay good, back to the sexting thing... you have to decipher how far the woman is willing to go with it. You don't want to offend her if it's too soon for her. Maybe start out slow with something like, 'I thought about you all night after I dropped you off.' If she asks, 'What were you thinking?' she probably wants to play a little. But don't just jump right in and tell her you want to ram her with your man stick."

Rubbing a hand over my jaw, I nodded. "I can promise you that the words 'ram you with my man stick' will never even cross my mind," I said curtly.

"Well, that's a relief. Maybe there is hope for you yet," she said, patting my hand. "Like I said, start slow. Think of it like foreplay. Make it sexy. Like, 'I thought about unzipping your dress and sliding it slowly down your body.'"

I smiled and nodded my head. That did sound sexy, but not overly perverted. "I think I get it. I probably don't have to worry about that stuff with Charli, though. She's just so fucking sweet and probably not into the dirty talk."

"Au contraire, big brother. You have to watch out for the quiet ones; they're usually the ones that like to let their freak flags fly." My eyes widened, and Blaire giggled. "You'll be fine, bro. You're a smart guy and you're really sweet underneath all that growly exterior. Just remember that Charli isn't one of your bimbos that you can just fuck and dump."

"I know, Blaire," I told her, reaching down to stroke Danica's soft hair.

"Why don't you come back for dinner again tomorrow night? You're in a kind of safe zone here, so you can get to know her a little better without the awkwardness of a first date."

Blaire leaned over and kissed me on the cheek. "You're a good man, Beau Atwood. You deserve some happiness in your life. A partner who will take care of you like you take care of her. Someone who would make an excellent mother to your children," she said, waggling her eyebrows.

I almost choked on my own spit, and my sister laughed.

"I didn't mean to scare you, but that's something you need to consider when you're dating. I don't want you to end up with some stupid shrew that the rest of us have to deal with. Who was that girl I met at your house last month? Melinda or something?"

"Miranda?" I asked.

"Yes, that's her. When she asked what I did and I told her, she told me she thought she would make a good surgeon and was going to 'look into it.' Then she asked, 'do you, like, have to go to, you know, like, college and stuff to do that? Or can I, like, do it online?'" Blaire rolled her eyes theatrically.

I chuckled. "Yeah, Miranda's not going to be winning any academic achievement awards any time soon."

Blaire gave me a slightly evil grin. "I suggested she specialize in plastic surgery since it seemed to be something she was already familiar with."

"You did not," I said with a laugh.

"I sure as hell did, and she wasn't even smart enough to know that she was being insulted."

"This is why I love you, little sister," I told her, wrapping my arm around her. She curled up next to my side and put her head on my shoulder. "Thanks for talking to me. And for giving me a kick in the ass when I need it." I kissed the top of her head.

"It's my job as the bratty little sister to give it to you straight," she said, looking up at me.

As I drove home later that night, I thought about what it would be like if I had a woman to go home to every evening. A week ago, that would have scared the shit out of me, but now the thought of coming home to the same woman every day didn't sound bad at all. Especially if I could find someone who looked at me the way Blaire looks at Axel. Yes, I liked to give them shit for being so affectionate, but the truth was, it was pretty damned appealing.

With my mind made up, I was officially about to un-friend-zone myself from Charli Casper ASAP.

CHARLI

"What are you wearing tonight?" I asked Bristol on Saturday afternoon.

Through the phone, I could hear her sliding hangers around in her closet. "Uhh, let's see. I think I'm going to wear this tight black bandage dress. My ass looks amazing in it. Not as good as yours, but still."

I surveyed the outfits on my bed. "I think I'm wearing pants. I have some white fitted pants that are cut low. And let's see. Maybe my gold cropped tank. Show off a little belly. Or do you think that would be too much?"

"Hell no! But I think you should wear a skirt."

"I thought about it, but if this DJ is as good as you said, I plan on dancing a lot. I don't want my skirt flying up."

"That, my dear, is why you wear cute underwear," Bris said with her trademark sass. "Show off the goods a bit."

I laughed. "I don't think so. I'm not as confident as you."

"So, how are things in the Broxton household? I haven't had a chance to talk to you all week."

"Things are great. I love my job, but..."

"But what?" Bristol asked, zooming in on that one word.

"It's Beau. He's come over for dinner every single night this week, and, I don't know, Bris. I have the feeling he's coming to see me. I know that sounds conceited, but since I've been here, he's never come over every weeknight before."

"Be careful with the porn star, Charli. He sounds like a total player," she warned.

"I know, but you know how I told you he insists on calling me Peach? Well, every night when I go into my room, there's something peach-related on my pillow."

"What the hell? He's been going into your room?"

"I guess, but it doesn't seem creepy, you know? Just kinda... sweet. Wednesday night there was a pack of peach gummy rings, and Thursday I found a box of peach cookies from that amazing bakery near here. Then, last night he left a small cooler with peach ice cream and a plastic spoon."

"Was it Blue Bell?"

"Yeah, why?"

Bristol chuckled. "At least the boy has good taste."

I hesitated before telling her the next part, but Bris was my best friend. "Also, before he left last night, he asked me to walk out on the porch with him. He asked me out."

My friend was silent for a rare moment. "Asked you out as in 'Hey, you want to come over and bang?'"

"No. Like on an actual date. He wanted to take me to dinner one night."

"Whaaaaat? Are you serious? What did you say?"

"I told him no and that it was best if we stay friends. I felt like shit turning him down, because he seemed so nervous to ask me. I really wanted to say yes, but I can't date a playboy, Bris."

"No. You're right. You would just end up getting hurt, and then I would have to murder Mr. Porno."

I smiled, loving her loyalty. "Awww. Thanks, Bris. I would totally come visit you in prison if you killed someone for me."

"You better. It's in the best friends rule book, page thirty-eight, if I'm not mistaken. Right next to the rule about sharing ice cream when you talk about sexy men."

"My favorite rule," I said. "Look, I need to go, but I'll meet you at the club tonight. Text me the address."

"Sure thing, toots. I have a surprise for you, too," she sang, her voice trilling up and down on the last word.

"A surprise? What is it?" I asked warily. There was no telling with Bristol.

"If I told you, then..."

"...it wouldn't be a surprise," I finished. "All right, woman. I'll see you tonight."

That evening after the kids were down for the night, I got ready in my room. I was coating my lashes with mascara when I heard a light tapping on my bedroom door. "Come in," I called and turned as Blaire walked into my room.

"Charli! You look gorgeous, honey."

"Thank you, Blaire. I'm going out with my friend Bristol tonight. That's okay, right?"

"Sure, Charli. Your free time is your own. You're young, and you should be going out and having fun. If you ever need any time off for... oh, let's say... a *date* or something, you just let me know." She was grinning at me, and I felt a sharp frisson of guilt skirt down my spine.

"Oh, thanks, but I'm not really dating right now," I mumbled.

"Why not? You're a beautiful girl, and I know lots of men who would love to take you out. One in particular," she said, her eyebrows rising high on her smooth forehead. *Was she talking about Beau? Did she know that he had asked me out?*

"I... I'm new in town and don't really know many people," I stammered.

"What about my brother?" she asked directly.

Oh, shit. "Beau?"

A hint of a smile played around Blaire's lips. She knew I was hedging. "Well, yes. Do you like him?" *Damn, let's just get right down to it.*

"Um, he's very... nice."

"You think he's good-looking, right? Most women tend to find him irresistible."

I decided to just be honest. "That's the problem, Blaire. I think he finds women irresistible, too. *All* of them." I gave my boss a flat smile, and she returned it with a bright one.

"That's true, but I think my brother is ready to settle down." She sighed heavily and sat on my bed. I positioned myself on the edge of the bed with one leg tucked underneath me. "Beau is complicated. He's resisted real relationships in the past because he felt responsible for me and Carrie. Beau took me in when I was pregnant and alone, gave me a place to live. He basically gave up his life to be there for us." Blaire's voice was heavy with emotion as she spoke.

"That was a wonderful thing for him to do," I said quietly as my heart bloomed with renewed affection for her brother, and Blaire nodded and smiled at me.

"It was. Charli, please don't think I'm pressuring you at all. I would never do that. I just wanted to give you some insight as to why Beau is the way he is. If you don't want to go out with him, then don't. I know better than anyone that he's stubborn and bossy. Hell, I wouldn't go out with him," she said with a laugh. She reached over and laid her hand on top of mine. "But one thing about my brother, he's the most honorable man I know. If he were to start dating a woman, she could expect nothing but total loyalty from him. And I do think he's ready to change."

"Thank you for telling me all that, Blaire. I'm still not sure if I want to date right now, but that helped with my concerns about Beau. I'm just afraid of getting hurt."

"If you do go out with my brother and he hurts you, please let me know. I'll be happy to rip him a new butthole for you," she said, rubbing her hands together as if relishing the thought. "So, where are you going tonight?"

"Some new club that just opened up called 'Flame.'"

"Oh, I've heard that place is awesome. We've been wanting to go, but it's so difficult with Axel being recognized everywhere. The men think they're his best friends and want to talk football, and the women think they can stick their boobs in his face, and he'll automatically leave me for them. We can never just go out and enjoy being together."

I laughed at that. I had been out to dinner with the family a couple times, and I had seen the extreme flirtation firsthand. It was almost comical how ballsy some of the women could be while Axel's wife was standing *right beside him*. But that man only had eyes for Blaire.

"Anyway, I'll let you finish getting ready. I want to hear all about Flame tomorrow," Blaire said. "Do you want Axel to drive you? He can come back and pick you up when you're ready to leave, as well."

"No, I'm going to Uber. But thank you for offering." I pulled out my phone and opened the app. "I'll go ahead and order it now."

We walked out into the living room a few minutes later, and I glanced at my phone and frowned. "What is it?" Blaire asked.

"My Uber driver was in a fender bender, and there's not another one available that can pick me up in the next twenty minutes. I'm going to text Bristol and tell her I'll be late."

"No, don't do that. I'll get Ax to take you. He won't mind. I'll promise him sexy times when he gets back, and he'll do anything I ask," she said with a giggle.

"I hate to tell you, but I think he would do anything you asked anyway."

"Yeah, he's pretty dreamy," she sighed as she pulled out her phone and tapped out a text. I wasn't sure what she typed, but we heard Axel bounding down the stairs a few seconds later, and Blaire and I grinned at each other. He was wearing sweats and was pulling a wrinkled t-shirt over his messy-haired head. He realized he didn't have shoes on, so he pulled on his rain boots that were sitting near the door. "That's hot, babe," Blaire said with a teasing smile.

"I'll show you hot when I get home," he growled, giving her a hard kiss on the mouth. "And I'm leaving the boots on while I do it." I swear, these two were too freaking adorable.

Twenty minutes later, Axel pulled his black BMW convertible up in front of Flame. "Are you sure you don't want me to come in with you? Maybe I could start a new trend in clubwear with my outfit," he said, gesturing up and down his body.

I laughed as I got out of the car. "No, but thanks. You should get home to your wife. Thanks for the ride, Axel." I texted Bristol that I was there, and she met me at the front door, and thank goodness she did. This place was packed. It would have taken me an hour to find her in this crowd.

"This place is fantastic!" I yelled to her over the pulsing music. Along all the walls, flames of different heights were encased between two sheets of clear glass, giving the impression that the whole place was on fire.

"I know, right? We got here a little early and were able to get a booth. We're right back here," she said, dragging me to the right.

"We?" I asked.

"Yep. That's your surprise!" She did game show hostess hands as she stopped by a large, curved booth upholstered in a deep red leather, and I squealed when I saw who was sitting there.

"Aaron!" I yelled as Bristol's older brother stood and enveloped me in a hug that lifted my feet from the ground.

"Gnarly Charli! What's up?" He released me and grabbed both of my hands, holding them out so he could inspect me. "Dayum, girl. You are looking F-I-N-E." I giggled at his attention. Aaron had only gotten more handsome now that he was older. His dark brown hair was mussed stylishly, and his brown eyes were warm and affectionate. He was dressed in charcoal slacks and a thin, light gray sweater that was just fitted enough to show off an athletic build on his six-foot frame.

"And look at you! Are you still breaking hearts all over Denver?" He had moved there after college and become one of the most successful real estate brokers in the state of Colorado.

Aaron glanced at Bristol and asked, "You didn't tell her?"

She shrugged. "I was saving it for you, heartbreaker," she said sarcastically.

Her brother held his arms out and said, "I'm back, baby! I moved back to Dallas."

"Oh, Aaron! That's fabulous! I know your parents will be thrilled."

He buffed his fingernails on his shirt. "Yes, they are quite ecstatic that their favorite child has returned to the fold." Bristol smacked him on the head, and he rubbed the spot with a frown. "Ow. Watch the ring, you psycho." He turned back to me and cupped one hand around his mouth, but still talked loud enough that his sister could hear. "This is why I'm the favorite."

Bris rolled her eyes and gestured to the booth. "Sit down, prodigal son. I'm sure Charli wants to rest her feet before we hit the dance floor. You look fab tonight, Char."

"Thanks." I said as I sat to scoot into the booth.

"Scooch over, Charli," Aaron said, moving me farther into the booth and sitting right beside me. He flagged down a waitress as Bristol sat on my other side. "What do you want, babe?" he asked in my ear.

"An amaretto sour, please," I said, reaching for my debit card in the hidden inside pocket of my pants.

"Nuh-uh. You will not pay for a single drink tonight," Aaron said, pushing my card away. "I insist."

He ordered our drinks, and as the waitress started to walk away, I asked, "Hey, what is that?" I pointed to another table downing fire shots.

"We specialize in all kinds of flaming drinks," the waitress said. "We've got flaming B52, flaming Dr. Pepper, flaming Jesus, flaming Bob Marley—which is really pretty, by the way—flaming lemon drop, flaming giraffe. Those are some of the most popular. Scan this barcode with your phone, and you can see the full menu," she said, tapping a square on the table.

"Bring us a round of Jesus and Bob Marley," Aaron said, circling his finger in the air. The waitress returned a few minutes later, and we raised our Bob Marley shots first. "Let's do it, ladies," Aaron yelled over the bumping bass of the music before we downed the shot.

Bristol coughed. "Damn, I need some Jesus after that shot." She wrinkled her face and stuck out her tongue as she reached for the other shot, which she slugged back like a champ. I sipped on my amaretto sour for a few minutes before my tablemates finally cajoled me into drinking the flaming Jesus shot.

"Whoa! What all is in that one? It's strong," I said, shaking my head. Reading from the menu on her phone, Bristol informed us it was vodka, rum, grenadine, and lime juice. "Somehow, I don't think that one is actually approved by the Lord," I said with a tipsy giggle, but I wasn't too tipsy to feel Aaron's hand move to my thigh, squeezing lightly. "What are you doing, Are?"

"Just keeping you from tipping over, babe. Let's dance," he said, sliding from the booth and taking my hand. "I'm liking retro night. All this old music is the best." He put one hand around my waist and held our joined hands close to our bodies when we reached the dance floor. It felt weird to have Aaron's hand on the bare skin of my back, but I guessed that was what happened when you wore a crop top to the club.

"Me too. I like knowing all the words."

Aaron leaned forward and sang lyrics that had something to do with heaven, an old Warrant song, if I wasn't mistaken. During the instrumental part, he said, "You look really great, Charli." His fingertips stroked softly against my back, and it felt... good but a little strange. He rubbed his nose against my cheek. "I've always thought you were beautiful, but fuck, baby." He pulled me tighter against him, and I could feel his erection pressing against my stomach.

What the hell was going on here? This was *Aaron*. Bristol's *brother*. And he had an erection. And it was touching me! Aaron was a couple years older than us, but I had never known he ever saw me. Like *really* saw me. "I always thought I was just the annoying friend of your annoying little sister."

He chuckled, and his soft breath warmed my hair. "Maybe a little, but we're all grown up now." He drew back to look at me, and it was obvious he was having very grown-up thoughts in that handsome head of his. I smiled weakly, starting to feel a little bit uncomfortable, especially when his fingertips slid into the waistband at the back of my pants. My pants rode low on my hips, so that put his fingers right at the top of my... *Holy shit! Aaron Hopkins is touching my ass crack!*

"Aaron, don't..." I warned, and he moved his hand to a slightly more neutral position.

He gave me a crooked grin and said, "Sorry. I would love to take you out some time." His grin widened. "In fact, I would love to do a lot of things with you." His hand slipped down to my butt again, this time over the top of my pants.

I was rescued by Bristol, who appeared at our side. "Are you trying to touch my friend's ass, you perv?" I bit the inside of my cheek to keep from exploding with laughter at her brazenness. The song ended, and Aaron reluctantly released me as Bristol shoved a shot into my hand. "It's that giraffe one. Shoot it!" We linked arms and swallowed our shots, and Bris shoved both of our glasses into Aaron's hands, effectively dismissing him. I shot him an apologetic smile, but he took it in stride, winking at me before he walked off the dance floor and back toward our booth.

Bristol and I danced our asses off to a cool mashup of Donna Summer's "Bad Girls" mixed with Beyonce's "Naughty Girl." We were having so much fun, moving our bodies to the music, and I forgot all about the awkwardness with Aaron a few minutes earlier.

10

BEAU

I DIALED AXEL'S NUMBER, and a deep female voice answered, "You've reached Maxine's House of Pleasure. How may I direct your call?"

I grinned. My sister thought she could fool me with that fake-ass voice.

I put on my heaviest drawl and asked, "Uh, yeah. I would like to place an order. Y'all still got that two-for-one Saturday night special?"

"Why yes, we do, sir. Do you prefer blondes, redheads, or brunettes?"

"I'm not picky. Hell, she could be bald, as long as she's got a nice rack."

I could hear the smile in her voice. "Nice rack. Yes sir. I've got that down. Any more requirements?"

"Um, you got anyone with a cool accent? I like to feel fancy when I'm getting it on."

I heard a snort on the other end of the line. "I think we could accommodate that request."

"And, let's see... oh, are any of your girls named Bambi?"

"Of course, sir. We have a Bambi and a Buffy available for tonight. Bambi has a lovely Scandinavian accent, and Buffy is half-French on her mother's cousin's side. I'll just need your credit card number, along with the expiration date and the three-digit code on the back."

"Sure, let me just get that for you. Oh, and can they handle a man with a really big—"

My sister cut me off, reverting to her normal voice. "Ewwww! Gross, Beau! Shut up."

I laughed heartily. "You started it, sis. Can I talk to Axel?"

"No. The big goof left his phone here accidentally. He should be back in a few minutes though."

I bit the edge of my bottom lip. "I wanted to see if you were going to the Wranglers game tomorrow. Maybe I could go with you, if Ax could swing an extra ticket?" I asked hopefully.

I wanted to hang out with Blaire and Carrie, but I didn't want to go to their house. Not with Charli there. Not after she had shot me down like a flying squirrel. I mean, I *wanted* to see Charli. It surprised me how much I ached to see her, but damn, it hurt to be rejected.

"Carrie and I are going, and I'm sure Axel can get you a ticket. I'll ask him when he gets home."

I looked at the clock on my oven and frowned. "Where is your husband this late?"

"Oh, he gave Charli a ride to that new club, Flame. Have you heard about it? Some of the interns at the hospital were talking about it. I'm dying to try some of their flaming shots."

I attempted to control my breathing as my sister blabbed on about the nightclub. *Charli is going out? Jesus, why does that make it so hard for me to breathe?* During a break in Blaire's diatribe, I said absently, "Yeah, sounds cool. Hey, just text me and let me know what Ax says. Hopefully, I'll see you tomorrow."

My mind swelled with a thousand thoughts when I hung up the phone. Who was she going with? Was she meeting someone there? If so, was that someone a man? What was she wearing? I bet she looked amazing. Of course, she always looked amazing. Would she dance? She could probably really move that tight little body. What if other guys looked at her or tried to touch her? And I knew they damn sure would. On and on the thoughts poured unfiltered through my brain.

Fuck! Why was this woman under my skin like this? Without knowing what I was doing, I went into the living room and stood over Cam, who was watching ESPN.

"Why you hovering, dude?" he asked, looking up at me with suspicious eyes.

"Charli went out," I said simply.

"Like on a date?"

"I don't know. I just talked to Blaire, and she mentioned that Axel had given her a ride to a club called Flame. So probably not a date, unless she's meeting someone there." I was all too aware of my chest rising and falling more heavily than usual.

"Yeah, I've been to Flame once. It's incredible. Lots of hotties there looking to…" His voice faded away as he took in my stiff demeanor and angry stare. "Sorry. Uh, you want to go check it out? I could do with a cold one."

I nodded once and headed to my room, calling over my shoulder, "Ten minutes."

Nine minutes later, we were walking out the door. I had showered, shaved, dressed, and put on some aftershave.

"I called the guys. They're meeting us there," Cam said as I cranked up my truck and put it in drive.

"Why the fuck did you do that?" I practically shouted. I didn't want them to know about my weird attachment to Peach. It was bad enough that I had spilled my guts to Cam. I didn't like anyone knowing I had… *feelings*.

My friend shrugged as I took off down the street in front of our house, the V-8 engine roaring. "Thought we might need backup if you decided to take out every man in the bar for looking her way," he said with a touch of amusement.

I allowed myself a slight smile. It was like Cam could read my damned mind. "Yeah, might not be a bad idea," I grudgingly allowed. The club wasn't far, and we arrived within minutes.

We got inside, and I looked around at the sea of people. "Fuck," I said loudly, and Cam nodded.

"Let's split up. You head to the right, and I'll go left. The bar is that way, so I'll grab us beers."

I started walking swiftly, my eyes swiveling left and right with razor-sharp intensity. Using my height to my advantage, I weaved between people, searching booths and tables. Vaguely aware of women's eyes sliding up and down my body as I worked my way through the crowd, I got to the edge of the dance floor. Sweeping my eyes across the mass of writhing bodies, I searched for a little blonde head… and there she was.

Christ almighty.

I shot Cam a text.

Shark: Target acquired. Right side of the dance floor.

Cam: OMW. The guys are just pulling up.

I glanced at his reply and then focused my eyes back on Charli. Correction: I was focused on the hand of some prick who was rubbing all over her back, imagining all the ways I could separate his fucking hand from his body. They were slow dancing to a love song, and my stomach roiled with nausea. Cam arrived and shoved a beer into my hand, placing a restraining hand on my shoulder as he took in the scene.

"Well, fuck. Sorry, Shark." The guy was leaning in close to her, and then he yanked her up against his body. My jaw clenched, and my body shook almost uncontrollably with the urge to act. Cam's hand tightened on my shoulder. "Stay calm, bro."

Our other friends arrived then, shouting greetings over the loud music. "Hey, is that Charli?" Woody asked excitedly. Cam gave a sharp shake of his head and then jerked his chin toward me. "Huh? Ohhhhh. Oh, damn. So…" The realization hit him, and quickly spread to my other friends. We had been team members or co-workers for over ten years, so they knew me better than almost anyone. We could communicate without words. And my clenched hands and the tight set of my jaw as I watched Charli told them everything they needed to know.

I closed my eyes and tilted my head back, downing half my beer when the prickfuck slid his fingers down into the back of her pants. "Goddammit! I'm going to fucking jail tonight," I growled.

I felt Tank's beefy hand on my bicep. "Calm down, Shark," he said in my ear. "Look, she's handling herself."

I watched as she said something, and the fingers moved back up to her back. Her bare back.

Fucking Christ! What the hell was she wearing? Those tight white pants hugged her every curve, including that tantalizing ass. I couldn't really blame the guy for wanting to touch it, but that didn't mean I didn't want to send him to the hospital with his fucking arm in a trash bag. And that gold top made her look like a freaking goddess, especially with all that long, blonde hair draping down her back. Not to mention those cherry red lips. I had never seen Charli with lipstick on before, and the effect was near torture as I thought about her on her knees in front of me, my cock smearing that lipstick all over her pretty face.

Fuck me with a chainsaw. I wanted her. Badly.

A waitress appeared beside us, and I heard Hawk order a round of beers and shots. I downed the rest of my bottle and stared at the guy grinning at my Peach.

She returned his smile, but her head was pulled back, as if to put space between them. At least there was that.

I relaxed marginally when another woman approached, and the handsy douchebag released Peach. The girls did a shot together and laughed before sending the guy on his way. He walked right by us with a smug smile that I wanted to wipe right off his goddamn face, when I felt Tank's massive hand squeeze my arm hard. "Easy, brother. We've got your back, but let's try not to start any shit."

The waitress returned, and I felt a shot glass and a beer bottle being shoved into my hands by one of my friends. I downed the shot and chased it with some beer to try and calm my nerves. It worked. A little.

I looked up at Tank, but his eyes were back on the girls, who were dancing now. He tipped the neck of his beer bottle their way and muttered, "Who's Charli's friend?"

I tore my eyes away from Charli's shaking ass long enough to look at the other woman. She was a few inches taller than Charli, so maybe around five foot six-ish. Her long, dark, wavy hair had a bright blue streak framing her face on one side. She looked like one of those pin-up models from the old calendars, but with an edge.

"Dunno," I said.

Tank smiled as he took a big swig of his beer. "She's cute."

I raised an eyebrow and punched him in the arm. "Go for it, big guy."

His smile turned reluctant, and he shrugged a shoulder that was as big around as a cantaloupe. "Nah. She's probably..." He shook his head, not finishing the thought.

I turned to the other guys and said, "Somebody get Tank another shot. Loosen his big ass up so he'll stop being a pussy."

He glared at me. "I'm not the only one," he said gruffly. "Looks to me like you're pretty content to stand on the sidelines instead of going for what you want." His eyes returned pointedly to the dance floor, and my gaze locked onto Charli as she moved her sweet, lithe body to the music. *Bad girls. Naughty girl.* The lyrics surrounded me as I watched her, the pulsing strobes spotlighting only her on the dance floor, leaving everyone else in relative darkness. At least that's what it seemed like to me. I didn't see anyone but my sexy little Peach.

Fuck, she can really move.

I drained my beer, slamming the empty bottle down on a nearby table. "Fuck you, I'm going in," I announced as the DJ cranked up 'Super Freak.'

Taking a deep, calming breath, I climbed the two steps up to the elevated dance floor.

11

CHARLI

"You were right, Bris. This DJ is awesome!" I yelled, my hands over my head in the universal dance move of drunk girls everywhere.

The song changed, and Bristol and I looked at each other with wide eyes just before screaming simultaneously, "It's Rick James, bitch!" We fucking loved this song. My hips bumped and swirled to the funky beat, the alcohol making me feel loose and free.

I noticed Bristol's mouth drop open as she looked at something over my shoulder, but before I could turn to see what had interested her, I felt two strong hands wrap around to the front of my hips.

"Hello, Peach." *Beau freaking Atwood. No wonder Bris was staring.* His deep voice rumbled through my entire body as his warm lips skimmed the shell of my ear. "Are you a bad girl or a naughty girl?"

Holy hell. His voice and his words had wetness seeping between my legs in an instant. With liquid courage running through my veins, I turned my head and said saucily, "It depends on how many shots I've had." My nose was right at his neck, and *holy moly,* he smelled delicious.

His low chuckle made goosebumps rise on my arms, and I tried unsuccessfully to control the shiver that ran down my spine. "And how many have you had tonight?"

"I'm about one shot past naughty and well on my way to bad girl status. Though another shot would probably elevate me all the way to super freak level," I said with a giggle. His hands held me to his crotch as our hips circled in perfect rhythm. I could not believe I had just said that out loud. It must be a combination of the alcohol and the long, hard thing pressing into my back that was making me say brave, foolish things.

"Then please allow me to buy you another shot," he said smoothly, kissing the damp skin underneath my jaw.

What the fuck is happening right now?

"After this song is over, 'kay?" I asked, pressing back into him. I felt his sharp exhale and sensed, rather than heard, a groan from deep inside his chest.

"Whatever you want, Peach. I could do this all night." I released a groan of my own, intuiting that he wasn't just talking about dancing. I realized I still had my face twisted up into his neck like a sniffy little pervert, so I turned back to the front, noticing that Bristol was staring, her amethyst eyes wide and curious.

"Holy fucking shit," she mouthed at me. She fanned her face with one hand, and I pressed my lips together to avoid bursting into a nervous giggling fit. I should probably introduce them. I turned my head back to Beau, and he leaned his head down to give me his ear.

Damn, he smelled really good. Yes, there was the scent of cologne or something, but underneath that was a deep, masculine smell that I couldn't quite define. It made me want to lick him. *What the... where had that come from?* I had never had the desire to lick a person before.

Cut it out, Charli. He's your friend. That's it.

Yeah, a friend with a huge erection that he was grinding into my backside. His thumbs were making tiny circles over my bare stomach, and that, combined with the rich, dark aroma of his skin and his hips moving in tandem with mine, was making me lose my damned mind.

"Did you just lick me?" he growled suddenly.

I jerked my head back an inch. *Holy shit. Had I?* "Uh, no. Well, maybe, but it was an accident," I babbled. *Jeez, I'm a fucking idiot.*

His grip on my hips tightened as he spoke seductively into my ear. "Are you hoping I'll reciprocate, Peach?"

That conjured up some images that made me feel like someone had set me on fire, tiny flames flickering over my flesh and making me want to yell, "Yes!"

Okay, focus, girl. Say something to take your mind off this man's tongue. "This is my friend Bristol," I said in his ear, careful to keep my stupid tongue to itself this time. I nodded to my friend, who was grinning like this was the best entertainment she'd had in years.

Beau released me with one hand and stuck it out toward Bristol, who grasped it and shook enthusiastically. "Nice to meet you. I'm Beau Atwood," he yelled over the music.

She blinked twice and then darted her eyes back and forth between us. They finally settled on him. "The pleasure is all mine. Well, I guess it's all Charli's, actually, by the looks of *you*," she said with an exaggerated eyebrow wiggle.

Oh, shit, Bris. Shut the fuck up. But Beau just laughed and pulled his hand back, wrapping that arm around my waist and gripping the opposite hip while his other hand splayed across my stomach, anchoring my middle to his muscular body.

I gave Bristol an intense glare, but she just continued talking, damn her. "Sooo, you're *the* Beau?"

Jesus, take the damn wheel.

He smirked down at me. "I don't know, Peach. Am I *the* Beau?"

What the hell was I supposed to say to that? "I have to tell you something," I said conspiratorially. "Bristol is a drunk and a pathological liar. She's quite unstable. We've tried to get her help, but I'm pretty sure she's hopeless." I said, cutting my eyes toward my loudmouth friend.

Beau just chuckled and let me off the hook. "Damn, and she seemed like such a lovely girl." He turned me in his arms and rested his hands on the strip of bare skin at my back. "I understand about embarrassing friends. You've met my buddies, right?" I curled my arms around his shoulders and looked up into his dark green eyes.

I could lose myself in those flinty, forest-green irises.

"Where are they tonight?" I asked, and he jerked his head to the side. I looked that way and saw all five of his buddies grinning at us. Woody and Bode waved, and Cam saluted us with his beer. "I feel like we're in an exhibit at the zoo or something," I said, pulling my eyes back to Beau.

"Don't worry about it," he grumbled. The song ended, and he stepped back and took my hands in his big ones. I felt so small when I was with him. "Let me buy you a drink?"

I nodded. "Okay, we have a booth. Do y'all want to sit with us?"

"Sure," he said, his full lips tipping up in a pleased smile as he looked at Bristol over my shoulder. "Hey, Charli invited me and the guys to sit with y'all. That cool?"

"The guys?" she asked, and he pointed to his friends. I saw her eyes sparkle with interest. "Well, hell yes, you can sit with us. Introduce me," she said squeezing between us and hooking her arms with ours as we walked.

All of the men greeted me happily as Bris eyed them speculatively. I noticed she paid extra attention to Tank, her eyes taking an inordinately long time to sweep his six-foot-eight frame as Beau introduced her to everyone.

"Guys," Beau said. "These lovely ladies have agreed to let us sit with them. Charli and I are going to the bar. Be nice." His glare was stern, and they all nodded. Except for Tank who was staring at Bristol like she was a particularly tasty dessert. But men always looked at Bris like that. She was hot and innately sexy.

Beau put his hand on my lower back and guided me toward the bar, which was lit from underneath with a deep red glow. He found an empty stool and lifted me onto it. "Okay, Super Freak. You relax, and I'll get some drinks for the table," he said with a smirk, running his finger down my nose before working his way down the bar to try and find a bartender.

I watched him walk off and attempted not to drool. He was wearing dark wash jeans that hugged his thick thighs and spectacular ass. He seriously must do a hundred squats a day to get an ass like that. His tight, black microfiber t-shirt showed off a tapered body, trim at the waist and wide through the upper back and shoulders. It was the kind of body made for sin, and I wasn't exactly feeling wholesome.

In fact, I was feeling all kinds of thirsty.

"Can I get a glass of water?" I croaked out as a bartender with a full, dark beard scooted by.

He paused, quickly poured a glass, and slid it toward me, throwing a "There ya go, sweetheart" my way before moving to the other end of the bar.

My eyes automatically drifted in the direction Beau had gone, only to see a female bartender leaned over the bar toward him, her overly-made-up eyes running hungrily over his body as he said something to her. She threw back her head and laughed, and I wondered what the fuck was so funny.

I averted my eyes from the flirt-fest when I heard a voice beside me. "Say, baby. My friend would like your number," the blond man said, his breath laced so full of alcohol that it almost knocked me off my stool.

"Your friend wants my number?" I asked, lifting a skeptical eyebrow, arching my neck backward to put some space between us. I hated close talkers. *Unless they look like Beau Atwood. That man could get all up in my business.*

"Yep," Bourbon Breath said. "He needs to know where to get a hold of me in the morning." He grinned like he had just delivered the greatest pickup line in history, and I tried unsuccessfully not to roll my eyes.

All of a sudden the man was gone. Just disappeared into thin air. Swiveling my head, I saw Beau Atwood holding Bourbon Breath by the back of his hair with his right hand, his left hand holding another man in the same fashion.

He yanked both muscular arms outward before snapping them together and bonking the men's heads together à la The Three Stooges. The thud sounded like someone hit a watermelon with a sledgehammer, even over the loud bass of the music.

"Motherfuckers," Beau growled, dropping the men's limp bodies to the floor.

My eyes practically bulged out of my head. *What the...?*

"What the fuck, dude?" The bearded bartender was back, scowling at Beau and reaching underneath the bar for God knows what.

Beau jerked his head down toward Bourbon. "This asshole was distracting my friend while the other one slipped something in her drink." He pushed my glass of water across the bar, and the bartender's demeanor changed from one of aggression to one of apology.

"Fuck. Hold on, and I'll get security up here."

Holy shit! They were trying to roofie me?

The bartender took the glass and poured me a fresh one as he pressed a small microphone on his collar and spoke urgently into it. In seconds, three security guards appeared out of nowhere.

Beau turned his attention back to me, cupping my chin and holding the glass up so that the straw was at my lips. "Drink, Peach." His voice was low and authoritative, and I felt a pulse deep inside me spring to life. I wrapped my lips around the straw and sucked as his gaze became heavy-lidded. "More," he commanded, and I drank the rest of the cool water. He smiled, his thumb stroking my jaw. "Good girl."

I melted a little at his praise and his gentle touch.

As he turned to put the empty glass back on the bar and speak with the security guards, I heard a hiss in my ear. *Bristol.* "Charli Casper! Are you okay? And why didn't you tell me what a hunk Beau is?"

"I'm okay," I said. My hands were shaking a bit due to the near miss, but I was otherwise fine. "And I did tell you," I claimed, widening my eyes at my friend.

"Yeah, I guess you did, but mere words cannot describe what a fucking stud muffin he is. And that commanding voice. Aghhh!" She feigned a deep voice, "Drink, Peach."

"I know. I feel like I want him to follow me around and say bossy shit to me all day."

Bristol groaned, "Yessss! And when he called you a good girl, I thought I was going to come in my panties."

I giggled. "Me too, and I'm not even wearing any panties."

She looked at me, shocked. "Why, you dirty whore!" A wicked grin curled onto Bristol's face. "I think the man deserves a nice, long blow job for his Superman act."

I shoved my friend away playfully. "Shut up, you slut. And stop saying embarrassing shit in front of Beau. I'm not sure I'll ever be able to look him in the eye again after all your comments. I told him you were unstable and needed professional help."

She roared with laughter. "Who knows? Maybe I inspired him, and he'll show you a really good time."

"Trust me, he already felt quite *inspired* when we were on the dance floor. His extremely large 'inspiration' was poking me in the back the entire time."

"Lucky bitch. Hey, I wonder if that Tank guy is big *all over*?"

"I have no doubt you'll find out, you skank," I said with a smile.

Beau returned to my side, wrapping his arm possessively around my waist as he guided me toward the booth with Bristol hot on our heels. "You can say goodbye to everyone, and then I'll drive you home and make sure you get in safely."

I looked up at him, confused. "But I'm not ready to leave, Beau."

"You're leaving," he said sternly.

Oh, hell no! Who the fuck did he think he was? "No. I'm. Not. And you can't make me."

"Wanna bet?" he growled, pulling us to a stop. "You don't think I could throw you over my shoulder in a heartbeat and haul your little ass right out of here?" He glared at me, and I glared right back, which was ridiculous because he could probably eat me in one bite. And why did that thought make me wet?

Nonetheless, I stuck my finger in his face and used the strict voice I always used with the triplets. "You listen to me, Beau Atwood. I'm not going home to sit around and feel sorry for myself. I need to relax and have a good time after what happened." The air crackled between us, and it was much more than just anger.

"Don't point your finger at me." He nipped the end of my finger with his teeth before taking it between his gorgeous lips, sucking softly on the tip and soothing the sting of the bite. When his tongue drew a little circle around the end, all manner of happy things began fluttering in my vagina.

"You bit me," I accused.

"You licked me first," he said with a smirk.

Shit. I was hoping he'd forgotten that.

I softened a little and pressed my hand against his chest. "I'll be perfectly safe if you stay with me."

His eyes searched my face. "Fine." He heaved out an exasperated sigh, and then his voice turned demanding again. "But you will stick to my side like glue, do you understand?"

"I will. Thank you, Beau." I could think of much worse things than being stuck to Beau Atwood's side all night. He put his hand on my back again and started walking us back to our booth.

"You two are so fucking hot together," Bristol piped up.

"Shut up, Bristol," Beau and I said in unison.

"Just sayin'," she chirped.

The next two hours were filled with laughter and fun as we all told stories, speaking loudly over the blasting music. Beau bought me a couple of peach shots, and then I switched to drinking Sprite. I really didn't want to have a hangover when I had to take care of the kids tomorrow. They were loud little toots, especially Max. That kid's volume was permanently set on blast.

Beau managed to effectively cockblock all of Aaron's attempts to talk to me, his arm draped around the back of the booth as his fingers drew enticing little circles on my shoulder. Aaron finally stomped off when his sister slunk out of the booth and slid onto Tank's lap.

I watched as Bristol and the big guy made out hard and raunchy, his hand sliding down to her ass and squeezing as their lips stayed glued together.

"Biggie's got game," I whispered to Beau, and he grinned.

"Who knew?" he said, raising his eyebrows at me. "Let me know when you're ready, and I'll drive you home."

"You don't have to do that, Beau. I was planning to catch an Uber."

"It's not up for discussion, Peach," he said, his brows knitted together on his stubborn face.

Pick your battles, Charli. I sighed and relented.

Tank and Bristol disappeared at some point, and Aaron never came back to our table. As the night went on, Beau's body had inched closer to mine until we were thigh-to-thigh, and his arm had drifted down from the back of the booth to my shoulders so his fingers could toy with my hair. He was leaned back in the booth with his legs spread, looking confident, masculine, and sexy as fuck. Any resistance I had to this man had left the building, right along with Elvis. When things were finally winding down, I heard Beau mumble to Cam, "Can you get Woody to drop you off? I'm driving Charli home." Cam gave him a mischievous grin but nodded.

In the parking lot, Beau lifted me by the waist into his big black truck, his fingers warm against my bare skin. After closing the door, he walked around to his side and got in. He cranked the truck but didn't put it in drive, just stared out the front windshield for a long moment as if he were steeling himself for something.

I wished like hell I could invade his brain to see exactly what he was thinking. I wanted to turn and look at him but instead kept my eyes focused forward. Beau pivoted toward me and tucked my hair behind my ear, stroking the backs of his fingers against my cheek. Unable to help myself, I tilted my face toward him and rubbed my cheek against his fingers, my eyes closed to savor this moment fully.

When he finally spoke, his words were quiet and deep. "I haven't gotten the chance to tell you how beautiful you look tonight." I opened my eyes and turned to meet his. He was smiling shyly at me, and I had the feeling that he didn't talk to women like that very often; it pleased me to no end.

"Thank you," I said, laying a tender kiss on his palm. He dragged his fingertips slowly down my arm, evoking a trail of goosebumps where he touched me, until he finally reached my hand and intertwined our fingers together. I squeezed, and his smile broadened. I liked this Beau. Bossy, demanding Beau got my panties wet; but sweet, shy Beau gave me butterflies in my stomach. Gigantic, hyperactive butterflies who had missed their last three doses of Ritalin.

My resistance? Freaking *gone*.

CHARLI

Beau held my hand all the way to the Broxtons', his thumb rubbing against mine. My body wanted to squirm at the gentle touch, but I held myself still. How would it feel to have him touch other parts of my body like that? Or to have his warm mouth on mine?

He pulled up in front of the huge house and helped me from the truck, putting his hand on my back as he led me up the sidewalk.

"I'll use the side door," I said quietly, pointing to the stone path that led around to my private entrance. "It opens directly to my room," I explained.

We arrived at my door, and I used my key to unlock it but didn't open it. I turned back to Beau, who was standing a couple feet back with his hands in his pockets. "Thank you for the ride, Beau."

"Anytime, Peach." He walked backwards a couple steps, and my heart clenched harder the further he got away from me. I wanted to beg him not to go.

He turned to leave, and I spoke his name softly. So softly, I wasn't even sure if he would hear it, but he did. His body stopped and then pivoted toward me. "Ask me again," I said when he was facing me.

A little furrow line appeared between his eyes. "Ask you what?"

"Ask me on a date." *Oh, God. What if he said no? What if he laughed in my face?*

He stood still for a few seconds before walking slowly toward me. He braced both his hands on the door behind me, his face only inches from mine. He ran his tongue over his bottom lip and then scraped it with his teeth. "Charli," he said, his balmy breath drifting across my lips, "would you go to dinner with me?"

"Yes," I said, "I would love to." He breathed a sigh of relief even though he had to have known I would say yes this time.

His gorgeous green eyes dropped to my lips and then lifted to my blue ones. "Can I kiss you, baby?" he asked, his voice husky with desire, and everything below my waist felt like I had been dipped in a vat of steaming hot water.

"Yes. Please," I said, somewhere between a moan and a sigh. *Oh, damn. That sounded desperate.* But maybe he was as desperate for our kiss as I was, because he wasted no time in covering my mouth with his. *Oh, thank you, sweet Jesus!*

His lips were warm and firm against mine, and his hands slid into my hair to hold my head firmly like he wanted it. I felt his tongue teasing my lips, and I opened immediately for him, dying to taste him. As soon as our tongues met, we went from zero to sixty in approximately two point five seconds. Beau's hands tightened in my hair as his body pushed tightly against mine, forcing my back against the door. He let out an animalistic grunt as his tongue thrust hard against mine, and the deep noise vibrated through me.

My nose was pressed against his cheek, and God, he smelled so freaking manly. His mouth was hot, tasting of mint and liquor, and I moaned at the myriad of sensations flooding my body. His tongue fucked into my mouth as I felt his cock swelling against my belly, driving me to near desperation.

"Fuck," he groaned into my mouth as his hands slid down to the backs of my thighs. He lifted, and my legs went impulsively around his waist, my ankles locking behind his firm butt. We ate hungrily at each other as his hips began circling, slowly and methodically grinding his arousal against my sex.

Damn, he's going to make me come right here against my door.

I pumped and rolled my hips in a demanding counter-rotation, feeling the solid ridge of his dick bumping across my clit every couple seconds as I chased my orgasm. I sucked Beau's tongue into my mouth and felt his hands tighten on my ass as we fucked at each other through our clothes. His mouth became impossibly wilder, biting and sucking my lips and tongue and triggering another rush of wetness between my legs.

And the growling. *Oh, fuck me.* This man growling into my mouth like an untamed beast was enough to undo me. My fingers dug into his shoulders and then moved up to grip his shortly shorn hair, urging him on... and on... and on.

His hands slid up my sides to roughly cup the sides of my breasts as he pinned me to the door with his grinding hips. The edge of an orgasm crowned deeply inside my vagina, and I whimpered my need for him against his lips. "Beau, please," I murmured against his lips as my core clenched tightly. *Oh, fucking yes! I'm com—*

But then his warmth was suddenly gone as he pulled my legs from around him and backed away. It took me a few seconds before I could drag my eyelids open, and I found him standing a few feet from me with a look of horror on his face, his chest rising and falling violently. I frowned as the beginnings of a beautiful orgasm faded into nothingness.

When he spoke hoarsely, I felt like he had doused my body with a bucket of cold water. "I'm sorry, Charli. This was a mistake. You don't deserve to be kissed like that. I'm... I'm so sorry." After two more retreating steps backward and a look of disgust, he turned on his heel and walked stiffly around the side of the house, leaving me confused and wanting.

What the actual fuck had just happened?

I stood with my back to the door until the cool night air chilled my skin to the point of discomfort, and then I went inside and locked the door. I stood facing the room with my fingertips pressed against my swollen lips. That kiss had been... amazing. I had never been kissed like that before. I had never had my body played like that either.

I collapsed on my bed and let my mind drift to all the good parts. Beau's raw, brutal strength when he lifted me like I weighed nothing. His mouth, hot and demanding. His dick enormous and demanding between my legs. His hard body pressing me to the door. The noises he made as he kissed me.

And then the not-so-good stuff started seeping into my brain. There wasn't much of it, but it was significant. The look of disgust on his face. His hasty retreat. His harsh words.

This was a mistake. How could he say that? If he had felt even a fraction of what I had during that kiss, he would have never called it a mistake.

You don't deserve to be kissed like that. What did that even mean? That I wasn't good enough for him? That he only reserves his mouth for women with long legs and huge boobs, and I was found lacking?

Well, fine! Beau Atwood could kiss my ass. Who needed an orgasm-inducing kiss anyway?

Me! Me! Me! My damned traitorous body was still calling out for him, and I knew the pulsing between my legs wasn't going away any time soon. On a long sigh, I stripped off my clothes and pulled my hair up into a messy bun on top of my head as I headed to my shower. When the water was hot, I climbed underneath the steaming spray, turning in a circle to warm my entire body.

I soaped up the washcloth with my floral body wash and cleaned between my legs. The slight roughness of the cloth against my hot, sensitive sex made me moan, so I did it again.

Oh, God. I needed... I slid the fingers of my other hand down there and cried out quietly as I brushed over my clit. *Well, this isn't going to take long.* I dropped my cloth and braced a hand on the shower wall because my knees were already trembling. I slid my fingers through my slickness, wondering if I had ever been this wet before.

As much as I tried not to think about *him*, the image of Beau kneeling in the shower before me—his head between my legs, his wicked tongue working me furiously as he looked up at me—flashed unbidden in my mind. I came with a jolt, my knees finally buckling, and my hand sliding slowly down the marbled beige tiles as I sank to the floor and quivered like a mass of jelly.

Damn you, Beau Atwood. Damn you for bringing me to my knees without even being here.

When I finally regained my damn senses, I slowly stood and got out of the shower, the aftershocks of my orgasm leaving my vagina tight and tingly. I dried off and wrapped myself in my robe, grabbing my dirty clothes to put in the hamper. I felt something wet and pulled my pants in front of my face to inspect them. Had I spilled something on them? I didn't remember... *dammit all to hell.* I realized that my pants were soaking wet in the crotch, not from a spilled drink, but from... *him.*

That's what you get for going pantiless and then letting a master player dry hump you to near orgasm. Except there wasn't much dry about the humping we had done, obviously. I took my pants and headed to the laundry room but heard movement in the kitchen. "Blaire," I called out quietly so I wouldn't startle her. She turned as I walked in, holding little Danica in her arms.

"Someone is colicky," she said in explanation. "I came down for the drops."

"Oh, poor little thing," I said, kissing Dani on her soft head as her tiny lip trembled, and she let out a squeaky wail.

"Did you have a good time tonight?" Blaire asked me as she gave Dani some medicine.

"Yes, the club was amazing," I said, not elaborating any further. "I just came in here to put my pants in the washer."

"Oh no. Did you get a stain on them?" my boss asked, reaching for my pants. "You know, with triplet toddler boys, I'm a virtual stain-removal guru."

I pulled them behind my back and said quickly, "No, just spilled some, um, Sprite on them. No stain, but I wanted to go ahead and wash them."

"Ugh, yes. There's nothing worse than sticky pants."

Especially when the pants are sticky due to your brother almost fucking me against the door of your house. Shit!

I escaped to the laundry room and started the wash cycle for my pants. When I returned to the kitchen, Blaire asked, "Did you catch a cab home?"

"Oh, uh, no. Actually Beau gave me a ride home."

"Aw, that's nice. Beau can be pretty handy to have around." *Oh, yes. He's quite handy.* "Hey, I have an extra ticket to Axel's game tomorrow. You should come with us. You like football, right?"

"I love football. I've never been to a pro game though," I said, starting to get a little excited.

"Alright then, it's settled," Blaire said, looking pleased. I really had the best bosses in the entire world. "You go get some rest. I'll bring you one of my Wranglers jerseys in the morning, and you can wear that to the game."

I went back to my room and plugged my phone to the charger when I noticed that I had unread text messages. From Beau. Sighing, I swiped and read.

Beau: I'm sorry, Charli. I left before I made sure you got in the house safely.

Beau: Are you okay?

Beau: Charli?

Beau: Where the hell are you?

Beau: Dammit, answer me. Did you get inside okay?

Good Lord, what was wrong with this man? He had gone from burning hot to ice cold in an instant, and now he was worried about me? And did he really think I couldn't find my way inside when I was literally standing against my door? Another text came through then.

Beau: I'm on my way back over there to check on you. I'll beat the goddamn door down if I have to, which will probably wake up the whole house. Or you could just answer my fucking messages.

Damn, what the hell is wrong with this fool? I hastily typed out a text to the overbearing ass.

Charli: Cool your jets, Rambo. I'm fine. Inside safely.

Charli: I was in the shower. I wasn't aware that I needed to ask your permission.

I shook my head and crawled beneath the sheets, ready to get this day over with.

BEAU

I GRABBED MY TRUCK keys and headed to my garage. I wasn't fucking playing around with her. I would kick the damned door down if she didn't answer it. I had to know that she was okay.

I knew she was probably freaked out after I had lost control with her. Jesus, what had I been thinking? I just attacked the poor woman, even after those fuckwads at the club had almost drugged her. Hell, she probably never wanted to see me again, but I had to make sure she was safe. Why hadn't I waited for her to get inside before I ran off with my tail between my legs? I knew better than that. Someone could have been waiting in the bushes for me to leave and then grabbed her or... God, I didn't even want to think about it.

My phone dinged, and I snatched it out of my pocket and almost collapsed with relief when I saw it was from her. Then I read her texts and grinned. *Rambo?* God, she killed me. Dammit, I really liked her, so why had I fucked everything up? Everything between us had been going so well until I kissed her and felt her soft tongue in my mouth, and then I had lost my shit.

Jesus, I had treated that sweet peach like she was some... tramp. As much as I liked her, I didn't deserve a woman like her. She needed someone who would treat her right. Someone who wouldn't lose control and hump her against a goddamn door. But fuck, the thought of her with anyone else made my blood boil in my veins. I shucked my clothes, throwing them angrily into the hamper.

Control. Yeah, I didn't have an ounce of that when Peach was around, especially when my mouth was on hers. I stepped into the shower and let the hot water beat down on my body. *I should probably be taking a cold shower right now*, I thought, looking down at my cock, which was still fully erect. I didn't think it would be going down any time soon, not now that she had texted that she had been in the shower. I couldn't draw my mind away from that image in my head.

I gripped my dick, squeezing the shaft as I visualized her naked, the water trickling down her beautiful body. Would her nipples be a soft pink or more of a rosy brown? Either would look excellent in my mouth.

Fuck, baby. I leaned my forearm against the tile and stroked myself slowly.

I closed my eyes and thought about how Charli had tasted. And felt. And sounded. *God damn.* I started stroking myself harder, gripping my dick tightly and pulling with force as my mind wandered to dangerous places. I'd loved the subtle taste of peaches on her tongue from the schnapps. The feel of her soft body trapped between me and the door. The warmth of her pussy against my crotch when she wrapped her legs around me. The little noises she made. All of it. She was fucking perfect.

But her mouth was the ultimate fantasy. Those damned cherry lips. They would look even more beautiful wrapped around my cock. I would force her to her knees in the shower before sliding into her mouth and watching her struggle to take all of me. But she would do it to please me. *Jesus.* Those big blue eyes would look up at me and beg me to fuck her throat. And I would give her exactly what she wanted, sliding my dick in and out of her lips as she moaned around me.

I felt my balls tighten up as I thought about fucking her hot mouth fast and rough and... *oh, God.* My cum gushed from the end of my dick like an erupting volcano. I groaned out my release while I continued to come, my legs literally shaking as I braced myself against the wall. *Fuck, Peach. You made me come so hard.*

I took several long, deep breaths to steady myself before drying off and getting into bed. As I lay there, I thought of Peach and how she had blushed and smiled when I told her she was beautiful in the truck. Damn, I found myself wanting to tell her that over and over just to see those cheeks turn pink again. To see the angle of those lips tip bashfully upward.

I slept fitfully but still woke up early, like I always did. Blaire had messaged that Axel had extra tickets for the game, so I was welcome to join them. I got up and got ready, dressing in my brother-in-law's number eighty-seven jersey before driving to my sister's house. I was looking forward to going to the game with Carrie and Blaire today. As much as I loved my nephews, it would be a relief to spend time with my oldest niece. She was the light of my life, but it was hard to hold a conversation with her with the triplets running around. They pretty much took over any room they were in, the feral little rascals.

I was met at the door by an ecstatic Carrie, who jumped immediately into my arms. "Uncle Beau! You're going to my daddy's game with us!"

"I know," I said, laughing. "Give me some sugar." She smacked me on the lips, and I hugged her tightly against me, my nose pressed against her head. This was exactly what I needed today. Blaire called it 'Carrie Therapy,' because this little girl never ceased to cheer me up with her spunky personality and bright smile.

I propped her on my hip and carried her out to my truck. "You look extra super-duper cute today, Care," I said, pulling one of her braided pigtails.

"Thanks," she giggled. "You look extra super-duper cute, too."

"I'm flattered," I said, putting her in the back of my truck and making sure she buckled her seat belt. "Is your mom being a slow poke today?"

"Yessir. She's being dramatic and kissing the little kids like she's never going to see them again," Carrie said with an eye roll.

"Like this?" I asked, kissing her all over her sweet face, causing her to shriek with joy. I closed her door with a grin on my face, but it dropped away when I turned and saw Charli following Blaire down the steps. Peach stopped when she saw me, her lips pressing together, and I gathered that she was as surprised to see me as I was to see her. I gave her a small smile because damn, she looked gorgeous in a football jersey and skin-tight jeans. Not returning my smile, she resumed walking, her eyes cast down in front of her.

Blaire reached me first and kissed my cheek. "Thanks for driving, bro. I'll just sit in the back with Carrie, and Charli can sit up front with you," she said, giving me a sly wink and walking around to the other side of the truck. *Oh, for fuck's sake.* I followed my meddling sister, and she stood on her tiptoes and whispered, "Thank you for taking care of her last night, by the way." She patted my arm and opened the back door of my truck. *Taking care of her?* I hoped she was just talking about giving her a ride home, and not what happened when we got back here.

Oh, I had wanted to take care of Peach in more ways than one, dear sister. With my mouth. My fingers. My cock.

I lifted Blaire up into the backseat of my jacked-up truck and closed the door. When I turned back around, Charli was standing on the sidewalk, seemingly uncomfortable with the situation. I walked over to her and took her hand, leading her around to the other side of the truck. "Looks like you're up front with me," I said, and she glanced up at me before nodding.

I tugged on one of her long blonde pigtail braids. "Cute," I murmured before helping her into my truck and going around to my side.

As soon as we got on the highway, "Cherry Pie" by Warrant blasted through the speakers, reminding me of Charli's red lips last night. I shifted uncomfortably in my seat. What the fuck was this woman doing to me? I was getting turned on by fruit now? God forbid I eat a fruit salad; I would probably come in my pants. I weaved through the traffic trying to think of anything but fucking peaches and cherries.

We arrived at the stadium and found our seats, which were down low and near the fifty-yard-line. Charli sat down, and I tried to sit right beside her, but much to my chagrin, Carrie squeezed in between us.

The game started, and as much as I tried to concentrate on the game, my gaze kept being drawn to Peach. She was totally into what was happening on the field, jumping up and yelling from time to time. When Axel missed a pass in the third quarter, Charli leapt from her seat, her arms flailing around, and hollered, "Interference! Throw the flag!" When the ref called the penalty on the defender, Charli flopped back down and grumbled, "Finally. I thought the officials had all gone blind. Number twenty-five was all over Axel like a cheap suit."

I looked at her, amused at her extreme fanaticism. "You're really into football, huh?"

She grinned and shrugged one shoulder. "All of my brothers played in high school, and Henry went on to play for West Point."

"That's cool. How many brothers do you have?"

"Three. And one sister," she said, keeping her eyes on the field.

The more I found out about Peach, the more I wanted to know. During the next timeout, Blaire took Carrie to the restroom, and I scooted closer to Charli.

"Do you want to talk about last night?" I asked quietly.

She closed her eyes and angled her face away from me. "I'd rather not. It's embarrassing."

I was taken aback. "What do you mean 'embarrassing?'"

She spared me a brief look before looking down at her hands in her lap. "You said it was a mistake to kiss me, and then you... you said I didn't deserve it. It made me feel like I'm not good enough for you." My mind scrambled to process her train of thought.

"Wait. You thought... back up a second, Peach. I know I didn't handle things well last night. I felt like I was too aggressive with you, and that's what I was talking about when I said that stuff. I kinda lost control, and it scared me. I would never think you weren't good enough for me, baby. In fact, I've been struggling with the fact that you're *too* good for me." I lifted her chin with my fingertips so that her tear-filled eyes were on mine. "Way too good, sweetheart."

A tear fell down one side of her face, and I felt like that tiny droplet was slicing me open. "I like you, Beau, but you hurt me last night when you said what you did and just walked off."

I caught her tear on my index finger and rubbed it with my thumb. "I didn't mean to hurt you," I said sincerely. That was the last thing I would ever want to do, and that's what scared me so much. Because I *cared*. But I didn't want to stay away from her either. I had promised myself I would, and I hadn't even made it one damned day. I leaned toward her, my arm going around her back and my lips to her ear, "Let me make it up to you, Peach. Have dinner with me tomorrow night."

She inhaled a deep breath and then let it slowly out. "Okay," she whispered, rubbing her cheek softly against mine.

I looked up and noticed Blaire and Carrie coming down the steps, so I straightened and removed my arm from Charli's back. "They're coming," I said from the corner of my mouth, and Peach tried to inch away from me to make room for Carrie. "No, stay," I said with a hand on her leg, not wanting to lose the contact between our touching thighs. As soon as my sister and niece scooted into our row, I picked up Carrie and sat her on my left leg so that she wouldn't worm her way between me and Charli. "Sit with me, pipsqueak," I said, wrapping an arm around her as she settled comfortably on my lap.

Blaire glanced down at my hand on Charli's thigh and let out a quiet squeal. "You're so cute together," she mouthed, and I narrowed my eyes at her in a not-so-subtle warning.

"Hush," I admonished on a hiss, but I couldn't stop the smile that curved my lips upward.

14

CHARLI

By the time we returned to the Broxton neighborhood, I was as giddy as a schoolgirl, and it had nothing to do with the fact that the Wranglers won and Axel had two touchdowns. I was experiencing sparks and tingles and all the other electricity-related clichés that you read about in romance novels because of *circles*.

Specifically, the tiny circles Beau Atwood's thumb rubbed on my thigh for the entire second half of the game. And the same little circles he rubbed on the back of my hand on the drive home. Who knew tiny geometric shapes could have such an effect on a woman's body?

From the self-satisfied look on his face when we stopped at a stop sign, Beau did. "Do you want to go get coffee or something after we drop the nosy duo off?" he asked under his breath.

"Oh, um. I should probably stay and help Blaire with the bedtime stuff."

The space between his eyebrows tapered to almost non-existence. He was not pleased with that answer. Parking in the driveway, he called out, "Blaire, do you think I could borrow Charli for a couple hours so we can go get a coffee?"

"Sure," Blaire called back cheerily. "Axel's mom is staying the night, so we have an extra pair of hands."

Beau held his hands palm side up at me, and I laughed. "Okay, that sounds good." He hopped out to help Blaire and Carrie out of the backseat, and when he climbed back into the cab of the truck, I asked, "Do you always get what you want?"

"Not yet," he said with a grin as he shifted into reverse.

Good Lord!

Beau drove us to a local coffee shop, and we found a cozy booth in the back near a fireplace and drank coffee and shared a chocolate chip muffin. He was sweet and affectionate, constantly holding or touching my hand, and I felt all my tension over him melting away. We talked more in depth about my family, and I told him how excited I was that my sister and brothers were coming for a visit in a couple of weeks.

When we got back to the truck, I was shivering from the night air, and Beau grabbed a black fleece jacket that he kept in his truck and wrapped it around me. I was trying not to be obvious about burying my nose in the collar and smelling it because I didn't want him to think I was some kind of jacket-sniffing weirdo. Even though I obviously was.

At the Broxtons' house, he walked me to the side door and waited while I unlocked the door. "So, I guess I'll see you tomorrow?" he asked. "I'll pick you up at seven."

"That sounds good," I said, looking down to where Beau was holding both of my hands in his. He took a slow step toward me, his gaze locked on my lips. *Please kiss me!* "Beau, will you show me how you think I deserve to be kissed?" I asked tremulously, thinking of his words from last night.

His eyes burned into mine, and I felt paralyzed as he slid his hands up to cup my face. He lowered his lips, hovering for a few long seconds before they touched mine, pressing firmly before pulling back with a gentle suction. Then he repeated the action. He tilted my head a little and sucked my lips again. And again. And again. For the longest time he kissed my closed mouth like that, my core clenching tightly with every soft suction of his mouth.

Oh. My. God. I had never been kissed with such... reverence. I felt his tongue press gently against my lips, and I opened for him, craving his strong tongue against mine again. He stroked it with just the tip of his, and my body automatically arched toward him, needing to feel his warmth. He lapped tenderly against my tongue, and I couldn't suppress the low moan that rose up from deep inside me.

He changed the angle again, but still kissed me with a gentleness that I couldn't get enough of. One of his hands slid to the back of my head, but the other stayed on my face, his fingers softly moving against my cheek. I was mesmerized by his mouth, by his touch. My hands slid to his back, clutching his jersey like I never wanted to let him go, and I felt the tension in the muscles of his back.

Beau continued to slowly worship my mouth, making love to it until every inch of my body ached for him. This kiss was so different than last night's but no less intense. I pressed tighter to him, and a low growl escaped from his mouth into mine as my stomach came in contact with his thick erection. *Good.* I was glad he was as affected by this as I was. I could feel his need, not just between his legs, but also in the slow, sensual movement of his tongue against mine.

Though the kiss seemed to go on forever, I was reluctant for it to end. His tongue retreated, but I boldly licked into his mouth, drawing him back into me. With another soft growl, he kissed me harder, but just as longingly slow. He wrapped the fingers of both hands around the back of my head, his thumbs caressing my cheeks as his tongue stroked mine with an aching hunger.

It was official. Beau Atwood was the best kisser in the history of the world.

When he ended the kiss with a final soft suction, our lips were still touching, each of us breathing in the other's air. "Wow," I uttered, because I was pretty sure a single syllable was all I was capable of right then.

"Yeah, me too," he said, kissing the corner of my mouth. "See? I can be a gentleman."

I rubbed my nose against his and gave him a peck on the lips. "I had no doubt you could. You don't give yourself enough credit, Beau. I think you're very sweet."

He frowned grumpily. "I'm not sweet."

Damn, he is adorable.

I rubbed my finger over the line on his forehead until it disappeared. "Yes, you are. You're sweet to me." Laying a kiss against the corner of his mouth, I whispered, "But FYI, it's okay with me if you want to be... less than gentlemanly at times."

His dick twitched against my belly, and he smiled a grin that had no doubt dropped a million panties in his lifetime. "I could definitely do that, Peach, and it won't be hard."

"It won't be hard?" I teased, pretending to pout.

"Charli!" he said with a shocked laugh at my double entendre. He grabbed my braids and pulled my face toward his for a long kiss. "I'm pretty sure you don't have to worry about that when I'm with you."

Holy schnikes! We were standing here casually discussing his penis. His hard penis. His big, hard penis.

I hadn't flirted in so long that I wasn't sure what to say next, so I took the safe option. "I'm a little nervous about tomorrow," I admitted. "I haven't been on a first date in a long time."

"Yeah, I'm not really experienced with the whole dating thing, but I'm glad…" He ran a thumb over my bottom lip as his eyes locked with mine. "I'm glad it's with you, Peach. I feel good when I'm with you."

"I feel good when I'm with you, too, Beau." His green gaze was so intense that I found it impossible to look away. It should have been awkward, just staring at each other like that, but it wasn't. It was like we were eating each other up with our eyes.

He finally broke the silence. "Besides, since it's our first date, I'll be a good boy."

"And after our first date?" I inquired with a flirty smile.

He tugged one of my braids so that my head tilted that way. Leaning over me, he nipped my earlobe and growled, "After that, I'll be whatever you want me to be, Peach."

They were simple words, but the implications were so dirty and delicious that I was still thinking of them long after his last sexy kiss, long after I crawled in bed with his jacket pressed against my nose.

15

BEAU

My mind was hazy when I finally got home and crawled in the bed. I didn't even remember driving to my house or undressing. I wasn't drunk. I was… shit, I didn't know what the hell I was.

Peach thinks I'm sweet. For some reason that made me giddy. And I didn't fucking get giddy. I was a former goddamn Navy SEAL, for fuck's sake. Hell, what was she doing to me? She was turning me into a pussy who got turned on by fruit and pigtails. *Oh, God, those pigtails.* I wanted to grab hold of those long blonde braids from behind and fuck the ever-loving shit out of her, pulling hard so that she slid back and forth along my dick.

I slapped my hand over my eyes. "Stop it, Atwood," I groaned. I inhaled to try and control my thoughts, but Charli's scent overwhelmed me. Damn, she was all over my hands, so soft and sweet. I couldn't get enough of her. Before I could even think about it, I pulled my phone off the nightstand and tapped out a quick text, holding the phone on my chest as I waited for her to respond. I sent up a thanks to my sister for her texting advice when Charli replied quickly.

> *Beau: Hey, just wanted you to know I was thinking about you.*

> *Peach: What were you thinking?*

> Beau: Lots of things. Our kiss.

> Peach: I was lying here thinking about you too. That kiss was amazing.

> Beau: Lying in your bed thinking about me? What am I to think about that, my sweet little Peach?

> Peach: Use your imagination.

Oh damn! I had a goddamn excellent imagination. How should I reply? I didn't want to say exactly what I was thinking because every thought was fucking filthy, and I was trying my damnedest to show her I could be romantic and not just a deviant.

> Beau: My imagination is pretty active. Maybe you could be more specific.

> Peach: You're going to think I'm a weirdo.

> Beau: No, I won't. Tell me.

> Peach: I forgot to give you your jacket back.

Okaaaay. Abrupt change of subject there, Peachy girl.

> *Beau: It's OK. You can give it back tomorrow.*

> *Peach: It smells like you.*

My grin was so big it was almost painful as I understood.

> *Beau: So, you're on your bed smelling my jacket?*

> *Peach: I'm blushing so hard. But yes. Are you blocking my number right now?*

> *Beau: No, baby. In fact, I'll see your jacket smelling and raise you a hand sniffing.*

> *Peach: You're sniffing your hand? WTF*

> *Beau: It smells like you. But it's nowhere near as good as the real thing.*

> *Peach: Fucking weirdo.*

I laughed out loud. I liked everything about this woman. Not only was she gorgeous and sweet, but she was funny as hell, too. I hadn't laughed as much in the last ten years as I had when I was with Charli. And she was so easy to talk to. I was a pretty quiet and stoic guy, but Peach made it easy to open up and talk. She made me *feel things—oh, the horror!*—I thought with a grin.

Beau: Pot, meet kettle.

Peach: Touché

Beau: At the risk of sounding like a total creep, what are you wearing?

Peach: T-shirt and panties. How about you?

Holy fuck. Now I was thinking about her panties. Would they be satin? Lace? Even plain cotton would be sexy on her beautiful little body. I was rubbing my dick through my underwear and realized I hadn't answered her for a while when I heard my phone ding again.

Peach: Hello? Did I lose you?

Beau: Sorry, you got me a little distracted there for a minute. I'm just wearing underwear.

And a giant fucking hard-on.

Peach: Let me guess. Ummm, boxer briefs?

Beau: Good guess.

Peach: What can I say? It's a talent.

I felt a surge of jealousy course through me when I considered that she might think about other men in their underwear.

Beau: Is this a well-developed talent, and do I want to know how you acquired it?

Peach: It's a very recently discovered gift.

Beau: How recent?

Peach: Approximately 30 seconds ago. I'm going to guess black ones.

Beau: Close. Dark gray.

Peach: Damn. I'm going to need to hone my skills.

Beau: If I can be of service in any way in the honing of the underwear skills, don't hesitate to ask.

Peach: Aww, thanks! Maybe I could use you to practice on.

Holy shit! I was pretty sure we were about to take this flirt game up a level. I closed my eyes trying to formulate a clever but sexy response when I heard a knock on my bedroom door. I pulled the thick navy comforter over my lap and yelled, "Come in."

Cam stepped in my room and asked, "Uh, Shark, were you expecting company tonight?"

"No," I said, frowning slightly before a thought hit me. "Is it Charli?" I could hear the brightness in my tone when I said her name. *You dumbass, of course it's not her.*

Cam pressed his lips together and shook his head, stepping farther into my room. "Miranda," he said in a low voice.

"Fuck!" What the hell was she doing here? I had absolutely no urge to see my long-time hookup. I felt like it would be akin to cheating on Charli, though we weren't exactly official. Hell, we hadn't even been on a real date, but still. I didn't want things to be casual with Peach, and that meant no playing around with other women. "Get rid of her," I hissed.

"I'll tell her you're asleep."

"I don't care what you say. Just get her out of here," I whispered adamantly. A look passed over Cam's face, and I glared at him. "Stop fucking smirking at me." He held up both hands and backed out of the room, closing it behind him. In the past, I would have never turned down an easy lay that showed up on my doorstep, and I knew he knew exactly why I was saying no tonight. I got up and put my ear to the door, trying to listen to their conversation.

"Hey, Miranda. I'm sorry, but Shark's in bed already."

I heard her throaty laugh. "Good. That's just where I wanted him."

Shit.

"He has to work early tomorrow and asked not to be disturbed," Cam said firmly.

There was a pause, and then I heard Miranda say suspiciously, "Does he have a woman back there?"

"No, Miranda," he said, exasperated, "he's alone."

There was a long pause, and then… "I want to see for myself. Cam! Get the hell out of my way!" she shrieked.

I heard a series of sharp smacks and my friend yelling, "Stop hitting me, you crazy bitch!"

Oh, for fuck's sake. I jerked open my door and saw Cam blocking the hallway with his body and Miranda slapping and shoving at his chest, trying to get him to move. But Cam was a brick wall. "I've got it, dude," I said, pushing past him to confront her. "Miranda, cut it out!" I barked, and she immediately stilled.

"Shark," she purred, looking me up and down, and I suddenly realized I was in my underwear. "Hi, baby."

"What are you doing here?" I demanded.

She pouted, rubbing her hands up and down my chest. "Why are you acting like this, Sharky?" *Sharky?* "I haven't heard from you all week, and I missed you. I thought I would come stay the night with you again."

"Miranda, it's a work night, and I really need to get some sleep, so you need to go, okay?"

"No. It's not okay. You let me stay on a work night last week. What's different this week?" she asked with her arms crossed.

Fuck. If you only knew what was different.

"Well, I've started seeing someone, so I'm not seeing anyone else."

"Like a *girlfriend?*" she sneered. I saw Cam standing behind her with his eyebrows somewhere near the international space station.

"We haven't exactly labeled it yet, but it's headed that way."

"So… what? You're just tossing me out like yesterday's trash? After I've made myself available for you to fuck every single time you've called me for the past three years?" She jabbed her pointy fingernail into my chest.

I pushed her hand away angrily. "Don't pull that shit with me. You knew it was just sex, and I gave you exactly what you wanted every time we were together, Miranda. Multiple times, if I remember correctly. Otherwise, you wouldn't have kept coming back and begging for more."

She lowered her eyebrows at me, and the corners of her pouty mouth angled downward. "Is that what you want? You want me to beg you?" She dropped to her knees in front of me, dragging her hands down my front, ending at the waistband of my briefs.

"Jesus fucking hell, Miranda. No, I don't want you to beg. Get your ass off the ground," I grunted, backing away from her.

She smirked at me. "If you're not official with the other girl yet, then you shouldn't mind if I suck your cock, right?" She started unbuttoning her shirt. "I'll let you look at my tits while you blow in my mouth." She looked over her shoulder at Cam and said, "You can watch, too, if you want, you kinky bastard."

"You're embarrassing yourself," I hissed, walking to the front door and opening it. "Get. Out. Now."

Miranda's mouth dropped open, and she slowly rose to her feet, wobbling a little on her stilettos. She stalked to the door I was holding open and spat, "Don't come crying to me when you need someone to fuck."

"You don't have to worry about that," I said mildly as she left, and I closed the door behind her. I turned back and noticed Cam standing in the same spot with his arms crossed. "What?" I snapped.

"So, you and Charli are a thing now?"

"Like I said, we're not official or anything, but we're going on a date tomorrow night. It doesn't feel right to be with someone else if I want to try to work this thing out with her."

He nodded. "I gotcha. Good on you, Shark. So, if Miranda makes another appearance?"

"Don't even open the goddamn door," I grunted and headed back to bed. I picked up my phone, hoping that Peach was still awake.

Beau: Hey, sorry. You still up?

After fifteen minutes with no reply, I rolled over and went to sleep.

I woke up early the next morning and went for a four-mile run with Cam before showering and getting dressed for work. On the way to my office, I called Axel.

"Hey, bro."

"Sup, Ax? You kicked ass yesterday, my man."

"Thanks. I'm glad you could make it to the game. What's up?"

"Well, I was hoping you could help me with something. I need a recommendation for an Italian restaurant. Like a good place to take a date."

"You have a date? Like with an actual *woman*?" I could hear the humor in his voice, the smartass.

"No, Axel. With a lovely German Shepherd I met at the park."

"Okay, so you need somewhere pet friendly," he said, roaring with laughter.

"Yeah, real funny, fucker. Are you gonna help me, or not?"

"Sure I will, but who's the lucky lady?" He'd stopped laughing, but I could still hear the amusement in his voice.

"Charli," I mumbled, knowing he was going to give me so much shit.

"Wait. Did you say Charli? Like as in *our nanny*, Charli? Oh, my God." He was howling now, and I was tempted to just hang up and take Charli to Olive Garden. I mean, breadsticks, right? "Blaire is going to be so pissed if you fuck this up. She's going to kick you right in the dick."

I rubbed my temple with my fingertips. "Axel..." I growled

"Okay, dude. Good luck with that. Let's see... if you want to impress her, take her to Terilli's. It's really nice, but not disgustingly pricey. Blaire loves it, and the food is great. Nice portion sizes for guys like us, too."

"Cool. Thanks, Ax. I'll call them now." He was still chuckling when we disconnected.

When I got to the office, I walked in to find our receptionist, Aspen, with her tits hanging out all over the place. "Hi, Beau," she purred. "Did you have a good weekend?"

"Aspen..." I warned. I hated having to get snippy first thing on a Monday morning, but the girl never seemed to learn. I didn't socialize with my female staff, and I was *Mr. Atwood* to them. End of story.

"Sorry, Mister Atwood," she said, drawing my name out and making it sound practically pornographic. "Anything I can do for you this morning?"

Yes, button up at least two more buttons on your top. I didn't say it; instead, I headed back to talk with my office manager.

"Good morning, Sandra," I said, greeting the gray-haired matronly woman who ran my office with an iron fist.

I pointed my thumb sharply back toward the reception area, and Sandra nodded. "I'm taking care of it." This was why I adored the woman. A simple hand gesture, and she read my mind. "And good morning to you, sir. Don't forget that you have your physical this afternoon at one."

"Thanks. I remembered." She handed me a slip of paper that detailed Aspen's dress code violation, and I nodded and handed it back to her. "How many write-ups is this for Aspen for the quarter?"

"Three," Sandra replied, looking significantly at me. Per our company handbook, employees were allowed four write-ups for small offenses per quarter.

Just one more, and we could get rid of her, I thought as I walked back to my office and turned on my computer. I was aware that Aspen's main goal in life was to snag a successful man, and I was currently the unfortunate sonofabitch in her sights. I had reprimanded her personally the first two times she had worn revealing clothing, but she seemed to view that as a victory because I had obviously "noticed" her. From that point on, Sandra had handled all dress code write-ups.

Aspen had argued with Sandra on several occasions, claiming that it was misogynistic that she was the only one who received those reprimands. Sandra had informed her, in no uncertain terms, that if any of the guys came to work with their dicks hanging out of their pants, she would be happy to write them up. I fucking loved Sandra.

My other female employee, Journey, bounded into my office and plopped herself in the black chair across from my desk. "What's up, bossman?" Journey grinned at me, her white teeth a sharp contrast to her dark skin and dreadlocks.

She was an assistant here, but business was so good, I was considering hiring two more assistants and promoting Journey to lead assistant. She was young and eager and had been working for me for three years now. "Hey, Journey. Did you have a good weekend?"

"Yessir. Me and Lynn went to a music festival downtown. It was pretty cool." I liked how her face glowed like a beam of sunshine when she talked about her girlfriend. "How about you?"

"Hmph. Went to that new club Flame Saturday night. It was nice, but I almost got arrested when some jackwagon tried to roofie a friend of mine."

"A female friend?" she asked in surprise.

"Yes, a female friend, Journey. She's my sister's nanny."

"Okay, cool." She said in her easygoing way as she slid a folder across my desk. "Here's everything you requested for the concert. Me and Lynn plan to go, by the way."

"I didn't know you liked country music," I said as I read through her reports.

"I'm eclectic," she said proudly. "I listen to everything from jazz to death metal and country to gangster rap. I'm not a huge fan of opera, though."

I grunted my agreement.

Our firm had been contracted to provide personal security for a huge country music star that was coming to Dallas in a couple months. "This is good, J. Ask Cam to put his eyes on it as well. Make sure we don't have any holes in the plan," I said, flipping to the last page and pausing to read over her final analysis. "Thanks for your extra effort on this. I appreciate it, J." I smacked the folder against the desk.

"Thank you, sir. I had Woody draw up the route from the hotel to the arena since he's good with the lines of sight stuff." Woody had been a sniper during our military days, and there was no one better at honing in on potential problem areas.

"Good idea. Like I said, run this over to Cam for final approval." I slapped the folder back in her hand, and she left with a look of pride on her face.

I picked up my phone and noticed that Peach had replied to my last text.

Peach: Sorry, I fell asleep. I hope you have a good day.

Beau: You too, Peach. We have a reservation for Terilli's tonight. Pick you up at seven.

Peach: I'll be ready. Gotta go. Dex is trying to eat my phone and Max is sitting on my head. Helppppp!

I laughed and texted back.

Beau: Sending SWAT team now.

16

CHARLI

"Are you sure about this?" I asked as Blaire took the final hot roller out of my hair.

"Yes, I used big rollers, so it won't make you super curly. It will just add some volume. Your face is tiny, so I promise not to give you big Texas hair," she said, grinning at me in the mirror. She ran her fingers through my hair to loosen the large curls, and I realized she was right. It had a wave to it, and the volume made my blue eyes look huge. "Now, just let me spray it." She spritzed it with so much hairspray I choked, and then she deemed me done.

"That looks great, Blaire. Thank you so much for helping me. I haven't been on a date in forever."

"You look fantastic, babe. Now go get dressed. You've got twenty minutes, and Beau is always early."

I had already done most of my makeup, so I slipped into my long-sleeved champagne dress and gold heels and applied some matte hazelnut lipstick with a shimmery gold topcoat. I looked in the mirror and took several deep breaths as I heard the doorbell ring ten minutes early.

Blaire busted into my room in a frenzy, and I laughed. She was as excited about this date as I was. "Zip me up, please," I whispered. She pulled up my zipper and turned me to face her.

"Perfection," she claimed, and I held my hands over my stomach, tugging at my dress. "Stop fidgeting," she hissed, swatting at my hands.

We walked out to find Axel coming down the stairs, and he winked at me and gave me a thumbs up. Beau turned when I walked into the foyer, and fortunately, he appeared as nervous as I felt. But he looked devastatingly handsome in a navy suit sans tie with a dark green shirt that matched his eyes. He walked forward, his eyes roaming my body before landing on mine. He kissed me softly on the cheek and whispered, "Peach, you are stunning."

Axel cleared his throat and said sternly, "Son, can I ask what your intentions are with our nanny?"

I erupted in a fit of giggles as Beau impatiently circled his tongue inside his cheek. He stuck his hands in his pockets and rocked back on his heels. "Well, *Dad*. I thought I would drink a fifth of Jack Daniels and drive too fast down the interstate while we smoked some weed." Axel narrowed his eyes as Beau continued, "I forgot to bring any money, so I thought I would take Charli down to one of the strip clubs and have my friend Cinnamon teach her some moves. Then maybe she can do some lap dances and earn us enough money for dinner at Mickey D's."

Ax pursed his lips and glared at Beau before finally nodding slowly and saying, "Okay, that sounds good. You kids have fun."

I raised my hand to Beau's solid shoulder. "Wait, was I supposed to bring the weed, or did you get it?"

Blaire handed me my purse and jacket. "I put it in your purse, Charli. Inside pocket."

The guys snickered at Blaire and I playing along with their little ruse. Beau helped me slide my camel-colored jacket on, and his eyes shone with affection as he put his hand on my lower back and led me to the door.

"Have her home by nine!" Blaire chirped, and her brother shot her a withering look over his shoulder. I expected to see his big black truck, so I was shocked to see a red vintage car sitting at the curb.

Beau noticed my face and grinned as I quickened my steps toward the cool-ass car. "You like?"

"I love! What is it? Is it yours?" I stroked my fingertips delicately across the metallic red paint.

He opened the door and helped me in before going around to get in the driver's side. "It's a '57 Thunderbird. And yes, it's mine. It was my dad's, and I rebuilt the engine myself. It took a couple years because I had to try to find parts and I pretty much just worked on it on weekends. Tank helped because he's really good at anything mechanical."

"It's fantastic."

"We can put the top down one day when the weather is warm, if you don't mind messing up your hair."

"That's why God invented hats," I said as he reached across the bench seat and put his arm around my back.

"My favorite part of the car is the bench seat so I can do this," he said, sliding me toward him until I was sitting right next to him.

"I guess you do that a lot," I said drolly.

Beau laughed as he cranked the car and the engine roared to life. "Actually, that was my first time. You're the only female to ride in it besides Blaire and Carrie—at least since I've owned it." He pulled out onto the street, placing his hand on my thigh, and said, "No wait, that's not true. I have let one other woman ride in this car."

"Who?" I asked, feeling irrationally jealous.

He grinned over at me. "Your mom. She said your dad used to have a T-bird, so we went cruising one day for old time's sake. We even stopped for milkshakes."

"So, you basically took my mom on a date," I said, amused. "How did your date with her compare to this one?"

"Well, Ms. Casper is a hard act to follow, but so far, you're holding your own," he said, squeezing my leg.

"Well, that's comforting."

Beau asked me about my dad, who had died of colon cancer a few years ago, and he laughed with me when I told him stories about what a prankster my father was.

We arrived at the restaurant and were seated at a table near the windows. The place was stunning and elegant, and I was glad I had decided to wear a dress. Beau sat beside me and took my hand, bringing it to his lips and kissing my fingertips. "You look really beautiful tonight, Charli."

"Thank you," I said, trying not to blush at his compliment. "You look very handsome in this suit." He really did. The way his jacket fit showed off his trim waist and broad shoulders, and I had noticed more than one set of hungry female eyes eating up my date as we had walked to our table. It probably had a lot to do with his confident swagger, as well. Confidence was sexy as hell on a man, and Beau Atwood exuded it from every pore.

He slid his hand up my arm and rested it on my shoulder, playing absently with my hair as we looked over the menu. We ordered Italchos with shrimp and basil to share as an appetizer, and while we sipped wine and waited for our food, I tentatively asked Beau about his parents.

He gave me a sad little smile. "They were the most in love couple I had ever seen. A lot like Blaire and Axel, actually. Always kissing when they thought we weren't looking," he said, his eyes unfocused with his memories. "My dad was very affectionate with my mom. He was in the military and could be gruff and formidable, but he had such a soft spot for her. They actually died on the same day, which was good, I guess, because I don't think either of them would have survived without the other."

"How old were you when they died?"

"I was twenty, and Blaire was sixteen. I was already in the navy, but I requested to be stateside until she finished high school so I could take care of her. Of course, the smarty pants graduated early, so it was only a year."

"So, you finished raising her?"

He shrugged like it was no big deal to take on raising a young girl by himself. "I guess you could say that, but I didn't really do much. Blaire was easier than most teenagers. She studied a lot and never partied, so I didn't have to do much in the way of discipline. I threatened a few guys who came sniffing around, bought groceries, and made sure the house was secure at night. That was about the extent of my parenting."

"No wonder you two are so close. Were your parents in a car accident?" His jaw tightened as his fisted hand dropped to the tabletop, and I quickly added, "You don't have to talk about it, if you don't want to," I said, covering his hand with my own and noticing that it softened and unclenched at my touch.

The waitress brought our appetizer then, and I thought Beau would take that opportunity to change the subject. Instead, he shook his head and said, "It's okay. I don't really talk about it much, but it's been fourteen years." He took a bite of the Italian nachos and a sip of wine before continuing. "They were caught in a bank robbery. The guy was armed and high on PCP, so he was pretty volatile. He had already shot one woman, and then he turned the gun on my mom."

I pressed my fingertips over my lips, and Beau paused for a few seconds. "My dad jumped in front of Mom just as the guy pulled the trigger." I squeezed his hand, and his fingers twined tightly with mine. "He fired twice and hit both of them, and they died within a couple of minutes of each other."

Oh. God. Way to bring up a heavy subject on a first date, Char.

"I'm so sorry, Beau." I dabbed my eyes with my napkin. Wanting to lighten the mood, I said, "So, tell me your favorite memory with each of your parents."

He grinned then, and my heart lightened as he told me tales of baking cookies with his mom and fishing with his dad. I responded with stories of my brothers taking me fishing, and he laughed when I told him about one time when I talked so much that Justin threw me out of the boat.

"Then Ethan and Henry got mad and jumped him, and they ended up capsizing the boat. We lost our cooler and all of our shoes. Mom was so ticked off she wouldn't speak to any of us for a week."

Beau found that hilarious. "Ms. Casper pissed off? I can't imagine it. She seems so sweet."

"She is now that she's older, but raising five kids… well, she had to be a little tough just to keep our house standing. My brothers were awful. I miss those days, though."

By the time we ate our entrees and shared a piece of fried cheesecake with amaretto and whipped cream, Beau and I were laughing and talking like we had known each other forever. He walked me out to the car with his hand on my back, but instead of opening the car door, he pushed my back up against it and pressed his hard body against mine.

Ooh, yes, baby.

"I may not be very experienced with dating, but I had a wonderful time with you tonight, Peach." He nipped at my lips, and I was pretty sure everything inside my body melted.

"Me too. I like being with you, Beau."

His lips found their way across my cheek and up to my ear. "Will you go out with me again?"

Hell yes! Fuck yes! OMG yes, yes, yes!

"I would love to," I said, impressing myself with how calm my voice sounded.

He pulled back and circled my nose with his. "Good," he whispered, before his lips took mine in a soft, sensual kiss. I shivered in his arms, and he pulled away. "I'm sorry, baby. You're cold." I didn't bother telling him that I wasn't shivering because of the cold. He opened the driver's side door and ushered me inside the car, climbing in after me while I slid to the middle of the bench seat. He grinned over at me as he cranked up the car and the heater.

Reaching up to tuck my hair behind one ear, he studied me for a long moment. "Your hair looks really pretty like this, Peach." He slid one hand into my hair and the other one trailed up the outside of my thigh as his mouth slanted over mine for a scorching kiss. Dear God, this man had a tongue that would tempt a saint... not that I was feeling very saintlike at the moment.

As soon as he pulled back, I started giggling, and he frowned at me. "Not exactly the response I was going for," he said dryly.

I covered my mouth with my hand, trying to stifle my laugh. "I'm sorry. We're just here in this old car making out like teenagers, and I suddenly felt like I was in an Archie comic book."

He chuckled. "You want me to take you to Lookout Point, and we can neck for a while?"

"Or the drive-in movie," I said with a grin. "So, am I Betty or Veronica?"

"Babe, you're a total Betty. I had the hots for her so bad when I was a kid." He leaned in for a chaste kiss against my lips and said, "But since I'm pretty sure there's not a Lookout Point in the greater Dallas area, I guess I should take you home."

Beau's phone dinged when we were almost to the house, and he said, "Grab my phone out of my pocket and see who that is. If it's Blaire teasing about me keeping you out past your nine o'clock curfew, text her back and tell her to kiss my ass."

He told me his lock code, and I dug his phone out of his jacket pocket and opened his text message. My smile froze on my face, and tears unwittingly filled my eyes as I read it.

BEAU

"Was it my sister?" I asked, glancing over at Charli. My heart skipped a beat when I saw the wetness in her eyes and the downturn of her pretty lips. "Charli, what's wrong?"

She shoved the phone back into my pocket and turned her head toward the passenger window. "It-it wasn't Blaire. It was a, um, private message. I think you should read it after you drop me off." Her voice was thick with tears, and I felt a moment of panic.

"Baby, what's wrong?" I asked, pulling up in front of my sister's house and slamming the car into park. I reached for Charli, but she was already sliding toward the other door. I grabbed her leg to stop her as I wrestled my phone from my pocket with my other hand. "Just wait, Charli." I looked down at the text, and my heart dropped into my stomach. *That fucking bitch.*

> *Miranda: Sorry about last night. I can't wait to get my hands back on what's inside those sexy gray underwear you were wearing. Call me, baby.*

"Dammit," I muttered. "Charli, this isn't what it looks like. She showed up at my house last night uninvited."

I heard her sniffle, but I still couldn't see her face. "It's none of my business who you invite to your house. It's not like we're... anything."

"Peach, look at me, please." She turned her head toward the windshield and looked at me out of the corner of her eyes, like it was too painful to view me straight on. I cupped her chin gently. "I *want* us to be something, sweetheart."

"Beau, please don't. I just... can't." Tears were streaming down her face, and I felt that tightness in my chest again.

"Hold on," I said fiercely, quickly dialing a number and putting my phone on speaker.

Charli's face snapped toward mine. "What are you doing? I don't want to talk to—"

She stopped when Cam answered with a brief, "Yo."

I spoke quickly. "Cam, I'm in the car with Charli, and you're on speaker."

"Hey, Charles. How's the date going? Is Shark minding his manners?" he asked merrily.

"Cam, I need you to tell Charli exactly what happened last night at our house." When he didn't say anything, I clarified, "With the unexpected visitor we had."

"You want me to... uhhhh..."

I kept my eyes on Charli's as I spoke. "Yes, I want you to tell her word-for-word what happened. Please."

Cam started talking, telling the story of Miranda showing up at our house and demanding to see me. He told her that I refused to see her until she started making a scene. "Then Shark stormed out of his room in his briefs and told her to leave. When she refused, he told her that he was seeing someone—and if you haven't been paying attention, sweetheart, that is *you*—and he said that he would not fuck around because he wanted to be with you."

Peach's eyes softened, and I nodded at her and took her hand, kissing the backs of her fingers. "Thanks, Cam," I said.

He took a deep breath and said, "Charli, I don't know what's happened, but I do know he turned her down flat and that he really, really likes you."

Charli looked at me and said, "Thanks, Cam. I really, really like him too."

"I appreciate it, buddy," I said into the phone. "I'll see you later and explain." We disconnected, and I pulled Charli closer to me. "I swear, Peach. Nothing happened. I want to see where things go with us, and I can promise you that you're the *only* woman I'm interested in."

My heart felt like it was shot straight back into my chest when Peach smiled at me. "I believe you. I'm sorry, but we were texting about what we were wearing, and then she *knew* what you were wearing and—"

"I know. I know, baby. I was so pissed at her for acting like a lunatic, I just stomped into the living room without even realizing I wasn't fully dressed. I totally broke things off with her, even though there wasn't technically anything to break off. But I let her know that I was absolutely done." I tilted my phone so Charli could see and blocked Miranda's number. "There. No more phone calls or text messages, okay?"

She tilted her chin down and looked up at me with those big blue eyes. "I'm sorry I got so upset, Beau."

I was a little peeved that she didn't believe me right away, but I had to admit that if the shoe were on the other foot, I would have probably blown the roof off the car. And there was no way I could stay mad at her for getting upset about another woman texting me. Hell, I was glad she was jealous. "It's okay, Peach. I don't blame you. Just tell me we're okay."

"We're okay," she whispered, lifting her hands to the back of my neck and pulling my face toward hers. *Oh, baby.* As soon as her tongue slid through my open lips, I felt a slow burn start between us. I had one arm wrapped around her waist and the other was sliding up and down her thigh. As her sweet tongue stroked against mine, I moved my hand up and up and up to the very top of her thigh until I could feel the heat between her legs. "Beau," she moaned.

"What, baby?"

We were both breathless when she pulled away and looked up at me, the twinkle in her eyes making my stomach flutter. "I still have your jacket. Would you like to come inside and get it?" she asked, her fingers kneading the back of my neck.

"Sweetheart, I would *love* to come inside and get my jacket." I swiftly opened the door and we both slid out of the car and hurried to the house. She had her keys in her hand, fumbling to unlock the door as I swept her hair away from her neck on one side, and sucked gently on her soft flesh.

"Beau, you're distracting me," she complained. "I can't find the hole."

I chuckled as I took the key from her and slid it into the lock on the first try. "I can help with that."

"You're disturbingly adept at hole-finding," she said teasingly as I opened the door and pushed us both inside. I turned her around and pinned her against the wall, leaning down to suck and nibble at her mouth.

"Why don't you get out of this dress?" I murmured against her lips, and I felt her sharp intake of breath. I cupped her face in my hand and kissed her forehead.

"I think that came out wrong. I just meant, why don't you put some comfortable clothes on?"

Peach gave me a shy smile as her fingers unbuttoned two of my shirt buttons. "I want you to get comfy, too."

Holy fucking fuck! She turned and asked me to unzip her dress, and as I slowly drew the zipper down, my cock felt like it grew to twice its normal size. I saw her smooth skin in the angle of her open dress and caught a glimpse of light blue lace panties and bra. My fingers twitched with the need to stroke every inch of her, but I reluctantly pulled my fingers away. She got something out of her dresser drawer and headed into the bathroom.

I took off my jacket and quickly unbuttoned and removed my shirt, wondering exactly how comfortable she wanted me to get. Would it be too presumptuous to take my pants off? *Jeez, I was shit at this.* I was still debating when Charli emerged from her bathroom wearing a pale pink satin tank top and shorts set, making my mouth go instantly dry. She looked so fucking soft and beautiful. She walked hesitantly toward me, so I met her in the middle, putting my arms around her. Without her heels on, she was over a foot shorter than me.

"You look gorgeous," I told her as she rested her hands on my bare chest.

She smiled crookedly up at me and said, "I was just thinking the same thing about you." She moved her soft mouth over my heated flesh, licking and kissing her way across my chest, her eyes closed as she sampled me. I had never felt anything more intimate, more *right*. When she raised up on her toes, I lifted her by the ass so she could reach my neck, dying to feel those supple lips on me some more.

She wrapped her legs around my waist as her tongue and lips teased the side of my neck. "Jesus, Charli," I groaned, pulling her tighter against me until she winced. "What's wrong, baby?" I asked, loosening my grip a little.

Charli looked down between us and then back up at my face. "Your belt buckle poked me." I laid her on the bed and proceeded to unbuckle my belt and unfasten my pants. I watched her face as I pulled my pants down to make sure she was okay with it, and I was struck with pleasure when her eyes widened at the bulge in my underwear.

I crawled up the bed toward her wearing only my boxer briefs. "All the hard stuff is gone." She gave me a dubious look as she eyed my erection, and I laughed. "Okay, so maybe I didn't get rid of *all* the hard stuff, but at least nothing will poke you now."

She giggled and said, "Well, damn."

I laughed as I stretched out beside her. "You have a dirty little mind, Peach, and I think I like it."

"I think I like you," she said, turning toward me and licking my lips with tiny laps. I sucked her tongue into my mouth and slid my hand down her satin-covered back before hauling her body tightly against mine. I was used to being demanding in bed, and women usually loved it, but this was Peach. I didn't want to scare her off.

"Is this okay, baby?" I asked, trying to control the urge to roll on top of her and grind my dick between her legs.

She moaned a long 'yes' into my mouth, so I deepened the kiss, grasping her behind the knee and hauling her leg over my hip, longing to feel her warm sex on my growing cock. And fuck me, she wasn't just warm; she was on fucking fire.

My hand skated down over her ass, and I reveled in the feel of the smooth skin on the back of her thigh as I dragged my fingers up and down, from her knee to her round butt. Her tiny hand smoothed over my chest and shoulder, finally coming to rest on my bicep. She tugged, rolling me on top of her, and *fucking yes!*

"Jesus, Peach," I said against her lips. I plunged my tongue deeply into her mouth, and she responded by parting her legs and cradling my hips between her thighs. I ground my dick against her sex, and she let out a loud groan. "Shhh, baby," I said, kissing my way across her face and circling my tongue over the pulse under her jaw.

"More, Beau," she panted, sliding her hands down my back to grasp my ass. I rolled my hips into her, abrading her clit with the hard ridge of my cock, and she pushed her heels into the mattress to lift her hips to mine. "Oh, God," she whimpered. I was so fucking turned on feeling her tiny body writhing under me and knowing that she wanted me like I wanted her.

"Feel good, baby?" I asked, sucking and licking the side of her neck, finding her most sensitive spots and worshiping them with my mouth.

"So good, Beau."

"Are you going to come for me?" Her hips were pumping back against me, and I gritted my teeth against the need to come.

"Y-yes," she said, her voice trembling.

"Say it, Peach," I growled.

"I'm going to come for you, Beau." The way my name rolled softly off her tongue drove me over the edge and I grasped her ass and pulled her tightly against my groin as I thrusted my hardness against her clit over and over.

"Let go for me, baby," I grunted, lifting my face to watch hers as her hips jerked against me and her head tilted back. I ran my tongue roughly up her exposed throat as she moaned my name in ecstasy, and I'll be damned if that wasn't the hottest fucking thing I had ever heard.

Her hips finally dropped to the mattress, and I followed her down with my hips, slowing my grind and kissing her through the rest of her orgasm until I had wrung every ounce of pleasure from her body. I felt her wetness seeping through our clothes and warming my dick, which twitched in appreciation. And need. Goddammit, I didn't want to come in my underwear.

I buried my face in her hair, immersing myself in her sweetness as her breathing slowed, and then I flopped over onto my back, biting my cheek hard enough to draw blood. Charli rolled toward me with her head on my shoulder as her hand explored my chest and abs.

"Sorry. I just need a minute. I was about to..." My words drifted off as her fingers slid lower and cupped my erection through my underwear. I stilled her hand with my own and said, "Baby, you don't have to do that," and my dick told me to shut my fucking mouth.

Her big blue eyes held a touch of shyness as she raised her perfect face to look at me. "But I want to, Beau." I removed my hand, and her eyes dropped to watch herself pull the waistband of my underwear down. Her breathing quickened as she wrapped her delicate hand tentatively around my thick cock.

"Holy shit, Peach." Even if she didn't move an inch, I knew I could come just from the feel of her warm, soft hand on me. But she did move, and all apprehension was gone from her touch as she stroked me firmly from the root to the tip. "Baby," I groaned, "that feels so fucking good."

She palmed the crown of my dick, gathering the pre-cum that was leaking copiously from my tip, and she used the moisture to lubricate her strokes on my long shaft. Her hand twisted and pumped me as she pushed against my face with her nose. I tilted my head to the side, giving her mouth access to suck on my neck. "You're so hard, Beau. I love touching you."

I grinned at the ceiling. "That's what happens when the hottest woman in the world has her hand on my dick."

She fucked me with her hand, harder, faster, until I was only hanging on by a thread. "Let go for me, baby," she whispered, repeating my words back to me and breaking my tenuous control. She sank her teeth into my neck, and the slight pinch of pain had me shooting off like a rocket.

"Fuuuuuck," I growled into the top of her head as her tongue drew firm circles on my neck, and I pumped my hips against her, my cum gushing all over my stomach and her hand. "Christ, Peach. Don't... don't stop, baby." She didn't.

She worked me until I was dry, then placed a gentle kiss on my neck before looking up at me. I realized I was clutching her ass with one hand, and I used it to drag her body up mine for a series of tender kisses. "That was amazing, sweetheart," I murmured against her lips. "You're amazing."

"I like making you come," she admitted.

I chuckled against her cheek before kissing her there. "That makes two of us. Any time you feel the need, you just let me know."

"That's terribly sweet of you," she said with a grin before rolling to the side. "I'll get you a towel. You're so damn messy," she mock-scolded.

I hooked my hand around the back of her neck and pulled her down for a hot, sloppy kiss. "Are you sassing me, woman?"

She grinned against my lips. "What if I am?"

"Then I might just take you over my knee." *Fuck. Did I just say that out loud?*

I expected her to run screaming from the room, but she just bit her bottom lip before asking, "Is that a promise or a threat?"

I ran my finger down her cute little nose. "It's whatever you want it to be, Peach." She gave me a timid smile, and I said, "Now go get me a towel since you caused all this mess." I gestured at the sticky cum all over my stomach.

She rolled her eyes as she climbed off the bed.

"Sass!" I called to her retreating form with a big grin on my face, and she giggled. Peach returned a few minutes later with a warm cloth. I cleaned up, and she took the linen back to the bathroom as I tucked myself back into my underwear, wondering what I was supposed to do now. Should I get dressed and leave? Oddly enough, I didn't want to.

I was still contemplating what I should do when Charli returned to the bedroom, chewing her thumbnail nervously. I realized she was worried about something when her eyebrows knitted together as she crawled back onto the bed.

"What's wrong, gorgeous girl?" I asked, sliding underneath the covers with her and rubbing away her wrinkles with my thumb.

"I just… I've never done… *stuff* like that unless I was farther into a relationship with someone. I don't want you to think I'm… slutty." Her blue eyes were wide on mine, seeking reassurance.

Oh, my sweet, sweet Peach. I knew a thing or twenty about sluts, and she was the absolute farthest thing from that.

Cupping her face with my hand, I inched my face closer until our noses were almost touching. "You shut that down right now, Charli Casper," I said firmly. "You're fucking perfect, and everything we just did was perfect."

Her eyes softened, and she turned her head and kissed my palm. "I liked it, too," she said shyly. "I can't seem to control myself around you. I've never felt this kind of attraction before."

My head swelled. My heart swelled. Something farther south swelled, as well, at her admission.

I cuddled her to my side so that her head rested on my chest, loving the feeling of her soft, warm body against mine. *Who knew I would actually enjoy snuggling?*

"It's hard to control myself around you, too, Peach, but I'll never push you for anything you're not ready for. I'm fucking crazy about you, and I wouldn't be able to live with myself if we got carried away and you regretted it."

She looked up at me, and I fell into those deep eyes. *God, what is happening right now?*

"I wouldn't regret it, as long as you don't think—"

"I don't," I assured her, capturing her eyes with mine. "Not even a little bit. We're dating, right?" She nodded, so I continued. "And we're attracted to each other, right?"

"A little bit," she giggled.

Pulling her tight little body more snugly against my hard one, I rested my hand on the curve of her hip. "We're both adults, and we're getting to know each other." I lifted her chin and took her lips in a soft, but demanding kiss. "I would love to get to know you a lot better."

"Me too," she whispered.

"Then we'll just continue to explore each other, and we can go as slowly as you need."

"Explore," she said on a sigh. "I like the sound of that."

"Me too," I said, tucking her head underneath my chin and kissing the top of her head. She rested her arm across my waist, and I stroked my fingers lightly up and down, from her hand to her shoulder and back again as she looped her leg over one of mine. "Never be embarrassed with me, Peach. If there's anything you want, I'll make it happen."

"M'kay," she said sleepily.

Letting out a deep, contented sigh, I reveled in everything Charli... her softness... her scent... her even breaths against my chest. I'd just stay here for a few minutes until she fell asleep, and then I would go. Reaching over and flicking off the lamp beside the bed, I buried my nose in her hair. As her quiet breathing slowed, I closed my eyes, actually enjoying the feel of her body on mine.

Just a few more minutes...

18

CHARLI

Mmmm. Delicious. That's how I felt when I woke up Tuesday morning. I was so comfortable, even though I was lying on a giant rock. But that rock was covered with nice... warm... skin? I pried my eyes open and saw an expanse of tanned flesh under my face. It was covered with a smattering of light brown hair and... *holy shit! Beau! He spent the night in my bed!*

I wasn't ready to leave my warm cocoon yet, so I snuggled closer and pressed my lips to his chest. "Good morning, Peach," he rumbled in his dark, sexy voice that caused a rush of moisture to gather in my panties. *How the hell did he do that?*

I looked up to see his gorgeous green eyes looking hazily down at me, a little smile tipping up one side of his mouth. I realized that his hand was down the back of my shorts, cupping one of my ass cheeks over my underwear. *How had that gotten there?*

I went to move my right hand, but realized it was inside his underwear, gripping his hip. *What the shit?* I slid it slyly out, hoping he didn't notice, but yeah... no such luck. He chuckled and said, "I kind of liked your hand there." Then he squeezed my ass with the hand currently residing in my sleep shorts. "I guess we even like each other when we're asleep."

He rolled toward me, his hand still planted firmly on my ass, and pressed our bodies together. I realized I still hadn't said a word, so I muttered, "Did you sleep well?"

He had a look of slight confusion when he answered, "Yeah, I did, actually. Very well. I never—" He cut himself off and leaned his face down to suck lightly on my lips, and I felt his morning wood twitch against my hip.

Good Lord, that thing is enormous. I remembered thinking the same thing when I held him in my hand last night, my fingers not even fitting all the way around it. What was I supposed to do with it this morning? Should I give him another hand job? My waking-up-with-a-man-in-my-bed etiquette was severely lacking.

I was distracted from my thoughts by his tongue invading my mouth. He kissed me long and slow, our tongues dancing unhurriedly with one another. "Mmmm, I think I like waking up with you," he said as his lips moved to my ear and nuzzled there. Jesus, his gravelly morning voice was simply orgasmic. "I never do this," he mused as he nipped my earlobe.

"Do what?" I slurred, my voice sounding drunken as he rolled me on top of him and stuck his other hand down the back of my shorts.

"Cuddle all night with someone. What are you doing to me, Peach?"

I know what I'd like to do to you, I thought, but didn't say it out loud. "Never?" I croaked as his lips moved down the column of my throat.

"Never," he confirmed

"Well, you're very good at it... the cuddling, I mean." His grip on my ass tightened, rubbing me against his hard length. "I'm sorry. I think I fell asleep on you last night."

"S'okay, baby. I'm definitely enjoying the benefits of waking up with you." He nipped my collarbone and then trailed his tongue smoothly up the side of my neck while he lifted his hips and pushed his cock against my sex.

I heard a noise from inside the house and groaned. "God, that feels good, Beau, but I think Blaire is up, and..." I trailed off when he bit the side of my neck.

"Shit," he said, giving me a peck on the lips. "It wouldn't be good for her to find me here. She'd probably cut my dick off."

"That would be an epic tragedy. I like your—" I clapped my hand over my mouth and felt my eyes turn into big, blue saucers.

Beau grinned and rolled us over, so he was half-laying on me. "It's okay, Peach. You can admit that you like my dick."

"Beau!" I said, feigning outrage. "That's not what I was going to say." It was *totally* what I was going to say.

He munched playfully on my neck, which tickled and made me squirm. "Don't deny it. You like it, don't you?"

"No, I hate it. It's tiny," I said, trying to keep my laughter quiet.

"Don't lie to me, Peach," he growled, slipping his hand under my shirt and tickling my ribs. "Admit it! Say, 'I love your dick, Beau.'" I squealed and tried to push him away with my hands, but it was like trying to move a boulder. "Say it!" he demanded, increasing the neck-munching and rib-tickling until I was breathless.

"Okay, okay! I love your dick, Beau. It's the most spectacular organ I've ever seen," I gasped.

He grinned down at me as he instantly halted all tickling activities. "There. That wasn't so difficult, was it?" His thumb brushed against the side of my breast, and his pupils dilated until I could barely see the green of his irises. He slid his hand out and cupped my face with it. "I should probably go before I get us in trouble," he said reluctantly. I nodded, and he lowered his lips firmly to mine. "What are your plans for the day?"

"Oh, I have to drop the boys off at mothers-day-out, so my day is pretty easy. Blaire likes them to get some socialization with other kids their age besides each other."

"Good, come by my office around noon. We can go to lunch together." It was a command rather than a request, but I agreed. "Cool," he said, flashing me a brilliant smile which would have made my knees weak if I'd been standing. "I'll text you the address." He rolled off the bed and dressed quickly as I admired the view.

He pulled me out of the bed and wrapped his arms around me, giving me a sweet kiss before saying, "See you at lunch, Peach." He opened the door and studied the doorknob with a frown. "You really should have a deadbolt on this door. I'll talk to Axel and let him know I'll install one for you."

"You don't have to—"

"No arguments. Do you know how easy it is to pick one of these doorknob locks?"

"Uh, no. Because I'm not a burglar or a serial killer."

He grinned and winked at me. "That's comforting to know," he said as he locked the door and left. The room felt somehow colder now that he was gone, and I hugged my arms around my waist. After staring at the door like a sad little puppy for a few minutes, I showered and got dressed in jeans and a blue off-the-shoulder shirt that made my eyes pop, pulling my hair into a high, full ponytail. I glanced over at the chair in my room and smiled before sending a text to Beau.

Charli: You left your jacket again. Is this a ploy to get yourself invited back to my room?

Beau: No, but that's a good idea.

Beau: Do we have to have an excuse for you to invite me?

Charli: No, you can come back any time.

Beau: That's the correct answer.

I smiled goofily at my phone for a full two minutes before heading into the kitchen.

I was cooking pot roast for the family tonight, so I put on an apron before prepping the veggies and putting them in the fridge. I wondered if Beau liked roast, and I decided to ask him if he wanted to come over and eat dinner with us tonight.

After getting the kids all situated, I followed the GPS to the address Beau had given me and found a sleek, modern building that was cool and yet somehow still inviting. My wedge heels tapped on the dark hardwood floor as I approached the black marble reception desk about ten minutes before noon. There was a tall brunette there with a snug-fitting black dress, big boobs, and gobs of makeup on her face. She smiled politely as I approached.

"Hi, I'm here to see Beau Atwood," I said, returning her smile, which suddenly faded from her face.

She looked me up and down and pursed her lips. "Do you have an appointment, *ma'am?*" she asked with fake sweetness.

"No, but he asked me to meet him here."

"Hmmmm. Of course, he did," she said, and I didn't miss the sarcasm lacing her words. "I'm sorry, but no one gets to see Mr. Atwood without an appointment. What is your name?"

"Charli Casper," I said, and she looked down her pointed nose at me before sitting and typing something into the computer.

"Nope. No Carli Casper in my system," she said with feigned sympathy.

"It's Charli," I repeated, and Pointy Snoot gave me the fakest smile I had ever seen.

"Her either," she said without even looking back at her monitor.

Well, I didn't like this bitch at all. I drew myself up to my full barely-five-foot-four-with-heels-on height and said firmly, "I probably won't be in the system. This is a *personal* visit, not business. Beau and I have a lunch date."

Pointy Snoot looked like she was sucking on a persimmon when she snapped, "Lovely. Just have a seat, and I'll notify Mr. Atwood that you're here as soon as he's available. He's a *very* busy man."

And you're a very bitchy slut, I thought.

I took a seat in one of the plush blue armchairs near a coffee table and looked through the magazines, selecting one and flipping through the pages without really seeing them. My mind was racing. The receptionist seemed to get testy when I mentioned that I was here for a lunch date with Beau. Were they an item? She certainly seemed to be his type, based on what I had seen of that Miranda chick he had been banging when I showed up at his house that day. Very fake and um... busty.

I glanced down at my barely-C cup breasts and felt a bit inadequate. I sat for fifteen minutes, occasionally glancing up at Pointy Snoot, who was patently ignoring my existence. It was five minutes past twelve, and she hadn't so much as picked up the phone. Maybe she had sent him a message on the computer letting him know that he had a guest. Should I text him that I was there? No, the receptionist had said that he was busy. He was probably running late and would get to me when he had time.

Another ten minutes passed, and she was filing her nails and still ignoring me. I heard what sounded like an angry bear stomping down the hallway behind the reception desk and noticed that Snooty hastily threw the nail file in a drawer and slammed it shut just before Beau busted into the room.

"Aspen!" he barked. "I'm expecting—" He noticed me, and his angry face immediately melted into a confused smile. "Charli, what are you doing sitting out here?" Beau crossed to me in two long strides and took my hands, pulling me from my chair. He gave me several soft pecks on the lips, and I resisted the urge to flip off Aspen, who was openly glaring behind Beau's back.

"I didn't have an appointment," I said, deliberately shooting my eyes at the receptionist.

Beau frowned. "You don't need an appointment, Peach. We were..." Realization crossed his face and he turned to face Aspen. "When Miss Casper arrives, she is to be shown to my office. Immediately," he said sharply.

"But Beau..." *Giggle, giggle.* "I mean *Mister Atwood*..." She said his name so breathlessly I wanted to stick a sock down her throat. A dirty one.

"I said *immediately*," he snapped before turning back to me, his gaze softening on my face. "Your eyes look really pretty in this shirt," he said. Beau's hands slid across my shoulders and down my arms until he was grasping my hands. He brought each of them to his lips, and I attempted to not visibly swoon.

Keeping one of my hands, he linked our fingers and headed toward the hall. "Come back here, Peach, and I'll show you my office."

With exaggerated politeness as we passed the reception desk, I said, "Aspen, thank you so much for your... help." She narrowed her eyes at me, and if looks could kill, my mother would be picking out my casket tomorrow.

As we walked down the hall, Beau murmured, "Have you been waiting long?"

"About twenty-five minutes," I said, not wanting him to think I'd been late, as he ushered me into an office and closed the door. I didn't even get a chance to look around before I was pushed against the door with a big, chiseled male pressed against me, his warmth infusing every cell of my body.

He kissed me hard, his tongue insistent as it slid against mine. He slid a knee between my thighs and separated my legs as his hands slid to my butt. "I was going crazy, Peach. I thought you had stood me up." He sucked my bottom lip into his mouth and smoothed it with his tongue.

I circled his neck with my arms. "I wouldn't do that, Beau," I said, barely able to speak because his mouth was working wonders on my neck now.

"I was so mad at you," he said, his teeth sinking into the flesh at the side of my neck. *Ow!*

"Are you still mad at me?" I asked, my hands moving across his broad, strong shoulders.

"Little bit," he said, biting me again.

"Why?" I asked, trying to figure out what I had done besides get sidetracked by his guard dog receptionist.

He lifted his head and looked at me with a cocky half-grin on his gorgeous lips, those green eyes sizzling with lust. "Because your legs aren't around me." He bent slightly, his hands going to the backs of my thighs, and lifted me with practically zero effort on his part. I wrapped my legs around him, and he smiled, kissing my lips. "Better. This is how you'll greet me from now on," he declared before working his tongue back into my mouth. *Jesus. Someone was feeling bossy—and amorous—today.*

We were interrupted by the phone chirping, and he bit out a curse before turning and carrying me to his desk. With me still wrapped koala-style around him, he pushed a button on the desk phone. "Yes?" he snapped irritably.

Aspen's nasally voice sounded through the room. "Mr. Atwood, the mail has just arrived."

"And?"

"I just thought you would want to know," she said sweetly.

"Aspen, give the mail to Sandra, just like you do *every fucking day*, and stop interrupting me. In fact, do not disturb me again unless the building is on fire or terrorists have breached the entrance. Am I understood?" he barked.

At her dejected "yes," Beau disconnected and shook his head. "Fucking nightmare," he muttered.

"Is she, um... have you and Aspen..."

The scowl on his face told me I was way off base. "Fuck no, Peach. That's never happened, and it never will. She's an employee, and that's it. If I have my way, she won't even be that for very long, but I have to be careful and do everything by the book."

He set me on his big mahogany desk and settled between my thighs. "But I don't want to talk about Aspen right now," he said, his deep voice seducing me into a trance-like state. His hands dragging me tightly against his obvious erection told me what he would like to talk about instead, but I asked anyway.

"What do you want to talk about?"

A smile I was becoming way too familiar with slid over his lips. "This," he whispered, drawing closer, millimeter-by-painfully-slow-millimeter.

As soon as he'd closed his mouth over my lips, we heard a knock at the door. "Fuck," he muttered, and I had to agree with him. He lifted me and put me into his buttery-soft leather chair behind the desk before going to the door and swinging it open.

A tall black woman with a pretty, round face entered and said, "Hey, bossman. I gave that paperwork to Sandra, and…" She spotted me and stopped. "Oh, sorry. I didn't know you were with a… client?" I was obviously not a client because I was sitting *behind* Beau's desk.

"It's okay, J. Come on in. This is…" he turned to look at me, probably trying to figure out who the hell I was to him. He turned back to the woman with a proud smile on his handsome face. "This is my girlfriend, Charli," he announced, and I almost fell out of the damn chair.

Did he just call me his girlfriend?

The woman grinned happily, and I was instantly put at ease by her. I stood as she walked swiftly toward me and stuck out her hand. "Nice to meet you, girlfriend Charli. I'm Journey, assistant extraordinaire."

"I'm pretty sure that's not your official job title," Beau said wryly but with affection as Journey pumped my hand enthusiastically.

"It should be," she shot back, and I automatically liked this woman very much.

"Next you'll be asking for a pay raise."

Journey crossed her arms and said thoughtfully, her dreadlocks sliding over one shoulder as she tipped her head to the side, "Well, I wouldn't turn it down."

Beau chuckled and said, "We'll talk about it. Now get the hell out of my office. I'm about to take Charli to lunch."

"Alrighty. I'll talk to you when you get back." She shot a finger gun at me and said, "So nice to meet ya, Charli. And you can call me J. Everyone does."

"Okay, J. It was nice to meet you, too."

As soon as she left, Beau took my hand and said, "Let's go get some lunch, Peach."

"Who's Sandra?" I asked, praying that she didn't look anything like Aspen.

Beau eyed me and said, "She's my office manager. Come on, and I'll introduce you." He led me to the office a couple doors down, and I was relieved to see an older, gray-haired lady seated behind a desk. "This is Sandra. Sandra, this is my girlfriend, Charli." The G-word rolled off his tongue much more easily that time, and I felt a jolt of something warm slide down my spine.

"Well, my heavens," Sandra said, rounding her desk and taking both of my hands. "Aren't you just lovely, dear?" She beamed at me and made me sit in a chair in front of her desk as she sat beside me and peppered me with questions while Beau sighed. "And how long have you been Beau's girlfriend?" she asked after learning about my job, my schooling, and my family. I was just waiting for her to ask my blood type and if I'd had any recent kidney stones.

"Oh, about six minutes," I replied, and she laughed heartily while Beau chewed on the corner of his lip, trying to fight a mirthful smile.

"Okay, if you're done with the inquisition, I would like to take Charli to lunch," he said pointedly.

Sandra patted my hand and said, "It was so nice to meet you. Now go on before your sweetheart chews his lips off. So impatient!" she tutted. As I turned to the door, I noticed her give Beau a grin and a thumbs up.

In the hallway, Beau drawled, "Well, Sandra seems to approve wholeheartedly." He intertwined his fingers with mine and said, "I'm starving. Let's go before my stomach tries to digest itself."

We passed an open door, and Woody called out, "Charles! What are you doing here?" I walked into his office with Beau huffily following me, still attached to my hand.

"Hey, Woody. I just came to have lunch with Beau."

"Awesome. I'm hungry as hell." He grabbed his keys off his desk and asked, "Where we going?"

"You're not invited," Beau snapped. "Since it's a nice day, *Charli and I* are going to pick up some sandwiches and eat at the park."

Woody eyed him with a wicked grin. "Like a picnic? Shark, that is so sweeeeeet," he said with an overly sugary voice.

"What's sweet?" Bode asked, walking into the office, looking like a tall, blonde drink of water.

Woody turned to him with a smirk and said, "Shark is going on a picnic with Charles. Isn't that lovely?"

"A picnic?" Bode picked up Woody's teasing tone. "Well, that's just divine! Are you going to put flowers in your hair and dance around the maypole, Shark?"

Oh, they were ripping on my sweet man for taking me on a picnic, something they apparently found too girly for a real man. Well, I would just show them.

"It was my idea," I lied, drawing Beau's harsh glare away from his friends. He looked at me questioningly, but I just pressed my body against the length of his and gave him a conspiratorial wink. I saw his lips twitch as he finally got it. "Thank you for taking me, baby, even though I know you didn't want to." Sliding my hand up the side of his neck, I kissed his ear and whispered loud enough for everyone in the room to hear. "I'll do that *thing* you like later."

Beau's eyes widened comically, and he said, "That thing where you use your tongue to—"

"Yep."

"And then your finger goes—"

I interrupted him before he said something that would set loose the giggles building up in my chest. "That's the one," I said, sucking his lips with a loud, slurpy noise.

"I fucking love that thing," he mumbled, grabbing two handfuls of my ass possessively as he gave me a long, sloppy kiss.

"Ay! Dios mio!" Woody said at the same time Bode uttered, "Holy fucking shit."

Beau gave me two pats on the bottom as we broke apart from our raunchy kiss. "You ready, Peach?"

"I was born ready," I quipped before looking over my shoulder as if I had forgotten the other men were there. I waggled my fingers at them. "Bye, guys." They were both standing there with their mouths hanging open as Beau led me from the room with one hand planted firmly on my behind.

"I'm taking an extra hour for lunch today. I have, uh, some errands to attend to," he said before closing the door. "Shhhh," he warned, putting his hand over my mouth when I started to giggle out in the hallway. We could hear their voices from inside Woody's office.

"What the fuck, man? Shark and Charli? Did you know about this?"

"Hell no. I mean, I saw them eye-fucking each other at Blaire's party, and then he went all caveman at that club, but... Jesus. What do you think she does with her tongue?"

"I don't know, but I'm going home to take a cold shower."

"I'm going to find a girl and take her on a goddamn picnic."

Beau grabbed my hand, and we sprinted down the hallway, finally erupting in laughter when we reached the parking lot.

"Oh, my God! Did you see their faces?" I gasped as we walked to his truck.

"You're a fucking savage, Peach." Beau opened his truck door and lifted me inside. "Also, I'd really like to talk more about this *thing* that you alluded to," he said, grabbing my hand and nipping the end of my index finger.

I kissed him on the nose. "I made it up, but it apparently involved my finger and my tongue."

"Uh huh. We're going to discuss it more later. In depth," he promised, closing the door with a grin.

Ay! Dios mio!

At the deli, we ordered our sandwiches and were told they would be ready in ten minutes. Beau led me outside and into the small department store three doors down. "What are we doing here, Beau?"

"Buying a blanket," he said, heading toward the back of the store. "I had been planning to eat at one of the tables at the park, but now that Woody mentioned it, we're going to get a blanket and find a quiet spot to have a real picnic."

Thirty minutes later, we were sitting on the most unmasculine fuzzy blanket—the only one they had in the store—in a grassy, secluded area of the park. We had just finished our sandwiches, and Beau was gathering our trash up and stuffing it into the sacks as I traced my finger over the lavender blanket covered with unicorns and rainbows. When he was done, he put his hand on my chest and eased me down onto my back, stretching out beside me and leaning up on his elbow.

He kissed my bare shoulder and then skimmed his fingers over the top of my blouse. "This color matches your eyes perfectly," he said. "Cornflower blue."

"Cornflower?"

"Yeah. That was my favorite crayon when I was a kid. I used that color on everything. People, dogs, houses. I made everything cornflower blue." He traced his index finger in a circle around my right eye, crossed my nose, and repeated it around the other eye. Then he dragged his finger down my nose, ending with it against my lips. I kissed it, and he put the finger to his lips and did the same before pressing it back to my mouth.

"You're being very romantic right now," I whispered, captivated by his attention. If I hadn't been on this blanket, I would have swooned to the ground by now."

"Am I? I'm not trying to be. I just like being with you, Peach."

"I like being with you, too, which is good, I guess, since I'm your *girlfriend*," I teased.

He frowned a little. "You don't want to be my girlfriend?"

I thought about it for all of two seconds before responding. "Of course, I do. It just surprised me when you said that at your office. We've only been on one date."

"Now we've been on two," he said, his fingers lingering on my cheek. "And we've had coffee and decided we want to go on more dates together. I'm not going to be seeing anyone else, and you're not either." An intense scowl crossed his face, sharpening his features, when he asked, "Right?"

"Right," I assured. "I don't want to be with anyone else." The tension eased from his face, and he looked so damned young and handsome as he smiled down at me. "So, I guess I have myself a boyfriend."

"Your boyfriend is dying to kiss you right now. What time do you have to pick up the kids?"

He held up his phone so I could see the time, and I said, "I have to get the boys in thirty-five minutes, and then I'll pick up Carrie on my way home."

He squinted his eyes as he did some mental calculations before he set an alarm on his phone and explained, "I'm going to make out with my girlfriend on this blanket for the next fourteen minutes before I have to take her back to her car."

Oh, Jesus. This man...

Beau wedged his arm under my head and slid his other hand down to my hip to roll me toward him. Our lips came together in a lingering kiss that went from soft to hard and back to soft again as our fourteen glorious minutes passed. He slid his hand up the back of my shirt as the other one wrapped around my shoulders until I was in a giant Beau cocoon that I never wanted to crawl out of.

By the time we got back to his truck, I was floating on air. It was as if I had taken a leap off a giant cliff and been caught by a big, fluffy cloud. Beau slid the folded blanket under his back seat and said, "For next time."

There was going to be a next time? I wasn't sure if I could stand it. I was already melting for this man.

As he drove me back to the Broxtons' SUV, which I used when carting the kids around, he held my hand and asked, "What are you doing for dinner tonight?"

"I'm making pot roast for the family," I said. "I was going to see if you wanted to come over."

He frowned. "Dammit, I love roast, but all the guys are coming over to watch the basketball game and eat wings. I was going to see if maybe you wanted to come." The furrow between his eyes got deeper. "I would skip it if it wasn't at my house. I really wanted to see you tonight."

"It's okay. Maybe another night," I said hopefully, and he nodded, but still scowled. "You could come over after the game, if you want. You know, to pick up your jacket?" I said tentatively.

His answering grin made things flutter in my stomach. "I would love to come pick up my jacket. I'll text you when I'm on my way."

19

BEAU

I went back into my office through the back door and sat behind my desk, feeling a little dazed from my lunch with Charli. I pressed two fingers against my swollen lips, which were still tingling from our make out session on the blanket. I jerked my hand down and put it on my keyboard as Cam walked into my office and sat down. He stood and leaned over, picking something out of my hair.

"Uh, Shark. Why do you have grass in your hair?"

I swiped at my head, dislodging a couple blades of green. "Charli," I told him with a goofy grin on my face.

"Charli put grass in your hair?" he asked, genuinely confused.

"No, we had lunch together and then made out on a blanket in the park. And I told her she's my girlfriend now."

"You mean you asked her?"

I glowered at him. "No, I *told* her."

Cam ran his tongue over his bottom teeth. "Of course, you did, you big fucking ape. So, you just bullied the poor girl into it?"

"Hell no, I didn't bully her. She said that she didn't want to see anyone else, and I don't either, so..."

"So, the Sharkinator is off the market."

"It seems so," I said smugly.

"I noticed you didn't come home last night. Did you seal the deal?"

I threw him a dark look for asking but shook my head. "No, I told you, she's different, and I'm not going to be pushy." I leaned my head back against my chair. "But Jesus, I want to push," I groaned.

"Blue balls?" he asked with a smirk.

"You're really enjoying this shit, aren't you?" He gave a little shrug. "If you must know, we fooled around a little. I fell asleep with her wrapped around me, and I slept like a fucking baby."

"So, there was snuggling involved."

"Yes, Cam," I gritted out, "there was snuggling, and *yes*, I liked it, so fuck off."

He held his palms out and said, "Hey, no judgment. Having a sweet little female curled up against you can make you feel really... manly." He was right. Waking up with Charli's head on my chest and my arms holding her protectively made me feel strangely masculine... like she trusted me to keep her safe.

"Yeah," I grunted.

"So, what's next?"

"I invited her over for the game tonight, but she's cooking roast for the family."

"She can cook, too? You sure you don't want to give her up and let your buddy Cam step in?" I growled at him, and he fucking laughed at me, the prick. "I'll take that as a no."

"Why don't you take it as a *fuck no* and get the hell out of my office so I can get some work done?"

He finally stopped laughing and asked, "Are you going to be a raging asshole all evening because you don't get to see Charli tonight?"

I tilted my head and said smugly, "Who said I wasn't going to see her tonight?" He lifted his eyebrows, and I continued, "She invited me over after the game."

He roared with laughter. "So, *she's* booty calling *you*?"

"It's not a booty call, goddammit," I roared. "Don't talk about her like that."

"Calm down, fucker. I'm just teasing you. You know I wouldn't disrespect Charli like that. Have you told the rest of the guys about y'all?"

"Woody and Bode know. They were giving me shit because I was taking her on a picnic." I chuckled as I recounted the scene in Woody's office to Cam.

He was grinning by the end of the story. "I like this chick."

"Me too. She's pretty awesome."

Cam stood and slapped the edge of my desk. "Alrighty then. I'll let you get back to work. You picking up the wings for tonight?"

"Yup. I'll see you at home, man." Sports night was a tradition with the guys. It didn't matter who was playing; we met just to hang out with each other. We usually gathered for Monday Night Football, but this week we were meeting on Tuesday night to watch basketball.

Tank, Bode, Woody, and Hawk shared a house, and we swapped out between meeting at my and Cam's house and theirs. When it was at our house, we supplied the wings, and the other guys brought dessert and drinks. Bode was always on dessert duty because the dude could bake like a boss.

After work, I swung by and picked up the food before heading home. Just before tipoff, the guys started arriving at our house, and all of them seemed to be grinning smugly at me. I was sure Bode and Woody had filled them in on me and Peach, and they probably found it hilarious that I had a girlfriend now. *Girlfriend.* That had sounded uncharacteristically wonderful when I'd said it out loud today.

Bode carried two dishes into the kitchen, and I followed him to get paper plates and a roll of paper towels. "You brought two desserts?" I asked as the rest of the guys piled up in the kitchen behind us.

"Yes, my brother." He uncovered a casserole pan and said, "Viola! *Peach* cobbler." Then he pulled the foil off a pie plate and said, "And *peach* pie."

I heard the sniggers from around the room and rolled my eyes. "Haha. Very funny, motherfuckers."

Tank said, "I got regular beer, and I also got some special beer for you, Shark." He put down a case of Miller Lite and a six pack of a beer I'd never heard of before.

I picked up one of the dark brown, longneck bottles and sighed. "Peach beer? Really, Tank?" He grinned and slapped me on the shoulder.

"Not to worry," Hawk said. "I stopped at the liquor store and got us a little something stronger in case anyone wanted some Crown and Coke." He put a twelve-pack of Coca-Colas on the counter and handed me a paper bag. I opened it suspiciously. Yep, just as I thought, Hawk had bought peach-flavored Crown Royal.

I glared at all the grinning faces looking back at me with amusement. "Maybe I should fire all your asses, and you could go get jobs as comedians," I snapped, grabbing one of the peach beers and stalking back into the living room. I twisted off the top and swigged down about half of it. It was actually pretty damned good.

My asshole friends followed me, and Woody slumped down beside me on the couch and punched my arm. "We're just fucking with you, Shark. We like Charli."

"Yeah, she's cool," Tank said, taking up the entire loveseat adjacent to the couch. "You should invite her over some time."

I eyed them speculatively, but I saw only sincerity reflected in each set of eyes. "I was going to invite her tonight, but she was cooking pot roast at my sister's house."

"Shit, I love pot roast. You think she would cook for us if we buy the groceries?" Hawk asked.

"I don't know," I said, giving him a deadpan look. "Do you plan on mercilessly harassing her like you're doing to me?"

"Yeah, probably," Bode said honestly, handing out paper plates to everyone. "This is a whole new world of entertainment for us. But we'll be nice about it, 'cuz she's a sweetheart."

"I'll ask her," I said grumpily. To be honest, I was secretly glad the boys liked Peach enough to want her to come to guys' night. If she was going to be a part of my life, she was going to be a part of theirs, as well. They were my true brothers, if not by blood, then by choice. I wasn't sure if she would want to hang out with a bunch of dumbass men, but I would put it out there and see what she said. In fact...

I pulled my phone from my pocket and sent her a text.

Beau: My friends are jealous because they want pot roast. They said they would buy the food if you would cook for Monday Night Football next week.

Peach: Sure. Sounds like fun.

Beau: Warning – they're a bunch of jackasses and will probably tease us a lot. They've never seen me with a girlfriend before, and they find it amusing.

Peach: I can handle it.

Beau: I'm sure you can. Can't wait to see you later.

Peach: Me too. XO

"She's in," I announced to the room as everyone piled food on their plates. "Next Monday."

"Fuck yes!" Cam said. "As much as I like wings, it will be nice to have a home-cooked meal. And the Wranglers are playing next Monday, too."

"If she cooks for all of us, she shouldn't have to clean up, too," I admonished with a warning glare around the room.

"We'll handle kitchen duty," Tank promised, and the other guys nodded their agreement while demolishing the wings and beer.

20

CHARLI

I heard a knock on the outside door to my room and leapt off the bed. I had showered, shaved my legs, and put on my pajamas, another satiny top and shorts set. I loved the silky feel of sleeping in satin, so my mom had bought me several sets for Christmas last year, including the sky blue one I was wearing tonight. It wasn't cornflower blue, but I hoped Beau would like it anyway.

I opened the door and found him leaning with one forearm against the doorframe looking delectable as all hell. "Well, hello ma'am. I was supposed to drop by and pick up a jacket from the lost and found?"

"Of course, sir. I have it right here." I handed him his jacket and closed the door in his face, trying to contain my laughter. After a beat, I heard a soft tapping on the door again. I opened it and looked innocently at him. "Was there something else you needed, Mr. Atwood?" He stared at me flatly, and I could no longer suppress my giggles.

Until he growled, "You," and pushed his way inside and locked the door behind him with a look of intense warning on his face. I couldn't tell if he was really angry or not, so I leapt on him, wrapping my legs around his waist as he caught me with his hands on my ass. "You remembered. Good girl," he said just before his mouth slanted over mine, his tongue sweeping through my lips.

We kissed like we were starving for each other, and when we finally came up for air, I leaned my forehead against his. "I know it's only been a few hours since I've seen you, but I missed you."

"I missed you, too, baby. Especially since the guys all brought peach stuff to my house tonight. Peach pie, peach cobbler, peach beer, peach whiskey. All I could think of was you."

"Okay, sorry, but that's kinda funny. Peach beer?"

"Yeah, it wasn't half bad." He rubbed a hand up and down my back. "Do you always wear stuff like this to sleep in?"

Shit. What if he's used to women wearing something sleazier to bed?

"Yes. You don't like it?"

"I love it, sweetheart. It's perfect and soft and pretty, just like you." His eyes skimmed over my face, eating me up like I was his favorite meal.

Oh, this big man could turn me inside out with his words.

"I like how it feels against my skin." I hesitated before pulling his shirt over his head and pressing my satin-covered body against his bare chest. "Like this," I whispered.

"Mmmm, fuck, baby." He kissed down my neck, swirling his tongue over my most sensitive spots. "You feel so good."

"I could get you some satin PJs to sleep in."

Beau chuckled against my collar bone. "I would rather you wear them and let me rub up against you." He sucked and kissed down my chest and looked up at me before closing his mouth around my nipple, sucking me through the satin.

Oh, my God. Yes!

I heard a light tapping against my bedroom door, the one that led into the house. "Charli, are you still awake?" I heard Blaire call.

Beau and I looked at each other with wide eyes for a split second before I dropped my feet to the floor and mouthed, "Oh, fuck!" I shoved Beau toward the bathroom, and he banged his knee against the edge of the footboard, a look of pain shooting across his face. "I'm sorry!" I mouthed. "But hide!"

"Are you okay, Charli?" came my boss's concerned voice from the other side of the door.

"Yes, I'm fine. Hold on just a second," I called out just as I got Beau into the bathroom without causing anymore bodily damage to him. I was about to close the door when he grabbed my wrist and nodded at my chest. I looked down, and *fuuuuck!* My nipples looked like bullets pointing through the fabric, and one of them had a huge wet spot over it from his mouth. It looked like I was lactating from one boob.

I crawled quickly onto my bed and sat up against the headboard with the covers pulled up to my chest, effectively concealing my aroused nips and wet spot. "Come in," I called out just before I noticed Beau's shirt lying on my floor. *Shit!* I reached down and swept it up, cramming it under my pillow a second before Blaire walked in my room.

I snatched my phone off the bed and pretended to look down at it. "Hey, Blaire. What's up?"

"Is everything okay? I thought I heard voices."

I laughed like that was the silliest thing in the world as she sat on the edge of my bed. "I was just watching TikTok videos. Have you seen the ones with the cats that are afraid of cucumbers? Those really crack me up." Jeez, I sounded like an idiot, and why the hell did my voice sound so high. At least that was better than my boss knowing that her brother was hiding in my bathroom and that he'd had his mouth on my booby not even twenty seconds ago.

"No, I guess I haven't seen those. I just wanted to remind you that this Friday is when I'm using my birthday present from Beau and Cam." I tried not to let my eyes dart toward the bathroom when she mentioned her brother's name.

"Oh, yes, I remembered," I said.

"Well, it's going to be easier than you expected. Carrie is staying the weekend with Evan."

Blaire swept one hand in a semi-circle like she was Vanna White and announced, "Aaand your mom is taking the boys to stay with Axel's brother in Houston. He has a son the same age. "

"So, I'll just have Danica?"

"Yep. And Axel has talked me into staying an extra night at the hotel, but I didn't want to be away from Dani two nights in a row. Ax is going to come pick her up Saturday afternoon while I go to the spa, and she'll stay Saturday night with us in the hotel."

"I don't mind keeping her both nights, Blaire."

"I know you don't, but it's hard being away from her when she's so little. And that will give you Saturday night all to yourself in case *someone* asks you on a date," Blaire said, pumping her eyebrows at me. *Shit.* I knew he was hearing all this.

"Don't get too excited. We've only been out once."

"He's being nice to you, right? Because if he's not, I'll kick his butt." I thought I heard a noise from the bathroom, and I blinked rapidly to keep my eyes from jumping in that direction.

"He's been a perfect gentleman," I said, faking a smile. *Except when he dry humped me to the most fabulous orgasm I'd ever had. Oh, and then when I jacked him off. But other than that...*

"Good. I'll let you get back to your videos. Oh, and let me know if you don't want to stay here at the house by yourself this weekend. If you don't feel comfortable with Beau staying here since y'all are just starting to date, I can get one of the other guys to stay here with you. Maybe Hawk or Cam?"

Okay, I definitely heard a noise from the bathroom that time. It sounded like someone tried to strangle a cat, but Blaire didn't seem to have heard it. "Thanks, but I'll be fine," I managed to say as she stood. We said goodnight, and she left. I waited until I heard her going upstairs before I ran to the bathroom and opened the door to a very angry looking Beau.

"I'm not letting another man stay here with you this weekend," he huffed as he stomped into the bedroom with his hands clenched tightly at his side. "I don't care if Hawk and Cam are my friends. It's not going to fucking happen."

"I know," I said calmly, rubbing my fingertips across his stubbly chin.

He wrapped his arms around me, seemingly soothed by my touch. "But I don't want you and the baby to have to stay here by yourself either."

I gave him a shy smile. "Then maybe you should stay here with me." I nipped his jaw with my teeth. "All weekend."

"Okay," he said, and I could hear in his voice that he was pleased as I ran my tongue across his chest. He inhaled a quick breath when I circled my tongue around one of his nipples. The adrenaline of almost getting caught had my thoughts directed southward, toward the magnificent erection I could feel behind Beau's zipper.

I sucked the opposite nipple into my mouth and let my teeth graze the very tip. I inherently knew that he liked his sex with more than a little bit of edge and a whole lot of control, and that was confirmed by his deep growl.

"Peach, what are you doing?" he asked when I dropped to my knees in front of him, running my hand and mouth across his hard, cut abs.

Dear, God. This is the finest specimen of man I've ever seen in my life.

"Didn't you say we're supposed to be getting to know each other better?" I asked, looking up at him with a coy smile.

He returned my smile and said, "I feel like I'm about to lose my 'perfect gentleman' status."

"I'm not complaining," I said, unbuttoning his jeans and running my tongue down his sexy little happy trail. I looked back up at him from under my lashes and said, "I want you to take control, Beau. I want to be exactly what you want."

He stopped breathing for a few seconds, and I wondered if I had said the wrong thing. "You're perfect just the way you are, Peach," he said, his voice raspy as he cupped my chin with one big hand. "You're already exactly what I want."

"Please," I said meekly, and he groaned out a sound from deep inside his chest.

He ran a hand over the top of his head. "My fucking conscience is telling me to stop this right now."

I rubbed my hand boldly across his crotch, gripping his hard length through his jeans. "And what is *he* telling you to do?"

One side of his lips pulled up a fraction. "He's saying he wants you to take your top off, but he's a dirty bastard." I reached for the hem of my top and pulled it slowly over my head, holding it out for him with one hand once I was bare from the waist up. He took it, but his eyes were locked on my bare chest. "Dear God, Peach. You're even more stunning than I imagined," he said, his voice barely above a whisper.

He held my silky top in his tight fists, as if he were trying to stop himself from touching me. After a moment, he closed his eyes and brought the garment to his nose, inhaling deeply before tilting his head back and rubbing my satin top all over his chest and stomach. His movements were sensual and erotic, and I felt a gush of wetness between my legs. This was the hottest fucking thing I had ever seen.

When Beau opened his eyes again, he almost looked like a different person. Harder. Taller, somehow. He removed his pants and underwear without a word, his actions swift but controlled. His face was tempered a bit when he leaned down so that we were at eye level and cupped my face in his hands.

"I care about you, Peach. A lot. You're soft and sweet, and I'm... not." His forehead wrinkled with his thoughts.

"It's okay. I like you hard." When his lips turned up into a wicked smirk, I blushed furiously. "You know what I mean," I mumbled.

"I do," he said simply. "If you don't like anything I do, tell me and I'll stop immediately. Do you understand?" I nodded, and he said, "Say it out loud, Peach. Tell me you understand."

I clenched my thighs at his commanding tone. "I understand, Beau."

"Good girl." He lowered his head and sucked my lips, his mouth resolute and slow as his tongue swirled briefly, brushing the insides of my lips. He released my mouth with a soft pop and stood, towering above me with his extremely angry-looking cock right in front of my face. His face was a mask of steel as he looked down at me and commanded, "Hands behind your back. Cross your wrists behind your butt."

I did as he asked, and a tiny smile cracked the hard veneer of his gaze. "Good, baby. You look so fucking beautiful like that, on your knees in front of me. You look like every wet dream I've ever had." He reached out and softly stroked my hair, and more wetness dripped from my pussy and slid down the insides of my thighs. Beau Atwood was fucking sexy as hell all the time, but when he was in full control, spitting out commands but still touching me so gently… *Lord have mercy!* This man had me in the palm of his hand.

He gripped the base of his dick and pointed it directly at my mouth. Unable to stop myself, I leaned forward and swiped my tongue through the thick pearl of precum beading on his tip, savoring the salty taste of him. "Fuck," he hissed, and his harsh curse urged me on. I sucked his swollen crown between my lips and swirled my tongue around and around his head, prompting more curses to fall from his lips.

"Always look at me while you're sucking me off, Peach," he grunted, and I lifted my eyes to his. "Do you have any idea how sexy you look with my dick in your mouth?" He pushed in another inch and groaned. His grip tightened in my hair even as he cupped my chin and gently rubbed my cheek with his thumb. "More," he demanded just before pushing his hips forward and forcing me to swallow almost his entire length.

I gagged at first, and he pulled back, peering into my eyes. "You can do it, baby." I nodded and pushed forward slowly, remembering to open my throat and breathe through my nose.

I had only given a handful of blow jobs in real life, but Bristol and I had practiced on giant pickles when we were in high school after watching her brother's porn DVDs.

My skills were definitely being put to the test with Beau Atwood tonight. His girth was about the same as the thick pickles, but he had several more inches in length. I paused when I was almost all the way down on him and then sucked hard, pulling him the rest of the way into my mouth. I felt a stream of pre-cum slide down my throat as he groaned.

"My God, Peach. Your mouth is so fucking hot." His breathing was labored, but his movements were measured and precise as he slid out to the tip and then pressed back into the back of my throat. I wanted to make him lose control. I wanted to make him want me more than he had ever wanted anyone.

The next time he pulled out, I worked him with my mouth, rapidly flicking the heavy ridge on the bottom of his cock with the tip of my tongue. He was already stretching my mouth wide, but when he fed me his length again, I tightened my lips as much as possible. "Fuck, fuck, fuck," he said through gritted teeth.

He wrapped my pajama top around the back of my head like a strap, using it to pull my head forward as he thrusted into my mouth over and over. His gaze was hyper-focused on my mouth as his lips parted and his abrasive breathing fell into the same rhythm as his hips.

I pulled back about halfway up his shaft and applied the deepest suction I could manage, and he dropped the silky top onto the floor behind me. Both of his hands went to the back of my head, his fingers tightening in my hair as I felt his control starting to slip.

"Goddammit, that's good. I need to fuck your sweet mouth hard, baby." I nodded, and his body curled forward as he rode my mouth hard and fast, his dick dripping pre-ejaculate all over my tongue as he slid against it.

He twisted my hair in a near-painful grasp as he fucked my mouth roughly. I had never been more turned on, and I squeezed my thighs together as he growled and grunted with every deep thrust. His eyes were glazed over as he watched himself disappear into my mouth, but they cleared for a moment when he dragged his gaze up to my eyes.

"I'm going to give you a mouthful of my cum, Peach," he warned, and I hummed my *yes* around the giant dick in my mouth. His eyes rolled back, and he released a long, "Ohhhhhh," as he swelled, and then the first squirt hit my tongue. "Yes, baby. God. Fuck, yeah." His thick cum was streaming heavily into my mouth and down my throat as I struggled to swallow it all. But it was worth it to see him lose himself like that. The harder he pulled my hair and the more his legs trembled, the more powerful I felt.

Mirroring my thoughts, he slowed his motions as I sucked the remainder of his cum from his head. "You own me now, Peach," he admitted in his deep voice. "That was fucking amazing."

I own him? My heart fluttered like a tiny hummingbird in my chest as I sucked him deep once more for good measure.

"Ah, cut that out unless you want to go for round two," he groaned as his semi-hard cock twitched in my mouth.

Round two? But he just... Surely, he couldn't go again.

I let him slide from my mouth and blinked up at him. "Maybe I should invest in some knee pads, because I plan to do that a lot more." He slid his hands under my armpits and lifted me off the ground, up and up until I was eye level with him. *Fuck, he's strong.*

"Legs," he ordered, and I immediately curled my legs around his waist. He wrapped his arms around me and held me tightly to his body as a slow smile etched itself across his face. "You want to do it again? I was afraid I was too rough with you." A little frown creased his features, and I kissed the furrow between his eyes. "I'm sorry. I didn't want to lose control like that. Not with you."

"Don't apologize. I liked it," I admitted, and his soft smile returned.

"You're my perfect little Peach," he uttered before his lips covered mine and his tongue eased into my mouth, licking sensually. I was struck stupid for a moment before I started kissing him back. The one time Hayden had come in my mouth, he refused to kiss me for the rest of the night.

Beau turned and crawled onto my bed, kneeling and leaning me back until my head touched the pillow. He kissed me deeply as he rested on one forearm while the other hand stroked up and down the back of my thigh. When his mouth moved to my neck, sucking and licking my heated flesh, his hand slid back up my leg and into my shorts. He slipped a finger underneath my lacy underwear and moved it back and forth over the curve of my ass.

Something deep inside me clenched deliciously, and I wondered how in the hell this man could be undoing me with the stroke of a single finger. "Your skin is so soft, baby. I want to touch and taste every inch of it," he murmured as his head lowered. He placed a tender kiss on each of my nipples, urging my back to arch off the bed. I wanted his mouth on me. Everywhere.

I didn't have much experience with receiving oral sex, but what I did have wasn't stellar. It had been... disorganized, for lack of a better word. Just a bunch of fumbling around, a few licks here and there but never hitting exactly where I needed it. I had never orgasmed from oral, but now I was on the edge of a climax just from thinking about Beau's mouth on me. He was assertive and confident, and I knew deep down that he knew how to pleasure a woman.

I had the feeling that things would be different with Beau Atwood. *Very* different.

21

BEAU

Charli's scent surrounded me as I traced my tongue around each of her dark pink nipples. Her hips were pumping against me, and I could smell the luscious aroma of her arousal. I would get to that. Soon. But first, I needed to explore her beautiful tits. I licked along the supple skin underneath one of them, my eyes closed as I enjoyed the feel and taste of her silky skin against my rough tongue.

"Beau, please..." Her sweet little voice broke me out of my trance, and I glanced up at her as I rubbed my tongue across one taut nipple. "Yesssss," she hissed on a long exhale, her chin tipping up toward the ceiling. The woman had just given me the best head of my life. The blow job of the fucking century. Hell, I was surprised I had held on as long as I had because I had almost come in my pants the moment she dropped to her knees.

My Peach kneeling in front of me had been a fantasy that had invaded my brain like a cancer since the first time I laid eyes on her beside the pool. And the reality was even better than any fantasy I could have dreamed up. Her mouth was soft and wet. Eager. Demanding. I planned to return the favor and make her come all over my face. Multiple times.

She moaned loudly when I closed my lips around her nipple and sucked. Sliding one hand up to her face, I pressed my thumb over her lips to remind her to be quiet. It seemed like I always wanted to be touching Peach's face—something that I had never felt with another woman.

Tits? *Yes.* Ass? *Affirmative.* Pussy? *Fuck yeah.* But I had never in my life wanted to stroke a girl's cheek while I pleasured her.

She sucked my thumb into her mouth, and my dick roared back to life, hardening against the mattress. When she sucked my thumb harder, I increased the suction on her nipple, and her back arched off the bed with a low groan. I took my signals from her, and the harder she sucked my thumb, the harder I went on her peaked nipple. Her teeth scraped across the pad of my thumb, and I bit down on her nipple, earning me another of her sweet moans.

Fuck! My precious Peach liked it a little rough. I couldn't help but wonder if she liked *everything* rough, and that made my cock grow another hard inch. I moved to her other breast, knowing what she enjoyed now, and worshiped it with the same attention I had given the other one.

As much as I loved sucking her perfect tits, I needed my mouth on her cunt. Now. Her legs were still wrapped around my back, and I unwound them as I swirled my tongue slowly down her stomach until I was met with the silky fabric of her little shorts. I hooked my fingers into the waistband and started to ease them down.

"Beau…" the tremble in her voice made me look up at her apprehensive face.

I leaned forward, letting my chest press against her firm tits, and kissed her lips. "I need to taste you, Peach. All of you. Let me," I said gently, somewhere between a request and a demand, and she nodded.

"I'm just nervous," she whispered, and I kissed her again.

"It's okay, baby. I'll take care of you. I've got you."

But the truth was, she had *me*. Hook, line, and sinker, I was hers.

I suddenly realized why she might be apprehensive about me going down on her. It was a very intimate act, and she wasn't the kind of girl who would give that part of herself away to just anyone. Maybe she needed reassurance that this wasn't some stupid fling.

I cupped her face in both of my hands and said, "To me, this isn't just about sex or what feels good, Charli. I'm having serious feelings for you. Yes, I want to pleasure you beyond your wildest imagination, but I also… shit, I'm not very good at this." She gave me a gentle smile, which boosted my confidence a notch. "I just… I want to feel close to you." I had never said things like that to a woman because they had never been true. I may have been a dickhead, but at least I was always an honest dickhead.

Peach's face relaxed, and her nervousness seemed to melt away. "Oh, God, Beau. I'm having feelings for you, too. I don't do stuff like this very often because it means something to me."

God, she is so fucking sweet. "I *want* this to mean something to you, Peach. It does to me." A question perched on the tip of my tongue, but I wasn't sure if I wanted to know the answer. I asked anyway. "How many men have you been with?"

"Two," she said, and her cheeks flushed.

Shit! That wasn't very many, especially compared to me, but it was still two too many in my mind.

"I'm going to need their names because I'm going to kill them both," I said, and she giggled. I think she thought I was joking, but I seriously wanted to bury anyone who had ever touched her before. Irrational? Yes, because she was twenty-seven years old and a fucking knockout. Of course, she'd been with other men.

I kissed her before she could ask me the same question. I didn't know the exact number, but even a ballpark estimate would send her running for the hills. What I had intended to be a gentle kiss to soothe her soon turned into a sexy make out session. I was still naked, and the feel of her soft shorts against my dick had it as hard as a steel pipe against her lower stomach. She lifted her hips to press against me, and I groaned into her mouth.

Charli's hands skated up my back and gripped my shoulders as our kiss turned hotter. I lifted my head and traced an unhurried line from her forehead to her chin with my index finger. "This is perfect." I slid my body down and cupped her breasts, placing a kiss on each nipple. "These are perfect." She watched me as if mesmerized as I went even lower to her belly button. I circled my tongue around it and then sucked. "This is extremely perfect."

I looked up and saw her gazing at me with amusement. "My belly button is perfect?"

I stuck my tongue in the shallow divot. "It's the cutest belly button I've ever seen. I will have dreams about this belly button."

She giggled as I nibbled at her stomach. Sitting up on my knees and hooking my index fingers in her shorts and panties, I slid them slowly down her legs as I watched her expression. Her eyes were wide, but her tongue stole out of her mouth and moistened her bottom lip just before she sank her teeth into the soft flesh there.

When she was totally bared to me, I put my hands on the insides of her knees and spread her legs wide. Her hot arousal was dripping from her and coating the insides of her thighs like a glaze, and I almost blew my load as soon as I saw her. This was the first time I was seeing her totally naked, and I raked my eyes up and down her, trying to memorize every detail. I had never seen anything more beautiful in my life.

I positioned my head between her legs and let my tongue skate up her thigh, tasting her for the very first time. And *oh, fuck me*, she tasted like pure heaven. Hearing a small whimper from her lips, I eased my hand up her body and cupped her face while I licked every trace of her arousal from her thighs. I turned my head and buried my nose in her slit, inhaling the scent I would like to bottle and carry around with me every fucking day.

I couldn't hold back anymore. I needed my tongue in her sweet cunt, wanted to devour her like she was my last meal. Circling my tongue at her entrance, I licked all the way up to her clit. She sighed a long, "Yesssss, Beau," and all I wanted was to hear that beautiful sound again.

I continued my slow assault on her pussy, licking her up and down until her fists were clenching the sheets beside her. I wanted to make her have one of those long, drawn-out orgasms. The kind that started deep inside and built up until it took over her entire body. I wanted her to ache for me. I wanted her to need me like I needed her.

I patiently worked her sex with slow strokes of my tongue, feeling her desire awakening with every caress. When I knew she was close, I swirled my tongue in deliberate circles over her clit until I pushed her over the edge.

With my mouth still on her, I watched her face as she orgasmed. She cried my name out once, and I rubbed my thumb over her bottom lip to remind her we weren't alone in the house. Biting into the pad of my thumb, she moaned a little *oh* with every throb of her clit against my tongue.

Her climax seemed to go on forever, and it was the hottest fucking thing I had ever seen. The deep flush that crept up her chest and over her face. The tightness of her neck as her head arched back into the creamy pillowcase. Her blonde hair wild around her. Her entire body shaking furiously.

My cock was full and throbbing from watching and tasting her, and I pressed it into the mattress to get a little friction while I licked her down from her climax with the flat of my tongue. I lapped up every drop of her sweet cum that was flowing from her little pink pussy as I grinded my hips against her soft sheets.

"Oh. My. God," Charli panted. She grabbed my hair with both hands and pulled me up her body.

"Ow, baby. Don't be so rough with me. I'm delicate," I teased.

"Shit, Beau. That was so fucking awesome," she said raptly into my face. "Can you do it again? Please?" she asked, her eyes hungry and her voice threaded with desperation.

"Hell yes, I can." I grinned at her and gave her a peck on the mouth before sliding back down her body, eager for my new task. *Fuck slow and easy this time.* I was going to give her a fast, brutal orgasm that would make her never want another man.

I gave her several hard licks from her asshole to her clit, and her thighs tightened around my head. I slammed them open, holding them to the mattress firmly with my hands as I sunk my teeth into the soft flesh of her pussy lips over and again. "Oh, God," she groaned at my savagery, and her hands went to my head, not to push me away, but to hold me there.

I circled my tongue around her clit and then sucked on it mercilessly as she tried to squirm beneath me, but I held her down and made her take it. "Coming," she squeaked, and I felt a gush of wetness spill over my tongue.

"Fuck yes, baby," I growled into her, losing all control. "Come on my tongue, my tasty little Peach." I rammed my tongue inside her tight channel and fucked her as deeply as I could while she contracted around me. I was still holding her thighs to the mattress, but her back arched and slammed back down to the bed several times as she came hard and fast.

I heard muffled noises and looked up to find that she had grabbed a pillow with one hand and smashed it against her face as she screamed her release. I watched as she finally pulled the pillow away, her face pink and her hair all over the damned place. *Shit, she is fucking stunning.* I couldn't wait to see what she looked like when I made her come with my cock buried inside her.

"Beau," she panted, "you have an incredibly talented—and long—tongue." I curled my tongue inside her, licking her front wall in a lewd demonstration as she moaned out her pleasure. "Come kiss me so I can taste myself on your mouth," she said, tugging gently on my hair.

Holy fuck! My girl is dirty.

I crawled up her body, pressing my raging boner against her stomach. I was well aware that I could lift and tilt my hips, and my dick would be right at her soft opening. *But no.* We hadn't even talked about birth control or any of that, and I hadn't even had my fingers inside her to get her ready. If this were any other woman, I would already have a condom on and have my dick shoved in her by now.

But this was *my Peach*, and I wasn't going to take her like that the first time we were together. I hoped to God she was on the pill or something because I wanted to fuck her raw without any barriers between us. I'd never wanted to go without a condom before. In fact, the very idea had always repulsed me. But the thought of being inside Charli and feeling every single inch of her... well, that had my dick leaking like a motherfucker.

I rubbed it against her as I lowered my face so that she could taste herself. Her little tongue licked her wetness from my chin like a kitten lapping up cream. "You sure are a kinky little thing, Peach," I said, as her tongue slurped up more of her arousal from my cheek. *Yes, I had gotten a little messy down there.*

She giggled as she moved to my other cheek. "I've never really been kinky before."

"Well, you're with the right man because I'm kinky as fuck."

Charli edged her hand between our bodies and scooped up some of my sticky pre-cum from her stomach. She stared at my mouth while she rubbed my own fluids over my lips. I tried not to recoil because, fuck... that was just... But then she pursed her lips and rubbed them against mine.

"Now we can see what we taste like together," she said softly.

Holy Jesus. My little Peach had just fucking out-kinked me in the sweetest way possible. I mean, I had tasted a slight saltiness on her tongue after I came in her mouth and then kissed her earlier, and that didn't bother me. But this was different. She had just blatantly rubbed my own dick juice on my mouth.

She ran her tongue around and around my lips before it retreated back into her own mouth. "Mmmm, it tastes like *us*."

Not to be outdone, I licked the evidence of our combined desires from her lips and was surprisingly not repulsed in the least at tasting myself. Because it was from Charli's sweet lips, and her essence mixed with mine. "We taste good together, baby," I said honestly, wanting even more.

I rose up above her, leaning on one hand while I took my cock in my hand. "Close your mouth, baby." She did, and I rubbed my wet tip all over her lips. "Don't lick it off," I warned. Then I lowered myself between her legs, spreading her folds with my fingers and coating my lips with her sweet nectar.

I lay back on top of her and rubbed our lips together, combining our juices again. We licked and sucked at each other, and then we were kissing hard and deep and wild, my body pressing her back into the mattress. That had by far been the hottest thing I had ever done, and we weren't even fucking. *Yet.* I wanted her more than I had ever wanted anyone in my life, but I needed to make sure she was ready.

I reached between her legs and pressed the tip of my middle finger into her opening. "Mmm, what a soft little cunt you have, Peach." I pushed my finger up to the second knuckle, and it felt like my finger was caught in a vice. "Jesus, baby. You're fucking tight." I slid my body to the side of her so I could have more room to work.

"It's been a while," she said. "And I've never been with anyone..." her eyes drifted down my body and back up to my face before she finished with, "...*big* before." She bit her bottom lip anxiously.

Oh, fuck me running. Had she been thinking about taking me inside this tight little hole? My dick was hard against the outside of her thigh, throbbing her name. *Char-li. Char-li.*

I pushed my finger all the way in and felt her grow even wetter. She gasped when I curled my finger forward, searching for that tender spot inside her and finding it with ease. I slid my other arm under her head and pressed my lips to hers. "Feel good, baby?" I pumped my finger in and out, stroking her G-spot over and over.

"God, yes. Beau." She thrust her tongue into my mouth as her hips lifted against my hand. I took over the kiss, dominating her mouth as my finger worked her pussy.

I felt her get impossibly tighter as she moaned into my mouth, and I knew she was close. Dropping my mouth to her ear, I bit her earlobe and growled, "Come for me, Peach." Her hips jerked as her lips parted in a loud moan. I quickly covered her mouth and swallowed her bliss as her body writhed against the sheets.

"You're so loud," I said with an affectionate chuckle when I pulled back and kissed her nose. "But I love making you lose control."

Her chest was heaving, her perfect tits rising and falling as she gulped in lungfuls of air. "It surprised me. How did you do that without touching my, you know, my clit?" *Was she serious? She had never had a penetrative orgasm?* It didn't even matter if she had only been with small-dicked assholes. I had just made her come with a single finger. And neither of the pricks she had been with had taken the time to learn to please her like she deserved?

"I rubbed your G-spot, sweetheart. Do you know, uh…"

She smiled up at me. "I know what it is. From magazines and stuff. I just thought maybe I didn't have one or maybe it was a myth like the Loch Ness Monster. I was obviously mistaken."

"Obviously," I said, probably more pleased with myself than I should have been as I pulled my finger out and sucked her sweetness from it. "The Loch Ness Monster?" I asked amusedly.

"Or maybe Bigfoot," she said with a giggle.

"Chupacabra?" I suggested, lightly running my fingertips up and down her side. I liked this… this bedroom banter. I had never had that before. My sexual experiences consisted of fuck, come, leave. It had always been enough. But not anymore. Not with Peach.

"I thought I was weird or something," she said bashfully, not quite meeting my eyes.

I tapped my knuckle underneath her chin until she looked at me. "You're not weird, baby. It's the man's job to find out everything that makes his woman tick. Like a pirate with a treasure map."

She laughed as I kissed down her neck and across her chest. "You're an excellent pirate, Beau."

"I found *your* treasure," I said brazenly, sucking a perky nipple into my mouth and growling, "Arrrrgghhh." *Who the fuck am I right now?* I didn't know, but this was fun. And I was still hard as a rock against her leg. I slid my hand down her stomach until I was cupping her sex. "Again?"

She nodded eagerly and said, "Yes, please."

"Good. I'm going to put my mouth on your clit when you come this time, so it will make it even more intense." I nodded to the pillow beside her and said with a smirk, "Use that if you need to get loud."

I knelt between her legs and ran two fingers through her wetness before trying to push both of them inside her cunt. *Holy fucking Christ, she's tiny down here.* She winced, and I immediately pulled my fingers out and lowered my mouth to her sex, coating her with my saliva.

This time I circled my slippery thumb on her clit as I eased my fingers slowly into her sweet little channel. "Better?"

"God, yes," she said and then yelped when I found and stroked her G-spot. Her legs spread wider for me as I started to fuck her with my fingers. Even with my saliva lubing her up, it was so fucking tight that I was afraid she would snap my fingers in half when she came.

Totally worth it.

When she was finally stretched out a little, I started pumping her harder, the muscles in my arms flexing as I worked her over, my fingertips massaging that most sensitive spot on the front wall of her vagina. "Beau. Oh my God. I want you so bad."

Ah, hell!

I leaned up over her on one arm and bent to kiss her lips. "I want you too, Charli. But we can't yet."

Yes, we can, my dick practically yelled at me.

"Please, Beau. Please fuck me."

Jesus, baby. Never in my life had five words caused me so much conflict.

"God, I want you more than anything. Touch my dick, Peach. Feel what you do to me." Her hand wrapped around my length, and we both moaned. "I've never been this hard and swollen, baby. If I didn't know I would hurt you, I would already be inside you so deeply you wouldn't know where I started and where you ended."

Oh, yes. That. Do that, my dick insisted.

"Soon?"

"Very soon," I promised, still stroking her hard with my two fingers. I needed to do some preparations to make it good for her. "If I fuck you now, I'll break your vagina."

"Oh, fuck yes. Break me, Beau," she wailed. God help me, I wanted to. I wanted to fuck her so hard she ripped in half. Her pussy walls tightened around my invading fingers, and I knew I needed to make her come ASAP before I did something incredibly stupid.

After another swift kiss on her lips, I pushed back and knelt between her legs again. I lay a tender kiss against her mound, stealing a soft whiff of her incredible scent before closing my mouth around her clit. I noticed her fingers flexing and releasing in the sheets, and I reached over with my free hand and linked our fingers together, rubbing my thumb soothingly against her index finger.

I let my tongue slide over her little nub as my lips sucked greedily on it, and she exploded with a vicious orgasm, arching her back and crying out into the pillow. I fucking hated that she had to practically suffocate herself when she came that hard, but even though we were downstairs and tucked away down a hallway, I was afraid someone would come downstairs and hear her cries of pure ecstasy. Blaire or Axel. Or, God forbid, Charli's mom. That would be humiliating as fuck.

But for now, I had a more pressing problem. My goddamn dick was painfully hard, and I was about to come all over Charli's sheets, but I used every bit of control I had in my body to hold off until I finished taking care of my Peach. I slowed my hand between her legs and licked her softly as she came down from her intense orgasm.

Charli finally pulled the pillow off her face, and I rose up on my knees to look at her, her hair all disheveled, cheeks hot pink, and her lips swollen from my rough kisses. She looked sated, and when she smiled the most satisfied grin I had ever seen, everything below my waist tightened at the knowledge that I had put that look on her face.

I straddled her thighs and grabbed my thick cock, groaning, "Fuck. I'm about to come all over you, baby." The thought of marking her with my seed had my penis twitching like it was having a seizure.

Her sweet voice said, "I want to do it." To my surprise, she reached between her legs and gathered some of her slick wetness on her fingers. She smeared it on my cock and proceeded to use it as lubricant to jack me off with long, hard strokes.

Dear Mary, Mother of God. Having her sweet pussy juices on my dick was just too fucking much, and went I cross-eyed, my vision doubling as I exploded like my dick was a cannon. The first shot hit her flat stomach, and the second landed on her perfect left tit.

She sat up then and took my engorged head in her mouth, literally sucking the rest of the cum out of me. "Fuck, Charli! Oh God, suck it all, baby." I pulled her hand away from me before grabbing the back of her head and fucking her mouth deeply as I was hit with another orgasm before the first one had even ended. I just kept coming, and she just kept sucking until I had nothing left in the tank.

Holy hell. This is the woman of my dreams.

22

BEAU

I COLLAPSED ONTO MY back beside Charli and tried to get some air into my lungs. "Damn, woman. That was fucking phenomenal." I put my hand on my chest and said, "Let me relearn this whole breathing concept, and then I'll clean you up."

I drew in several deep breaths before turning my face toward her to find her looking back at me. "Hi," she said shyly.

"Hey, Peach." I rolled onto my side and picked up her hand, laying a kiss on her knuckles. "You're a dirty, dirty girl, you know that?"

She giggled. "I thought I was kinky."

I kissed her fingers again. "You're everything." My smile faded and my face turned serious. Charli was *everything*. This gorgeous, wonderful woman had taken up residence in my heart in the short time I'd known her. A few weeks ago, that thought would have scared me shitless, but now... the only thing that scared me was the thought of losing her. "You're everything," I repeated, my voice thick with emotion and truth.

"What are you thinking about?" she asked, her voice raspy.

I leaned over and kissed her softly. "About how lucky I am. I'll be right back, beautiful." I crawled off the bed, my legs still a little shaky, and went into her bathroom. I got a warm cloth and came back into her room to reluctantly wipe my cum from her body.

"Thanks, baby," she said in a hoarse voice when I was done. It was no wonder her voice was weak. I had fucked her throat, come in her mouth twice and given her... what? Three screaming orgasms? No. Four. *But who's counting right?* I climbed off the bed and slipped on my underwear. "You're leaving?" she asked worriedly, a frown crossing her pretty features.

"I'm not leaving unless you want me to, Peach. I'm just going to get you some water." I kissed her forehead before wandering out to the kitchen and pulling down a glass. I added a little ice and then filled it with water from the dispenser on the high-end refrigerator.

"What the fuck?" came a deep voice from behind me, and I whirled around, bobbling the glass but catching it before it hit the ground.

I looked up to see my brother-in-law standing in the kitchen in his underwear glaring at me. "Shit, Axel. I'm sorry, man. I was just getting, um, some water." I grabbed a dish towel and started wiping up the floor.

"You scared the shit out of me, Beau. You don't have water at your house?" he hissed.

"Oh, yeah. About that. Uhhhh..." I had nothing. No explanation as to why I was half-naked in his kitchen in the middle of the night.

He seemed to finally notice that I was only wearing underwear. *Oh, this looks bad.*

"Were you sleeping on our couch? Blaire didn't tell me—" Realization dawned in his eyes, and he grinned roguishly. "Ohhhh, I see what's going on here. You and Charli." He waggled his finger at me.

I swiped a hand over my face. "Fuck!"

My brother-in-law laughed. "Beau, you're a grown fucking man, and as long as you're good to Charli, I don't care what you do." He shrugged and said, "Besides, I have no room to talk. I just banged the shit out of your sister."

Gag.

The asshole smirked at me before heading to the laundry room and returning with a pair of pajama pants. "Here," he said, tossing them to me. "For when you feel the need to walk around my house in the middle of the night."

"Thanks," I mumbled as I pulled them on. Remembering the measly lock on Charli's door, I asked, "Ax, can I talk to you about something right quick?"

"Sure," he said, adding ice and water to a glass.

"I noticed that Charli doesn't have a deadbolt on her outer door, and I wondered if I could install one for her."

"Course you can. I didn't realize. Just let me know how much it costs."

"I'm not worried about that. I just wanted to run it by you since it's your house."

"Alright, thanks, Beau. I'm going to go back upstairs and see if your sister will let me tap that ass now."

Knowing he was just trying to get a reaction out of me, I replied, "Good. At least you can't get her pregnant again like that."

He toasted me with a slight tilt of the glass in his hand. "Good one, bro. But if Blaire's walking funny tomorrow, mind ya business." I could hear his laughter all the way up the stairs.

Asshole.

Charli was just coming out of the bathroom when I got back. I noticed she had put her panties back on, so I handed her the glass and pulled off the pajama pants I was wearing. She had put her hair in a ponytail in the bathroom, and I glided my hand down it, curling the end around my finger as she downed the water.

"Will you stay with me tonight?" she asked, setting down the glass and crawling into bed.

"Of course, I will." I climbed in behind her and pulled her back to my chest.

"I know you don't like to cuddle, but would you hold me until I go to sleep?"

I nuzzled my face against the back of her neck. "I'll hold you all night, Peachy." And with a contented sigh, she fell asleep in my arms.

I woke up early Wednesday feeling refreshed, like I had gotten the best night's sleep of my life. And maybe I had. I didn't wake up at all, a rarity for me. In fact, I hadn't woken up the night before either. *Hmmm, what's the common denominator here?* I smiled to myself and tightened my arm around Charli's waist, pulling her tightly to me. Even the half-inch of space between us seemed like too much.

I knew I needed to get up, but fuck. I wanted to stay here for a while. I never lingered in bed, something ingrained in my psyche from my military days. *Get your ass up and get your ass moving, Atwood.* But my Peach was so soft and warm against me, a sweet temptation I couldn't seem to resist.

I kissed the back of her neck, letting my tongue dart out for a brief taste of the skin there. A little salty, no doubt from our extended activities last night. And a lot sweet, because that was just Charli. She pulled away from me, and I frowned until I realized she was just rolling over to face me. She nestled herself against my chest, making a soft noise that was innately feminine and clutching onto me with one arm around my waist.

I felt her nose circling into the hair on my chest, and she let out a little, "Mmmm," before kissing me there and dozing back off. While my brain was telling me to get out of bed, I allowed my body the time to just hold her and enjoy the feel of her tiny body clinging to mine. I looped my leg over hers to get just a little bit closer to her and rubbed my hand softly up and down her bare back.

Fifteen minutes later Peach stirred and lifted her face to mine for a kiss, which I gladly obliged. "Sorry, I fell back asleep," she murmured against my lips.

"'S'okay, baby, but I really should get going before everyone wakes up," I said, reluctantly disentangling myself from her and climbing from her nice warm bed. As I got dressed, Peach got up and went into her bathroom, returning a few minutes later wearing a long, ratty terry cloth robe.

"Well, this is sexy," I teased, grabbing her by the lapels of the faded green monstrosity and kissing her.

She looked down at herself. "I know. It's hideous. I keep saying I'm going to buy a new one, but I guess I'm not good about buying stuff for myself. I wasn't allowed..." Her voice trailed off into nothing, and her lips pressed together in a tight line.

"What do you mean you weren't *allowed*?" I asked, something dark and disturbing rising up in my belly. Her eyes were focused on my chest, her mouth unmoving. I ducked my head to meet her eyes. "Is this about your ex?" When she nodded, it took every ounce of self-control I had not to fucking erupt.

"He wasn't always like that. It was after he got a promotion at work that he started drinking. He monitored every nickel I spent, and he would get angry whenever I bought something for myself, even if it was a cheap pair of earrings from the dollar store."

One word flashed brightly in my mind. "He got *angry*?" She nodded. "Did he... did he hurt you? Did he put his fucking hands on you, Charli?" I could hear the furious timbre of my voice cut through the space between us and hoped I wasn't scaring her.

She bit her bottom lip so hard I thought she was going to break the skin. I tugged gently at her chin, and she released it. "Just once, and then I left. I thought he loved me," she finished lamely.

I cupped her precious face in my hands, forcing her to look at me. "No man should control you, Peach. And no man should *ever* put his hands on you. That's not love, baby."

THIS is love. What I have for you is love.

I did the only thing I could do to keep from blurting those words out like a maniac. I kissed the fuck out of her. I kissed her with a passion I didn't even know I possessed, my tongue seeking and finding hers and making it mine. I didn't tell her I loved her with my words, but I told her with every slow stroke of my tongue against hers. I told her with the way I held her gorgeous face tenderly in my big, rough hands.

When I finally broke the kiss, I pressed my forehead against hers for a long moment, my eyes closed and my mind reeling. I loved Charli. I *loved* her. I had always thought love, if I ever found it, would feel heavy and oppressive, but it was just the opposite. I felt lighter than I had in years.

"I have a job for you," I said, kissing each corner of her mouth.

"A job?"

"Yep. I want you to go buy something today. Something for yourself, not for anyone else."

She frowned. "Like what?"

"Like anything you want, as long as it's totally frivolous and something you absolutely do not need."

"Beau, I don't know…"

"Okay then, let's make it a challenge. I'll buy myself something, too, and then tonight we can show each other what we bought. See who got the silliest item."

A grin broke across her face and my heart tumbled around in my chest at the sight. "You're on. Bring it, Atwood."

I loved that smile. I would do fucking anything for that smile.

Including going shopping. Ugh.

Things at work were going really well. We got a new high-profile security account with a major tech company located in Austin. Now Cam and I were sitting on the couch eating tacos, which made the day even better. And to top it all off, Peach texted to let me know I had "forgotten my jacket" and told me I should probably come over tonight to retrieve it. I smiled. This jacket routine was becoming our own little private inside joke. Hopefully, she would be wearing the lingerie I sent her today.

A couple of hours later, I was knocking on Charli's door. I heard the slide of the new deadbolt I had installed, and the door opened to reveal a vision in peach. I had known that robe would look gorgeous on her with her tanned skin and blonde hair, and I was so fucking glad to be right.

Her face was devoid of all makeup except for a soft peach lipstick, which made my dick as hard as stone. I closed and locked the door behind me and then arched an impatient eyebrow at her before she jumped and wrapped her legs around me.

Good girl.

I rewarded her with a long, hot kiss, our tongues curling around each other as her hands slipped up the back of my shirt. Her touch was feather-light as her fingers skimmed across my skin, and I marveled at how good it felt to have her hands on me like that.

"How was your day, Peach?" I asked when we finally stopped kissing.

"It was good. The boys were… energetic today."

"Is that code for 'they acted like little turds?'"

She laughed. "Maybe a little bit."

Pulling her hands above her head and holding them there easily with one of mine, I slid my free hand up her thigh and under her robe. "What are you wearing under this pretty new robe, sweetheart?"

She widened her eyes and looked at me sympathetically. "Oh, gosh. Don't be upset, but I seem to have a secret admirer. He sent me lingerie and said he was going to come to my room tonight to see it. He should be here any minute now."

I smiled against her skin. "When he gets here, I'm going to thank him for having such excellent taste, and then I'm going to kill him."

She laughed, and it was the most beautiful sound in the world. "The list of people you're going to murder seems to be growing by the day."

I lifted my head and smiled darkly at her. "Baby, you have no idea. Now, did you do what I asked you to do today?"

She struggled against me, and I let go of her and let her stand up. She slid the robe off and revealed a white babydoll tee with a butterfly in brightly colored sequins on the front. "Nice," I said. "Very frivolous."

"And it does this," she said, shifting her hand up the shirt to reveal the reverse side of the sequins, which were in a pastel rainbow pattern.

"Hey, that's cool," I said, moving my hand up and down her chest to switch the sequins.

She giggled. "You just like it because it gives you an excuse to touch my boobs. Now, what did you buy?"

I started stripping off my clothes. "First of all, I don't need an excuse to touch your boobs. They're mine now, and I'll touch them when I damn well please." I loved the way her eyes roamed over my body and her mouth went slack when I took off my shirt. I pulled off my pants and stood with my hands on my hips, proudly showing off my dark green satin boxers with a duck on the front of them. When I turned around, the back of them had "Butt Quack" written across my ass.

I mock-glared at her when she giggled, and she pinched her lips together and looked up at me. "I like them."

"The fucking satin has been rubbing against my dick since I put them on, and I haven't been able to stop thinking about you in your pajamas. There is some serious eagerness going on down there," I said, indicating the large tent in my shorts.

"Well, the boxers are certainly frivolous, and I like how you really put yourself out there." I lifted my eyebrows at her double entendre, and she bit her lip to hide her smile. "So, I declare you the winner."

"And what's my prize, Peach?" I growled at her. She pulled off her t-shirt, and my jaw hit the floor when I saw her in the peach bra and panty set. "Fuck, baby. You look absolutely stunning."

She sank to her knees in front of me and crossed her hands behind her butt, looking up at me with those big blue eyes and a not-so-innocent smile.

I ran my fingers gently through her long, blonde hair before gripping it tightly in my hand. My voice was raspy and dropped an entire octave as I lowered my shorts. "I think I like this game, Peach."

CHARLI

I HANDED BRISTOL A bottle of water and sat at the kitchen bar with her. "So, you never told me how it went with Tank that night at the club. Y'all just disappeared on us."

She gave me a sly smile before finally speaking. "We went back to my place."

"And?"

"And we fucked. But it was just a one-night thing. He's texted me a few times, but I haven't responded."

"Not good?" I asked. Bris stared at the ceiling for a long time before I finally prompted, "What aren't you telling me?"

She finally brought her eyes back to mine. "It was good. He's fucking enormous. Ev-er-y-where. He couldn't even get it all the way in at first. He was really sweet about it and took it slow until I told him I wanted it all. I think it was like a challenge for me or something, to see if I could take all of him."

"And was the mission a success?"

"Huge success. And I do mean *huge*. He pushed my knee up and told me to hang on right before he shoved the whole monster inside me. He grunted like the big fucking bear that he is, and it was the hottest thing I'd ever heard."

I closed my eyes and groaned, "I love the grunt. Beau is a grunter, and it's so damn sexy." I focused back on my friend. "So, he made you come. What's the problem?"

"He told me he wasn't stopping until I came at least once more." She looked at me deadpan. "I came *two* more times."

"Yeah, that sounds awful. I can see why you haven't texted him back," I said sarcastically.

"Don't get me wrong. The sex was totally excellent, and he's hot as fuck. I mean, he has muscles on top of his muscles. He was just too... sweet."

"Oh, the horror!" I cried out, doing the Home Alone face at her.

"Shut up, bitch," she said with a laugh. "You know I don't like to get emotionally involved, and he was just saying the sweetest stuff in my ear. It was like he was fucking his girlfriend or something. Actually, it was more like making love." Her face scrunched up at the thought.

Ever since Bristol had lost her fiancé in an oilfield accident three years ago, she had been like this. She rejected any kind of relationship with a man, choosing mostly one-night stands instead.

"So, because he was nice while he was giving you multiple orgasms, you're not seeing him again?" I asked wryly.

"Bingo," she said, pointing a finger at me. "I just can't deal with..." she waved her hand around vaguely, "all that." She bit her bottom lip. "I kinda want to, though, to be honest. It was the best sex of my life. And," she sighed, "I let him stay the night, which I *never* do, and we ended up doing it two more times." I raised an eyebrow in question. "And yes, those two times were just as magnificent as the first," she admitted reluctantly. "I thought it would be awkward waking up with him, but it wasn't. It was just so comfortable and easy, and that freaked me out a little."

"Bris," I said, gently taking her hand, "it's okay for you to move on now. Jared wouldn't want you to be alone forever."

"I know. I'm totally fucked up. Banging different guys when it means nothing doesn't bother me, but if a man tries to get too close or shows me the least bit of affection, I feel like I'm cheating on Jared. I know," she said, holding her hand up, "it's totally ridiculous to feel that way; it even sounds stupid and irrational to my own ears, but I can't help the way I feel."

I nodded. "I get it. Feelings aren't always rational. That's why they're called *feelings*. But if you ever decide to date again, Tank is a wonderful man."

"I know," she said, her voice almost a whisper. "That's what scares me."

"Puh," Danica said from her portable bassinet on the floor, and Bristol and I immediately burst into laughter at the adorable interruption.

"That's right, Dani. Auntie Bristol is full of puh," I cooed, picking her up and settling her on my lap.

"Puh. Puh. Puh," she babbled, proud of the attention she was garnering.

"Damn, the Broxtons sure make pretty babies," Bristol said, as Dani started gnawing on my knuckle.

"I know. It's almost ridiculous, right?"

"So, tonight's the start of your weekend alone with Beau, huh?" Bristol asked, a wicked smile playing across her lips.

"Well, not totally alone," I said, settling Dani in the crook of my arm and putting the bottle in her mouth. "We're babysitting this angel tonight, and then she's staying at the hotel with Blaire and Axel tomorrow night."

"Have you guys done the nasty yet?"

I smiled slyly. "Not exactly."

"What does that mean?"

My eyebrows arched dramatically. "Let's just say his tongue is considered a weapon of mass destruction in sixteen countries."

Bristol's mouth formed a little O.

"But he won't have sex with me yet. I apparently have a microscopic vagina, and he said I need 'preparation.'"

"That's good, Char. It sounds like he's putting your needs first."

"What I *need*, is to finally have sex with him," I said, exasperated. "Though I appreciate that he doesn't want to hurt me."

"I'm sure he's dying to bang you, Charli. You're a hottie of the first order." I bit my bottom lip, and she narrowed her eyes at me. "What? Tell me."

"I know he wants to. His dick wouldn't stay down last night. I gave him two blow jobs and a hand job, and the damn thing just kept getting hard."

"Dear lord. A magical tongue, a big cock, and stamina? That's like the sexual trifecta, girl. He's going to wreck your vajayjay."

"I know," I said with a giggle. "I've never had my hoo-ha wrecked before. Hayden wasn't exactly... wrecking material."

"He was a pencil dick. Is that what you're telling me?" Bristol asked with a self-satisfied smirk.

"Yes," I laughed, "but apparently I have a pencil pussy, so I never knew the difference."

Beau came over that evening as soon as he got off work. He knocked on the front door and I swung it open and jumped on him, wrapping my legs around him. He dropped his overnight bag and caught me, squeezing my ass as I attacked his mouth.

"Mmmmm, that's quite a greeting, Peach. Did you miss me?"

"Mmhmmm, I did," I said, rubbing my nose against his. "Did you miss me?"

"I thought about you all day, baby," he said, closing and locking the door, before carrying me into the living room and settling on the couch with me straddling him. "I wanted to talk to you about something, Peach," he said seriously, and my heart lodged somewhere near my voice box.

Oh, shit. What?

His eyes searched my face and sweat beaded on his forehead before he finally spoke. "I don't know if your mind is headed the same direction as mine, but, um, I thought maybe we should discuss birth control?"

"I'm on the pill," I said, and he breathed out a sigh of relief.

"I always used condoms, Charli. Every single time, but…"

"But what?"

He drew in a deep breath and then exhaled it slowly. "But I don't want there to be anything between us. I brought a box of condoms, and I'll use them if you want."

"But you want it to just be us."

Serious Beau had taken over, and he cupped my face with both hands, his green eyes deep and intense as they searched my own. "Yes. I do. But I'll do whatever you want, Charli. It's totally your decision." I couldn't help the smile creeping over my lips.

"So, we're going to… be together? Tonight?" A shiver of thrill trickled through my body when he nodded.

"If you want to."

"I do want to. And, um, I've always used condoms, too. But… I don't think I want to have anything between us either. I want to feel *you* inside me."

Because I love you. I felt him hardening against my sex, and I rocked intuitively against him. *This is crazy, Charli. You can't love him. You've only known him a couple weeks.*

Beau's hands went to my hips, guiding me back and forth along his hard length as his lips found mine. *Could I be in love with him? Did I know him well enough?* I knew he treated me better than I could have ever imagined. I knew he cared about me, or else he would have just had sex with me the first time I told him I wanted him.

I realized he was looking up at me expectantly, as if waiting for me to reply to something. "Sorry. I was in a bit of a daze. Did you ask me something?"

He smiled indulgently. "I just asked why you were on the pill if you used condoms anyway. Or is that too personal?"

Nothing's too personal with you, Beau.

"Oh, no. It's ok. Uh, I have very heavy periods, and the pill helps regulate them." I tried to shake the insane thoughts from my head. *I. Could. Not. Be. In. Love.* I had just gotten out of the relationship with Hayden about a month ago, though to be honest, I hadn't loved him for a very long time before that. In fact, I hadn't even *liked* him for the past two years.

Beau's mouth on my nipple helped to rid my brain of unwanted thoughts. Thoughts that would have probably sent him running away in two seconds flat. I looked down and realized that my bra and both of our shirts were lying on the couch beside us and wondered when that had happened. Then Beau sunk his teeth into my nipple, tugging on it while our hips undulated against one another.

"God, just the thought of being inside you is driving me crazy, Peach. You've got me so fucking hard right now." His mouth moved to my other breast, and I arched my back as I continued to ride him faster. I slid my hands over his shoulders and chest, loving the feel of his skin and his hard muscles beneath my palms.

We both froze when Danica's soft cry echoed through the baby monitor on the coffee table. I looked at him apologetically. "Sorry, she's probably hungry."

He gave my nipple one last kiss and tugged my shirt on over my head. "I'll get her while you fix a bottle." He lifted me off his lap and patted my ass before standing and heading upstairs.

I tried to make sense of the outrageous thoughts bouncing around in my head as I prepared Dani's bottle. I didn't think this was merely infatuation or lust, though there was plenty of the latter when I was with Beau. I had never felt so sexually charged around another human being as I did around him. But no, this felt deeper than that. I really thought I was in love with this man. I remembered something Bristol had said just this morning: *It's totally ridiculous to feel that way; it even sounds stupid and irrational to my own ears, but I can't help the way I feel.*

And I couldn't help how *I* was feeling. As I walked back into the living room, those feelings were confirmed tenfold. I paused at the edge of the room and just watched Beau. He sat leaned back against the arm of the couch, still shirtless and holding Dani in one massively muscled arm. With his other hand, he was tracing her cheek with one thick finger. So. Gently.

I had to clamp my hand over my mouth to restrain my ovaries from climbing up my throat and screaming, "Impregnate this woman now!" He was talking to the baby, who was no longer crying as her uncle soothed her like a pro. He would occasionally lean down and brush his lips across her forehead or her cheek, and I was overcome with emotions. I had seen Beau hold Dani before, but never like this. Never without a houseful of kids and adults swarming around. This was private and sweet, and my heart seized in my chest, my emotions all over the place. I shut down the twinge of sadness that threatened to surface and put on my happy face.

Beau must have sensed my presence because he looked up at me with a serene smile on his face. "Hey. Come sit with us, Peach," he said quietly, and I walked to him, allowing him to pull me down onto the couch between his legs. He wrapped his free arm around me, taking the bottle and holding it to Dani's darling little mouth. Tilting his head down so that his cheek rested on the top of my head, he released a little sigh of contentment.

Me too, Beau. Me too.

When Dani had finished half of her bottle, Beau lifted her to his shoulder to burp her, and she proceeded to spit up all over his shoulder. "You little monster," he said, with the utmost affection in his voice. "You must hold in all your spit up until Uncle Beau holds you."

"You're special," I told him wryly. "She hardly ever spits up on me."

"I'm her favorite. Isn't that right, baby girl?" He nuzzled his nose against her chubby little cheek, and she blessed him with a gummy smile while my uterus did a little shimmy in my abdomen.

After dinner, we bathed Dani together, and as Beau pulled her out of the tub to dry her off, she peed all over him. Then she grinned, and I lost it, doubling over with laughter. He gave me some serious stink eye when I gasped, "I guess this is another way she's proving you're her favorite, huh?"

"Puh!" Dani said enthusiastically and peed a little more, and I had to sit on the edge of the tub to keep from falling over. Beau, to his credit, just patted her little naked butt before wrapping her up in a towel and stalking into my bedroom. By the time I had composed myself, he had his niece on the bed with a diaper on, and he was blowing raspberries on her tummy.

"I'm glad you got a diaper on her before she pooped on you. Otherwise, you might be named Uncle of the Year." Then the giggles overtook me again.

I could see Beau biting his cheek, but he totally ignored me, leaning over Dani with his forearms resting on either side of her body. "Your nanny thinks she's really funny, doesn't she? I think she might need her pretty little butt spanked. What do you think, Dani-boo?"

Dani grabbed his hair in her chubby little fists and kicked against his chest with her tiny feet. Then she went still as her face screwed up and turned red. Unmistakable sounds emanated from her diaper region, and Beau fell sideways on the bed, laughing hysterically as the baby calmly pooped in her diaper. I fell down on the other side of Dani, holding my stomach.

Beau stroked his finger down her downy cheek and said, "You're killing me, smalls," and Dani farted and then smiled proudly, sending another wave of laughter through the adults in the room.

After I changed her diaper, Dani's little eyes got droopy, and I sent The Uncle of the Year off to get a shower while I put her down for the night. After putting the sleeping baby in her crib, I grabbed the baby monitor from the coffee table downstairs and took it into my room.

Beau was still in the shower, and I stood in the middle of my room in confusion. Should I put on some sexy lingerie? Shit. I actually didn't have any sexy stuff besides what Beau had sent me and a few pairs of lace panties. I slipped on a pair of ivory lace underwear and found an ivory satin spaghetti-strap sleep shirt in my drawer. I couldn't find the matching shorts, so I just spritzed on some perfume and turned off all the lights except for a small lamp on my dresser as I heard the shower turn off.

Climbing into bed, I pulled the sheet up to my waist and curled up on my side facing the bathroom door. Beau emerged a few minutes later, steam billowing from the door behind him, and my mouth went dry. He had a white towel around his waist, his tanned, muscular torso on full display. He looked absolutely yummy, and a nervous energy fluttered throughout my body.

He prowled toward me, all lean muscles and sharp angular features, and crawled onto the bed, coming to rest with his knees on either side of my hips and his fists on the pillow beside my head. "Are we done with all the funny business now?" he growled.

I lifted my head and slicked my tongue up the side of his neck before nibbling on his ear. "All done," I whispered, and he turned his face to mine, pressing my head back to the pillow with his nose against my cheek. He smelled clean and warm, and as I ran my hands up and down his back, his skin felt balmy and moist from his shower.

"Good," he said, his lips resting against the corner of my mouth. Another slight turn of his face, and he was kissing me hard and deep. My body turned into warm butter and melted right into the mattress.

BEAU

Charli's body went loose and soft as I kissed her. My body, on the other hand, was a study in taut nervousness. I wasn't sure exactly why I was so anxious about being with her. I knew the mechanics of the whole process. Tab P goes in Slot V. But...

I wanted our first time together to be different. Special. I wanted to *make love* to Charli. Sounds reasonable... unless you factor in that I had never actually made love to a woman in my life. Even my first time had been a rough, raw affair in the backseat of my girlfriend's car in high school. I was a freshman, and she was a senior, and we had fucked doggy-style like animals while parked in a dark corner of the high school parking lot after a football game.

I peeled back the sheet and groaned as I saw her lying there in creamy satin and lace. I rested my forehead against her stomach and said, "Sweetheart, you could tempt a saint."

"Are you likening yourself to a saint?" she asked, strumming her fingers through my damp hair.

"Hardly," I said dryly, pressing a kiss to her belly.

"Good," she said, her fingernails scratching softly over my shoulders. "I wouldn't want my bed to be struck by lightning."

Her little joke eased my tension a bit. I was with my sweet, funny Peach, and if I was with her, everything was going to be okay. I lay to the side of her and rolled her body toward mine. I kissed her tenderly while exploring every inch of her body with my hands. I'd had my hands on her every night this week, and I knew every curve and every tender feature with my eyes closed, but it felt somehow new tonight, knowing that I was finally going to have her.

I lifted her shirt off over her head and explored some more, my mouth and hands on her soft breasts, before kneeling between her thighs. Her big blue eyes looked up at me, and I locked my gaze with hers as I slid her lacy panties down and off her body. Without breaking eye contact, I pulled her legs over my shoulders and lowered my mouth to her sex.

Her sweet taste overwhelmed me, and I could have eaten her all night, but my poor cock was thumping insistently between my legs. Charli's thighs were shaking, and I knew she was close. "Come for me, Peach," I said against her flesh before double-timing her clit with my tongue and bringing her to a hard, rolling orgasm.

"God. Beau," she moaned. "So good."

I added two fingers, stretching her and getting her ready to take me before I added a third finger and lapped slowly at her hot little button. When she was writhing with as much need as I felt, I covered her body with mine, the tip of my erection resting right at her entrance. Cupping the back of her head with one hand, I stroked the backs of my fingers down her cheek with the other. *I love you, baby.*

"You have to let me know if I'm hurting you, okay?" She nodded at me, her eyes full of emotion. "I'll try my best, but I don't know how to be sweet and gentle."

"Yes, you do, Beau." Her tiny hands cupped my face, and her simple yet vehement statement and the look of pure trust on her face strengthened my resolve. I could do this. For her.

I pressed my hips forward, just a couple inches, and her lips parted, not with pain, but with pleasure. "Beau..." My name was delivered on a sweet sigh, and I pushed into her soft heat a little further. Dear God. I had no words and a million words in my head all at the same time.

Perfect. Mine. Beautiful. Tight. Warmth. Forever. Sweet. Mine.
Love.

Yes, there were words there, but I was incapable of speaking them in any coherent way, so I just whispered, "Charli..." I tugged at her lips softly with my own, pulling my hips back an inch before taking more of her. I heard a soft whimper and circled my hips to stretch her as my lips sucked sweetly on hers, drinking her in. When our tongues touched, my hips moved of their own volition, taking her fully. I swallowed her low moan, stilling my body over hers to allow her to accommodate my thick intrusion.

"I'm in, baby. You okay?" I rested my forehead against hers and felt her nod.

"There's... so much of you." I had known it would be a tight fit, but the way her pussy hugged me was indescribable. A thousand times better than I could have even imagined. I gyrated my hips some more until her moans became ones of pleasure, rather than of discomfort. "Beau, I love having you inside my body," she said, and her sweet words almost undid me.

I knew at that point that I could go slow with her. *For* her. But also, for me. I wanted to feel every single inch of the inside of her. I didn't want to miss a single detail with hard, pounding, uncontrolled thrusts. Every moment, every touch would be ingrained in my memory for the rest of my days.

Burying my face in her neck, I started to move. A deep thrust followed by a slow, grinding revolution of my ass, and then withdraw. Thrust, grind, withdraw. Over and over until her voice was reduced to deep, throaty cries against my shoulder. I lifted my head, looking down into the face I had grown to adore with everything in me.

"Look at me when you come, Peach. I want to know your pleasure is all mine." *Mine, mine, mine.*

"All yours, Beau. Just don't stop," she groaned.

I continued my sensual movements inside her body until her vagina gripped me to the point of pain and her fingers dug into my spine. Her eyes widened and then fluttered as her orgasm overtook her. But she never closed her lids fully, holding my gaze like I was her anchor. And I knew for damn sure that she was mine. She cried out my name against my lips as I grinded deep inside her, riding out and extending her climax for as long as possible.

"That was the most beautiful fucking thing I've ever seen in my life," I whispered reverently. It was an inescapable truth that I *would* see it again before I was done. I would make certain of it. I reached down and captured the back of her knee, guiding her leg around my waist.

Angling my hips to make sure the crown of my dick would hit her G-spot with every movement, I thrusted deeper than before, evoking a cry from the back of her throat. Long, slow thrusts. In and out. Using my back to roll my hips and ensure maximum sensation against every part of her.

"Oh, my God. Beau. I'm... oh God... yes!" Her head was pressed hard into the pillow, eyes closed, as my hips nailed hers to the mattress.

"Watch me while we come together," I demanded, my voice harsh as I tried to maintain enough control to get her there before I exploded like a fucking bomb. As soon as our eyes met, I felt connected to her in a way I could have never imagined, like strong, invisible wires ran between our eyes. "Now," I whispered, and for the first time in my life, I spilled myself inside a woman.

She cried out her own release, but I was only vaguely aware of it as I was almost buried by my own soul-bending orgasm. I continued pumping unhurriedly, feeling her rippling and squeezing out every drop of cum I had for her.

I looked down at her lying beneath me, our bodies trembling and our breaths coming in small, ragged gusts. I pushed a sweat-soaked strip of hair away from her forehead, not moving my green eyes from her deep blue ones. I could read it there. She had been just as affected by our lovemaking as I had been. And not just physically.

Swaddled in each other's arms, contained in our own little bubble where nothing else existed, I softly said, "I love you, Charli."

"Ohhhh," she said on an exhale. *Was that good or bad?*

She smiled at me. *Good. Definitely good.*

Then she started laughing. *Okay, let's go with bad.*

A heavy frown settled on my face, but she lifted her hands to my cheeks and pulled me down for a kiss.

"I thought I was insane, Beau. I was having all these feelings for you, and I thought I must be losing my mind. My heart was telling me it was love, but the logical part of my brain was telling me it was too early." With our foreheads pressed together, she said, "Crazy or not, I love you, too, Beau."

Okay, that's very, very good. Excellent, in fact.

I couldn't restrain my grin as I rolled us over with me still buried inside her and her body pressed to mine. "You love me?"

"Yes," she said, and the pure honesty in her eyes threatened to undo me.

My fingers traced every stunning feature of her face, my eyes following the movement. "I want you to know I didn't say that because of what we just did. I really mean it, Peach. I love you so fucking much."

"I know, Beau." She smiled, and I felt like it lit me up from the inside. Her smile was my own personal sunshine. Charli's lips pressed against my forehead. "I know you here." She bent and fluttered little kisses over my heart. "And I know you here." Her glistening eyes lifted to mine. "You're a man of few words, Beau Atwood, and I know you don't waste them with things you don't mean."

She gets me. This woman really fucking gets me. I felt myself start to harden and lengthen inside her, and she sat up, a look of wonder crossing her face. *Yes, baby. That's all for you.*

"Again?"

"If you want." *Please want. Please, please want.* "If you're not too—" She swiveled her hips then, and I bit out a loud groan. "Christ, Peach. Do that again," I said, gripping her waist.

Charli's hands slid up and down my abs as she started to ride me, tentatively at first, and then with a little more hip action. "So good, Beau. So fucking deep."

My cock was back at full attention, raring to go as she moved on me, her hips rotating and her ass grinding against my balls. My Peach looked so beautiful with her head tossed back, eyes closed and lips parted, like feeling me inside her was all that mattered in the world right then.

"That's it, baby. Ride my dick," I grunted, unable to keep my hips from thrusting upward, as she ground down on me. We found our own unique rhythm that was primal and perfect, our bodies taking and giving as Charli let out a little "Oh," on each downstroke. I put one hand on the small of her back and the other on her chest, applying gentle pressure to lean her back and change the angle of entrance.

Her eyes shot open as she gasped, "Right there, baby. Ohhhhh. Yes." She lifted her chin to the ceiling, her long hair spilling down her back and brushing my thighs as she rested her hands there behind her. "Touch me, Beau. Please. Everywhere."

God, she is fucking beautiful like this.

I loved how she wasn't too shy to tell me what she wanted, and I obliged her request, moving my hands up and down her exquisite body. "You're my goddess, Charli," I said, touching her face gently with one hand as my fingers plucked roughly at one taut nipple. "So wet and hot and sexy."

She sucked my thumb into her mouth, conjuring up images of her perfect lips wrapped around my cock, which was currently pulsing like a motherfucker inside her. When she bit the pad of my thumb, I pinched her nipple hard, giving it a little twist. Screaming my name, Charli bucked her hips against me, fucking me so hard and fast that I could barely keep up.

Fuck! This woman is a bonafide sex machine.

I slid my thumb between us, pulsing it against her clit as she came all over me, flooding me with her sweet wetness and triggering my own intense orgasm. "Shit, baby. You're so... oh goddamn. Fuck, Charli," I roared, painting her inner walls with my heated semen.

I gripped her hips tightly, shoving my cock as deeply as I could go as she spasmed around me, and I emptied myself into her wet heat. "Ohhhh, God. Beau, I've never..." Her words trailed off as she collapsed forward onto my chest. "Love you," she mumbled as I slipped out of her, and she curled up on top of me. And then she was asleep. Or maybe in a sex coma. I wasn't sure.

I smiled down at her as I stroked her back and hair with my hands. She had gone from wild sex goddess to sleepy little kitten in the span of about five seconds, and it was adorable as fuck.

"I love you, too, Peach," I murmured, kissing her hair and relishing the feel of her sleeping soundly on my chest.

25

CHARLI

When I woke up, I sensed it was daylight, though any rays of light were blocked by the huge body hovering over me. I was flat on my back now, and Beau was on top of me, his erection heavy against my belly. "Good morning, Peach," he said against my neck in his sexy sleep-laden voice. His tongue and lips were doing wondrous things to me, and my libido was suddenly wide awake, even though the rest of me was still halfway entrenched in dreamland.

He lifted his hips a little and slid his dick between my legs, sliding it over my pussy until I was wet and panting. Just when he put the tip inside me...

WAAAAHHHHH!

We both glanced over at the baby monitor, willing it to stay silent, but then came another wail from upstairs. "Cockblocking baby," he grumbled, giving me a swift kiss before rolling off the bed and pulling on some pajama pants.

"You get the bottle, and I'll get Dani." I threw on Beau's shirt from the night before and jogged up the stairs to the baby's nursery. "Well, good morning, pretty girl," I said, picking her up and holding her on my shoulder. She quieted instantly but rooted around and sucked on my cheek. "I know, darling. You're hungry, aren't you?"

I got back downstairs to find Beau stretched out on my bed with a pillow propped up beside him. I put Danica down on it and lay on the other side of her as I held the bottle to her mouth. She sucked hungrily as we lay and watched her. Beau picked up her tiny foot and kissed the bottom of it. "I love baby toes," he said, rubbing his nose over her pudgy digits.

It made my heart sing and ache at the same time to see him with his nieces and nephews. My hand went involuntarily to my belly, and Beau's sharp eyes noticed. "Does your stomach hurt, sweetheart?"

"No," I said, faking a smile. "I guess I'm just hungry. Would you like breakfast?"

His eyes brightened. "Can you make a Spanish omelet?"

"I will make you a Spanish omelet so good you might just cry," I said confidently, rising from the bed. "You finish up here, and I'll meet you in the kitchen."

I busied myself cutting and sautéing bell peppers, onions, garlic, and potatoes before cooking the omelets. When they were almost done, I chopped some fresh cilantro to sprinkle on the top of the dollop of salsa I added to them. Beau wandered in, carrying Danica in one arm, and I shot him a questioning look.

"Yes, Miss Smartass. She tried to spit up on me, but I remembered to put the burp rag on my shoulder first." He put Dani in her baby swing and turned it on as I set our plates at the dining table. Beau dug in immediately and groaned, "Shit, this is good. I think I love you even more than I did yesterday."

I smiled as the casual declaration of love rolled easily off his tongue. "Just wait til you taste my pot roast. You'll be declaring your undying love for all things Charli."

"My love is already undying, sweetheart," he said, leaning over and kissing my cheek. "Whether you cook for me or not." Those huge, hyperactive butterflies returned to my stomach, along with a sick sense of dread. Would he be saying that if he knew... everything?

I pushed those thoughts away as I got Danica ready for her daddy to come pick her up. An hour later, Axel arrived, and I handed him the baby and the diaper bag. As he headed out to his truck in the driveway, he called back over his shoulder, "You kids don't do anything I wouldn't do."

"Do you have an itemized list?" I asked, causing Beau to practically choke on his tongue and Axel to laugh uproariously.

"Please don't answer that," Beau called out to Axel. "And stop calling us kids. I'm older than you, for shit's sake." He closed the door and turned to me. "You really shouldn't encourage him. It only makes him worse."

"Oh, hush," I said, slapping his chest. "He and your sister are the most adorable couple."

"They're repulsive," he shot back, though the hint of a smile teased his lips.

"You're repulsive," I said, poking him in the ribs and then turning to run when he narrowed his eyes menacingly at me. I made it two steps before he grabbed me around the waist and tossed me over his shoulder like I weighed no more than a handbag.

He swatted my butt, and I squealed as he toted me back to my bedroom and tossed me on the bed. "Are you done manhandling me?" I asked with a pretend pout.

He stalked toward me with a feral smile. "Oh, Peach. This man isn't nearly done handling you."

Thirty minutes later, we were lying on my bed, naked, sweaty, and sated. Round three of sex had been just as orgasmic as the first two, but more… fun. We had laughed and rolled around on the bed, nipping and teasing each other as we explored each other with mouths, hands, and, um, other body parts.

"I've never had playful sex before," Beau said as we faced each other with our limbs tangled together.

"Me neither. All I've ever had was boring sex." At his raised brow, I clarified, "I meant *before* you."

He grinned and propped himself up on his elbow, his hand trailing up and down my side. "Okay, so we'll skip the boring sex and stick with the good stuff. What else do we need to mark off our list?"

"Let's see. Last night we had sweet-sweet-loving sex."

"Yeah, we did," he said proudly. "And then when you were on top, we had you-fried-my-fucking-balls sex." He tapped his fingertip against my nose.

"How about monkey sex? I'm pretty sure that entails hanging off some light fixtures or something."

"I'm down with that, but I also want to try sleepy-morning sex."

I leaned forward and pressed my lips against his. "Mmmm, that sounds delicious."

"You sound delicious," he said, licking my lips. "Oh, that's right. We mastered oral sex all the way around."

I frowned slightly. "Though I don't think we should take it out of the rotation. We don't want to get rusty."

"Oh, heavens no," he said, pretending to be horrified. "We couldn't have that. So, what else do you want to do with me?"

"Decisions, decisions…" I said, tapping my lips thoughtfully with my index finger. I knew what I wanted, but could I say it out loud? *Meh, what the hell.* "How about rough-and-dirty sex?"

Beau blinked hard three times before staring at me like I had just told him I wanted to visit Jupiter next weekend. "You want it r-r-rough?" he stammered, his breathing hitching up a notch.

Oh, he likes this idea.

"And dirty," I reminded him. Tracing my finger down his chest and following the movement with my eyes, I said, "I've never been with someone so..." I circled his nipple before dragging my eyes back up to meet his hazy green eyes, "...masculine. And strong. I want to feel how powerful you can be with me. Tonight."

A strange noise came from his throat, as if he had swallowed a large bird. "Peach," he croaked before clearing his throat and trying again. "Peach, I don't know if I can be like that with you."

I pouted shamelessly. "But it's what I've been fantasizing about." There was that bird swallowing noise again. "I've always wanted to be with someone who wanted me so much they couldn't control it."

Beau's nostrils flared, and his jaw clenched. "Do you want to know how much control I have right now, Charli?" he snapped. He held his thumb and forefinger a quarter inch apart right in front of my face. "About this much right here."

I pinched his thumb and finger between mine until they were touching, and then I arched a challenging brow at him.

"Jesus H. Christ on a popsicle stick, Charli. I'm going to need a drink... or six. And a cold shower," he grumbled. He closed his eyes tightly, apparently trying to hold on to that tiny thread of control he still owned. Well, he could squinch his eyes and clench his jaw all he wanted. I was going to snip that thread. *Tonight.*

26

CHARLI

OPERATION: FLIRT AND GET *Fucked Dirty* was firmly in place.

After the movie, we walked to a cozy pub near the theater, our arms wrapped firmly around each other. We found an intimate little booth near the back, and Beau went to the bar and ordered burgers and drinks, a margarita for me and a Jack and Coke for himself. When he came back, he sat on the same side of the booth as me, looping an arm possessively around my shoulders.

There was talking and drinking and eating and laughter—so much laughter—coming from our booth as the night went on. And I was flirting my ass off. My breast brushing against his arm. My hand sliding up and down the inside of his thigh.

"You're a little naughty tonight, Peach. You know what happens to naughty girls?" Beau asked, his face a mere inch from mine.

I moistened my lips with my tongue. "Do they get punished?"

He growled before pulling my hand from his thigh. "You'll have to wait and see, won't you?" He placed a swift kiss on my lips before standing, and I noticed the considerable bulge behind his zipper. *Yum.* "I'm going to grab us another drink. Then home," he said, giving me a look full of heat and promises before heading to the bar.

I picked up my phone and saw I had notifications from Instagram. I had posted a picture of me and Beau in the bar a little while ago, our faces pressed together, looking like the happy couple that we were. I laughed as I read the comments from Blaire and Axel.

DocBlaire – Awwww, my fave couple.

AxMan87 – Hey!

DocBlaire – Hush. Look how happy they look.

AxMan87 – I would be happy if you put your phone down and got ur ass in this bed with me.

DocBlaire - *winky face emoji* Have fun, B&C! Gotta go.

AxMan87 – Rawr.

Beau returned to the table and set our drinks down, his hard thigh hot against mine as he sat next to me.

I lowered my voice, which caught his attention, and he turned to face me straight on when I said, "I have a confession." His tongue slid slowly over his top teeth as I gave him a half smile. I leaned in and whispered in his ear, "I'm not wearing any panties under this skirt."

Beau's head jerked back, and his eyes widened almost comically, his attention completely diverted from his drink now. His gaze ping-ponged between my lap and my eyes as if he could discern the truth of my undergarment status with a look. "Seriously, Peach?" I nodded, and he grabbed his drink and downed it in one swallow. Grabbing my hand, he stood and said, "We're going. Now."

Gesturing to my drink, I said, "But I haven't even—"

"Nowwwww," he grunted like some sex-starved Neanderthal, which was kinda hot, to be honest.

I clicked on my Uber app and ordered a ride home as soon as we cleared the door. "Two minutes away," I announced, and he grabbed me around the waist with one arm.

"That gives us a hundred and twenty seconds to discuss this no-panty situation." He snapped open my purse and peered inside. "Are they in here?"

"No," I laughed, swatting his hand away. "And haven't you been taught that it's inadvisable to snoop in a woman's purse?"

He slid a hand into my purse, his curiosity piqued now. "Why? Are you hiding something from me?"

"No, but you might come across a tampon or something equally frightening to men." He yanked his hand back like something in there might bite him, and I stifled a giggle. "And to satisfy your curiosity about my panties, I never put any on after my shower."

"So, you've been… commando all night? In a skirt?" he asked way too loudly, and I shushed him.

"I thought you would like it," I said, sulking a little.

Leaning down to capture my earlobe between his teeth, he whispered, "Oh, I like it, baby. I like it so much, you're lucky you're not up against that building with my head underneath your tiny-ass skirt."

Whooo boy!

The absolutely carnal look on his face was both alarming and arousing. Luckily, the car arrived just then, and Beau opened the door and ushered me into the back seat. As soon as he had entered and closed the door, he pulled me over to sit across his lap with my knees facing the door. Using the darkness and shadows to his advantage, he parted my legs with his hand and slid it up the inside of my thigh.

When I tried to squirm back into my seat, his firm hand on my hip halted me, as did the unadulterated lust on his face. Into my ear, he hissed, "Don't look away from me, and don't come until I tell you to." He stroked through my slick sex with a single finger, his smile dark and dirty. "Soaked," he mouthed, furtively putting that finger into his mouth and sucking it with a look of pure satisfaction.

Oh, sweet Jesus!

His hand snuck beneath my skirt again before I could even take a breath, and that finger circled my clit in a stealthy tease. When he finally slid it inside me and tickled my G-spot, I let out a rush of breath that had him biting his bottom lip.

Over and over, he slowly taunted me to the edge of insanity before pulling his finger out and sucking it... tasting me. Then his hand would slip right back under my skirt.

When we were a couple blocks from the house, he finally grunted quietly, "Now," and it was like someone had flipped a switch. I came with a rush of wetness all over his finger, my mouth open in a silent scream. His face slowly transformed into a look of heated approval as he sped up that wicked, curving finger inside me.

"We're here," the driver announced, and I dazedly looked forward, finding her looking at me in the rearview mirror. "Have a nice night," she said with a wink.

Oh, holy hell. She knows what we've been up to in her backseat.

Beau opened the door and slid my feet to the ground, following me out after a quick, "Thank you," to the driver.

"Beau, I'm not sure I can walk after that." He mumbled something about me not being able to walk tomorrow as he swept my knees out from under me with one forearm. The other arm smoothly caught my waist, and he carried me around to the door to my room. I slid the key into the lock, and within seconds we were inside, my back shoved against the door with a large, provoked man between my legs.

With his body pinning me to the door, Beau grabbed both of my hands and pulled them above my head, trapping them there with one big hand before sliding the other down my body to squeeze my breast. He opened his lips wide, encompassing my entire mouth before sucking hard, drawing my lips into his mouth as his fingers plucked at my nipple and sent electric sparks directly to my clit. His tongue moved harshly over my pursed lips, and he groaned, "Mmmmm, I want to devour every fucking inch of you, Peach." Dragging the tip of his nose across my cheek, he nibbled along my jaw as his lower body pressed me against the wood with deep rolls of his hips.

"Beau," I moaned against his cheek, and he gave a deep grunt of satisfaction when I lifted and wrapped one leg around his waist, opening myself for him. Matching the rhythm of his hips with my own, I tried to pull my hands out of his grip, desperate to touch him, to feel his hard muscles beneath my fingertips.

"Stop squirming," he growled into the side of my neck before lifting his head to look at me. His green eyes pierced me with a look that was almost animalistic, the green irises deep and intense. "Do you have any idea what I'm going to do to this pretty little pussy tonight?" He inched his hand down to grip my ass beneath my skirt, holding me tightly against him, and I could feel the wetness between my legs soaking the rough fabric of his pants.

I leaned my head forward for a kiss, sucking on his tongue and tasting the sweet and warm remnants of the whiskey there. Knowing I was fully under his control, he released my hands and gripped the hair at the top of my head as his mouth took over mine. He plundered deeply, licking into the deepest recesses of my mouth as he tilted my head back. I felt his other hand slide around and fumble with the button and zipper of his jeans, and then he was there, his hot cock sliding between my slickened slit, pushing my arousal to a fever pitch.

Lifting my hips, I tried to push myself down onto him, but he pulled his hips back. "Not yet, my little Peach." His voice was deceptively soft. "First, I'm going to feast on your tasty little cunt until you come on my face." Oh, holy shit! His tongue snaked out and licked my lips. "I'm going to drink down every bit of your sweet cream while you scream my name." Another wet lick against my lips.

"God, Beau," I groaned, working my fingers into his short hair.

"And then I'm going to fuck you like you've been wanting all night. Hard. And rough. And deep. So fucking deep, Peach." He nipped my bottom lip. "I'm going to fuck you until you can't think of anything but having my cock inside you. You'll be feeling me for a week."

Fuck yes.

He swung around and tossed me on the bed. "Hands and knees," he demanded, and the tone in his voice left no room for argument. Sweet mercy, I had gotten my man wound up, and I was about to suffer the naughty consequences.

Kneeling behind me, Beau scrunched my skirt up around my waist and rubbed his hands over my bare bottom. "God, this ass. If you knew the thoughts I had about this ass..." I felt his hot breath there, and then his tongue lapping against my back entrance.

"No, Beau..." I started before I felt a sharp slap against my butt cheek. "Ow, what was that for?"

"For telling me no." Another smack. "And for wearing that little skirt that made me lose my fucking mind all night." Smack. "That's for going without panties and not telling me." With each slap, the wetness between my legs escalated until it was coating the insides of my thighs. Jeez, why was getting spanked so damned hot? I was nothing but a trembling bundle of hormones.

He pushed my shirt up and licked up the center of my spine until his lips were at my ear. "Do you like teasing me, baby?" I nodded, and he chuckled. "I like it, too. What about when I spank you? Does that turn you on and make your pussy wet?" *Um, yes!*

"Why don't you put your tongue there and find out?"

He nipped my earlobe and laughed. "I think that's an excellent idea, Peach." His mouth was on me seconds later with long, hard licks from my clit to my asshole. When I buried my face in the pillow, Beau grasped my hair and pulled my head back. "We're alone, baby. Let me hear you tonight." Then he went back to work between my legs, his tongue buried in my pussy while his scruffy chin scraped across my sensitive clit. His fingers dug into my ass, his nails a pleasing bite of pain. All the sensations coalesced into a knot of tension that finally untied and slithered up my spine. A scream tore from my throat at the intensity of the orgasm that slammed into me like a truck.

Beau groaned into me. "That's it, baby. Scream for my tongue." Another cry from my lips, this one longer as his tongue slipped under my clit to suck it into his mouth. I couldn't even catch my breath before his firm suction pushed me over the edge again.

"Beau, God yes!" His mouth was so relentless that my arms buckled, and I dropped to my elbows. His tongue finally slowed into long, gentle licks, ending with a gentle fluttering against my back hole before he rose up behind me.

"Stay just like that, baby, with your beautiful ass up in the air for me," he said, smoothing a hand over my butt cheeks. I felt the bed shift as he stood and quickly removed his clothes. He climbed back up behind me and slid my shirt off over my head. "I'm leaving this sexy little skirt on you while I fuck you," he said, grabbing the waistband and using it as leverage to pull me back onto his waiting fingers. Two fingers at first, and then three… filling me… stretching me.

"I need you, Beau. Please," I begged.

"You still want it rough, Peach?" he asked, twisting his fingers inside of me.

"Yes, baby. Fuck me," I said, my words breathless, yet firm. I wanted this. I wanted him to take control of my body and dominate me.

I felt a hand on my lower back and the thick crown of his cock rubbing through my sensitive lips a second before he drove into me with a loud, "Unnnngh!" and then a muttered, "Holy fuck." I couldn't even make a sound because he had knocked all the air out of my lungs with his vicious thrust.

Then he was moving into me with deep, driving thrusts. Hard. Fast. *Hard. So fucking hard.* The first few knocked me forward on the bed until Beau's big hands clutched my hips to steady me. He was stretching my inner muscles to their absolute limits, taking me exactly how he wanted, so deep it hurt. But it was an exquisite pain which quickly faded to a pulsing heat. And that was so damn good.

"God, I love fucking your hot, tight pussy, Charli." Sharp snaps of his hips punctuated his next words. "You're. So. Fucking. Sexy. I. Love. You." The sounds of his hips slapping against my ass and the banging of the headboard into the wall was the most erotic percussion I had ever heard, and I felt something starting to build again, deep in my core.

Beau slid one hand up my back to press between my shoulder blades, and I surrendered myself fully to him, pressing my cheek and chest against the mattress. "Fuck. Yes," he grunted, the sound low and guttural as he fisted a hand roughly in my hair. "Tell me you're mine, Charli."

"I'm yours. All yours, Beau."

"Yessss," he hissed, his movements slower now, but somehow deeper. The head of his dick was hitting me hard and high, pushing me closer and closer to the edge of something vast and all-consuming. My hands squeezed the sheets, trying to hold on for dear life. "Forever," he rasped.

Huh?

Beau curled his chest over my back, sliding his hands over mine and linking our fingers, his hips never breaking their punishing rhythm against my backside. His open mouth rested on the side of my neck as the hair on his torso rasped against my back. "Tell me you'll be my little Peach forever," he said plaintively, sucking my flesh into his mouth like he could suck the answer he wanted right out of me. I hesitated. *He was talking about forever already?* "Please, baby. I couldn't live without you." His soft admission tore my response from my lips.

"Forever, Beau." It was an easy admission. *How the hell could I love him like I do and not want to be with him always?*

My man let out a desperate moan against my neck. Then he wasn't my man anymore. He was an animal, grunting and growling and rutting. And I was coming and coming and coming, my toes curling and my hands clenching. My insides had formed a big mass of orgasm that he was pulling relentlessly from my body, and it felt like his large frame covering my small one was the only thing keeping me from floating to the ceiling.

With an unholy cry of, "Fuck. Goddammit, you're so good, baby. Mine. *Mine,*" he roared his release before clamping his teeth down on my shoulder, marking me, claiming me.

He was still buried deep inside me when his mouth softened into a tender kiss where he had bitten me. His lips skimmed up my neck and to my cheek. "You okay, baby?" he murmured, his hot breath washing across my face as he panted from our intense fucking.

"Mmmm," was all I could come up with, and he withdrew from me and turned me over, slipping back inside and letting his body rest against mine.

"Was that a good mmmm or..."

"It was an excellent mmmm," I said, gripping his face and pulling it down to mine for a long, leisurely kiss. "You made my toes curl. My toes have never curled before."

He grinned happily. "And you came like a damned waterfall." He moved his lower body against mine, our combined fluids slicking our thighs and lower stomachs. "I like that, but we probably need a shower."

"And fresh sheets," I said wryly.

He lifted us from the bed without breaking our connection. "In the morning. We'll just mess them up again, because I'm not done with you yet, Peach."

I groaned as he carried us into the bathroom and turned on the shower. "I'm already going to need crutches to walk tomorrow," I groaned. At his wicked smile, I glowered at him. "Why do you look so damned smug about that?"

He walked us into the shower and put me on my feet before kissing my lips softly. "Because I like you knowing where I've been. Where only I'll ever be." He soaped up his hands and started cleaning me, leaning down to kiss me sweetly. "Just me, Peach. I'm the only man who will ever touch this beautiful body." He swept his hands down my sides and between my legs, touching me with the utmost gentleness. "Mine," he whispered.

"Yours," I confirmed. "Forever." I liked that he was washing me with his hands instead of with a cloth. It made everything seem so much more intimate. He turned me under the water and then swept his big hands all over me again to wash the soap away.

Beau cupped my face and lowered his lips to mine, planting sweet kisses there. "I love you, Charli. With all my heart." *Oh, this man melted me like a snow cone in July.*

I laid my hands on his massive chest and kissed along his sharp jawline. "I love you, too, Beau."

"I'll never understand why you love me, but I feel like the luckiest man in the world."

He was always selling himself short, thinking he was incapable of being loved. I rested my cheek over his heart and said, "Because you have the kindest heart of any man I've ever known. You love so fiercely."

Wrapping his arms around me, he held me tightly against him, his lips settling on the top of my head. We stood like that until the water ran cold, and then Beau took me back to bed, covering my body with his and making slow, sweet love to me. I hadn't thought I could want sex again for a while after the pounding he had given me earlier, but I found myself unable to get enough of him. Every slow thrust, every *I love you*, every caress of my face.

I could tell we were both close when Beau rested his forehead against mine, his face almost in pain. "I feel like I'm on fire every time we're together." He gave me a long sucking kiss as he rocked into me. "Burn with me, Peach."

And I did.

27

CHARLI

I WAS HAVING THE most wondrous flashbacks to this weekend. *Beau and his big, sure hands. His amazing mouth. His hot body covering mine. His incredibly huge...*

I snapped out of my reverie and gathered my things for my evening at Beau's. I was supposed to stay the night at his house after the football game and return to the Broxton's early tomorrow morning. My phone rang as I was putting a Wranglers jersey that Axel had given me into my bag to change into after I finished cooking. I answered with a cheery, "Hello."

Beau's rich, warm voice greeted me and sent chills down my spine. "Hi, baby. How is your day going?" He had left my bed early this morning, but it seemed like days since I had spoken to him.

"It's good. We just finished getting your filthy, muddy nephews bathed and down for a nap."

I could hear the heartfelt affection in his voice. "I love seeing kids having fun and getting all dirty. Playing outside is so much better for them than stupid video games."

"I agree. I was just packing, but I might... I don't know... I might come back here and stay," I said uncomfortably. *I don't think I can sleep in the bed where you've fucked other women.*

There was a pause and then, "I know what you're thinking, Charli, and I've already taken care of it."

No way he knew what I was thinking. "Took care of what?" I asked curiously.

"You don't want to sleep in my old room in my old bed."

"Oh... what?"

"Last week I moved into the spare room in our house. I got a new bed, new linens, new pillows... everything."

"You... you switched rooms for me?"

"And for me, Peach. I didn't want to stay in that room anymore either," he said softly.

I chewed my bottom lip. "And did you have a priest come and bless the old room?" I blurted out.

His warm laughter filled my ears. "No, but that's a good idea. I'll get on it."

"I love you, Atwood."

"I love you, too, Peach. Oh, and what I was calling for... I have to work late, so can you come by my office and pick up a key to my house? I know you'll need to get started on dinner soon."

Half an hour later, I was walking into Beau's office and was greeted with a fake smile from Aspen, the bulldog receptionist. "Can I help you?" she asked with saccharine-sweetness, like she didn't even recognize me.

"Hello, Aspen," I said, matching her fake nice tone. "Beau asked me to stop by and pick up something."

"Do you have an appointment?"

Oh, this bitch...

"If you'll remember, he told you last week that I don't need an appointment," I said, still sweet but with a slight edge to my voice.

She put a perfectly manicured nail to her lip and said, "Hmmm. And what was your name again? *Beau* is awfully busy today." I noticed she emphasized the fact that she was calling him by his first name.

Okay, that was it. I placed my hands on her desk and leaned over right in her face. "If you're not smart enough to remember me, *Aspen,* then perhaps I'll have a picture of my face blown up and put on your fucking desk." She was bending back in her chair with her eyes wide and her mouth gaping open. "You wouldn't want to risk angering *Mr. Atwood* because you upset me, right?"

"O-oh, Miss Casper. Right. Okay, go on back."

I straightened and brushed my hands down the front of my black cropped jacket. "Thank you so much. Have a nice day," I said, sashaying down the hallway toward the offices. I don't remember ever sashaying before, but it felt good. I was totally working the sashay into my walking repertoire from now on.

I knocked on Beau's door, and he called for me to enter. He came around from behind his desk and was on me in three long strides. "Hi, baby," he purred, lifting me so that I could wrap my legs around him.

He pressed his lips to mine and curled the fingers of one hand around the back of my head, holding my face to his as he delivered soft, slow kisses to my lips. Sliding my tongue against his pillowy lower lip earned me a deep growl, and next thing I knew, Beau was shoving his tongue roughly into my mouth. I sucked on it, and he groaned, gripping my ass with one big hand and pulling me up and down his dick, which was rapidly hardening beneath his black dress pants.

"You missed me," I said against his lips.

"More than you know," he said, carrying me around his desk and setting me on my feet as he settled back into his chair. "Did you miss me?"

"Of course, I did," I said, putting my hands on the arms of his chair and kissing his ear.

I heard the unmistakable sound of his belt being undone and looked down to see him undoing the button and zipper on his pants. He lowered his briefs and said, "Enough to get on your knees under my desk and suck my cock while I make a phone call?" He wiggled his eyebrows mischievously as he grabbed himself and gave a long, slow stroke, making my mouth water for him.

Well, someone is feeling playful.

I nibbled on the tip of my finger and said, "I'll do whatever you want. I really need this job, Mr. Atwood."

His eyes darkened to a deep glass green and he jerked his chin toward the wide space under his desk. "Then I suggest you get to work and suck it like you own it, Miss Casper." A slow, wicked smile spread across his face as I dropped to my knees and backed under his desk.

Beau slid his chair up to the desk and picked up the phone as I ran my tongue up his straining length. "Yeah, Jim. Hey, it's Beau Atwood."

I ran my tongue around the head of his dick repeatedly, tasting the smooth saltiness of his precum, and he widened his legs, brushing my cheek with the backs of his fingers. "Uh-huh, that's fine. I just wanted to make sure you were still coming by at five today."

When I pulled the thick crown into my mouth and sucked softly, Beau's voice changed to a slightly higher pitch. "Of course. I'll have Journey email you the projected figures on that so you can look them over before the meeting."

Sliding my lips down his shaft, I took him inch-by-inch until he touched the back of my throat. A weird sound emanated from his lips, and he quickly cleared his throat. *Oh, this is fun.*

"No, no. I'm fine. Everything's fine. What did you ask me again?"

I grinned around his cock and then pulsed him against the back of my throat. "I'm not sure about that, Jim, but you can call Sandra. You have her number?"

Opening my throat, I let him slide down into it, evoking low groans that he managed to turn into actual words on the phone. "Mmmmmmkay. That sounds ahhhhhhmazing." I felt his hand rest against the back of my head.

I slid my lips back to the tip and then deep-throated him again just as I heard the door to his office open. When I tried to pull back, his fingers tightened in my hair, holding me in place. "Okay, Jim. I'll see you tonight. Gotta run, though. Cam just walked into my office... yeah, okay... bye."

Cam? Cam was in the office with us? Holy shit! I heard the squeak of leather as he settled into a chair across from the desk. It was one thing to be doing this while Beau was on the phone, but with Cam only a couple feet away?

Beau hung up the phone and said, "Hey, man."

"Hey, Shark. You ready for this meeting tonight?"

I tried to pull away again, but Beau shoved my head down onto his thick cock. "Yep. Just got off the phone with Jim. I think we should be able to wrap this deal up with him tonight." He slipped off one loafer and wedged his socked foot between my legs, pressing against my sex.

Oh, you wanna play, buddy? It's on like Donkey Kong, Atwood. I sucked him deep and bobbed my head, looking up at him from underneath the desk. Sweat was starting to bead on his top lip, but he managed to keep his eyes firmly on his friend.

"Hell, I hope so," Cam said. "Jim has some excellent connections. How did you manage to get this meeting?"

I drug my lips slowly up the shaft, working my tongue against the underside, and Beau's hand tightened in my hair. "Uhhh, the... the meeting?"

"Yeah. The meeting tonight. Jim's used RD Security for as long as I can remember. Why did he agree to meet with us?" He paused for a second and asked,

"You okay, Shark?" I fisted the base of Beau's erection and pumped him hard as I sucked his head with lots of sloppy tongue action.

"Uh-huhhhh. I'm fine. Guess I have a little... indigestion or something." He pressed right against my clit with his big toe.

"You want me to get you some Rolaids?" Cam asked, his voice concerned, and I tried not to giggle.

"Naw, I'm good." *You're about to be better than good, Mr. Atwood.* "Jim wasn't happy about that screw up..." I fisted him faster and sucked harder, flicking my tongue on that sensitive spot on his crown as Beau attempted to finish his sentence. "That screw up with RD and the... the actress. Whatsername."

"Maxine Day?"

I scraped my teeth lightly up Beau's shaft and felt him swell in my mouth.

"Yeahhhhhh, that's it," he said with a clenched jaw as his hand tugged my hair, forcing me down on him as he filled my mouth with his hot cum. He bit his bottom lip as I swallowed and licked him clean.

I heard the scrape of the chair against the floor as Cam stood up and turned to leave. "All right. I'll be back in here a little before five so we can strategize about what we're going to say." I heard the door open just as I let Beau's dick slide from my mouth. "Bye, Charli," Cam called with a grin in his voice.

Fuck. "Bye, Cam," I said, my voice not much more than a squeak from under the desk.

The door closed, and Beau peeked under the desk. "That was fucking hot, Peach."

"That was fucking embarrassing," I hissed. "Did he know I was down here the whole time?"

"Probably. Cam's a dirty bastard. He usually has a fairly accurate radar for any kind of debauchery going on in his midst." He helped me out from under the desk before standing and settling me into his chair. He tucked his dick back into his pants and refastened them.

"Dirtier than you?"

He leaned down and kissed me. "Sweetheart, I'm practically a saint compared to Cam. He has some... uh, voyeuristic tendencies."

"Um, should I be worried about staying at your house tonight?"

Beau walked over and locked the door to his office. "I've already threatened him. No peeking allowed. Though he will probably listen to us."

"Seriously?" *Why were my panties getting wet thinking about that?*

"Yep," he said, slowly walking back toward me like a lion stalking a gazelle. He had *that look* in his eyes. That look that told me I was about to be a very happy girl. "Does that bother you?"

"No," I said, and my cheeks heated at the admission. Beau gave me a dark smile as he spun the chair to face his desk.

"I love my dirty little Peach," he said, sinking to his knees in front of me and pushing my maroon circle skirt up around my waist. "Put your feet up on my desk and spread your legs." I did, and his eyes locked firmly on my sex, which was covered with black tights. "I'm going to owe you a pair of tights," he said a split second before he ripped a huge hole in the crotch.

Holy sexy hell!

"You're lucky I didn't wear panties under them today." He leaned forward and swiped his tongue through my slit. "Correction. I'm the lucky one," I groaned.

"Mmmm, I love eating your pussy, baby. I like devouring you first thing in the morning so that your taste is on my tongue all day long." He buried his face between my legs, his tongue and lips sucking and licking like he would never get another taste of me.

I clutched the arm of the chair with one hand and stroked the other through Beau's thick hair. "That feels so good, baby," I panted.

He sucked on my clit, and I felt a sudden gush of wetness, which Beau quickly lapped up. "Fuck yes, baby. Give me some more of that sweetness." He fucked me with his long, tongue, and I had to pinch my lips together to keep from crying out.

Beau's eyes met mine when the phone on his desk let out two sharp rings. "Grab that phone for me, Peach. I'm busy," he said casually, flicking his tongue over my clit.

"Beau, I can't answer your phone."

"Sure you can." Two more quick rings and a scrape of teeth against my clit. "That's the interoffice line, probably one of the guys." He gave me a little smirk before putting his tongue back to work inside me.

I reached over and picked up the receiver. "Atwood's phone. This is Charli," I said, proud that my voice sounded relatively normal, despite the things Beau was doing between my legs.

"What's up, Charli? Can I talk to Shark for a second?" Beau was shaking his head at me as he flexed his tongue up and down inside my vagina.

"Oh. Hey, Hawk. He can't come to the phone right now."

"Are y'all fucking in his office?" he asked, sounding amused. Beau sucked hard on my clit, and my hips lifted six inches off the chair.

"Of course not," I said, hoping my voice didn't sound as breathless as I thought it did. "He's just... in the middle of something right now." Beau grinned and rolled his tongue over my sensitive little bundle of nerves. "He'll call you back in five minutes." My sexy-as-fuck boyfriend held up three fingers, and I said into the receiver, "He said make that three minutes."

Hawk busted out laughing and said, "He's a cocky bastard, isn't he?" before hanging up the phone. No sooner had I replaced the receiver than Beau amplified his efforts down below. He pushed a thick finger inside me and greedily devoured my clit, triggering a hard, fast orgasm to throb from my pussy all the way down my legs.

"Shit. Beau. Oh, my fucking... Ohhhhhh," I moaned as quietly as I could. "So good, baby."

KNOCK KNOCK KNOCK.

"Christ," Beau hissed, standing up and pulling my feet off his desk before straightening my skirt. "It's like Grand Central Fucking Station here today." He grabbed a tissue off his desk and wiped his mouth before heading to the door and swinging it open.

Aspen strolled in like she owned the place and quickly ran her narrowed eyes over me and Beau. We both looked decidedly rumpled, and Aspen's lips pressed into a hard line before she turned to her boss.

Shooting her eyes at me, she asked my boyfriend, "May I speak with you in the hallway about a private matter?" Beau sighed and followed her out into the hall. She lowered her voice but kept the door open so that I could easily eavesdrop. "Did you need me to stay late tonight, Beau? For yours and Cam's meeting with Mr. Belew?"

"It's *Mr. Atwood*, and no, you do not need to stay late. I've already told you that, Aspen."

She put her hand on his chest and said, "I would be happy to, if I could be of service, Mr. Atwood."

He removed her hand and said firmly, "I've told you repeatedly, you cannot be *of service* in any way, shape, or form that you are alluding to. You can do your job by showing Mr. Belew to my office, and then you can leave. Understood?" She nodded and flounced away angrily.

Beau's face was stony when he re-entered his office and closed the door. "Fucking nightmare," he said, through gritted teeth. "I swear, the next receptionist I hire will be male or over the age of sixty."

"I must say, I like that idea very much," I said standing and crossing to him. "I don't like you working with her."

He wrapped his arms around me. "You have nothing to be worried about. You know you're the only woman for me, Peach."

"I trust you, but I don't trust her as far as I could throw her. She doesn't even try to hide that she wants you," I said, crossing my arms over my chest.

Beau unfolded my arms and wrapped them around his waist. "That's why I don't let her stay late and why none of my men are allowed to be in a room alone with her. We're not stupid."

"I know you're not." I lay my head on his chest. "I could stand here cuddling with you all day, but I know you have work to do, and I need to get started cooking."

"I'll walk you out." We got to the lobby, and Beau laughed. "I almost let you leave without giving you this. You had me a little distracted," he said, pulling a pink key from his pocket. He snagged my keys from my hand and added it to the ring. "Key to my house. I had a copy made for you, so you can keep it."

I heard Aspen make a little derisive noise behind him and saw her shooting daggers from her eyes. For her benefit as much as my own, I raised up on my tiptoes and pressed a kiss to Beau's lips. "Thank you, baby. I'll see you tonight."

"Love you, Peach," he said with an adorable wink.

"Love you, too," I said, turning to the door. I refrained from sticking my tongue out at Aspen because I was a mature woman. Though I was flipping her off in my head as I walked to my car.

28

CHARLI

I was searing the roasts in the two Instant Pots in Beau and Cam's kitchen when I heard a knock on the door. *Shit! Was I supposed to answer that?* I walked into the living room and called, "Who is it?"

"It's Bode."

I unlocked the door and was greeted by Bode's huge grin and swift kiss on the lips. I was taken aback, but he just strolled into the house. "Hey, pretty lady. Shark sent me here early to assist with the vegetable-cutting duties." He held up his long-fingered hands. "My hands are your slaves."

"I could use them," I said with a laugh, leading him into the kitchen.

"Mmmm, it smells good already, Charles."

"I'm just searing the roasts now. You can help with that, and then we'll get on the vegetables." We chatted and cooked, and I realized how much I liked Bode. He was sweet and quirky and so easy to talk to. When we were done, I added the beef broth and seasonings and started cooking the meat on the high-pressure setting. "We'll let those cook for a while and then add the veggies, so they don't get too soggy."

Bode started cutting onions, for which I was very grateful because they always made my eyes water. I peeled potatoes and cut them up, and then Bode got to work on the carrots while I cut celery. A while later, I felt strong hands grip me from behind and a pair of soft lips that I recognized against the back of my neck. I tried to fight my grin.

"Cut it out, Bode. Beau will be here any minute, and he'll catch us."

I heard a low growl and then turned in my boyfriend's arms and smacked him on the forehead with a stalk of celery.

"Gotcha," I said on a laugh, earning me a swat on the ass.

"Not funny," he grunted, but I saw the hint of a smile beneath his scowl. "You almost got Bode's ass whooped."

Bode wielded a carrot stick like a weapon and said, "Come at me, bro." Beau swiped the celery from my hand, and they proceeded to have a vegetable sword fight around the kitchen while I released the pressure on the cookers. I added the veggies—minus Beau and Bode's current weapons—to each pot and turned the machines back on for another forty minutes.

"What the hell is going on in here?" Cam asked, entering the kitchen just as Bode dramatically faked his death on the floor.

"Beau killed Bode with a piece of celery," I reported.

"True story," Bode said, cracking one eye open.

"Cool," Cam said, grabbing Bode's carrot sword from his limp fingers and taking a bite of it.

Beau grabbed me around the waist and said, "I have defended your honor, m'lady. I expect a reward." He dipped his head for a long kiss, and Cam pretended to gag.

"I'm out," he said, stopping near the kitchen door and turning back. "Unless you're gonna bang her on the counter, Shark. Then I'll stay and watch."

"Out!" Beau ordered, and Bode peeled himself from the floor and stood up.

"I feel the love in this room, and I like it. Shark, do you realize I haven't had to cleanse your chakras in almost two weeks?"

"I'm going to remove your chakras and stick them up your—"

"Okay, I'm leaving," Bode interrupted as Beau lifted me up in his arms and placed me gently on the counter.

When we were alone, he wedged himself between my thighs and kissed my lips softly. "How was your meeting?" I asked.

"Good," he said with a grin. "We got the account. Though I had to keep my chair under my desk because every time I heard Jim's voice, all I could think of was your lips around my cock. I couldn't get it to go down."

"I'm glad," I said. "About the account, not your unfortunate penis situation," I clarified.

"You're not going to think it's unfortunate later tonight," he said, nibbling on my neck. We hadn't had sex last night since I was sore from Saturday night's vigorous activities, but Beau had stayed over anyway. Going without for one night was apparently too much for him, though, because he was hard again between my legs.

His hands slid under my shirt just about the time Tank, Woody, and Hawk busted into the kitchen. "Give it a rest, you two," Hawk said.

"Goddammit, is five minutes of privacy too much to ask for?" Beau snapped, pulling his hands from my shirt and tugging it down.

"But we come bearing gifts. We've got beer and Bode's famous cream puffs," Tank said, setting down a covered tray that smelled delicious. I hopped off the counter and snagged one of the delicate pastries, and Tank pretended to swat my hand.

"Hey, I've been slaving away in the kitchen. I need sustenance," I said, sinking my teeth into the flaky, creamy delicacy. "Ohmigod, thass so good," I said around a mouthful of yumminess.

Beau leaned in and licked a dollop of the soft cream from my top lip. "I'm stealing a couple of these and hiding them in the bedroom for playtime later," he whispered, slipping his hand under the cover and pulling out two of them and sneaking out of the kitchen.

"Charli, we didn't know what you liked to drink. We have beer, but I could run down to the corner and get you some wine or something, if you want," Tank said. He was such a sweetheart.

"Duh, it's a football game. Of course, I'm drinking beer. Only sissies drink wine during football."

"My homegirl," Woody said, giving me a high five. "It smells fucking good in here."

"I cooked two roasts in the Instant Pots. They only have to cook a little over an hour, and they come out so tender." I checked the timers. "Okay, I'm going to change clothes right quick." I headed to Beau's room, where I had stashed my bag earlier.

"Whatcha doing, babe?" he asked when I walked in.

"Changing into my football clothes," I said.

"You need help?" he asked, pulling my shirt over my head.

I laughed. "I'm pretty sure I can manage. I've been dressing myself for quite some time now."

"It's more fun if I help you," he said, unzipping my skirt and pulling it and my torn tights down my legs. I reached for some panties in my bag, but he stopped me with a hand on my wrist. "No panties." His voice had dropped lower and so had his hands. He cupped my bare butt and said, "Easier access for later."

"Okay, but don't you dare rip my leggings like an animal. These are my favorite ones," I warned, lowering my eyebrows at him as I pulled my black Lululemon leggings on.

"Don't you give me scary eyes, Peach. I'll rip them off you, and you'll damn well like it."

"No. I won't," I said, poking him in the chest. "They cost like a hundred dollars. I'll buy some cheap ass ones at Walmart if you want to play caveman sometime."

"That sounds like a fun game. I could just grunt at you while I'm fucking you."

"You do that anyway," I said with a giggle as I slipped the jersey on. "But I like it."

"Come on, Captain Caveman! Y'all are gonna miss kickoff," Cam called from the living room.

"We really need better fucking insulation in this house," Beau muttered as we walked hand-in-hand down the hallway.

"No, we don't," Cam disagreed. "Otherwise, how am I going to hear you and Charli playing the caveman game later?"

"Shut up, fucker," Beau growled, plopping down on the couch and pulling me onto his lap. Someone passed us a couple beers, and we settled down to watch the game. I heard the timer go off in the kitchen during the first quarter and got up to release the pressure valves. When I had the food transferred to two large glass pans, I called the guys into the kitchen.

They paused the game and flooded into the kitchen, descending upon the food like a flock of vultures. "Damn," I said, fascinated as they jockeyed for position around the center island, grabbing meat and vegetables and coating everything with gravy. "It's like feeding time at the alligator farm."

"Yeah, you hog asses," Tank said, holding a plate with a chunk of roast big enough to feed a family of four. "Make sure to leave some for Charli."

I glared at Woody's plate. "You didn't get any vegetables."

He frowned and forked up two chunks of potatoes and a tiny sliver of carrot. "There. Happy, mom?"

"Ecstatic, son. Don't you want to grow up to be a big boy like your brothers?" I asked with a smirk.

He flashed me a naughty grin and said, "I'm already big enough where it counts."

Beau cuffed him hard on the side of the head and said, "Respect, asshole."

Woody grabbed me in a one-armed headlock and said, "Charles knows I'm just messing around, dontcha?" He kissed the top of my head affectionately, and Beau growled at him. "Hey, calm down, caveman. We're cool." They had been calling him caveman ever since they heard our little conversation earlier, and Beau rolled his eyes.

"Call me caveman one more fucking time, and I'll kick all your asses out of here. Without food."

"No bueno, cave—uh, Shark," Woody said, and they all hustled into the living room with their plates piled high before Beau could make good on his promise. I fixed my plate, grateful they had left me a decent-sized chunk of meat and plenty of veggies.

"Sorry they're such assholes," Beau said with a scowl.

"They're just having fun." I kissed his cheek. "*I'm* having fun. Thank you for inviting me."

"You really don't mind being around them?" he asked, his tone brightening.

"Of course not. I love your friends. It reminds me of being around my brothers. Oh, I've been meaning to ask you. My sister and brothers are coming to town a week from Thursday, and we're all having dinner together. Do you want to go so you can meet them?"

"Sure," he said a tad apprehensively. "Do you think they'll like me?" I hesitated before answering, and Beau jumped on it. "You paused. Why did you pause?"

"They can just be a tad… overprotective since I'm their little sister. They really didn't care for Hayden, but I'm sure they'll like you." I kissed his jaw. "I love you, and that's all that matters."

"So, your family is going to hate me. That's what you're telling me," he said sullenly.

"They won't hate you, and I'll be right there with you the whole time. They will be glad to see me happy and with someone who loves me like you do."

"Would you two stop playing kissy face and come on?!" Hawk called from the living room.

"I fucking hate them," Beau said with a laugh as we picked up our plates and headed to the living room.

"Holy crap, Charles. This is the best roast I've ever eaten," Cam said.

"Seriously," Tank said. "Friggin' delicious. What seasoning do you use?"

"Well, I rubbed it with oil and fresh garlic cloves and then coated it with sea salt and coarse-ground black pepper. Then I seared it on the sauté function on the pressure cooker."

"I helped with that," Bode said proudly, and everyone clapped sarcastically.

I laughed. "Bode was an excellent assistant. Anyway, you just add beef broth and a packet of onion soup mix. That gives it a richer flavor."

"That's too much to remember. I'll just get you to make me roast when I'm hungry for it," Cam said, nodding his head as if the matter were settled.

"She's not your personal chef, nimrod," Hawk said.

I shook my head. "No, really. I don't mind. But maybe we could do a trade for services?"

Cam grinned deviously. "If Shark doesn't mind sharing, I'm up for it."

Beau glared so hard at Cam I was surprised he didn't catch on fire. "Try it, fucker. See what happens." he said over his bottle of beer before tipping it up and taking a long drink.

My green-eyed—literally and figuratively—man was seated on the couch, and I was on the floor between his feet, so I reached over and patted his leg soothingly. "Not *those* services, obviously, Cam. I was talking about self-defense lessons. Beau said you're a good teacher."

Cam gave me a genuine smile this time. "Sure thing. I'd be happy to."

"Come on, Ax!" Hawk yelled at the TV, and I turned my attention to the game just in time to see my boss catch a pass and dodge two tackles on his way to a twenty-eight yard scamper.

"Hell yes!" I yelled, rising to my knees and smacking my hand on the coffee table. "He's got to be one of the top tight ends in the league in YAC."

Just then the commentator announced, "That was Axel Broxton on the reception. He leads the entire NFL in yards after catch this season." I nodded proudly before noticing that every eye in the room was looking at me in amusement. "What?"

Beau laughed and pulled me up into his lap, kissing my temple. "My girl really likes football," he explained.

Bode tipped his beer at me and said, "You're the perfect woman, Charles. You know football, you can cook, and you're hot." At Beau's glare he amended, "I mean nice. You're really nice," and all the other guys chuckled.

The boys cleaned up the kitchen during halftime, and then we ate way too many cream puffs while we watched the second half. Axel had three more catches, and the Wranglers won by a touchdown. "That was a great game," Hawk said. "And thanks for cooking, Charli."

"Yeah, thank you," Tank said, giving me a hug. In fact, all the men hugged me before leaving, and Beau didn't even growl at any of them.

As soon as the door closed behind them, Beau pressed his chest against my back and wrapped his big hands around my hips. "You really are the perfect woman, Peach," he said into my ear. I pinched my lips together to hide my emotions.

Oh, Beau. If you only knew.

29

BEAU

I TURNED CHARLI IN my arms and took in the look on her face. "You're really terrible at taking compliments," I teased, making her smile. *God, I love that smile.* "Let's go to bed, baby."

Leading her by the hand to my new bedroom, I caught Cam's eye, and he mouthed, "Leave the door open." I flipped him off. Fucking perv. I closed the bedroom door firmly behind us and stripped off my shirt.

Charli ran her hands up and down my torso, kissing and sucking me softly as her mouth moved across my chest. "It's really a crime to cover all this up," she said. "It should be a law that you walk around shirtless all the time."

"The feeling is mutual," I said, pulling her jersey off over her head and running my hands up her sides to cup her perfect tits. "Get on the bed," I demanded gruffly. She climbed up and lay on her back, and I sat on top of her, straddling her hips.

"I want to restrain you while I'm fucking you tonight. Are you okay with that?"

"You're going to tie me up?" she asked nervously.

I shook my head as I reached beneath her and unhooked her bra, slipping it down her arms and tossing it aside. Sliding my hands up her arms, I pressed her hands into the bed. "You think I can't hold you down?" I growled, and something flashed in her eyes. Excitement? "Does that turn you on?"

"Yes," she whispered, and I had to fight my urge not to pump my fist in triumph.

"Good," I said, licking up the side of her neck. "Me too." I pressed a quick kiss on her lips before reaching over to my bedside table and grabbing the two cream puffs I had stashed there earlier. I nibbled the top off one before turning it upside down and squeezing the cream out onto her right nipple. I grinned at her and popped the rest of the pastry into my mouth.

Charli frowned at me and mumbled, "No fair."

"Don't worry, baby. I got you," I said, repeating the action with her left nipple and holding the delicate pastry to her lips. She opened her mouth and took it, dragging her teeth and lips across my finger and thumb. "Fucking tease," I grumped, and she laughed as she chewed the flaky dessert.

I leaned down and smeared the sweet cream over her rosy nipples with my tongue before sitting up to admire my handiwork. "Beautiful," I proclaimed before deliberately sucking every bit of the cream from her tits. "Mmmm, and delicious. But I can think of something else sweet and delectable that I would like to eat even more." Her back was arched off the bed, and I smoothed my hands over the supple skin there before sliding down her body and taking the waistband of her leggings in my hands. I gave her a devious look, earning me the cutest glare ever.

"Don't even think about it," she said strictly, and I obediently slid her pants down without ripping anything.

I flipped over onto my back, taking her with me so that she was straddling my head.

"Beau. What are you doing?" She gasped, and I pulled her down onto my face, licking her with fast, sharp flicks of my tongue followed by long, curling ones against her clit.

I gave her an especially long, hard lick and grunted, "Fuck my tongue, baby."

"Beau," she said in a feeble attempt at protest as she moved her hips tentatively.

"That's it, Peach. Ride my mouth," I coaxed, gripping her slim hips and pulling her gently back and forth across my face. On every back movement, I curled my tongue upward against her clitoris, and soon she was riding my face like it was her job, her hands pressed against the wall behind the bed.

"God, yes! I'm coming, Beau," she moaned loudly as a stream of her sexy juices flooded my mouth. Fuck, she tasted like goddamn heaven.

Charli let out a little squeak when I sat up, my arms wrapping under her butt and my hands holding her upper back. I held her firmly against my face as I fed hungrily on her, and she held onto my head for dear life. "God Beau, you're the master of the oral universe," she moaned just before she exploded against my tongue once again.

She was still sobbing my name when I lowered my arms to the bed to gently lay her down, pressing soft kisses against her swollen sex. I crawled up her body and crushed my lips to hers, and she lapped herself from my mouth with her warm little tongue. "You need to fuck me. Now," she snapped, tugging at the button on my fly.

"You seem to think you're the boss here," I said with a grin, kneeling and flipping her over onto her stomach.

"I am," she said, smartly, and I popped her on the ass with the palm of my hand.

"What did you say?"

"I'm the boss," she said, smirking at me over her shoulder, and I spanked her other butt cheek, leaving a pretty red handprint on her soft flesh.

She let out a low moan as I teased her with two fingers inserted shallowly in her pussy. "This soaking wet cunt tells a different story, Peach." I heard her gasp when I pushed the fingers knuckle-deep and massaged her G-spot before pulling back out to just the tips. "Say the words if you want more, baby."

"Beau, please," she begged.

I smacked her sexy ass once more and barked, "Say it!"

"You're the boss, Beau," she panted.

"Fuck yeah, I am," I said, plunging my fingers deep while my thumb massaged her clit.

I heard Cam call out through the wall, "I don't think she learned her lesson, Shark. Spank her again."

"You are not a fucking participant, Cam. Shut the fuck up," I yelled. I leaned down to Charli and whispered, "Do you want to stop?"

"No, let him listen," she said, loud enough for my friend to hear. "Poor little Cam is over there all by himself without a woman."

"I'm about to come in there and spank you myself, Miss Smartass," Cam shot back, and Charli erupted in giggles, which quickly turned to moans when I sped up my fingers and thumb between her legs.

"Don't come yet." I worked her harder and faster until I felt her starting to clamp down on my fingers, and I pulled them out.

Charli whimpered. "Please, baby."

I stood from the bed and quickly shucked my shoes, socks, jeans, and underwear. "I'll let you come, Peach, but you're going to come on my dick while I'm buried balls deep in your hot little pussy."

"Well, hurry up," she groaned.

"You're getting bossy again, Charli," I warned.

With the sweetest voice she could muster, she purred, "Pretty please, won't you shove your gigantic cock inside me and make me come?"

"That's better," I said with a chuckle, kneeling on the bed behind her and spreading her legs wide. "Lift your hips for me, baby." She did, and I wedged a couple pillows beneath her hips to lift her tight little hole right where I wanted it. "Since you asked so nicely..." I said, sinking slowly into her wetness.

"Shit, Beau. That feels amazing."

"Hands beside your head," I commanded, and she immediately did as I asked. "Such a good girl. I'm going to fuck you so hard you'll still be coming tomorrow."

I grasped her wrists in my hands and straightened my arms, holding her down while I spread my knees for better traction. I pulled out to the tip and then slammed back into her, triggering a loud squeal from her lips. "Fuck, baby. This tight little pussy is my heaven." I pulled back and shoved into her again. Hard.

Circling my hips, I ground deeply into her until she was begging for more. I complied. Hard and fast. She came with a scream, and I pounded her through the orgasm, my hips slapping against her ass as she cried out my name.

Holding her down.

Hearing her scream for more.

Feeling her tight, wet cunt squeezing me.

All these things coalesced into a coil of pressure at the base of my spine that made me almost dizzy and tightened my testicles up against my body. "Can't hold back anymore, baby. Fuck, you feel good." I lowered my body to hers and humped against her ass with my dick buried so deeply in her that I wasn't sure if I could ever find my way out.

Charli tightened and spasmed again. "Me too, Beau," she whimpered, her fingers digging into the mattress as I sucked the sweet flesh on the back of her neck into my mouth. "God, yes! Just like that."

She rippled gloriously around my hard length, and I poured myself into her with a loud grunt as we came together. "Damn, you're beautiful when you come, Peach," I panted, kissing the side of her face over and over. "So fucking sexy."

I drug my quaking body off her and lay beside her, rubbing her back until her breathing returned to near-normal.

Charli turned her face to me and smiled softly. "Beau?"

"What is it, my gorgeous girl?" I asked, kissing her adorable nose.

She looked at me with all the seriousness in the world and said, "I need another cream puff."

I huffed out a laugh and said, "Yeah, that actually sounds pretty good right now. Come on." I patted her affectionately on the butt and rolled out of bed, tossing her my t-shirt and her panties as I pulled on a pair of pajama pants from my drawer. She quickly dressed, and we snuck down the hall to grab a couple of the tasty pastries.

I stuck an entire puff into my mouth, but Charli sunk her teeth into hers slowly, savoring every bite. Why was watching her eat so damned hot? "Mmmm, so good," she moaned. "These are almost orgasmic." Then she winked flirtily at me and whispered, "Almost."

"You're gonna make me jealous, Peach," I told her, wiping my thumb across a smear of cream on her upper lip and sucking it off.

She ate the rest of her dessert and kissed my chin. "Don't worry, baby. You're still my favorite snack."

My cock twitched to attention, and I buried my nose in her hair and inhaled. "Don't tempt me, sweetheart. We both have work tomorrow."

"Okay, bed," she said, nuzzling against my neck. I lifted her, and she wrapped her legs around me so I could carry her back to my room. I positioned myself behind her on the bed and wrapped my arm around her waist as our legs tangled together.

"I love you, Charli."

She sighed happily. "I love you, too, Beau. Even more than all the cream puffs in the world."

CHARLI

I WOKE UP SUDDENLY as a gripping pain wrenched through my abdomen. *Noooo, not yet!* I wasn't due to start my period until tomorrow. My pills kept me pretty regulated, but I occasionally started a little early. I carefully pulled Beau's arm from around me and struggled through the pain to sit up. I felt a gush between my legs and cursed inwardly.

I climbed off the bed and looked down to see a large red spot on Beau's light blue sheets. *No. No, no, no. Dammit to hell.* Another wave of pain hit me, and I doubled over, unable to stop the cry of pain. Beau's eyes opened and a frown crossed his gorgeous features. "What's wrong, sweetheart?" He spotted the blood on his sheets, and his eyes widened.

Fuck, this is mortifying.

He slid quickly to the edge of the bed and pulled my head to his shoulder, where I sobbed, "I'm sorry, Beau. My period." I tried to stand, but my body folded over again. "Let me just get your sheets in the washer. I'm so sorry," I gritted through the excruciating pain wrapping around my middle.

Beau scooped me effortlessly into his arms. "I'll do it. Let's get you into the bathroom. You're hurting, aren't you?" he asked. I looked at him, seeing only concern instead of disgust in his eyes, and nodded.

"Please let me do it. Oh, God. I'm sorry."

"Stop apologizing, Peach. For Pete's sake, it's just a little blood. I'll spray some stain remover on them and throw them in the washer." He carried me into the bathroom and set me down before turning the water on in the bathtub. Then he held my face and kissed my forehead sweetly.

When the water was ready, I climbed into the tub and wrapped my arms around my legs, pressing my forehead against my knees. I sensed Beau kneeling beside the tub even before he stroked my hair. "Hey," he said softly, and I looked up at him. "It's okay. I'll take care of you. Are your cramps always this bad?"

"Yeah, usually."

"Do you need some, uh, gear or something?" I had never heard feminine products called "gear" before, and that made me smile.

"Just put my overnight bag beside the toilet, and I'll handle it. And can you hand me a ponytail holder from the side pocket?"

"Sure. And what about some medicine?"

"Advil. Those are in my bag, too." He returned a few minutes later with the medicine and a glass of orange juice. "I have endometriosis," I blurted. "That's why my periods are so bad."

"I've heard of that, but I'm not sure exactly what it is. Just that it's some kind of female thing." He lay his hand gently across my slightly swollen lower abdomen, and the touch felt reassuring and comfortable.

"The tissue inside the uterus is called the endometrium, but with endometriosis a tissue similar to that grows outside the uterus. It causes pain during menstrual cycles," I explained.

His hand moved in soothing circles over my belly, and I relaxed against the back of the tub. "Is there anything else I can do to help? I want to take care of you."

Oh, God. He's just so fucking sweet.

"No, I'm okay," I said, leaning back against the back of the tub and closing my eyes, letting his gentle hands and the warmth of the water soothe me.

"I'm staying home from work today."

My eyes shot open to find his concerned green eyes locked on my face. "No, Beau. You don't—"

"I'm staying," he said sharply, his tone leaving no room for argument.

"Stubborn ass man," I mumbled, and he chuckled in agreement.

On Thursday morning, I woke up in my bed with Beau curled around me. He had been so sweet and protective the last two days. He had held me captive in his room after I woke up from my nap Tuesday afternoon, only letting me up to go to the bathroom. I even ate in his bed when he brought me soup, crackers, and more medicine.

I made him go to work on Wednesday, but he brought me toast and eggs in bed before he left. I had felt better by noon yesterday, so I went to work at the Broxtons', listening happily as the triplets talked all over each other, trying to tell me about their trip to the Dallas World Aquarium.

I felt kisses along my shoulder and closed my eyes. "Good morning, Peach," Beau said, dropping his hand to my belly, which wasn't nearly as bloated today. "How are you feeling this morning?"

"Perfectly fine," I said, turning in his arms and nestling my face in his sexy chest. "Especially since I'm waking up with you."

"Mmmmm, my favorite part of the day," he said. I loved the way his chest rumbled deep and low in the mornings. Beau's hand slid up the back of my t-shirt, and he asked, "Do you need a back rub?"

"What self-respecting woman would turn down an offer like that?" I asked, rolling over to my belly as Beau rose up and straddled my hips. He pushed my shirt up around my neck and started massaging me with his big, strong hands. "Damn, that feels good," I said on a low groan.

He dug his thumbs into my lower back, and I let out a long moan of pure bliss. He leaned down to whisper in my ear, "You need to stop all that sexy fucking moaning, or I'm going to come all over your back, sweetheart." Beau was wearing only his boxer briefs, and his erection was pressing heavily against my ass.

"Maybe I could take care of that for you," I said seductively, reaching behind me and rubbing my hand up and down his leg.

"You... what... you can do that? Like while you're..."

I giggled as he stammered. "The south entrance may be closed for business right now, but the north entrance is open," I said, pulling his hand up to my mouth and sucking one thick finger deeply into my mouth.

"Damn, baby," he growled as his dick twitched against my bottom. The door creaked open, and Beau scrambled off my back and leaned against the headboard, pulling the sheet up to cover his lap.

Carrie popped into my room like a beam of sunshine and gasped with delight. "Uncle Beau! What are you doing here?"

His hand was rubbing leisurely up and down my back. "Charli's back was hurting, so I came over to rub it for her."

"Does that feel good, Charli?" the little girl asked innocently, climbing onto the bed and sitting beside me in her little kitty cat pajamas.

Fuck.

"Oh, um, yes. It's very nice. Uncle Beau is an excellent masseuse."

"My daddy is too. I went into their room in the middle of the night last week, and Mommy was saying, 'Oh, Axel. That feels sooooo good.' When he saw me, he told me he was giving her a nice massage."

I buried my face in my pillow to muffle my laughter, and Beau patted me softly on the back. "That's... great," he croaked out.

"Daddy had his shirt off, just like you, Uncle Beau. Do you have to take your shirt off when you're massaging someone?" she asked curiously, and I bit the pillow to stave off the giggles that were trying to escape. I finally got myself under control and turned my head to look at Beau's reaction.

He was biting his bottom lip and breathing through his nose. "Well," he said, his voice carefully measured, "it helps. So the shirt doesn't, uhhh, restrict the arm muscles during the, ah, massage." He flexed his arms and said, "See? Check out these guns, Care Bear. No shirt could contain them."

She giggled and punched his big bicep with her tiny fist. "Ow! Watch out there, Rocky," he said with a fake wince. He pulled my shirt down and patted my back chastely. "Okay, I think you're good to go for the day, Charli. Call me if your back starts acting up again, and I'll come right over and take care of it."

"You're a treasure, Beau Atwood," I said with a sly grin before turning my head to Carrie. "Why don't you go get dressed for school, and I'll start breakfast."

"Okay! Can Uncle Beau stay for breakfast, too?"

"Sure he can. Now run upstairs and get your clothes on." I rolled over and sat up against the headboard as Carrie climbed off the bed. She turned back to us and put her hands on her little hips, looking back and forth between us. "Are you two boyfriend and girlfriend now?" she asked seriously.

I felt Beau glance at me before he beckoned the little girl to his side of the bed. He lifted her and set her on her knees right between us. "We are, Carrie. What do you think about me and Charli dating?" he asked warily.

A wide grin split her precious little face. "It makes me feel happy," she said, wrapping an arm around each of our necks for a sweet group hug. "You're my favorite two people in the whole wide world. Besides Mommy and Daddy, of course."

Oh, this kid...

I looped an arm around her waist and snuggled my cheek against hers as Beau put a hand on the back of her head, stroking her messy, bedhead curls. He kissed her forehead, and with a voice thick with emotion, he said, "You're our favorite, too, baby girl."

She sat back and fisted her hands on her hips. "I'm not a baby, Uncle Beau."

"I don't care how old you are. You'll always be my baby girl," he said, poking her in the ribs and making her giggle. "Now skedaddle before I tickle the pee out of you." She squealed and scampered off the bed just as Blaire came through the open door.

Taking in the scene, she said, "Carrie Lexa Broxton, what are you doing in here?"

Carrie's eyes widened at hearing her full name being called. "I was just coming to say good morning to Charli, and Uncle Beau was here. He came over to give Charli a back rub like Daddy gave you that night." Blaire's mouth dropped open.

"Well, not *exactly* like that," Beau said dryly as his sister blushed.

"Yeah, but Uncle Beau keeps his underpants *on* when he's doing massages," Carrie said matter-of-factly, and I had to stick a pillow over my face to muffle my laughter.

"Upstairs, missy," Blaire said, and Carrie dragged herself from the room. When the kid was headed upstairs, my boss turned back and said in a low voice, "Sorry, guys. Perhaps all of us need to be more conscientious about locking our bedroom doors during *massages*." A smirk played across her face as she turned and left the room.

"It really was just a back rub," Beau called out as the door closed, and we could hear Blaire laughing as she went down the hall.

"Well, that was humiliating in so many ways I can't even count them," I said, getting off the bed and heading to the bathroom to get ready for breakfast, which was always a raucous affair in the Broxton household.

We managed to make it through the meal with only one spilled orange juice and a minimum of food in anyone's hair. Plus, I had my handsome man right beside me, and he couldn't seem to keep his eyes off me.

What a way to start my day.

CHARLI

A WEEK LATER, I was in my bathroom fastening a silver clip into my hair when Beau called out from the bedroom, "So, what are your plans for the day?"

"I'm going to get dressed and then get my day started. Elizabeth is picking me up this afternoon."

"Is your mom going shopping with y'all?"

"No, she said she wants me and my sister to have some time together. We're picking her up for dinner, though. You're meeting us at Matt's this evening, right?" I anxiously peeked my head back into the bedroom.

Tonight was the night Beau was meeting my sister and brothers, and I would be lying if I said I wasn't a little bit nervous. I really wanted them to like each other, but my brothers could be... difficult. We were supposed to meet at a local barbecue restaurant called Matt's Meat House. Everyone was happier while eating BBQ, right?

"Of course, baby. I wouldn't miss getting to meet the rest of your family." He was sitting on the edge of the bed and sounded a little anxious as well. I decided to put my newfound sashaying skills to the test to distract him and strolled back into the room topless.

I boldly straddled his lap and said, "I love you, so they'll love you, too." *I hope.*

"Love you, too, sweetheart," he said, circling my nipple with his nose and then kissing each peak softly. "As much as I'd rather stay here and nibble on you all day, I really need to get to work."

On his way out the door, Beau kissed me goodbye and said, "Don't forget to buy yourself something when you're shopping with your sister today. Something fun that makes you smile."

"You make me smile," I said.

"Well, I'm way too expensive for you to afford, Peachy," he teased as he walked out the door.

God, I love that man.

I slung open the front door to find my sister standing on the Broxtons' massive porch. "Lizzy!" I squealed, and Elizabeth wrapped me in a huge hug.

"Oh, Charli baby! It's so good to see you!" I pulled her into the house and closed the door as she looked around. "Damn, this place is massive." She strolled into the living room where children's books were scattered on the coffee table and one of Dani's baby blankets was draped across the arm of the couch. "But not stuffy at all."

I smiled. "Yes, the Broxtons are super wealthy, but so down-to-earth. I love it here." Just then a herd of elephants came down the stairs, and we turned to see our mother following the triplets into the living room. Excited to see a new person in their house, they surrounded Elizabeth with eager eyes until she squatted down to meet them. "This is Rox, Max, and Dex," I introduced, laying my hand on each of their little heads in turn. "Boys, this is my sister, Elizabeth."

"Izabuff?" Max tried, and my sister laughed.

"You can call me Lizzy."

"Wizzy," Rox said.

"Close enough," Elizabeth said with a grin, giving the boys hugs before standing and being engulfed by our mom.

"Oh, my sweet Elizabeth." She covered my sister in kisses. "I've missed you so much."

"I've missed you, too, Mom." Lizzy let my mom fawn all over her and drag her to the couch in the living room. We sat and talked for a while before Axel walked through the front door, and Elizabeth's mouth dropped open. "Holy shit," she mouthed to me.

The boys attacked their dad, and he rolled around on the floor with them as Lizzy murmured, "Dear Lord, my ovaries are freaking out right now." I stifled my laugh and had to admit that my boss was a very good-looking man.

"Simmer down, sis. He's *so* taken," I whispered.

"My brain knows that, but my eyes don't," she said with a snicker, never taking her eyes from Axel.

"Girls, hush!" my mom hissed, giving us a disapproving look.

"Hey, it's not me. I've got my own hottie."

"Yes, let's talk about that, shall we?" Lizzy said, turning her sharp eyes on me. "Mom said you're dating a man? Our brothers are *not* pleased."

"We'll talk about it later," I said under my breath, scowling at her. "And it's none of their business."

My sister rolled her eyes in such a dramatic fashion that I was afraid they would stick like that. "Oh, come on. Have you met our brothers?"

Her attention was diverted as Axel pushed himself gracefully from the floor and walked over to the couch. "Hey, I'm guessing you're Charli's beautiful younger sister?"

Lizzy stood and said something that sounded like, "Flubbaguh," her eyes locked on Axel's handsome face.

"This is my sister, Elizabeth, Lizzy for short," I said, trying to suppress my grin. "Lizzy, this is Axel Broxton."

My sister finally untied her tongue and said, "Mr. Broxton, I'm a huge fan." She extended her slim hand for a shake.

"Please, call me Axel. We're practically family now," he said, grabbing her hand and pulling Lizzy in for a hug and a kiss on the cheek, at which point my sister almost fainted.

I took Lizzy by the shoulders and said, "Okay, maybe that's enough excitement for now. Why don't we head out for our shopping trip?"

After visiting the salon and three stores, we settled into overstuffed chairs at a local coffee shop with hot caramel macchiatos. "So, tell me about this new guy in your life."

"Well, what did Mom tell you?"

"Just that you were dating a man named Beau and she liked him a lot."

"She adores him, and I do too. He's sooooo dreamy, Lizzy. He treats me like a princess, and he's all gruff and protective."

"Mmmm, gruff is hot. What does he look like?"

I pulled up my pictures on my phone, and my sister's mouth dropped open. "That's it. I'm fucking moving to Dallas. You live in the house with Axel friggin' Broxton, and you're dating this hunk? Jesus, have mercy, little sis."

I laughed. "Yeah, he's the hottest man I've ever met. I have no idea what he's doing with me."

"Oh, whatever! You are flipping gorgeous, Charli. Have you... you know..." She wiggled her eyebrows up and down, and I pressed my lips together and nodded. "And?"

"He knows what he's doing. That's all I'm going to say."

She held her hand over her chest and groaned, "Oh, give me strength. I love a man who knows what to do with a woman. And this one looks like he would be all alpha and dominant."

"He is. But he can be really sweet, too. Did Mom tell you he's Blaire's brother?"

"No! Are you serious? So, you're dating your boss's brother?"

"Yep. And Blaire loves us together. She even helped me with my hair and outfit for our first date, and oh my God, Lizzy. She gave me a pair of YSL heels that were too small for her. They are to die for."

"Hot guys and designer shoes? Tell me again why I'm a teacher instead of a nanny."

"Because you love it," I said, squeezing her arm. "And you're so good at it."

"Yeah, I do, and I am," she said. "Hey, we'd better get a move on and pick Mom up for dinner. Are you nervous about the guys meeting Beau?"

"A little," I admitted. "They still think of me as a kid, even though I'm approaching thirty. Let's try to get there early so maybe I can beg the bros to be nice."

"Good idea."

Twenty minutes later we had Mom in the backseat, and we were stuck in gridlock traffic. I was doing my very best not to drop F-bombs in front of my mother. Beau was going to be so pissed.

BEAU

I walked into Matt's Meat House and looked around the dining room for Peach. I didn't see her, but I recognized her three brothers from pictures she had shown me. They were all sitting on one side of a long table. Henry, Ethan, and Justin, from left to right, sitting there like blonde guardian gargoyles just waiting to pounce.

Okay, I can do this. Peach will be here in a couple of minutes. I wasn't physically intimidated by her brothers, even though they outnumbered me three to one; I just wanted to get along with them. My eyes moved over them, assessing, gauging. Justin and Ethan were a little shorter than me, but Henry was about my height. All three of them seemed to be in good physical shape, though none of them had the muscle mass that I did.

Just be nice. Don't be your usual grumpy asshole self.

Pasting on a smile, I strode confidently to their table and stood across from the men, sticking out my hand to Ethan in the middle. "Hi. I'm Beau Atwood. I'm guessing you're Charli's brothers?"

They stood as one as if it was choreographed, and each of them shook my hand, squeezing entirely too tightly to be polite, though I didn't flinch a bit. I could have easily broken the majority of the bones in their hands without even trying, but I merely kept my grip firm and steady.

They stood until I was done shaking hands with all of them and then sat all at once, none of them speaking a single word. *Did they practice standing and sitting in unison?* I was tempted to ask, but *no*, I was going to be the mature one here and not a smartass.

"You guys doing okay?" I asked as I sat down in the chair across from the middle brother.

Ethan sat back with his arms crossed over his chest, Justin rested an elbow on the table and curved his index finger over his lips, and Henry sat forward with his hands clasped on the table. The latter at least looked like he was interested in talking to me, though none of them spoke. *So, this is how they're going to play it? Alrighty then.*

I had struggled with what to wear tonight, my first inclination being to wear a dress shirt and slacks to meet the family, but we were eating barbecue, and that would have looked like I was trying too hard. I had settled on nice jeans and a navy blue polo with a gray Northface jacket. I unhurriedly removed my jacket and hung it on the back of my chair before leaning forward and resting my arms on the table, showing off my muscled biceps and thick forearms.

Ethan's eyes dropped to my arms before returning to my own, and I thought he almost raised his eyebrows. I wanted to get along with Charli's brothers, but I also wanted them to know they weren't dealing with some pansy ass.

"So, you're going with the silent intimidation tactic?" I asked, pursing my lips and bobbing my head in a slow nod of approval. "I've had pretty good results with that, but to really sell it, you need to have a good glare. Yours isn't bad," I said, pointing at Ethan. Looking at Justin, I said, "It's much more effective if you push your eyebrows together really hard. Touch that spot just between your eyebrows," I said, demonstrating. "If it doesn't feel spongy, you need to frown a little harder."

Justin actually raised his finger and pushed the area I indicated until Ethan shot him a look, and his hand immediately dropped to the table. "You can practice it at home in front of the mirror," I said, and Henry snorted, covering the sound with a fake cough. "If you're not going to introduce yourselves, can I call you Huey, Dewey, and Louie?"

So much for not being a smartass.

Henry raised his clasped hands to his mouth to cover what I was sure was a smile, and I was positive I saw Justin's lips twitch underneath his finger. I grinned winningly. "I'm kidding, guys. You're Ethan, Justin, and Henry, right?" I asked, pointing at each of them and purposely getting their names mixed up. It was an old interrogation trick. Act like you knew something but get it slightly wrong.

Most people couldn't help but correct you because it was human nature to want to be right. It worked.

These guys had no fucking idea who they were messing with.

Ethan let out a long sigh as if it was just so much trouble to tell me their names. "I'm Ethan. Justin. Henry." He jerked a thumb at each of his brothers.

"Very nice to meet y'all," I said politely. "Just to let you know, I have a little sister, so I know exactly where you're coming from. You want to make sure Charli's safe and secure and happy, right?" I saw Justin nod once in agreement. I held my palms up and said, "So, what would you like to know?"

Henry dropped his hands back to the table and finally spoke. "What do you do, Beau?"

"I'm in private security."

"So, you're like a mall cop or something?" Ethan sneered. My phone rang before I could correct him, and I held up one finger before pulling out my phone and seeing that it was Charli calling.

"Hey, Charli."

"Beau, oh my God. We are stuck in traffic on 635. Are you at the restaurant yet?"

"Yeah, I'm here with your brothers, sweetheart."

"Shit. I'm so sorry. I was trying to get there before you to tell them to be nice. Are they?"

"Of course, Peach. We're getting along *just fine*," I said, giving each of them a long look, and they managed to look chagrined. "Be safe and don't rush, okay? We're not in any hurry."

Please hurry the fuck up!

"We'll be safe. I promise."

We disconnected, and I turned back to her brothers, who I was apparently stuck with until traffic cleared up a bit. "The ladies are stuck in traffic," I announced. "I guess we have a little more time to talk until they get here."

"How old are you?" Justin asked, speaking for the first time.

"I'm thirty-four."

Justin's eyebrows shot up, and Ethan's nostrils flared. *Dammit. They think I'm too old for their sister.*

"Have you ever been married? Do you have children?" Ethan asked.

"No to both."

"Ever been engaged?"

"Nope."

"And how many serious relationships have you been in?"

"Including Charli, one." Justin's eyebrows were now in the stratosphere, and Ethan looked like he was about to chip a tooth from gritting his teeth so hard. Yep, I was definitely raising some red flags with these guys. I didn't really like to put my private business out there, but I understood where they were coming from.

Here goes... "I took care of my little sister after our parents died. She was in high school, and she was my priority until she graduated from college." All of their faces softened a little bit. "Then she got pregnant, and I moved her to California with me because I was stationed there. I wanted her near me so I could help her with the baby while she continued her education." Henry was nodding. "She's been happily married for a few years now, but I've never found a woman I wanted to get serious with. Until Charli."

"So, you would classify your relationship with our sister as 'serious?'" Justin asked.

"Yes. I'm very serious about your sister, Justin," I said honestly, and he kind of frowned and smiled at the same time, evidencing his mixed feelings about that.

Henry spoke up. "You said you were stationed in Cali. Are you in the military?"

"Retired from the navy."

"What did you do in the navy?"

"SEAL team," I said shortly. Six eyebrows raised, and I tried not to smile. "I can tell by your responses that you know what that means, so you're probably realizing by now that I'm not easily intimidated."

A waitress stopped by the table and said, "I know you're waiting for the rest of your party, but can I go ahead and get you gentlemen some drinks?" Henry and Justin ordered beers, but Ethan asked for a Dr. Pepper. I could have really used a beer, but I settled on unsweet tea, because I wanted to keep my mind clear for the rest of this conversation.

As soon as the waitress dropped off our drinks, the interrogation continued. "Have you ever been arrested?" Henry asked, and I smirked.

"No."

"What about drinking and drugs?" Justin asked.

"I've never touched drugs in my life, not even marijuana. I drink occasionally, but I always call a cab or an Uber if I'm out somewhere when I'm drinking."

Ethan leaned across the table and asked quietly, "Are you fucking my sister?"

Oh, no the fuck he didn't.

I leaned across the table as well, until we were practically nose-to-nose. "I don't see where that's any of your goddamn business, since Charli is a grown-ass woman," I growled.

"Stay the fuck away from her."

"No," I said flatly but firmly. Ethan and I stared each other down for what seemed like an hour before I felt soft hands cover my eyes.

"Guess who?" I recognized the voice and the perfume. *Blaire.* I stretched one hand up behind me and felt my sister's head and face, making sure to muss her hair as much as possible.

"Ummmm, Danny DeVito?"

"You jackass!" she said, smacking me on the top of my head before settling in the seat beside me. We exchanged cheek kisses before she grabbed my glass and took a big drink, wrinkling her nose at the taste. "How do you drink this shit with no sugar?" She poured two packets of sugar into *my* tea glass and stirred it around before drinking some more. "Mmmm, that's better."

"By all means, help yourself to my tea," I said flatly.

"Shut up. I'm thirsty from carrying this fat baby around." She had Danica strapped to her front in one of those baby carrier things.

"Don't call my girl fat," I protested, taking Dani out of the carrier and settling her in the crook of my arm. Charli's brothers were looking at me in confusion and a large vein was pulsing in Ethan's temple, so I made the introductions. "Guys, this is my sister, Dr. Blaire Broxton. And this little sweetheart is my niece, Danica." I turned to my sister. "These are Charli's brothers, Henry, Ethan, and Justin."

They all stood and greeted Blaire warmly, and I noticed they were much more polite to my beautiful sister than they had been to me. All of a sudden, it was like a light bulb went off over Henry's head.

"So Blaire, you're married to Axel Broxton?"

"Yep. That's my man. He's got the other heathens next door at the toy store. They should be here any minute. I came in to get us a table." Blaire rested her chin in her hand, her eyes sparkling, and said, "Is this some kind of brotherly inquisition? Are there lots of awkward questions and snarling? Can I watch?" The men seemed taken aback by her eagerness to have them pummel me with questions—and possibly their fists—so she graciously explained. "He used to scare the shit out of any boy that showed the tiniest bit of interest in me. The glaring, and oh my goodness, the damned growling!" She waved her hand impatiently and batted her eyelashes at the guys across the table. "Please continue."

But her fun was interrupted when Axel made his appearance with the other four children in tow. Blaire scowled at the massive number of toy store bags in his hands. "What did you do, Broxton?"

"They were being cute. I couldn't help it," he said sheepishly, leaning down to kiss his wife.

"You're a damn sucker," she said.

"Swear bank, Mommy!" Carrie said loudly, and my sister dug a dollar out of her purse and handed it to Carrie, the anti-cursing enforcer in the family.

"You have a swear *bank?*" Ethan asked, looking amused.

"Yeah," Axel sighed. "A swear *jar* just isn't big enough for my wife's mouth. So far we have enough money in the swear bank to send all five kids to college with approximately one point seven million dollars left over."

The three guys howled with laughter, and I had never been happier to see my pain in the ass brother-in-law in my life. Blaire shot him a look and muttered, "Asshole," under her breath.

"I heard that," Carrie said, and Blaire stuck another dollar in her direction without even breaking the glare directed at her husband.

"Blaire, honey, we should probably get a table and let the boys run off some of their energy in the play area," Axel said. The restaurant had an awesome play area right near our table, complete with a giant Jenga game and a life-sized Candyland game board on the floor.

"Why can't we sit with Uncle Beau?" Carrie whined.

"I think they're having a family dinner, sweetie," Blaire explained.

Henry, clearly enamored of Axel, jumped up excitedly. "No, please join us. Let's just pull that other table over." He and Axel lifted another table and scooted it over next to the one we were occupying.

After placing their drink orders, Axel took Carrie and the triplets to the play area, and Blaire took Dani for a diaper change, leaving me alone once again with Charli's brothers.

"Guys, I just want you all to know that I really do understand where you're coming from. If my sister had been treated like that fucker Hayden treated Charli, I would be wary of any man she was with." I shook my head roughly as I darted my eyes toward the play area.

There was a long pause before Ethan said through gritted teeth, "Exactly how did he treat our sister?"

Oh. Holy. Fuck. Charli hadn't told her brothers how Hayden had treated her? *Way to open your big, fat mouth, Atwood.*

"Uh, maybe you should talk to Charli about that," I hedged.

"We're talking to *you* asswipe," Justin said gruffly. "Spill."

"Fuck, I thought you knew," I muttered, turning my face to see Carrie leading her brothers through the Candyland game. "I don't know the specifics," I said honestly. "She doesn't tell me much, but a couple little things have slipped out that concerned me. I know the prick was was fucking controlling. What she could eat, what she could spend. Shit like that."

Three sets of eyes widened, and Henry muttered, "That fucker. We never did like him."

"Oh, God," Justin whispered, pressing his fist over his mouth as if he were about to be violently ill.

Jesus, I couldn't imagine how they were feeling. If anyone had ever done that to Blaire... I thanked my lucky stars just then for Axel Broxton. He may pluck my last nerve sometimes, but I knew that my sister and her kids were safe with him. He fucking adored them.

"They lived so far away. We never knew," Ethan said, his eyes hollow, and I nodded sympathetically.

"How could he control her like that without us knowing?" Henry asked, his brow furrowed.

"Like Ethan said, they lived in another state. It's not your fault at all. Men like him are manipulative, but I'm taking steps to make sure she's safe from him."

"What steps?" Ethan asked, leaning forward.

"Of course, I've investigated him. I have his face memorized," I said, tapping my temple. "If he ever shows up around here, I will recognize him."

"And then what?"

"Let's just say he would be safer wearing pork chop underwear while sandpapering a lion's ass than to come anywhere near Charli." All three men chuckled.

Ethan drew in a deep breath and said, "I'm still not sure about you, Atwood, but I do feel better knowing that you can protect Charli."

"And I would. With my life," I said honestly, looking the big man in the eye, and he nodded.

A couple minutes after Blaire returned to the table, my heartbeat picked up a notch, and I turned my head and saw Peach wending her way through the tables.

I stayed seated as Charli's brothers stood and greeted her, though it took a lot for me not to jump right up and grab her. But I had just seen her this morning, and her brothers hadn't seen her in almost a year. They hugged and squeezed her, and she cried as she kissed each of them. I'm pretty sure I even saw Henry swipe a few tears from his face with his palm, and Ethan flashed the most genuine smile I had seen from him since I met him.

While they were having their reunion, Ms. Casper introduced me and Blaire to her other daughter. "Lizzy, it's so nice to meet you," I said, rising and kissing her cheek.

"You're even hotter in person," she said, looking me up and down, and then she clapped her hand over her mouth, her eyes widening. "Shit, did I say that out loud? I'm so sorry."

I laughed good-naturedly. "It's okay. That's the best thing I've been called all day."

"The bros giving you a hard time?" she asked sympathetically.

"Nothing I can't handle," I said with a grin. "And Henry almost smiled at me. I think he might be in love with Axel, though."

"Who wouldn't be?" she quipped and then pressed her hand over her mouth again. "Dammit, I must be high on all the testosterone floating around the room."

I liked this woman. "The genes are strong in your family. You look just like a tall Charli." Lizzy's facial features were remarkably similar to my girlfriend's, though Charli had a bit more sweetness in her face. And Elizabeth was five or six inches taller.

"Actually, I'm older, so she looks like a short me," she said with a smirk. "Our dad always said he and mom ran out of material by the time they got to Charli, and that's why she's so much smaller than the rest of us."

"Charli's told me a lot about him, and he sounds like he was a wonderful and funny man. I wish I could have met him," I said, taking her hand.

She squeezed and said, "Thank you for saying that."

"Hey sis, find your own man," came the sweetest voice from behind me, and I turned to find my Peach walking around the table toward me. She bounced once and then she was in my arms. And damn, did it feel good.

I lifted her to my eye level and bent to her ear. "I would like my proper greeting, Peach."

"Would you also like to be involved in a brawl with my brothers in the middle of this restaurant because they saw me wrap my legs around you?" she whispered back.

I drug my nose across her cheek, inhaling her, until it rested against hers. "Okay, but you owe me," I said with a grin, which she returned. We stared happily at each other until I couldn't stand it anymore. My lips pressed against hers in a series of slow, soft pecks. I could have kissed her like that all night, but someone cleared their throat, and Charli pulled back, her cheeks flushing.

That's when I noticed her hair. She had gotten a couple inches cut off, though it still reached the middle of her back. But she had also gotten some slightly darker blonde streaks done, and it set off her gorgeous eyes even more than usual. I ran my hand through it, and it felt like fine silk. I wanted to feel it on various parts of my body that I really shouldn't be thinking about in the middle of a crowded restaurant.

"Your hair..."

"Do you like it?" she asked, worry tinting her voice.

"I love it, Peach. It's beautiful. You're beautiful." She smiled gently at me, and I kissed her lips once more before letting her slide down my body. There was more throat clearing from the table, and I turned to see Ethan glaring at me like I had just bent his sister over the table and had my way with her. Justin's eyes darted back and forth speculatively between me and Charli, and the edges of Henry's lips curved up just the tiniest bit.

Henry is definitely my favorite brother.

I pulled out the chair beside mine, and Charli sat, frowning at Ethan. "Oh, calm down, Eeth. It was just a couple kisses." He made a disapproving sound and averted his eyes as Justin put his hand on his shoulder and squeezed.

I felt a million times better now that Peach was here.

33

CHARLI

"Here, Peach. You eat the last piece of brisket," Beau said, sliding the smokey meat toward me. We had split Matt's Monster Meat Platter, and I was proud to say that I had done my part in helping Beau polish off almost every bit of the brisket, ribs, and sausage.

Our table was a hub of activity with me, Beau, my family, and the entire Broxton clan laughing and talking loudly. Ethan was being a big fat grump, but other than that, we were having a blast. Henry was enamored with Axel, and the two of them talked football the entire time.

"I really wish you could all stay longer," my mother said gloomily.

"We've got to get back because Henry's team has a playoff game tomorrow night," Justin said.

"Yeah, we're playing in Allen, which is up this direction, but I have to get home and ride the bus with the team," Henry explained. My middle brother was the head football coach for a large high school in Waco.

"Wait! You're playing in the Dallas area, and you didn't tell me?" I almost shrieked.

"That's only about an hour away from us," Beau said speculatively. "We could go, if you want. I've heard that stadium is the shit."

"Swear bank!" Carrie yelled from the other side of me, and her uncle dug his wallet out of his pocket and handed her a dollar. "Can I go to the football game with you, Uncle Beau?"

"Sure, you little moocher," he said affectionately before turning to Blaire. "Charli and I are taking her fishing Saturday morning, so she can just stay at my house after the game Friday night. That okay?"

"Heck yes. Take all of my children, if you want," she said, forking up a bite of potato salad.

"You really want to come to our game?" Henry asked Beau incredulously.

"Of course. You're Charli's brother," Beau answered.

"Well, that doesn't concern you," Ethan uttered, and I shot him a glare. "Just saying," he mumbled.

"If it makes Charli happy, it concerns me," Beau said mildly. I was proud of him for not taking the bait offered up by my oldest brother, who was honestly starting to annoy the piss out of me.

Carrie turned her attention to Henry. "What kind of offense do you run?"

Henry appeared confused at having to explain football to an eight-year-old girl. "Uh, a pretty balanced approach. We have one of the best tailbacks in the state, so we rely on him a lot, but we also have some great receivers."

The little girl nodded wisely. "And what about your quarterback? Is he a pocket passer, or can he scramble?"

Looking amused, Henry said, "He can scramble. He has over a thousand yards passing this year and about seven hundred rushing."

"That's pretty good. Is he a smart player?"

I could tell my brother was fighting a smile. "Very smart."

"Good," Carrie said approvingly, her curls bouncing as she nodded her head. "You want someone who can read the defense and change the play at the line when necessary."

Henry chuckled. "You ever thought of being a football coach when you grow up, Carrie?"

"Sure. Or I might be a doctor like my mommy." She beamed a smile up at Axel. "Daddy said I could be whatever I want." Axel stroked her hair affectionately.

"Your daddy is a smart man. I would hire you," Henry said with a grin.

Beau looked down the table and said teasingly, "Ms. Casper, I brought the Thunderbird tonight, if you want to ride to the house with me and Charli."

My mom flushed with excitement. "I would love to, Beau. Thank you for asking. If I weren't so full, I would insist on stopping for milkshakes." My boyfriend chuckled. I loved that he and my mom got along so well. My sister seemed to adore him, too. Hell, women of all ages were mesmerized by Beau Atwood. Now, I just needed to get my brothers on board.

Henry seemed to be the most amenable to my relationship with Beau, but the jury was still out on Justin. Ethan was going to be the real test. He had barely spoken the entire meal, except to throw verbal jabs at my boyfriend.

"What kind of T-bird do you have, Beau?" Justin asked. He was the 'car guy' out of all my brothers, so maybe this was a good thing.

"Swap seats with me, Jus, and y'all can talk about it," I said, imploring him with my eyes. We traded seats so that I was right beside Ethan. While Justin and Beau discussed engines and paint and interior, I leaned close to my oldest brother, bumping my shoulder against his arm. "You okay?"

He crossed his arms defiantly over his chest, keeping his eyes on Beau. "Not really. I don't like him."

"What is it that you don't like?" My stubborn ass brother simply shrugged. "Well, that's a compelling reason," I said sarcastically, earning me a smirk.

He kept his voice low. "He's old."

"He's younger than you," I shot back, making him pause.

"It worries me that he's never been in a serious relationship, Charli."

I nodded because that was a fair point. "True. But does that mean he should never be allowed to have a relationship?"

"So, you're going to let him practice on you? Then what?"

"Then we see how it goes. That's how relationships work, Ethan."

He let out a long-suffering sigh. "I didn't like Hayden. He kept you away from us, and now you're jumping right back into a relationship."

"Trust me, Beau is the farthest from Hayden I could get. I know I didn't tell you much about our relationship because I was embarrassed, but... he wasn't very nice," I said on an exhale. Ethan looked at me for the first time during this conversation, uncrossing his arms and twisting his body toward mine to give me his full attention. "I won't ever be that stupid again."

"You're not stupid, sweetheart," he said, tucking a strand of hair behind my ear. "You're the smartest person I know. You have so many brilliant ideas and dreams."

"And Beau supports them. He supports *me*. I've never been with a man who believed in me before." Ethan scowled insolently, and I grew even more frustrated. "Do you want me to be alone forever, Ethan? Would that make you happy?"

His eyes widened just before his entire face softened, and he pulled my head to his chest, kissing the top of my head. "No, baby sister. That's not what I want at all. I want you to be with someone who makes you happy and treats you like you deserve to be treated." He blew out a frustrated breath before continuing. "I've watched you together, and he barely takes his eyes off you for two seconds. He seems to want to... take care of you. I know you're all grown up and don't need someone to take care of you, not physically anyway. But it's like he centers himself around you."

He frowned angrily, prompting me to ask, "And why is that a bad thing?"

"It's not. I'm just pissed because I'm trying really hard not to like the guy."

That made me giggle as I looked up at him. "I love you, my stubborn ass brother."

"Love you, too, baby sis," he rumbled gruffly, kissing my forehead.

"So, you'll try? For me?"

"For you," he agreed. "But I'm still going to give him shit every chance I get."

"I would expect nothing less."

Ethan released me and leaned across the table, growling, "Atwood. Outside. Now." Beau eyed him, his jaw tightening before his eyes flashed to me in a look that said, *I'm sorry, but I'm about to fight your brother in the parking lot.* Then Ethan's lips tipped up on one side. "Show us this car you've been going on about."

Thank you, Ethan.

Blaire insisted that my siblings come back to their house for a while after dinner. Ethan hesitated but finally relented. Henry had no problem accepting because he would get to spend more time with Axel, and I was pretty sure my brother was developing a bro crush on my boss. Justin was all in when Beau said he could ride to the house in the T-bird.

"I'll call the security gate and tell them we're expecting guests, so just give them my name when you arrive," Axel said, giving Ethan the address as we all headed toward our vehicles. Beau helped Mom into the front seat, and Justin and I climbed into the back of the vintage muscle car. By the time we arrived at the Broxtons', Justin was firmly on Team Beau. Not only did he have a cool ass car, but he treated my mother with the utmost respect.

Blaire, Axel, and Beau quickly wrangled the triplets and Danica through their nighttime routines while Mom and I visited with my siblings, and then they joined us. "Beau's friend, Bode, sent over a chocolate cake that's to die for. I'll make some coffee to go with it," Blaire announced to the room before heading to the kitchen. She came back a short time later, and we all stuffed our already-full bellies with dessert and coffee.

Carrie was allowed to stay up a little later than the younger kids, and she was perched in Lizzy's lap, discussing children's books. When Blaire told her it was time to go to bed, my sister offered to take her up and let Carrie read to her. Lizzy, being an elementary school teacher, was a huge advocate of reading, and I was sure she would be impressed with Carrie. "You're going to love my book collection, Ms. Lizzy," she said, dragging her toward the stairs.

"It's more like a mini-library," Axel said with a laugh just as the doorbell rang. "I'll get it," he said, pulling himself from the recliner and heading toward the door. A few seconds later, he popped his head in the living room and said, "Charli, it's for you."

I pushed myself off the couch and headed to the massive foyer, wondering who in the world would be at the door for me at nine o'clock at night. I pulled open the partially open door and froze.

No.

It couldn't be.

"H-Hay-Hayden," I stammered, my heart hammering against my chest as I stepped onto the porch and closed the door behind me.

"Hello, Charli." He smiled, his hands in his jacket pockets.

I looked Hayden over carefully. He appeared to be sober. There were none of the usual signs. Red eyes. Raised voice. Questionable balance.

I straightened my shoulders and lifted my chin. "How did you find me, Hayden?"

His unassuming smile faded into something dark, like a shadow of hatefulness fell over his face. "Are you fucking that Broxton guy?" he snapped.

"No, Hayden. That's my boss, and I'm not fucking him. Now answer my question." I was impressed with myself. My voice sounded strong and imperious. I didn't feel like that on the inside, but at least I was putting on a good show on the outside.

Keep your chin up, Char. Do not appear weak or meek. He'll only feed on it.

"You used our Uber account to and from this address last weekend. I knew your mom worked for the Broxtons, so I figured this fancy neighborhood must be theirs. I gave their name at the security gate, and they let me right through."

Shit, I hadn't even thought about that.

"What do you want, Hayden?" I asked insolently.

"You left without a word, sweetheart, and I think I deserve an explanation," he cooed with false sweetness, his hand reaching out to brush my hair back over my shoulder.

"I left you because you're an asshole," I spat, wrenching away from his touch, and Hayden's eyes narrowed dangerously before he schooled his face into a placid mask once again.

"I'm afraid I don't understand, sweetheart. I thought we were planning to get married and start our lives together."

Jesus, could he be more clueless? Keeping my voice low, I said, "Hayden, I left because I was tired of being controlled. Food, money, my career, who I talked to. You controlled every aspect of my life, and I couldn't live like that anymore. And then you hit me, and that was the last straw."

He ran a frustrated hand through his hair. "You know how I get when I drink, Charli, but I'm doing better now. I haven't been drinking as much, even though I've been stressed out since you left me. I wanted..." He sighed heavily. "I want you back, Charli. I promise I'll be better. It's almost Thanksgiving, and you should be with me." He took a step toward me and rubbed a hand up and down my arm. It gave me chill bumps, and not in a good way.

"I don't want to be with you anymore, Hayden, and I really need you to leave now."

"But I came all this way," he said, his left hand tightening on my arm to the point of pain. "I need you to get in the car and come home with me. Right. Fucking. Now."

"No," I said firmly. "This is my home now."

Everything after that was a blur. Hayden's right hand emerging from his jacket pocket. A glint of metal. The sound of a door opening. A deep voice yelling my name just before a loud boom cracked the night wide open.

And my vision went black.

But before that—a split second before—my mind registered only redness.

Blood.

So. Much. Blood.

All over Beau Atwood's face.

BEAU

I shoveled a piece of chocolate cake into my mouth, my eyes automatically finding her across the living room. Charli tossed back her head and laughed at something Justin said, her soft hair brushing almost to her tailbone, and my breath stalled in my lungs.

Would I ever get used to this feeling? This urge to stare at her without blinking, out of fear of missing one of her perfect smiles? As if my thoughts compelled her, she turned her head and looked at me, her cornflower blue eyes sparkling as she gave me a sweet smile that made the breath I'd been holding expel heavily from my chest.

"*I love you,*" I mouthed.

"*I love you, too.*"

My head turned sharply at the sound of the doorbell. *Who the hell is coming over this late at night?*

"I'll get it," Axel said, rising from the recliner on the other side of me and walking swiftly to the door before they rang again. God forbid they wake up the little kids; no one wanted the triplets to wake up once they were down for the night.

A few seconds later, Axel stuck his head in the living room and called out, "Charli, it's for you." My girl gave him a quizzical look before heading to the front door.

"Honey, can you get more coffee while you're up?" Blaire asked, and my brother-in-law nodded and turned toward the kitchen.

I sat silently for half a minute until I couldn't stand it anymore. Following Ax into the kitchen, I asked, "Who was at the door?"

He shrugged as he poured water into the coffee machine. "Some guy looking for Charli."

"What guy?" I snapped, and Axel stopped what he was doing and turned to me.

"A man about our age. A little overweight. Brown hair. I'm sure it's okay, Beau. Probably one of the dads from the neighborhood. People around here are always looking for babysitters, and everyone knows how good Char is with kids." He chuckled. "They're always trying to steal her from us."

A mental picture of a man flashed through my brain, causing panic to rise in my chest. A slightly chubby man with brown hair. Hayden Harrison, Charli's ex, the abusive sonofabitch. I had his fucking face memorized in the hopes that I would run into him one day. But now all I hoped was that it *wasn't* him because Charli was alone with him.

There are millions of chubby men with brown hair, Atwood. Cool your jets.

Yeah, but how many of them knocked on the Broxtons' door at this time of night? Fuck it. I took off at a sprint to the front door with Axel right on my heels. "Beau, what is it?" he hissed, trying not to alert the rest of the house.

"Might be her ex," I hissed back, slinging the front door open and having every one of my worst fears coalesce into a ball of truth before my eyes. It was indeed Hayden Harrison, and he had my girl by the arm as his right hand lifted from his pocket. There was a glint of metal—a Glock 21, my mind instantly registered as my military background kicked into overdrive—and I roared, "Charli!" as I launched myself at the fucker.

There was a loud pop, and I shoved his hand to the floor of the porch as we hit the ground with me on top of him. The weapon skittered away, and I rammed my fist into his fucking face. I did it again. And again. I kept hitting him until I felt strong arms pulling me away and heard Axel's voice. "Beau, that's enough. Beau!"

Ax had his arms bound tightly around me. My brother-in-law was fucking strong to restrain me; I'd give him that. Because I was goddamn feral by that point, wanting to do nothing more than kill the motherfucker who had dared to touch my Peach. To threaten her with a fucking gun.

The loud pop! Oh, my God! The gun had gone off! Charli!

I broke Axel's hold on me and whirled to where she was sitting a couple feet away with her hands over her face. *Jesus, please don't let her be...* She uncovered her face, locked eyes with me, and immediately started screaming. I ran to her, almost stumbling over my own feet to get to her. Kneeling and pulling her into my arms, I pressed my cheek to the top of her head.

"Baby, are you okay? Please, Peach. Stop screaming and tell me what hurts." I pulled back to inspect her, and almost fainted at the sight of blood streaking her light blonde hair. "Fuck, baby! Did you hit your head? What did he do to you?" My hands scrabbled gently through her hair, looking for the wound. She was conscious and screaming, so I was pretty sure it wasn't a gunshot wound, but where the fuck was all this goddamn blood coming from?

"Ax," I sobbed, "get Blaire. Charli's hurt. She's hurt."

But Blaire was already running from the house. Her eyes widened as she looked at us on the ground, and she let out a loud, guttural wail.

Fuck. It must be really bad for Blaire to make that noise. My sister was always calm and cool, even in the face of the most gruesome situations. Turning quickly back to Charli as my sister knelt beside us, I redoubled my efforts to find where Charli was bleeding.

"Help me, Blaire! I can't find where all this fucking blood is coming from." Charli had stopped screaming, but her eyes were as wide as saucers as she looked up at me in fear. I was vaguely aware of a commotion behind us and Axel telling everyone to stay back and let Blaire work.

My sister grabbed my shoulder. "It's you, you big idiot! You've been shot in the fucking head! You're bleeding all over Charli."

What? I reached my hand up to the side of my head and winced at the pain that manifested there all of a sudden. With all the adrenaline pulsing through my veins, I hadn't even noticed it before. Pulling my hand back, I saw that it was covered in blood.

My blood. "Oh, thank God," I breathed.

Looking back at Charli, I felt my heart shatter when I saw the dam of tears break and streak down her face. "Beau," she croaked, scrambling into my lap and curling into a tiny ball.

"It's okay, Peach. Can you tell me if you're hurt?" I wrapped my arms tightly around her, kissing her forehead even as more red liquid dripped down the side of my face and onto her.

"Would you fucking be still? I'm trying to look at your head!" my sister snapped. "Axel! Grab my bag and some towels and get an ambulance here right fucking now! Then run upstairs, check on the kids, and make sure Carrie doesn't come down here and see this."

That was my sister. In charge like a fucking boss now.

"Yeah, I want to get Charli looked at," I said, nodding and earning me a smack on the shoulder from Blaire.

"I said, be still," she yelled as her fingers prodded my scalp. "And the ambulance is for you, dumbass."

"I'm fine. It's just a flesh wound," I grunted. "And stop slapping and yelling at the guy who just got shot."

Charli's shaking hand reached up and swiped at the blood that was pouring down my cheek. "Beau, you got shot," she whimpered.

Thank God she's finally talking.

"Yeah, Peach. I'm all right. Just grazed me. Did he hurt you, baby?"

She shook her head. "He shot you. Hayden shot you."

"Uh-huh. I'm not his biggest fan right now."

A tiny smile flashed across her lips, and the tension in my chest eased infinitesimally. "Stop making jokes." Then her face turned somber, anger lighting those soft eyes like I had never seen before, and she leapt from my lap. Marching over to Hayden's unconscious body, she said in a low voice, "I hate you." She toed him lightly in the side. "I fucking hate you Hayden Harrison!" she said a little more loudly, this time with a hard kick to the ribs.

I scrambled up from where I was sitting, and my sister let out a frustrated huff of displeasure but didn't otherwise protest. Placing my hands on Charli's shoulders from behind, I squeezed gently, giving her my strength, my unending support. "I hate you, you bastard," she screamed, landing a series of kicks to his side and stomach as tears flew wildly from her pretty little face.

"That's it, Peach. Let it out, baby." I wasn't about to stop her. She needed this. She fucking *deserved* it. After a few more hard blows of her foot to the bastard's inert body—complete with some pretty impressive curses and insults—she seemed to lose steam and turned, pressing her face against my chest as I wrapped her up tightly. "Feel better, precious?"

She nodded. "He hurt you, Beau. I wanted to hurt him back."

God, this sweet, beautiful woman. Harrison had mentally abused her for years, and what finally snapped her control was when he hurt *me*. I loved her with every single cell in my body.

"So, you were defending my honor?" I asked, smiling against her hair, and she raised her tear-streaked face to mine.

"Nobody messes with my man unless they want me to go beast mode on them."

I grinned and pressed my lips to hers. "I love Beast Mode Charli. She's kinda hot."

I heard the din of voices from behind me and swiveled my head to find Charli's brothers and mother hovering nearby. Though it almost killed me to do so, I released my possessive hold on her. "You need to talk to your family, Peach."

She nodded and took two steps toward them, and they rushed her. Ethan got to her first, engulfing her in his arms for a long while, his face a picture of pain as he whispered to her before releasing her to Ms. Casper, who was smacking impatiently on his shoulder. The oldest brother approached me, and I eyed him warily.

"Atwood," he croaked, his voice breaking on my name.

"Ethan," I said with a nod.

His face crumpled, and he grabbed me in a rough hug. "You took a fucking bullet to the head for my sister."

"Just a flesh wound," I mumbled, patting his back awkwardly. "No big deal."

"It's a *huge* fucking deal, Atwood." He pulled back, and I noticed that I had bled all over the guy, soaking the shoulder of his shirt. *Wow. I'm bleeding like a stuck pig here*, I thought. *Maybe I should have that looked at.* "I just... thank you. So fucking much. You're all right, Atwood."

"Thanks," I said quietly, giving him a respectful nod before my sister broke in.

"*Atwood* needs to sit his ass down because he's been shot," she snapped, pointing to a nearby chair. "Now!"

"Yes ma'am," I said, swiping some of the blood from my face with my shoulder.

"Ethan, hold this light for me," she ordered, handing him a pen light. "Right there," she said, guiding his hand as she dug into her bag. "Fucking shot in the head. Won't even go to the hospital. Goddamn fool ass brother," she was mumbling as she drew up something in a syringe. "Oughta poke this needle through your skull to see if you have any fucking brains left in there."

"You know I can hear you, right?" I asked as she cut my shirt off and draped a towel over my shoulder. "And I liked that shirt."

She gave me her infamous death glare, and I shut my mouth. Blaire drenched my head with some kind of saline, squirting and dabbing and cleaning me up before applying what felt like battery acid to my scalp. "Okay Beau, I'm going to give you a shot to numb the area before I start suturing." Her voice was gentler now.

"I don't need a... ow! Shit, Blaire. The gunshot hurt less than that needle." But a few seconds later, I didn't give a damn as the numbness set in.

BEAU

Two hours later, I had been sutured, police statements had been made, and that shithole Hayden Harrison had been carted off in an ambulance under police guard.

I was at my house with my woman, in the shower, the water pouring off of us stained pink from my blood. Charli's hands were gentle as I bent so that she could wash my hair, being cautious around my head wound.

"You don't have to wash my hair for me, Peach."

There was a heavy pause as she rinsed the shampoo from my hair. "I want to, Beau. I want to take care of you."

Swiping the water from my face, I leaned in for a kiss. "It's my job to take care of *you*, baby."

She rolled those blue eyes at me. "Okay, I'll let you be in charge of beating the hell out of people. But no more jumping in front of bullets," she said, a frown marring her beautiful face. "You scared the hell out of me."

Taking a step closer to her, I kept my eyes keenly on hers. "I'll do whatever is necessary to keep you safe, Charli. I've fought people with guns before, and I would fight a million armed men if they tried to hurt you. I would do anything for you."

Her blue eyes burned with love and hunger as she pressed her sweet little body to mine. "And I would do anything for you, Beau Atwood." My cock instantly responded to the feel of her, my length hardening against her stomach. I had told myself we were taking a break from sex tonight because she had been through enough, but goddammit, I couldn't help how that fucker between my legs behaved when presented with Naked Charli. She was his favorite thing in the world.

"And you're in charge of things like washing my hair for me?" I asked, smiling down at her and letting my hands rest on her lower back, a relatively safe zone.

Charli's head tilted to the side, and she gave me a coy smile, her teeth denting her lower lip seductively. "Among other things." Sinking to her knees, she kept her eyes on mine as her hands slid down my body and her fingers bumped along the hard ridges of my abdomen.

Holy fucking shit. This is not helping my resolve to keep my hands off her tonight.

"Peach, you don't need to do that," I said huskily, and I could practically hear my dick groan at my attempt at being noble.

She put one sassy hand on her hip and lifted her eyebrow at me. "I can suck it if I want to. It's mine." Her tongue stole from her mouth and licked the ever-growing swell of my crown.

Fuck, that feels good.

"Is it, now?" I growled.

Her eyes narrowed, and she tickled her fingers across my belly before firmly gripping the base of my cock. "Isn't it?" she asked, her lips pursing forward to kiss my tip. Then she leaned back on her heels. "Because if it's not..."

"It's fucking yours," I grunted as my erection lengthened even further in search of her hot little mouth.

Giving me a satisfied smirk, she canted her head forward, taking the end of me into her warmth and giving me a long, slow slurp. "Now that we have that settled..." She wrapped her lips around me and swallowed me deeply.

I slammed a hand against the tile wall for support as my knees threatened to buckle from the pure, raw pleasure of being inside Charli's mouth. "Fuck! That's my good girl," I said, stroking my fingers through her freshly washed hair. She hummed her pleasure at my praise and began to work me over with long, tortuously slow bobs of her head, allowing me to feel every soft caress of her tongue over my heated flesh.

Sliding the backs of my fingers down her pink cheek, I let my thumb rest on her bottom lip, reveling in the sensation of my hard dick gliding over her supple lips. "You're so fucking perfect, Charli. You're my goddess."

She moaned around my dick and then closed her eyes and loved me with her mouth, her lips pressing and releasing gently as she suckled me over and over like

I was the last fine meal she would ever have. It was the most tender and intimate moment of my life. I didn't want to tarnish it by fucking her mouth like an animal and coming down her throat, so when I was close, I eased my penis from her mouth.

Giving my cock a nice, hard squeeze, I waited until her eyes found mine. "Do you want me inside you tonight, baby? If you're tired, I can just hold you and we can go to sleep."

The words were barely out of my mouth before Charli was on her feet, leaping into my arms and wrapping her legs around me, letting the heat of her core press exactly where I wanted. "No. I need to feel you alive and strong on top of me. Inside me. Please."

She didn't have to fucking ask me twice.

Slamming the faucet off and without even bothering with towels, I carried Charli to my bed and eased her onto the sheets, my body following her down. Resisting the urge to take her roughly, I parted her legs with my knee and pressed the tip of my cock against her clit, allowing her to feel the synchronized throbs as our heartbeats found matching rhythms between our legs.

Rocking my hips, I pulsed against her over and over, stimulating her clit until she begged me on a plaintive cry to enter her. Shifting a little, I found her hole dripping with desire, helping to ease the way as my thick cock pushed into her, inch by inch, stretching her out as he sought the deepest part of her.

When my balls were pressed against the peachy skin of her ass, a deep rumble of satisfaction rose from my chest. I had never felt more complete in my life. As our lips touched with reverential kisses, I held myself up on my elbows and cupped her precious face.

I was buried deep inside her, not even moving yet, but every fiber of my being knew that this was life-affirming sex. Peach had said it herself. She wanted to feel me *alive* and strong on top of her. And I wanted her to know exactly how I was feeling.

I'm not what you would call a hearts and flowers kind of guy. I wasn't good at the sweet talk. But the new and improved version of me loved Charli Casper, my sweet little Peach, and I wanted to tell her. We had exchanged *I love you*s, but this need I had was deeper. It was *more*.

Moving my body over Charli's, I pulled back before pressing forward again and closed my eyes for a brief second at the sensation of her wrapped snugly around me. When I reopened my eyes, her cornflower blue ones were staring up at me, reflecting so much love and trust that I could barely breathe.

I stroked my thumbs over her cheekbones as I thrust deeply into her and began to whisper against her lips. I didn't know how to do romantic talk, so I simply said what I was feeling and hoped it was enough.

"I feel so close to you right now, Charli. I feel like we're one person." My words and my dick seemed to have hit the right spot at the same time because Charli's body began to tremble as her pussy clamped tight around me, a perfect, intense orgasm spreading through her. I kissed her as I fucked her through it, slow and deep, my cock loving every single tremor and clench from her pussy walls.

Trailing my lips across her cheek, I continued talking into her ear, feeling more confident with my words now that I'd seen how they affected her. I was in my motherfucking sweet-talking element.

"You're not just under my skin, baby. You *are* my fucking skin. You hold me together, Charli Casper." We clutched each other tightly, her arms and legs wrapped around me as I continued to make love to my woman. I had never felt the way I did when her beautiful, gentle eyes spilled over with tears. My voice was thick and hoarse with emotion when I spoke again. "You are my goddamn *life*, Charli. I promise I will love and protect you forever."

Okay, that last one got me. *Fucking forever.* That's what I wanted with Charli. Just the thought of it had me coming like a tsunami. Pressing my face into the pillow beside her head, I roared my completion as I filled her up, giving her all of me. My heart and my soul.

"I love you, Beau," Charli was panting repeatedly as our connected bodies quaked with the force of our emotional lovemaking, and I lifted my head and circled my nose around hers.

"I love you, too, Peach. You make me happier than I ever thought I could be."

Two thin lines appeared between her eyebrows, and she stroked my face with her small hands. "My handsome man was sad before?"

God, she's sweet. What did I do to deserve her?

"No, not really sad. It wasn't like I moped around all the time. I just didn't have anything to look forward to every single day." I kissed her tenderly.

Her pretty face brightened, her eyes sparkling up at me. "And now you have Beast Mode Charli."

"That I do," I said with a chuckle, sliding off her and shifting to the side.

"Uh-uh. Switch sides with me so you don't have to sleep on this side of your head," she said, her fingertips running gingerly around my wound.

I crawled over her and hauled her back against my front. "Happy now?"

"Mmhmmm," she said, snuggling her blonde head against my bicep. "Except I'm leaking down there. It's going to get on your sheets."

"Can't have that," I said, wrapping my arm around her hip and pressing two fingers up into her, effectively plugging her pussy. "There. My body made that cum especially for you, Peach. Don't want to waste it."

I heard her giggle as she reached over and flipped off the lamp. "That's kinda dirty and sweet at the same time."

"That's me in a nutshell," I said, nuzzling my face against the back of her neck. "I'll never stop loving you, Charli. Not even on the day I die. I'll come back and stay in your room, watching you sleep like some kind of perverted ghost."

She wiggled her tiny body back against me. "Go to sleep, you weirdo."

36

CHARLI

Soft lips feathered across my shoulder as the spaghetti strap of my pajama top was eased over the curve and down my arm. "Happy Thanksgiving, Peach," Beau said in my ear, his voice deep and gravelly with sleep.

I nudged my butt back against his large erection and murmured, "Feels like it's going to be a very happy Thanksgiving."

"Mmmhmmm," he said, getting his tongue into the act, swirling it around my shoulder and up my neck. "Forget the turkey. You're my favorite thing to stuff."

Smiling in the darkness, I said, "I'm not sure if that was supposed to be funny or sexy."

He slid his hand down into my pajama shorts and rubbed my clit with his fingers. "How about now?" he whispered in my ear, and I moaned.

"Leaning toward sexy, but I might need a little more convincing."

I could feel him smile against my cheek at the seductive challenge. He slid one thick finger inside me as his other hand slid under and around me and pushed my shirt down under my breast, cupping me and toying with my nipple. His lips sipped at my skin, and he grinded his hardness against my ass. "How am I doing?"

"Not bad," I teased, and he nipped my jaw with his teeth.

"I'll show you not bad," he growled, pushing another finger into my pussy, which was dripping with desire by that point.

"I think you would be much more convincing if you were naked," I suggested.

"I usually am," he said, pulling his fingers out and working my shorts and panties down my legs. I kicked them off under the covers as he removed his underwear with one hand, the other hand still firmly on my breast. He slipped his dick between my legs from behind, holding it tightly to my body with his hand as he rocked against me. "Fuck, you're wet, baby," he groaned as the thick head prodded my clitoris with every soft pump. "You're soaking me." In the quiet room, I could hear the slickness between my legs as his hardness slid through my pussy lips.

"I need you inside me, baby."

"Not yet," he said, sucking on the pulse point below my jaw as his hips gained speed beneath the sheets. He was hitting my sensitive nub with every stroke, and I felt all the blood in my veins rushing to the area between my legs. "Almost," he said, as I panted his name, begging him for more. "Come, baby," he finally murmured, and I felt a deep heat spreading from the apex of my thighs, like a pot bubbling over.

"Ohhhh. Yes, Beau. That's it."

As soon as I started coming, Beau slipped his erection inside me with a groan. "Fuck yes. Come on my cock, Peach." Burying himself deeply from behind, he pumped gently as I spasmed around his thickness, his fingers massaging firm circles against my clit. "Christ, you feel good. So tight and hot."

I could feel him straining against me, struggling not to come yet. "You don't have to hold back, Beau. Come in me."

His dick twitched inside me, and his breathing became ragged. "No. I need more of you," he gritted out. He had been like this since the incident with Hayden last week. Beau had always been a highly sexual man, but since he'd saved me from my ex, his sexual appetite for me was in damn overdrive. Every morning he woke me up like this.

And the nights. Oh, good Lord, the nights! Where the morning sex was sweet and loving, the things he did to me when we went to bed were damn near unmentionable. Our fucking was hard and so freaking dirty. A couple nights, he had insisted that we stay at his house because he said he wanted me loud. And I was. Much to Cam's delight, based on the crude teasing comments he made the following mornings.

But the morning lovemaking was simply... beautiful. Beau was softly kissing the back of my neck when we heard a light tap on the door. "Yeah?" he called out quietly, stilling his hips and pulling the covers up over our shoulders.

Axel stuck his head in the door and asked, "You ready, buddy?" He and Beau were going to put the turkeys on the outdoor smoker, a tradition they had apparently been doing since Axel and Blaire had gotten married.

"Yeah," Beau said hoarsely, "give me five, okay?"

Axel chuckled and said, "I'll give you ten," before closing the door behind him.

Beau rolled us until I was on my stomach, and he was lying on my back. He widened his thick thighs, spreading me out for him as he began hitting me deep with long, slow strokes. Wrapping both arms underneath me, he held me tightly and possessively against him.

"You are my life, Charli. I love you so fucking much."

"And you're mine, Beau. You're so perfect."

The thick crown of his dick was rubbing sensuously across that tender spot deep inside me with every long push and pull, and I felt a hell of an orgasm building low in my belly.

"I'm far from perfect, baby, but I will spend every day of the rest of my life being the best man I can be for you," he said, plunging somehow deeper inside me as the bedsprings squeaked rhythmically beneath us.

His sweet promise brought tears to my eyes, and a quiet sob escaped. "I love you, Beau. God, I love you so much."

"Charli..." he moaned. "Oh, Christ, Charli. I need you to come." One of his hands slid between my legs to stroke my clit, and I came a few seconds later, my back arching as Beau's hips slapped against my ass. He pulled out as soon as I was done and released himself all over my butt with a quiet grunt.

His soft, sweet kisses on the back of my neck made me shiver as he rolled to the side of me. Turning my face away from my pillow, I breathed, "Have I told you how much I love morning sex?"

"Me too," he said, pressing his firm lips to my cheek. "Let me get a towel and clean you up."

Beau pushed himself from the bed and returned a minute later with a warm cloth. After wiping his cum from me, he murmured, "Come here so I can kiss you." I turned toward him and received a soft, sucking kiss against my lips. "This is our first..." Another kiss. "Holiday together..." A little tongue now. "The first of many." Then his tongue was rolling around mine in a seductive dance as he twitched against my hip.

"Does that thing ever rest?" I asked against his lips.

He glanced down to where we were joined. "Not around you. He's quite a rascal, always looking for a good time."

"I think you're a rascal," I giggled as he pulled me close and nuzzled my hair.

He chuckled against my ear. "I can't deny that allegation. Unfortunately, this rascal has to go get the turkeys in the smoker." He peppered tender kisses across my face and whispered, "But I'll be back after Axel leaves." Ax had a game today and would be leaving for the stadium soon. Beau pulled away with a reluctant groan. "Mmmm. Why can't I just stay buried inside you all day?"

"Because that would make Thanksgiving dinner a wee bit awkward," I said.

"But it would be a lot more fun," he said, rolling off the bed and patting my hip before heading into the bathroom.

"I'm not sure my brothers would agree," I called out and heard him laugh before he turned on the water in the sink.

A few minutes later, he emerged from the bathroom fully dressed and kissed my temple. "Sleep a little more, sweet girl. I'll be back."

I scooted over to his side of the bed and nestled into his pillow, falling asleep with his masculine scent surrounding me. I wasn't sure how much time passed, but a while later, I woke up with a head between my legs. "Beau?" I asked, lifting the covers up and finding his green eyes scowling up at me.

"It'd better be Beau," he growled, biting the inside of my thigh. Then he nipped the soft flesh of my lips, his teeth sinking into me before he smoothed the area with his tongue. "God, you smell like hot fucking sex," he moaned, sliding his tongue against my clit. "And you taste like you've been thoroughly fucked recently."

"As a matter of fact…" I panted as he began to eat me with gusto. "Damn, Beau. That feels so… oh, God… so good." He brought me to the edge with his lips and his tongue and his teeth. I felt my face and chest flushing with an impending orgasm just as the door to my bedroom swung open.

"Rise and shine, little sister," Lizzy said, flipping on the light switch. "I'm here to… oh, my fuck…" Her words trailed off and her eyes widened as she noticed the Beau-sized lump under the covers.

The cheeky bastard popped his head out with his adorably rumpled hair and grinned at my sister. Oh. My. God. His lips were glistening from… me.

"Happy Thanksgiving, Lizzy," he crooned.

"Uhhhh, yeah. Apparently happier for some of us than others," she commented, backing through the doorway and pausing, taking one last look at my boyfriend's totally unembarrassed face before she flipped off the light. "I'm just gonna..." She locked the door and closed it behind her.

From the hallway right outside my door, I heard Justin say, "Hey, is Charli up yet?"

Oh, holy shit.

"Uh, she's not decent right now." Well, that's the damn truth. "Come on. She'll be out in a few minutes," she said loudly.

Beau kissed up my stomach, his lips leaving a wet trail from my hip to my nipple, which he took between his lips. "You know, door locks are amazing things," I said sarcastically.

"You know what else is amazing?" he asked around my breast. "Thanksgiving shower sex."

"That's not a thing," I said, brushing his hair away from his forehead and catching a whiff of cherrywood smoke.

"It's totally a thing," he replied, releasing my breast with a pop before climbing off the bed and gripping both my hands to pull me up with him. "Come on. I'll prove it to you."

37

BEAU

"Your sister, my sister, and Bristol tried to kill me today," Charli whined, her voice muffled because she had collapsed face down on her bed after the girls had hazarded the Black Friday crowds.

I shuddered as I sat down beside her and patted her bottom. "I can only imagine. You couldn't pay me enough to get out in all that mess."

"I shoulda been a guy. Then I could just sit around, drink beer, and watch football all day."

"You can stay home with me next year. We could make that another tradition," I said, stretching out beside her on my side, my hand slipping underneath her shirt to stroke the smooth skin of her back.

Charli twisted her head and peeped at me with one big, blue eye. "Like the Thanksgiving morning shower sex tradition? I still think you made that up."

Leaning forward, I pressed my lips to her temple. "So what if I did? It's our thing now."

She buried her face in the mattress again and groaned. "And getting caught with your head between my legs by my sister? Is that going to be a tradition, too?"

A deep laugh escaped my throat. "Oh, come on. Elizabeth thought it was funny. What *wasn't* funny were all of Cam's little innuendos in front of your brothers."

"Jesus, I wanted to kill him," she snarled, rolling over and frowning at the ceiling. "That reminds me. I think my sister is interested in Cam. She was asking about his status today."

"Hmmm, you probably want to discourage her. Cam's… complicated."

"You mean kinky?"

"And then some. You know he likes to listen, right?"

"Uh, yeah. I'm aware," she said dryly.

"Well, he also likes to watch."

Charli was silent for a moment while I glided my fingers through her sleek ponytail. "Have you ever let him watch you?"

Well, fuck.

"Yeah, I have." Her eyes widened at my admission. "You know I was no angel before I met you, Peach."

"You're not an angel now either," she said with a smirk. Then her face turned serious. "How many times?"

"A few," I said. *A few dozen.*

A slight frown creased her beautiful face as she stared at my chest. "Did he ever do more than watch?"

"Do you really want me to answer that?" I asked warily, and her eyes lifted to mine, reading the answer there.

"I guess that would be a yes." She tilted her head forward until her forehead rested on my chest.

"I'm sorry, baby. If I could go back and change my past, I would."

"You like that kind of thing?" Her wary eyes lifted to mine and searched there.

"In the past," I said carefully. "But not anymore."

"You can't just turn off what you like, Beau. I'm afraid you're going to get... bored with me. I feel like *just me* isn't enough for you." She was staring at my chest again.

I kept my eyes on hers for a long while until she finally looked up at me. Then I spoke the truest words I had ever uttered. "You shut that down right now, Peach. I never knew what I was missing until you. Until *us*. Nothing from my past even compares to being in love with you."

"You're sure?"

"I'm positive." I leaned down to suck on her luscious lips, letting my tongue play at the seam. "After you take a little nap, I'm going to fuck you so long and so hard, you will never have another doubt." I kissed her deeply, licking into her mouth as she plastered her body against mine. I grasped her behind the knee and wrapped her leg over my hip, desperate to have as much body contact as possible with her.

When our lips parted, Peach snuggled her face into the side of my neck. "Can I ask you one more question, snookums?"

"Yes on the question. No on the snookums," I said with amusement. She had been trying out different pet names for me, none of which impressed me. So far, we had discarded schmoopie, love chunks, pooky bear, honey buns, and now snookums. I had jokingly suggested King Dong or Super Dick, but she said she refused to call me those names in public.

"This bachelor party you're going to Saturday night... it's at a strip club, right?"

"Yes, and none of those women hold any interest at all for me. None. I'm only going because it's for one of my old military friends, and that's what his best man planned for him. I'll be on my best behavior. I'll even keep my eyes closed the whole time, if that would make you feel better."

"You don't have to do that. I want you to go and have fun, as long as there's no touching."

"I promise, there will be absolutely no touching, okay?"

She nodded. "Okay. I trust *you*, but I don't trust other women around you. You're just so... hot."

"I'll just frown a lot and act like an asshole to discourage any women from approaching me."

Charli rolled her eyes. "You are so clueless. That's the absolute worst thing you could do. Women like a broody bad boy."

"So, you want me to smile at the strippers?"

"No! Don't you dare smile. Just try to look... I don't know... neutral or something."

"Neutral, huh? I'll work on that," I said with a laugh as her eyes drifted closed and I held her sweet body against mine.

38

CHARLI

Saturday evening, I was sitting on Beau's couch waiting for Bristol to come pick me up. We were going to dinner, and then we were having a few drinks at a martini bar while Beau went to the bachelor party.

I looked up as Beau entered his living room, and my mouth instantly watered. I stood, rubbing my hands up his soft black dress shirt. "Damn, you look good. I'm not sure I should let you out of the house looking like this." I leaned in to kiss his exposed throat and inhaled his heavenly scent. "Or smelling like this. Women are going to be throwing themselves at you." I planted a soft kiss on his Adam's apple.

"No one is going to get close enough to smell me, Peach. Not until I get home to you." He bit my earlobe and growled, "Speaking of that, I want you naked in my bed when I get home. And your pussy better be fucking dripping for me."

"Isn't it always?" I teased, making him groan.

"Let me feel it one time before I go," he said, sliding his hand into my leggings and toying with me over my underwear.

He slid my panties to the side just as Cam walked in. "Don't mind me. I swear I'm not looking," he said, his eyes trained on Beau's hand in my pants.

"Fucker," Beau mumbled, pulling his hand free and kissing my lips.

"You look nice, Cam," I said, turning toward him. He was wearing charcoal dress pants and a crisp white button-down, while Beau was in solid black, looking sexy and dark. Both of their shirts were fitted enough to show off their muscular physiques.

"Thanks, Charli. If you were a stripper, would you want to bang me?"

Beau shot him a withering look, but I studied him. "Ummm, undo one more button on your shirt. And maybe add some jewelry." I turned to Beau and scowled. "And you need to fasten your buttons all the way up, please."

"There will be no stripper banging. I promise," he said, kissing my nose.

"Speak for yourself," Cam said with a dirty grin, going to open the front door when the doorbell rang. "Hey, Bristol," he said to my friend. "If you were a stripper, would this outfit make you want to fuck me?"

Her gaze drifted down and back up his body. "Hell, I'd do you, and I'm not even a stripper." She reached up and undid one of his buttons, exposing more of his hard chest. "There. Now you're totally fuckable."

"Cool. Thanks, Bris."

"If you're going to a sleazy strip joint, you might want to wear some gold chains, though," she said thoughtfully. "And possibly a pinky ring."

"That's what I said," I piped up.

"We're not going anywhere sleazy," Beau said, getting exasperated with our conversation. "It's called Vibration, very upscale. They have a steakhouse attached, and we're having dinner there before we, uh, you know."

"Before we go check out the tits and asses," Cam said helpfully.

"You're not helping," Beau spat. Turning to me, he said, "I'll be good, baby. I can't promise that Cam won't come home with at least five different STDs, but I know how to behave."

"I've heard there's one woman there, and when she bends over, glitter shoots out of her ass," Cam said, looking heavenward and sighing happily, and I couldn't help but giggle.

I patted his arm. "I hope all your sparkly ass dreams come true, Cam." Then I turned to Beau and glared. "And Mister, I'm checking every inch of you for glitter specks when you get home."

"I'm looking forward to it," he said, pulling me toward him for an achingly long kiss.

"Aw hell, you guys," I heard Cam mutter, and Bris grunted in response. "Shark, we've gotta jet. The limo will be at Gavin's house in fifteen minutes." I was glad to hear that they wouldn't be driving at least.

Beau rested his forehead against mine and said, "I gotta go, Peach. Don't forget how much I love you."

"Don't *you* forget how much you love me," I said pointedly, but with a smile. "Now go have fun. I love you, babe." I smacked him on the ass, and he gave me one final smiling kiss before turning to Bristol and giving her a friendly hug.

"Keep my girl out of trouble," he said with a wink.

"Oh, you know me. I'll keep an eye on her."

"That's what I'm afraid of," he said, only half-joking. "Let me give you my number in case you need it."

"Why would I need your number, Beau?" she asked with a smirk as he punched his name and number into Bristol's phone.

"I don't know. In case y'all drink too much and need a ride or something."

"I can just call my brother," she said, and Beau's jaw tightened noticeably. "Besides, what are you going to do? Come pick us up in a limo filled with guys covered in ass glitter?"

"If you're lucky," Cam broke in with a laugh. "Come on, Shark. Your little Peach will be fine for one night. Let's go."

"We're leaving, too," I said, grabbing my purse and following them out the door. "We're getting dressed at Bristol's house tonight."

As we climbed into my bestie's Toyota, we watched the guys get into Beau's big black truck, their asses looking tight and lean in their dress pants. "I don't mean to worry you, Charli, but those two look way too yummy to stay out of trouble tonight."

"I'm not worried. Not about Beau anyway," I said. "Cam's a different story. He's a fucking deviant."

"But a damned fine one," she said, putting the car into drive. "But not as fine as Tank."

"So, have you had another magical night of multiple orgasms? Y'all seemed pretty, um, close a couple weeks ago." Bristol made a noncommittal noise and kept her eyes studiously on the road. "Bris?"

"Fine! Yes, okay? Are you happy? We fucked again." She sighed. "And it was awesome."

"Then why do you sound like someone kicked you in the vagina instead of doing, you know, *good stuff* to it."

"I don't know. The way he is with me. I think he's catching feelings. But we're not really talking right now."

Knowing better than to try and argue with her about it, I nodded and changed the subject.

Two hours later, we had our hair and makeup done, and Bristol was sliding a skimpy red dress over my head. She stepped back and looked me over, her lips curling up wickedly. "Girlfriend, you are on *fire*."

Looking at the hem of the dress skimming the tops of my thighs, I asked, "Is this a shirt?"

"No. Well, maybe it *was* a shirt on *me*, but on your little pipsqueak self, it's definitely a dress. And the red looks great with your blonde hair. You just need fire engine red lipstick."

I tugged the bottom of the dress/shirt down a little, and Bristol slapped my hand away from my fidgeting. She lined my lips, something I never did, and filled them in with a tiny lip brush. "There. Now I'm insanely jealous."

"Whatever, bitch. You look like a damned supermodel." She was wearing a deep blue dress that was the same color as the streak in her hair and equally as short as mine, showing off her mile-long legs. Her dark wavy hair was full, and her makeup was on point, as usual, with red lipstick about five shades darker than the one I was wearing.

"Let's go give my brother a heart attack," she said, dragging me toward the living room, almost making me stumble in the ridiculous red heels I was wearing. "Aaron, please tell Charli she looks good."

Her brother was sitting on Bristol's blood red couch reading on his iPad, and his eyes widened when he looked up. "Fuuuuck," he said, his voice little more than a groan before he cleared his throat and tried again. "Yeah, it's fine. You're fine. Very fine. Um, and nice." His head was bouncing up and down like one of those bobblehead dolls, his eyes locked somewhere near my crotch.

"Told ya," Bristol muttered under her breath. "Watch this." Speaking more loudly to Aaron, she said, "You can't see her panty line, right? If so, she can just take off the lacy thong and go commando."

He grabbed a throw pillow off the couch and pulled it onto his lap to cover his crotch. "I don't see anything," he said quickly. "Not that I'm looking or anything. Uh, where are you girls going tonight? You want me to come with you?"

"Nope, sorry bro. It's girls' night. We're going to dinner and then for drinks."

"So you don't have dates?" he asked, looking pleased.

"No, Charli's boyfriend is going to a bachelor party."

"Boyfriend?" he asked, looking much less pleased.

"Yes, you met Beau that night at Flame."

Aaron scowled, and I could see his mind turning. "I didn't know that meathead was your boyfriend."

"Well, he wasn't then, but he is now. And he's not a meathead," I said sternly.

"Uh-huh. And where are they going?"

"Some strip joint called Vibration."

Aaron's eyes widened. "Did you say Vibration? Are you shitting me? The girls there are smoking hot. I went once. It was my friend's idea," he added quickly.

I gave him an exaggerated eye roll. "What is it about guys and strip clubs? I mean, I just don't see the appeal of looking at someone you can't have."

"Oh, but at this place you *can* have. If you have enough money and a reservation to The Vibe."

"Wait," I said, confused. "What's The Vibe?"

"It's like a club within a club. Vibration is the main club, and it's very classy. Well, considering there are titties everywhere. But they're classy titties."

"I'm sure they are," Bristol remarked flatly.

Aaron lowered his voice like he was afraid someone was outside with some kind of listening device. "But *anything goes* in The Vibe. Parties can reserve the room, and they're the only ones allowed in for the rest of the night."

"What do you mean *anything goes*?" I asked, feeling a bubbling in the pit of my stomach.

"I mean fucking, sucking, threesomes, whatever. My friend Stone went with a bachelor party, and he said it was the wildest night of his life. He said most of the guys in their party opted for getting blow jobs because, *fuck yeah*, right?"

Threesomes? And Cam would be with him? I felt sick to my stomach.

"Holy shit! So, you're saying they have bedrooms back there and people can just... I don't even know how that would work? You pick a stripper and ask her to go to a room with you?" Bristol asked her brother.

"Nope. It's all one big room with couches and lounge chairs so everyone in the room can see what everyone else is doing. It adds to the debauchery. Each guy has their own personal girl called a liaison. It starts with lap dances and then progresses from there to however far they want to go."

"Well, Beau didn't mention that they were going to some kind of VIP room or anything, so I'm sure they're just going to the regular part of the strip club."

"You'd better hope so, because if your boyfriend goes into The Vibe, he's getting his dick sucked... or worse. Or maybe I should say better, depending on your point of view," he said with a chuckle. Noticing the look on my face, Aaron flattened his lips and softened his tone. "But I'm sure they're not going back there. It's very expensive, and like I said, they only allow one group back there per night."

"Yeah, it's probably fine," Bristol said, rubbing a hand up and down my arm as her brother excused himself to go to the bathroom.

"The groom's brother Grayson is the best man, and he planned the whole bachelor party. I know he's rich. Like super rich," I said worriedly. "Should I text Beau and… fuck… I don't even know what I would say. 'Hey, babe. Are you planning to go back into a secret orgy lair and have sex with a stripper whore? Just let me know. K, bye.'"

"Charli, he loves you. I don't think Beau would cheat on you."

"I don't think so either, but…" My mind was still stuck on the threesome thing. Beau had admitted that he liked having threesomes in the past but insisted that all of a sudden, he's not into that anymore. "I need to know, Bris. I think I'm going to call the club and ask the name of the party in The Vibe tonight."

I picked up my phone to Google the number, but Bristol snatched it out of my hands. "No. You can't do that. If this place is supposed to be, like, super exclusive, they're not going to just blurt out that information to anyone on the phone, especially a woman."

"Well, I have to know, dammit. I'm not going to be able to have any fun tonight because I feel like my brain is going to explode."

My friend's eyes brightened. "Hold up. I have a plan that might keep your brain intact. What if we get Aaron to call and say that he's with the bachelor party, and maybe he can find out if they're going to the secret sex room."

I chewed my bottom lip nervously. "I don't know. Do you think your brother would do that?"

"Do what?" Aaron asked, walking back into the room. When Bris and I shared a glance, his eyes narrowed. "What kind of hare-brained scheme are you two trying to get me involved in?"

"We want you to call Vibration and pretend to be a member of the bachelor party. See if you can find out if the party has The Vibe room reserved," Bristol said.

He crossed his arms over his chest. "And why would I do that?"

"Seriously, Aaron? Tell me you're not going to pull some bros before hos bullshit, because you don't even know these guys. But Charli is our friend."

"She is." His eyes ate up my body, top to bottom, and a slow grin curled his lips when he finally settled on my face. "I'll do it if you go out with me," he said with finality.

My mouth dropped open in surprise. "Aaron, I have a boyfriend."

Bristol stood with her hands on her hips, facing off against her brother. "That is sleazy as shit, Aaron Hopkins!"

He held up his hands, palms out, and said, "Hey, I'm just saying, I would like to take Charli out if this goes south and she doesn't have a boyfriend anymore." He gave me a boyish grin. "I've always liked you, Charli, and I just want to take you out for a nice dinner if you become single again. That's it. Nothing sleazy." Then he raised his eyebrows and said, "Certainly not as sleazy as a guy blowing his load in a stripper's mouth. Or tag-teaming a woman with one of his friends, all while a bunch of other guys watch."

Fuck. It's like Aaron was reading all the darkest fears in my mind and putting a voice to them. Beau had promised me no touching, but faced with that kind of temptation—the kind of temptation he admitted he used to like—would he keep his promise? He had tried to mask it, but I had noticed that heated glimmer in his eyes when he was talking about being watched. And he would potentially have a whole room watching him tonight.

My Beau loved getting head. If he was watching all his friends getting sucked off, would he be able to resist? Images of him with his legs spread obscenely wide with a scantily-clad woman licking and sucking his big dick flitted through my mind. Would he twist his fingers in her hair like he loved doing with me? When he started losing control, would he tighten his fist and shove roughly up into her mouth? Would he growl her name when he came? Shit... would he even *know* her name?

And I didn't even want to think about him and Cam fucking a woman at the same time. How did they share women in the past? Did Beau ride her from behind while Cam took her mouth? Or vice-versa? *Dammit, I said I wasn't going to think about it!*

"Okay, Aaron. If you help me find out what's going on, *and* if Beau and I break up, I'll go out with you. But just as friends, okay?"

Bristol and Aaron both stared at me in astonishment before Aaron stammered out a rapid, "O-okay. What's the groom's name?" I told him, and he looked up the number and hit the call button, putting it on speaker.

"Vibration. How may I serve you?" a seductive female voice said.

"Yeah, hey. I'm with the Gavin Keats bachelor party tonight, and I'm running a little late. I think Gav's brother said something about a VIP room. How do I get in there if my buddies are already inside?"

"Let me just check something here…" We heard a keyboard clacking on the other end of the line, and then the sultry voice was back. "Ohhhh, yes sir. Your party will be in The Vibe. You're a lucky boy," she said with a giggle as my heart dropped. "We have everyone's names as provided by Mr. Keats. As long as your name is on that list, we will have someone escort you back to The Vibe where you can join in the fun."

Oh. Damn. I had held out hope that the guys would just be staying in the regular part of the club, but now I was faced with the reality that the man I loved would probably be tempted beyond his limits tonight. And then it would be over. I nodded at Aaron's questioning look, and he maintained eye contact with me when he said, "My name is Beau Atwood. Can you check to see if my name is on the list?"

"Certainly." *ClickClickClick.* "Yes, Mr. Atwood. You're on the list." If my heart wasn't already low enough, now it felt like it was dragging the ground with that confirmation.

"You okay, babe?" Aaron asked after hanging up.

It was weird. I was so sad, but I couldn't cry. My tear glands were drier than the Sahara. "I'm okay. Maybe… maybe he won't go back into that room. He could just stay up front, right?"

"Sure, babe," he said in an overly conciliatory tone that told me he didn't believe it at all. "He would have to be stupid to cheat on you."

Bristol's voice sounded angry. "Okay, Aaron. You've got to go down to that club and spy on Beau."

"What?" Aaron and I said in unison. "I'm not Sherlock Holmes, you crazy heifer," he said. "And have you forgotten that Beau and his friends have seen me?"

She waved her hand airily. "I can disguise you. I have all kinds of stuff from when I was doing hair and makeup for that community theater group. Come on." She grabbed his hand and dragged him toward her bedroom as he looked back at me with a *please save me from my crazy ass sister* look.

Twenty minutes later, Aaron and Bristol emerged from her room, her with a satisfied look on her face, and him with a blonde wig and unruly blonde mustache and beard. "I look like a reject from Game of Thrones," he muttered sulkily.

"Oh hush, bro. Women like some facial hair. It tickles our—"

He closed his eyes and held up one hand. "Please. Do not finish that sentence. I'm begging you, for the love of all that's holy."

I got up and circled Aaron, inspecting Bristol's work. "Bris, this is good. Really good." Aaron was damn near unrecognizable.

"It's what I do," she said modestly.

"You girls know I'm not going to be able to get into that room, right? My name is not on the list, so I'll have to stay out in the main room."

"And I'm sure watching naked women gyrating on a pole will be such a sacrifice for you," Bristol said with a condescending eye roll. "Just get going. Char said the guys were having dinner at Vibration, so you need to be inside before they're done. I'm going to take her to get something to eat while we wait for your report."

Thirty minutes later, Bristol and I were chowing down at a local taco shop. As I bit into my third chipotle chicken taco, I moaned. "Please stop me. I'm totally stress eating over here. And pass the hot sauce."

Her phone pinged, and she snatched it off the table. "Okay, Aaron said they're coming out of the restaurant now." She stared at her phone while I chewed anxiously. Her eyes widened and she looked up at me sympathetically. "Char, I'm sorry."

"What? What is it?" I asked, a hunk of chicken falling inelegantly from my mouth as she turned her phone toward me. I saw a picture taken from behind of a group of men standing in front of a door marked, *THE VIBE - Private. No admittance without invitation.* There were women scattered amongst the men, and right near the back of the group was the unmistakable form of the man I loved smiling down at a brunette beauty beside him.

I felt something rise up inside me. There was pain, of course, but it was being heavily overshadowed by anger. Hot, intense anger. "That motherfucker," I said loudly, and an elderly couple at the table next to us threw me an irritated glare.

Bristol looked just as angry as she tapped the screen with her fingernail. "And look at who's right beside him." Tank was standing there with his arm around a tall raven-haired woman who looked remarkably similar to Bristol.

"I thought you weren't talking to Tank right now," I said.

"I'm not," she said defensively. "I just... well, never mind. Come on. I know what will take your mind off of that cheating bastard." She grabbed her purse and pulled me toward the door muttering something that sounded like, "Fuck that big giant asshole with his big giant dick."

Considering what I was going through, that shouldn't have been funny at all, but I was finding myself amused by her reaction. Apparently, Tank wasn't the only one catching feelings.

39

BEAU

As we watched the women gyrating on stage, I leaned over to Lester, one of my teammates from back in my SEAL days. "Uh Les, did you know about all this?" I asked, sweeping my hand in a half-circle to encompass this VIP room or whatever the fuck it was.

"Nope," he said. "Gavin's brother just said we were going to have the time of our life."

I shifted uncomfortably. "I don't like that Grayson dude. He's a little too slick for my taste, and I don't like whatever is going on in here. See that chick on the middle pole?" Lester nodded. "Before we came in here, she said she was my liaison or some bullshit. What does that even mean? Liaison? Like we're brokering a peace treaty or something."

"I don't know, buddy, but it doesn't sound good. Allie was really uncomfortable about me coming here tonight, and I'm beginning to think she was right."

I grinned at him. "How is the lovely Allie doing? She enjoying being married to your ugly ass?"

"She's still way too good for me, but for some reason she thinks I'm the shit."

"Because you treat her like a goddamn queen, and rightfully so." I stroked my hand over my chin. "So, I have some news." I briefly glanced up at the women on the stage and then back to Lester. "I have my own queen now," I said with a satisfied grin.

"Shark! What the hell, man? Some lady has finally tamed your wild ass?" He slapped me on the shoulder like a proud father, even though he was my age.

"Yeah," I said happily. "Her name is Charli, and I'm crazy about her." I gave him a little shrug. "No, scratch that. I'm in fucking *love* with her. We haven't been together long, but I'm going to marry that girl one day."

"Does she know this?"

I laughed. "Not yet."

Some woman named Tasha came by and addressed us as Mr. J and Mr. M. and asked for our phones. "Why do you need our phones?" Lester asked. *And what was with the code names?*

"It's our policy," she said, putting the phones in little velvet bags with our assigned letters on them. "No one wants photographic or video evidence of what takes place in this room, right?" she asked with a sly little smile and a lifted eyebrow.

"And why's that?" I asked.

Her smile broadened. "Sugar, lots of things can happen here. Read the rules in the top drawers of your tables for the guidelines." She pointed at two tables that we had been using for our drinks. On closer inspection, mine had a J on it, and Lester's had an M. *Ahhhh, Mr. J and Mr. M.*

Tasha sauntered off to collect more phones, and Les and I opened the top drawers of our tables, which were filled with condoms and a piece of heavy ivory cardstock entitled 'Rules of The Vibe.' After reading for about fifteen seconds, we both got a pretty good idea of what The Vibe was all about, and our eyes met. Words like *'utmost discretion,' 'prophylactics required for any and all penetrative activities,' 'only soft bindings allowed,'* and *'consensual adults'* were littered throughout.

"Holy fuck," Les whispered and scooted closer to me. "Am I correct in assuming you're not okay with this?" he asked, waving the paper in my face.

"You are correct," I said. "Should we just leave?"

The music changed, and girls started streaming from the stage and spreading out around the room. "Too late. Incoming," my friend murmured as two gorgeous dark-haired women headed our way. "Shit, what do we... hold on. Do you trust me, man?"

"With my life."

"Then go with me here." The two women in black strapless dresses stopped in front of us and slowly pushed their dresses down their bodies, revealing white lace thongs and nothing else... well, besides their black stilettos.

Holy shitballs.

"Hi, guys," the one in front of me said. "I'm Cora, and this is Piper. You're sitting close together, so we're assuming that means you may be interested in some swapping?"

Lester spoke up. "Darlin', you are both just fabulously stunning, but..." My friend turned his face to me and gave me the strangest look. *Was he batting his goddamn eyelashes at me?* When he grabbed my hand and linked his fingers with mine, I almost pulled away and asked him what the fuck he was doing, until... *ohhh.* His plan became clear then. "We're just here for our friend's party, but we're not interested in any extracurricular activities. Not with women anyway." He let out a little giggle. An actual fucking giggle from six-foot-four, 230-pound Lester, and I had to bite my lip to keep from laughing out loud.

"Yes, but thank you, ladies. You're both wonderful dancers, and we've enjoyed watching you. Just because we're not into girls doesn't mean we can't appreciate true beauty when we see it," I said, laying it on thick.

"Awww, that's so sweet! Thank you, Mr. M and Mr. J, and we wish you all the happiness in the world," Piper said kindly.

"Thank you, sweetheart," Les said. "And we would appreciate your discretion."

"Of course," Cora said, laying a hand across her ample bosom. "Love is love, and what you do in your private lives is no one else's business."

"We agree wholeheartedly," I said, giving them a polite nod before they blew us kisses and turned to go back to the stage. Cutting my eyes at Les, I unwound my fingers from his. "You were just a little too good at that," I said out of the corner of my mouth.

"Shut the fuck up, Shark," he said with barely restrained laughter. "I just hauled both of our asses out of the fire." He shot me a dry glare. "You ever thought about using some hand lotion or something? I'm not going to hold your hand anymore if you don't start moisturizing."

"I'm heartbroken. No, really. I can hardly bear the disappointment," I said sarcastically, looking around the room. Everyone except us was getting lap dances. Well, Tank was just talking to his woman as she knelt between his legs. Looking toward the couch to my right, I caught Cam's eye, and he frowned at my and Les's lack of strippers on our laps. I just gave a sharp shake of my head, and he gave me a firm nod of understanding.

I heard laughter and looked forward to witness Grayson turning his brother's couch around so that Gavin was facing us. A chestnut-haired beauty sank gracefully to her knees in front of him and began sucking him off for everyone to see.

"Not to sound judgmental, but isn't he getting married next week?" I said to Lester.

"Fuck yeah, he is. I've never understood why some guys think it's okay to cheat on the woman they're about to marry just because it's their bachelor party."

I nodded my agreement. If you loved a woman enough to marry her, there's no way you should want another woman sucking your dick a week before your wedding. No wonder they took away everyone's phones.

Jesus. I was no prude, but I couldn't believe all this was happening. I needed to get out of here ASAP.

40

CHARLI

"Here! Drink another one, Char!" Bristol yelled above the music. "Fireball in honor of sexy firefighters!"

I downed the shot, which didn't burn nearly as much as the first three, and looked up at the shirtless firefighters on the stage. "Do you think they're actual firemen?" I asked with a giggle as the five huge hunks thrusted and grinded to a Pitbull song.

"Sure, babe. Let's go with that." The men yanked off their pants in unison, and Bris and I screamed our approval as the one closest to us walked to the edge of the stage and waggled his dick at us. He was wearing some tiny little underwear with flames on them, but you could still see the goods flopping around behind the fabric.

"This is, like, so fun, Bristol! I didn't know they had one of these places in Dallas."

Bristol edged her phone up over the edge of the table and furtively snapped a pic of the well-endowed, greased-up guy in front of us. The music changed, and the firefighters ran off, throwing kisses at the adoring audience.

The lights went dim, and a spotlight appeared over a man standing at attention in a naval uniform. "Oh, God bless the USA," Bristol groaned. "That guy's biceps look like friggin' boulders."

With an ultra-confident swagger, he walked to the front of the stage. Standing up and waving my arms, I yelled, "Oh, yeah! Walk for mama, big boy!" causing

Bristol to spew her Cosmopolitan across the table. She slapped my arm as she coughed, and I patted her back. "What? He walks soooooo sexy."

"You're so fucking drunk, Charli Casper, and I love it." I showed off my best drunk girl moves, hips swaying and arms in the air, moving my body to the beat as I watched the navy god grind his hips slowly. *Jeez, this guy is really good.* I let out another yell, and he looked over at me before pointing me out to a security guard.

"Oh shit, Bris. I think I'm getting kicked out," I hissed as the beefy security guard walked toward me. "Was I acting too rowdy?" My friend's eyes widened as the guard asked me to come with him. "Don't tell my mom. And come bail me out. I'll pay you back. I love you, Bris," I was yelling over my shoulder as the big dude dragged me by the hand away from our cozy little round table.

Would they just kick me directly out into the street, or would they take me in a back room and beat a confession out of me? Hell, I didn't even know what I was supposed to be confessing to. Eying the direction he was pulling me, I decided we definitely weren't headed to the front door, so it was either the beating or I was getting tossed in a back alley. Without warning, the guard lifted me by the waist… and right up onto the… stage? They were going to beat me onstage? That seemed a tad extreme, but maybe they were wanting to make an example out of me to send a message to any other women who decided to become unruly.

The navy guy walked up to me and took both my hands as he leaned forward to whisper in my ear. "Hi, beautiful. We're going to put on a show together, okay?"

"You're not going to hit me, are you?" I asked fearfully.

He laughed, and it was a warm, gentle sound. "No sweetheart, it's not that kind of show. I promise you'll be safe, and I won't touch you inappropriately at all. I'll come close at times, but it's all part of the show. Tell me your name."

"Charli," I said, still confused as to what was going on. Was I in trouble or not?

"I'm Joseph," he said, dropping low with his legs spread before I knew what was happening and then slowly sliding back up with his mouth an inch from my body, drawing *ooohs* and screams from the crowd. "See, you're doing great, gorgeous."

He led me by the hand to a chair that had magically appeared in the center of the stage. "You have really strong thigh muscles," I observed, and he chuckled.

"You ain't seen nothing yet, baby. Have a seat." I sat down, and he disappeared behind me as the audience whooped and hollered. *What was he doing back there?* I felt something on my head and realized he had put his uniform hat on me. He walked back around in front of me and tore his top open while he was facing me.

Holy hell, this guy is ripped. Chest. Abs. Everything was so... hard.

Someone in the crowd yelled, "Lucky bitch," and I was pretty sure it was Bristol. I looked for her and found her standing on her chair, screaming with glee. Joseph turned to face the audience and bent over at the waist, giving me a very up-close view of his spectacular ass.

"Those pants are really stretchy. Is that polyester?" I asked, and the stripper was grinning wildly when he turned to face me again.

"I don't know. Maybe you should take a better look." He yanked off his pants and tossed them to me, but I didn't bother to check the tag because I was suddenly faced with an enormous penis covered only by a navy-blue thong. He planted his feet on either side of my chair so I could more closely inspect his junk as he wiggled his ass, much to the delight of the audience.

"Jesus, do you have a squirrel in there or something?" I asked, pointing at the large member bouncing in my face.

He squatted down and rested his hands on the back of my chair, almost sitting in my lap, but not quite as he pretended to hump me. "Oh, Charli, you are fucking adorable," he murmured in my ear. "You really want to make them scream?"

"Um, okay."

"Pull my shirt off when I turn around. Do it slowly."

Oh, my God! He wants me to undress him. I'm not authorized for this kind of thing. Shouldn't I have some kind of permit or something? He turned around, and I was face-to-face with his tight ass. Or I guess it would be face-to-ass, right? I reached up and grabbed the shoulders of his shirt, sliding it slowly down his arms as the place went fucking nuts.

Joseph was rolling his hips, his ass almost brushing my nose with each rotation. He turned to face me again, and I asked, "Do you have a quarter I could borrow?" He looked down at his tiny briefs and then gave me a wide-eyed look as if to say, *where the hell would I keep a coin purse in this outfit?* "I'll bet I could bounce a quarter off that ass of yours," I said knowingly, and he smirked and held up one finger.

He turned and strutted—*literally strutted*—to the front of the stage, spreading his legs and squatting, giving the audience an excellent crotch view, which they obviously appreciated. He whispered something to the guard there, who looked perplexed before reaching into his pocket and drawing out a coin. Joseph lay down on his stomach, turning his face to me and beckoning with one finger until

I stood and took the quarter from him. I held it up so the audience could see and noticed that all of them were standing and yelling, "Bounce it! Bounce it!"

I straddled his thick thighs and bent over, aiming right for his left butt cheek with the quarter. Flicking my wrist, I released it, and the damn thing hit his ass and bounced up like it had been shot out of a cannon. I had to lean back to avoid being pegged in the head by the flat projectile.

A swell of cheering rose up from the audience, and Joseph flipped over with a huge grin and rose to his feet in one sexy, graceful movement. He held my hands and gently guided me to lie on my back on the floor.

Oh, holy hell. What's happening now?

Joseph straddled my feet and suddenly fell forward, catching himself with his hands less than half an inch before he crushed me with his massive, almost-naked body. Then he proceeded to do pushups over my prone form, his arms rippling as he stopped just a hairsbreadth from touching me every time.

After one final pushup, he shoved himself to a standing position with *just his fucking arms* and offered his hand to help me up. Despite his assistance, I wasn't nearly as elegant as I rose to my feet, but everyone screamed when Joseph lifted one of my hands in the air like I had just won a prizefight or something. He gave me a hug and a chaste kiss on the cheek before scooting me toward the edge of the stage, where the burly security guard lifted me to the ground.

On my way back to our table, everyone I passed high-fived me with huge smiles. Bristol threw her arms around me and screamed in my face, "That was the most epic fucking thing I've ever seen in my life. You and that damned quarter!" Her laughter was contagious, and soon we were both dissolving in fits of giggles.

I noticed the security guard approaching, and my nerves took over. Was I in trouble for the whole impromptu quarter demonstration? But he leaned down and said, "Joe said you can keep the hat with his compliments. He also said you can meet him backstage after the show is over." He glanced at Bristol. "Your friend, too." With a mischievous wink, he went back to his post in front of the stage as the next set of dancers lined up.

"Oh. My. God. That big hung-like-a-horse hunk wants you, Char!"

Bris had been right. This club was the perfect distraction because this was the first time I had thought about my maybe-wayward boyfriend for at least an hour.

"I can't go back there with that guy, Bris. What about Beau?"

"Fuck Beau," she retorted. "Aaron texted that he watched him go back into that VIP area, and you saw the picture of him talking to that woman."

"Yeah. You're right. Fuck Beau Atwood."

BEAU

"You think we can blow this joint now?" Lester asked. "I want to get back to my wife."

Shooting a long look around the room and finding everyone else 'occupied,' I nodded. "They'll never even miss us," I said dryly. I caught Cam's eye and motioned that we were out of here, and he gave a sharp nod before turning his attention back to the woman who was gyrating all over him. *Fucking Cam.* He was in his element here, and I felt way out of mine.

My only desire right now was for my sweet little Peach.

Lester followed me out of the room, and we collected our phones from the lady in the hallway. "Thank you for visiting The Vibe tonight, gentlemen, and we hope to see you back again soon."

"Not fucking likely," Les muttered to me, and I had to agree with him. We barely glanced at the women working the stages in the main Vibration room. After what we had just witnessed, mere nudity was fucking tame. "You wanna share a cab?" my friend asked. "We're staying at a hotel not far from your house."

"Sure, and why don't we meet for breakfast in the morning? I want you and Allie to meet my Peach."

"Peach? I thought you said her name was Charli."

I grinned, slightly embarrassed at my slip of the tongue. "I call her that sometimes. She's just so soft and sweet, and fuck... that voice of hers..."

Lester clamped a hand on my shoulder as we walked out onto the sidewalk. "You've got it bad, my friend. And that's a wonderful thing."

In the back of the cab, I checked my phone for the first time and frowned when I saw two messages from Bristol. Shit, I hoped Charli didn't need me while my phone was being held hostage outside the Room of Live Porn. "What the fuck?" I blurted out with a laugh when I saw a picture of a dude wearing only some tiny little underwear with flames on them.

Lester peeked at my phone and asked, "Dude, what kind of kinky shit are you into?"

"This is from Charli's friend Bristol. She texted, 'Strip clubs aren't only for men.' What the hell is that supposed to mean?"

Lester smirked at me and said, "I think it means she took your girlfriend to a male strip club tonight."

"No fucking way!" I shouted, earning me a glare from the cab driver, so I lowered my voice. "Charli would be blushing like crazy if she watched something like that." I scrolled down to the next picture and almost dropped my phone. "Charli?" I whispered to the phone like the picture of her wearing what looked like a navy dress uniform hat could hear me.

"Is that your girl?" Les asked, grabbing my phone from my limp hand. "Damn, she's hot. Don't tell Allie I said that," he added quickly. My fists balled up in my lap, and Les said, "And why don't you forget I mentioned it, as well." Staring at the picture, he hummed thoughtfully. "It looks like she's on a stage, but who is that dude?"

"That's what the fuck I would like to know," I hissed. The dude was practically naked, and he was standing right beside Charli.

"Well, I want to know if that's a squirrel in his pants," Les said, tilting his head a little until I snatched the phone back.

"It's not funny, Les. She's been... corrupted."

"From the smile on her face, it doesn't look like the corruption bothered her very much." I elbowed him hard in the ribs, forcing a low grunt from him. "I'm just sayin'..."

I read the text underneath the pic. 'Good thing Charli's into Navy guys, huh?' *Okay, I'm officially pissed.*

Slapping the seat in front of me, I barked at the driver, "Change of plans."

CHARLI

"Are you sure you're okay? I really hate leaving you at this house alone."

"I'm fine," I told Bristol, probably a little more harshly than I had intended. "I'm going to grab my bag and get a cab back to the Broxtons' house." I would have just gone straight home, but my bag had my toothbrush and my birth control pills in it, so I was stopping by Beau's house to pick it up. He was obviously *busy*, so I didn't have to worry about running into him. "Seriously, I'll be in and out in two minutes, and you live in the complete opposite direction."

"Okay, you seem awfully, um, calm about all this. It's freaking me out."

"I'll tell you who better be freaked out, and that's Beau fucking Atwood. The cheating bastard." I saw the lifted eyebrows of the cab driver as she looked at me in the rearview mirror. The poor woman had gotten an earful on the ride from the strip club to Beau's house.

I had no idea why I wasn't dissolving into tears, but I wasn't crying at all. I was too fucking mad. Now tomorrow? It would probably be a different story once all the alcohol I had consumed wore off. I would probably spend the entire day crying.

After hugging Bristol and assuring her once again that I was fine, I used the key Beau had given me to let myself into his house. *Just get in, get your bag, and get out.* My plan was thwarted when I ran into a solid wall of muscle as soon as I walked in the door. I shrieked, and the light switch flicked on, leaving me facing six-foot-plus of very angry male.

"Where. The fuck. Have you been?" he said in a low, scary voice.

Oh, he has some nerve. "After where *you've* been, I don't think it's any of your goddamn business," I said saucily, not intimidated by him at all.

"Would you care to explain this?" he asked, holding up a picture on his phone of me onstage with Joseph.

Really? He's pissed about that when he was out acting like a whore?

"Would you care to explain *The Vibe?*" I asked indignantly. I dug my own phone out and pulled up the picture Bristol had forwarded to me—the one of Beau and the rest of the party entering that disgusting room—and shoved it in his shocked face. "Yeah, I know alllll about it, Beau Atwood. And I know exactly what you did in there."

He squinted at the picture. "Where did you get that?"

"It was sent to me by... a friend. And to answer your other question, I went to a strip club, just like you, so don't you stand there being all hypocritical."

Beau crossed his arms and leveled me with a glare that probably would have been scary if I wasn't so pissed. He should be the scared one. "We'll talk about you and that fucking goon later, but what exactly do you think I did tonight?"

"I don't *think.* I *know.* There was a witness who saw you going into that room with a woman."

He softened his tone a little, which threw me off guard. "Peach, I didn't do anything with any woman." It was then that I noticed we weren't alone, as a big guy with sandy brown hair walked up to me and held out his hand.

"Hi, Charli. I know this isn't the best circumstance to meet someone, but I'm Lester, a friend of Beau's. He was with me the entire night."

I put my hands on my hips, refusing to shake his hand, and he slowly lowered it. *No telling where that hand has been if he was in that room with Beau.* "Were you with him when he got his dick sucked or when he fucked some bitch in The Vibe? Or did y'all have a threesome or a tensome or whatever?" I didn't even know if a tensome was a thing, but I was so mad, I didn't even care about the accuracy of my sex terminology.

They exchanged a bewildered look before Lester spoke again. "I can assure you, none of those things happened. Not with me or Beau. Don't get me wrong; there was a lot of that shit going down in there, but not with us. Your witness—whoever she is—must be mistaken."

"Who said the witness was a she?" I asked, and then clamped my mouth shut. Those damn shots had certainly loosened my lips.

To my dismay, Beau caught my slip, and he and his friend shared a look. Lester must be military too, because those guys had a way of communicating with each other with just a look.

"It doesn't matter who told me. All that matters is that you…" *Okay, the tears were threatening now.* I stifled a sob and did my best to glare at him.

Lester took a step toward me and said, "Charli, I know you don't know me, but I'm happily married. I love my wife more than my own life, and I would never, ever cheat on her. And Beau didn't cheat on you. He didn't lay so much as a pinky finger on another woman." He grinned at me. "You're all he could talk about."

A small inkling of doubt cracked through my resolve, and a seedling of hope planted itself in my heart.

"So, you didn't… partake? Either of you?"

They shared another one of those looks before Beau spoke. "Neither of us touched a woman tonight. In fact…" He glanced at his friend who closed his eyes and gave a reluctant nod. "We pretended to be a couple so that the women we were assigned would back off."

My eyes bounced back and forth between them like I was watching a ping pong match. "You pretended to…"

"Yep," Lester confirmed. "We even held hands."

I felt my lips curl up at the corners. "Oh my God. Did you kiss?"

"Hell no, I wouldn't kiss that ugly fucker," Beau practically yelled. "In fact, I think I might cut off the hand he held during that little charade."

"Well, it was no picnic for me either, asshole. Charli, don't you have some hand lotion or something he could use? Or maybe take him to get a manicure? It was like holding a fucking dragon's paw."

"Shut up, shithead," Beau said sarcastically. "I'll have you know that my hands are very manly, and you—" He cut off his tirade when I launched myself into his arms and wrapped my legs around him. "*Peach*," he said softly against my hair.

Lester chuckled as Beau's lips found mine. "I think my work is done here. Shark, call me tomorrow, and we'll take our beautiful women to breakfast."

Beau answered with a muffled, "Mmmfh," because he had his tongue halfway down my throat. As soon as the door closed behind his friend, he pushed my back against it and turned the deadbolt lock. "Please tell me that prick onstage didn't touch you, because I would really rather bury myself in you than have to go hunt his ass down tonight." He pumped his heavy erection between my legs, and a rush of wetness soaked my panties.

"He didn't touch me anywhere except my hands when he led me to the chair or helped me up. He was actually very... respectful."

Beau's mouth moved down my neck to nibble at my collarbone as his hands slid up my dress to cup my ass. "Well, I still hate him, but I love this fucking dress."

"Beau? Did you get a lap dance?"

He seemed exasperated with my questioning. "I told you, Peach. I didn't touch anyone, and they didn't touch me. I swear."

"Well, would you *like* a lap dance?"

"Of course not. I just want you, babe."

"No, I mean, would you want *me* to give you a lap dance?" I asked shyly.

His lips twitched as if the idea of me doing that was funny. "I would love for you to do anything you want to my lap," he said, sounding slightly condescending.

I tried to hide my smirk. He didn't think I could dance as raunchily as a stripper, but he was about to learn. My freshman year of high school, I joined a dance studio. They brought in guest teachers in different genres to teach us once a month, and one of my favorites had been burlesque. I was about to draw on those particular lessons to blow my man's damn mind.

Squirming out of Beau's arms, I grabbed an armless dining room chair and set it up in the living room. "Sit," I ordered, and he complied, looking amused as I tapped on my phone.

I'm about to rock your fucking world, Beau Atwood. You have no idea.

I turned on "Candy Shop" by 50 Cent and stood in front of him, swaying my hips innocently. "You're doing good, baby," he said encouragingly, and I dropped down to a squat with my legs locked primly together, my hands on my knees. Smiling sweetly at him, I waited for the beat, and then I popped my legs open wide, drawing the exact response from Beau that I had anticipated. Wide-eyed astonishment.

"Fu-fuuuck," he panted as I slithered my body upward, dragging my hands provocatively up my sides and giving my breasts a quick squeeze before pushing my fingers up into my hair. I tilted my head back and closed my eyes, sliding one hand down my neck and between my breasts, letting it finally come to rest obscenely low on my belly as I moved my hips in a wide figure-eight pattern.

I swiveled to face away from him and bent to grab my ankles, drawing a low groan from my man as I looked over my shoulder and trailed my hands up the outsides of my legs. When I reached the hem of my dress, I grasped it and pulled it up and over my head in one smooth movement, tossing it to the side as Beau took in my red satin thong and bra. "Fucking gorgeous," he breathed, reaching for me as I jiggled my ass enticingly.

"Uh-uh. No touching," I chastised, turning around and booping him on the nose with my forefinger. I walked sensuously around behind him and slid my hands over his broad shoulders and down his chest. "I'll be the one doing the touching tonight, Mr. Atwood," I whispered low in his ear. My drunken fingers didn't even stumble as I deftly unbuttoned his shirt and slid it off his arms.

Keeping one hand on his shoulder, I swung one leg over to straddle Beau's lap, continuing my hip and upper body rotations as his big hands slid up my thighs to cup my ass. I stopped my movements and slid off his lap, meriting a deep scowl from my boyfriend. "I said no touching," I sang, going around behind him again and sliding my hands down his arms, letting my fingernails scratch against his flesh.

"You're my girlfriend, and I'll touch you if I fucking want to," he growled. Before he knew what was happening, I had his shirt in my hand and was binding his wrists together with the long sleeves.

"I don't think so, Mr. Atwood," I purred in his ear. "You need to learn to follow the rules."

His arms jerked against the bindings, and he barked angrily, "What the hell do you think you're doing, Charli? I need to touch you." I pulled his face around to meet mine and soothed him with a long kiss, sweeping my tongue into his mouth until he relaxed. His voice was softer, almost pleading. "Please, baby. My zipper is going to be permanently engraved on my dick if I don't get some relief."

I knelt in front of him and removed his socks and shoes before unfastening his belt and pants. As soon as I got his pants unzipped, he released an audible sigh of relief. He lifted his hips as I slid his pants off, and I noticed that the end of his dick was sticking out the top of his black boxer briefs. *Jesus, I've never seen him this long and thick before.* As soon as I released his hands, I knew he was going to let me have it with that big cock, and I smiled in anticipation. But that was going to be a while because I was just getting started.

I had put the song on repeat, and it started over as I stood and slid one hand down to my inner thigh, the other lifted to my mouth where I sucked innocently on the tip of my index finger.

"Holy fuck. Who are you?" he croaked as I wove my hips in a serpentine pattern, keeping his attention on my lower body as I let my middle finger graze the deep red satin covering my most private area.

"I'm your sweet little Peach," I said with a coy smile, bending forward to give him an excellent view of my cleavage encased in the slick red fabric. I slid my hands up his thighs, dangerously close to his testicles. I let one thumb brush seemingly accidentally across his underwear, and he groaned loudly. "Are you done barking orders at me so I can finish dancing for you now?" I asked, letting my tongue trail lightly up his cheek.

"By all means, Peach," he said with a smirk as I settled on his lap again, my legs spread wide. Draping my arms over his shoulders, I started grinding against his hardness in slow circles with only our thin underwear separating us from what we both wanted. "Goddamn, your pussy is hot, baby. And so fucking wet."

I drew more urgent curses from him when I leaned back, arching until my hair brushed the floor between his spread feet, my hips never stopping their undulating movements against his crotch. Then I slowly made my way back up until my breasts were right in his face. Unable to use his hands, he slid his tongue inside the top of my bra, teasing my nipple.

Pulling my bra cup down under my breast to give him better access, I said, "You better make me wet because I'm sure you're going to fuck the shit out of me when I untie you."

"Damn right," he growled sucking hard on my nipple as I circled my hips in rhythm with the music. *Slow. Fast, fast. Slow. Fast, fast.* "Let me taste the other one," he grunted, and I lowered the other bra cup a half a second before he sucked my nipple roughly into his mouth. "Fuck yes. You're so damn sexy, baby." He bit the underside of my breast and sucked hard until he marked me. Running his tongue once over his handiwork, he looked up at me smugly. "Mine."

Sliding my ass back until it was resting on his knees, I leaned down and placed my mouth on his hard abs, so close to the tip of his exposed dick I could smell the musky scent of the pre-cum that was leaking all over his stomach. I sucked the taut flesh into my mouth and marked him like he had done to me. "Mine," I claimed as he shifted his hips, trying to push the head of his erection toward my mouth. I straightened and pressed my body against his, our genitals coming in contact once again. It was time to put this poor man out of his misery. Rolling my hips, I fucked him hard and fast through our underwear as I plunged my hands into his hair and sucked on his neck.

"Christ, baby. You need to slow down or I'm gonna come all over the place." Instead of slowing down, I pressed my lips against his and rode him like a bucking bronco, our tongues battling violently as I swallowed his deep moans. "Charli.

Stop, sweetheart. Seriously," he said, his words far removed from what his body was saying. He was moving with me, pushing his dick up between my legs and building up an orgasm in me that I was fighting against. For now.

"You don't want a happy ending?" I asked, biting his bottom lip and sucking it into my mouth as I drug my pussy over his thick hardness.

"Fuck! I can't hold it anymore, baby. Oh, God. Fuck, Ch-Char-Charli. Ahhhh, fuck yeah." He was coming all over his stomach, his breathing harsh against my lips. "Dear Lord, woman. That was... unexpected."

"You didn't think I could do it," I pouted, rocking gently against him.

"I knew you were the sexiest woman in the world, but I didn't know you could move like that." Narrowing his eyes, he said, "If you've ever been a stripper, please don't tell me about it. I don't think I could take it."

"We all have our little secrets," I said demurely, kissing my way down his chest. "You made quite a mess down here." I swirled my finger through the thick cream he had ejaculated and rubbed it on his nipples before taking my time licking and sucking it off. Beau's green eyes darkened as I continued scooping up his cum and spreading it across his chest and up his neck. I used the flat of my tongue to lick up every bit of it, and I felt him hardening between my legs again.

"Damn, baby. That's fucking sexy," he rasped, his head tilted back as I sucked the last of him from the side of his neck. "Can you untie me now?"

I wasn't sure where this vixen-like behavior was coming from. Perhaps from the flow of alcohol that was still swirling through my veins. I traced the hard muscles of his upper arms with my fingernails. "Who said I was done with you, Mr. Atwood?"

BEAU

I WAS PRETTY SURE my cock was about to spontaneously explode. Had my sweet angel just tied me to a chair, given me the hottest fucking lap dance ever, made me firehose all over my stomach, and then proceed to smear my own cum on me and lick it off? And now she was saying she wasn't done with me? *Holy. Fuck.*

Correction: she *looked* like an angel, but she was a wicked, wicked woman, and I fucking *loved* it. I felt an almost physical pain when she slid off my lap to pick up her phone and change the song. I couldn't help but grin when I heard the first sharp, metallic beats of "Milkshake" from her phone.

She turned and sauntered back to me with her own smile curving her gorgeous, swollen lips. "For the record, Peach, your milkshake better not bring any boys to the yard."

As she approached me, she purred, "Oh, I'm not interested in any boys. Just men. Actually, one *specific* man." She put those precious lips on mine, weaving her tongue into my mouth so that I could taste myself on her. Her hands tightened on my shoulders, and before I knew it, her small feet were on the seat of the chair, just outside of my hips. She broke the kiss and stood, bringing her satin-covered pussy level with my mouth... just where I liked it.

Then she started to move again. Those fucking hips of hers! Where had she learned to move like that? Standing on my chair and gyrating her cunt in my face, she looked like a goddess, and I intended to worship her. Her movements faltered when I bent my head forward to suck on a soft patch of skin on her hip that was exposed by those tiny ass panties.

I let my tongue slide into the crease at the top of her leg, and dear God in heaven, she smelled good. And tasted good. Her arousal was coating the tops of her thighs, and I voraciously lapped it up. First one thigh and then the other until her hands were buried in my hair as she rolled her hips forward and moaned.

I closed my mouth over her pussy, sucking her wetness from the fabric. "Let me taste all of you, baby," I practically begged, and since I couldn't move my damned hands, she quickly slid her panties off, exposing that slick pink flesh I was craving. Her legs almost buckled when I slid my tongue through her slit the first time. Yeah, my girl was already right on the edge. It wouldn't take much.

I lapped her with long, hard swipes of my tongue as she pumped her hips against my mouth. "Beau," she said with a sexy moan that had my dick throbbing like a sonofabitch. "I'm so close." I flicked my tongue rapidly over her swollen little peak and then sucked hard on it, feeling a rush of wetness against my chin as her hands tightened in my hair.

I knew my woman's body, and she was about to come, but her right heel was hanging precariously off the edge of the chair. I gave her a long lick and pulled my mouth away from her sweetness. "Hold on a second, baby. Just untie my arms so I can—"

Charli jerked my hair roughly until my face was between her legs again. "Beau, eat my pussy. Now!" Pushing her hips forward, she growled, "Don't. Fucking. Stop."

Holy fucking shit!

I'll be damned if her desperation for my mouth on her hot little pussy didn't have my balls swelling with need.

Okay, fuck it. I yanked my arms violently outward, ripping my shirt to shreds before I slung one of her legs over my shoulder and buried my face in her cunt, supporting her with my hands under her ass. She came as soon as my mouth closed over her, and I sucked and licked her hungrily as she screamed for me. Her orgasm lasted for a full minute, after which I let her leg go so that she could collapse down into my lap.

"So good," she murmured, licking her taste from my chin and lips with tiny little kitten licks.

"I'm planning on bending you over that couch and fucking you until you can't remember your own name."

"Yes, please," she murmured against my lips, so I stood from the chair and set Charli on her feet, reaching behind her to unhook her bra and pull it off. I gently guided her to her knees and kneeled to face her, pulling her hands behind her butt and commanding, "Leave them there."

Her tits jutted out alluringly in this position, so I leaned down and tongued each of them, ending with a long pull on the nipples. "Beau, touch me," she implored.

Placing soft kisses on her mouth, I surprised her by refusing. "No, baby. I'm not going to finger-fuck you tonight. I'm going to let my cock do all the work of stretching that tight little pussy of yours to its limits." She moaned and I plunged my tongue into her mouth, kissing her deeply as I cupped her face in my hands. "I love you, Peach," I murmured against her lips.

"Love you, baby," she replied, turning her face into my hand to kiss my palm.

My dick was becoming unbearably hard, so I stood and removed my briefs, freeing my erection to bob right in front of Charli's hungry eyes. I fisted myself and gave a couple long, slow strokes before threading the fingers of one hand into her hair to hold her where I wanted her. I painted her full, swollen lips with my precum and ordered her to lick it off. "Taste what you do to me, Charli. Taste how much I want you."

She moved her tongue slowly across her bottom lip and then the top one, and the sight made my cock twitch with need. I pressed my hardness against her lips. "Open up and let me in, sweet girl."

Charli's eyes closed, and I sharply tugged her hair. "Where are your eyes supposed to be when my dick is in your mouth?" I growled, and she looked obediently up at me with those giant cornflower-colored irises. Keeping her eyes on mine, she licked me from my balls to my tip before sliding her lips up and down each side of my thick cock. Then she took me into her mouth, slurping and moaning around me. It was wet and sloppy and loud… and so fucking hot.

Pushing deeply into her mouth, I hit the back of her throat. "Open for me, baby," I commanded as I surged forward, my tip sliding down into her tight throat. "Fuck, yeah." Three more deep pumps, and I was ready to blow, so I reluctantly pulled out and helped Charli to her feet. "I need to fuck you, Peach."

I backed her toward the couch and then turned her around so that the silky skin of her back was pressed against my chest. Pushing her hair over one shoulder, I peppered the other one with kisses and slid my hands up her slender body to cup her breasts. "You are so fucking beautiful, Charli," I murmured in her ear as I tugged at her nipples with my fingers. She tilted her head back to me for a kiss and I obliged, smoothing both hands down her taut belly all the way to her hips as my mouth ate at hers like a man starved.

She wrapped her arms back around me to grasp my ass and my dick slipped between her butt cheeks as she pumped back against me. "Beau. I need you. Please," she said breathlessly, and I bent her over the arm of the couch with one hand between her shoulder blades.

Taking my heavy erection in my hand, I squeezed the base as I rubbed the tip through her wetness until it was dripping with *her*. Lining up with her entrance, I surged forward, sinking half of my length into her tight sheath. "Fucking Christ, baby," I groaned as she whimpered beneath me. "You have the sweetest, tightest little cunt." I separated her ass cheeks with my fingers and watched myself disappearing deeper and deeper into her with each thrust, groaning at the sight of her pussy stretching to accommodate my thick intrusion.

"You feel so good inside me, Beau. Take me deeper." Pulling back to the tip, I rammed myself inside her all the way to the hilt as she pressed her lips together to stifle her cry.

"Don't hold back, sweetheart. I want to hear every bit of your pleasure," I groaned. The next time I slammed into her, she cried out loudly. "That's it, gorgeous. Tell me how it feels."

I circled my hips, stirring my dick deeply inside her as her hands clutched the couch cushion. "It feels hot and hard. And so thick. It hurts a little bit, but it's so good." Sliding my hands up and down her back, I reveled at the feel of her soft skin and the firm muscles beneath. I settled my hands on her slim shoulders and used them for leverage as I started to rut into her like a primal animal fucking his mate. The room filled with the sounds of hard sex… the deep moans and groans from both of us… the satisfying *smack smack smack* of flesh against flesh… the uttered filthy curses.

"Fuck yes. Take it, baby. Take all of this cock," I grunted. Angling my hips a little, I found her sweet spot as a killer orgasm began building deep in my core. I rode hard against her rounded ass, loving the hot slide and friction as my penis was fully claimed by her tight cunt.

I stuck my thumb into my mouth and coated it with saliva before sliding the slippery digit between her ass crack and massaging her back entrance. As soon as I pushed it into her, her voice deepened with unfettered desire. "Oh God, Beau. Right there. I'm. Gonna. Come." She was pushing back against me as I rammed into her, flexing and contracting my back muscles with each hard thrust and working my thumb in and out of her tight little ass.

Fisting her hair, I tugged her head to the side and ran my tongue around the shell of her ear. "That's it, baby. Let me see how beautiful you look when you come on my dick with my thumb in your ass." With her mouth wide open, she let out a piercing wail as her inner muscles clamped down around my plunging rod.

My girl was coming with a vengeance, so I started counting as I pounded her through it to try and distract myself from my own impending orgasm. Twenty seconds... forty... holy fuck, sixty-five seconds.

My climax, unable to be contained anymore, shot up through my dick and into my sexy woman. Swear to God, there was so much cum in that first shot, it was like I had ejaculated a fucking plum. I stilled my hips as I continued to release myself deep inside Charli with low grunts until I was empty.

Her legs buckled, and I pulled her body up against my chest, supporting her weight with my arms wrapped around her. Pressing my lips to her sweat-slickened cheek, I breathed her in.

My sweet, sexy little Peach.

CHARLI

I FREAKING *LOVED* ALLIE James. Lester's wife was fun and bubbly and a total smartass. I saw for myself what Les had told me last night. He adored his wife. Like, he was fucking gaga over her, and she felt the same toward him. They were just precious together.

He had told her everything that had transpired the night before, and as soon as we were shown to our table for breakfast, she offered to let Beau and Lester sit on the same side so they could hold hands. *See? Total smartass.*

Her long strawberry blonde hair was pulled back in a French braid, and she giggled when Beau pulled his hand out of his pocket with his middle finger extended. "Look Al, I got you a present," he said with a grin. Then he pulled her into an affectionate hug. "Wassup, Allie Cat? I see being married hasn't made you any less of a wiseass."

"If anything, she's even worse now," Lester said with absolutely zero bite to his words as we settled into the booth.

"I heard you went to a strip club, too, Charli," Allie said. "I was apparently the only one who didn't get to ogle naked people last night." Her freckled nose wrinkled into an adorable pout.

Her husband nuzzled the pout right off her face, murmuring, "You certainly did a lot of ogling when I got back to the hotel, babe. Among other things."

"I take it the honeymoon phase is still in full effect," Beau said, watching the couple across from us as his hand rested on my thigh and his thumb stroked my bare skin.

With his eyes locked on his woman, Les said, "Four years, and going strong. My little woman is still thrilled to have entered a life of sexual servitude to me."

"In your dreams, big guy," she said, though the sexual connection between the two was palpable. And fucking adorable. Pulling her twinkling eyes from her husband, she addressed me. "So, did you get pics of the hotties?" Both men snorted their disapproval, much to our delight.

"They're on Beau's phone," I said, picking it up and finding the pics Bristol had sent him last night in a fit of loyal outrage. I showed Allie the pic of the fireman stripper and her eyes widened.

"Wow! Why don't you ever wear stuff like that for me, Les?"

"Baby, you know my stuff wouldn't fit in those tiny little drawers," he said as Beau snickered. "There would be cock and balls hanging out every whichaways."

"That's true," she said with a coy smile as her teeth sunk into her bottom lip. I showed her the pic of the navy guy, and she snatched the phone right out of my hand, zooming in on it. "Dear God, is he smuggling a rabbit in there?"

"I think it's a squirrel," Les said, squinting at the phone.

"I think that's enough on the subject," Beau said sorely, grabbing his phone and sticking it in his pocket.

Looking at Allie with a sly grin, I said, "I'll call you next time, and you can go with us."

"There's not going to be a fucking next time," Beau growled, and Lester nodded with a frown creasing his forehead.

Turning to my boyfriend, I gritted, "You go to another strip club, and see what happens, Atwood."

"After last night, I don't need to," he said smugly, referring to my strip tease and lap dance skills, and I felt my face flush. *Had I really done that?* "And after this morning, I would think you'd learned your lesson about going to places like that." I had received a very sexy spanking earlier today for my misdeeds.

"That wasn't exactly a deterrent," I said, and his hand slid further up my thigh under the table.

"Oooh, let me guess," Allie said. "Punishment was meted out, right?" Then she sighed dreamily, "The penalty phase is the best. Sometimes I misbehave on purpose." We shared a knowing look and a giggle as our men shifted in their seats, obviously excited at the thought of spanking our little asses.

"Perhaps a change of subject is in order if we're going to make it through this breakfast," Lester said. "Shark, you bringing Charli to the wedding next weekend?"

"Yep. I can't leave this one alone or she might get into more trouble," Beau said, sliding his arm around my back and smiling warmly at me.

Over our delicious breakfast, Allie and I chatted about the upcoming wedding and what we were going to wear. In accordance with girl law, I accompanied her to the bathroom after we were done eating. "Oh, my God, girl! I love you two together," she gushed from the stall beside me. "I've never seen Beau like this before."

"Yeah, I understand he used to be kinda grumpy," I replied before flushing the toilet.

We stood at the sinks to wash our hands, and she smirked at me in the mirror. "Yeah, a bit, though he was always nice to me. I've never even seen him with a woman, though Les has assured me he, ummmm, dated."

With a genuine laugh, I said, "I wouldn't exactly call what Beau used to do 'dating.' More like banging anything that moved."

"And now he's found you. You're his lobster!" she cried, referring to an old episode of *Friends,* her fingers and thumbs mimicking Phoebe's lobster claw gesture. "He's such a good guy, Charli. And you're obviously so good for him." She gave me a warm, sweet hug.

Before we left, Allie and I exchanged phone numbers, and *boom!* I had a wonderful new friend. We texted a couple times that week, and by the time Gavin and Reana's wedding rolled around, I was really looking forward to seeing her again.

Allie and Lester were standing in front of the church when we arrived, and Allie ran up to me, a miraculous feat in the heels she was wearing. "Charli! You look stunning, sister!" she said, hugging me fiercely. I was wearing a deep purple fitted dress that Beau had already been threatening to peel off me.

"You do, too," I said, taking in her fuchsia A-line dress with long sparkly sleeves. "That dress is amazing on you, and damn, woman. Your skin is literally glowing."

"Thanks," she said, blushing and looking over at her husband. "And how hot are our men in those suits?" she asked, fanning her face.

"Pretty fucking hot," I muttered under my breath. I had ogled Beau the entire drive to Fort Worth, and he had finally told me to stop looking at him like that or he was going to pull over and fuck me in the back seat of his truck. I cheekily told him it was a good thing he had darkly tinted windows, and he glowered at me in that way that told me I was going to pay for my sass in the most delicious way possible.

Beau was wearing a navy suit with a light gray shirt and navy tie, and I wanted to do nothing more than grab him by that tie and yank him against me. He had let me put a little gel in his hair, and he looked sleek and totally edible.

The four of us sat together at the wedding, and we were also fortunately seated at the same table at the reception. "Let's get our beautiful women some drinks," Beau told Lester. "Do you want champagne, baby?" he asked me, and I nodded.

"Just a sparkling water for me," Allie told her husband, and the men headed to the bar.

"You don't drink?" I asked, and she gave a little shrug, her cheeks filling with color. "Oh, my God! You're pregnant!" I blurted, and her eyes widened comically.

"Shhhh! We haven't told anyone yet." She smiled beatifically. "We just found out two days ago, and Les is about to piss himself with excitement. We've been married for four years, so it's pretty big news."

"Well, I'm thrilled for you, but I promise I'll keep my trap shut."

After dinner, we all went out onto the patio and sat on couches around an outdoor fireplace. Allie and I were glad to prop our feet up for a while. "Who the hell decided that women should wear heels and men shouldn't?"

"I don't know," I groaned, "but it needs to change." I frowned at Beau, as if it were his fault, and said, "I think you should wear a pair of stilettos next time we go out."

"No fucking way, Peach. My legs are sexy enough without them," he said, looking at me over the rim of his glass and giving me that smile he reserved just for me.

"Hey, guys," Les said, glancing at his wife and then back at us. "We have some news and also something we wanted to talk to you about."

"Charli already guessed the news when I turned down the champagne," Allie said, putting her feet in Lester's lap.

Taking her foot and kissing her big toe, he said, "Well, I'm going to tell her again because I love saying it." Flashing a grin so big I was afraid his face would crack, he turned to us and said proudly, "We're pregnant! Well, Allie is, but I helped. A lot."

His wife patted his hand and said indulgently, "You were excellent, babe. Couldn't have done it without you."

"I was excellent, wasn't I?" he asked happily as they literally beamed at each other.

"You're having a baby?" Beau asked, his face lighting up.

"Yes, and we want you and Charli to be the godparents," Les said.

You could have knocked me over with a light breeze. "I... we... bu-but you just met me," I stuttered.

"But it feels like we've known you forever, and Allie adores you. And now that you're with Shark, you're the perfect choice for godmother. Plus, he told us how much you love kids, and we want someone who will adore our little love dumpling."

"Love dumpling?" Beau asked with a laugh, and Allie just rolled her eyes and jerked her thumb at Lester, indicating that he was the creator of the goofy nickname. Searching my eyes for a moment, he turned back to our friends and said, "We would be honored."

Beau spent the rest of the evening talking in a horrible Marlon Brando voice until Allie threatened to fire him from his short-lived godfathering position. "Fine!" he huffed, pretending to be offended. "I'll just ask this pretty lady to dance with me." He stood and extended his hand for me.

"That's an offer I can't refuse," I said, trying to make my own voice gravelly, and everyone groaned at my weak Godfather impersonation.

The band was playing Foreigner's "Waiting for a Girl Like You," and Beau pulled me snugly into his arms and rested his cheek against my temple. "I feel like this song was written specifically for me, Peach," he murmured. "I've been waiting for you all my life, even though I didn't even realize it." I squeezed my arms tighter around his neck as his hands played up and down my back. "I love you so much, sweetheart," he said in his low, gruff voice, turning his head to nuzzle my hair.

"I love you, too," I said, my voice cracking with emotion. *God, this man is simply divine.* "I think I'm ready to go upstairs."

He lowered his head to press a series of sweet kisses against my lips. "Me too." His eyes were full of fire and deep promises, and I lost myself in them until the song ended.

We said a quick goodbye to Allie and Lester, and Beau led me to the hotel elevator with his hand on the small of my back. As soon as the doors closed, he pushed me against the wall and pressed his hard body against mine. "All this talk of babies got me to thinking. We should probably start practicing, so when the time comes, we'll know exactly what we're doing."

If he noticed my startled look, he didn't show it. He just poured himself into a deep, steamy kiss that had my entire body forgetting his comment and singing with desire.

In our room, Beau undressed me slowly, almost reverently, before removing his own clothes and taking me to bed. Our lovemaking was achingly sweet, his eyes never leaving mine as he covered my body and cradled my face with his hands. Our mouths were touching, but we weren't kissing; we were just inhaling each other's soft moans and whispered *I love you*s. When he came inside me, his body shuddered powerfully over mine, and his eyes shone with something I hadn't seen much from him—vulnerability.

Afterward, we both lay sated, our bodies damp and limp, and he pulled me to lie half on top of him with my head on his broad chest. "How many kids do you want, Peach?" he asked, his hand stroking leisurely up and down my hip.

I tried to force my body not to stiffen as I turned my face into his chest. "I don't know. What about you?"

He linked the fingers of his free hand with mine and rested them on his flat stomach. "Mmmm. More than two but less than ten," he said, and I could hear the happiness in his voice at the prospect of children.

Oh, Beau. Honey...

I didn't sleep well that night, even though I should have after several glasses of champagne and a long round of satisfying sex. Beau wanted children, and I lay awake cursing my body for not being able to guarantee that I could give them to him.

BEAU

I WAS WORRIED ABOUT my Peachy girl. She barely said two words on the drive back home, claiming that she had a bit of a champagne hangover. She leaned her seat back and closed her eyes, but I never heard the deep, soft breathing I was so familiar with when she was sleeping. Yes, I was a weirdo who often lay in the bed beside her and counted her breaths as she slept.

She had asked me to just drop her off at my sister's house, so I did, but I texted Blaire to ask her to go check on her periodically. I woke up alone Monday morning for the first time in a while, and I didn't like it one fucking bit. I called Charli before I went to work, but she said she was busy getting breakfast for the kids and couldn't talk.

By dinnertime, it had been twenty-four hours since I had seen her, which was totally unacceptable, so I invited myself over for dinner. "Beau... hi," Charli said hesitantly as I walked into the kitchen, and I noticed that her smile didn't reach her eyes.

"Hi, gorgeous. Are you feeling better?"

"Yeah, I'm good," she said, turning to flip the fried chicken in the pan when I went in for a kiss. "I didn't know you were coming tonight."

Hurt, but not deterred, by the less-than-warm welcome, I pressed myself against her back, holding the fronts of her hips as I nuzzled against the side of her neck. "I like your hair up so I can do this," I said, nibbling at her soft flesh and inhaling her clean, fresh scent. Her body softened against mine for a brief moment, and then she stiffened in my arms. Determined to get a response from her, I slid my tongue up her neck to that spot just below her ear that always drove her wild. And I sucked.

"Beau..." she said on a protracted exhale. Steeling her voice, she said, "You're going to make me burn the chicken."

"But I missed you last night, baby. I missed holding you in my arms." I kissed that spot gingerly. "Touching you." I swirled my tongue before dropping my voice an entire octave. "Fucking you." My teeth sunk into that sensitive area, and her head dropped back to my shoulder as a full-body shiver worked its way down her form.

"Oh..." Her voice shook as I slid my hand around her belly to pull her back against my growing length.

"Uncle Beauuuuu!" I took a deep breath to steady myself before turning to see Rox dashing across the kitchen.

I dropped to my knees to accept his tackling hug and sweet kiss against my cheek. *Cute little cockblocker.* Then his two rascally brothers invaded the kitchen, and I knew the moment was over. For now.

After we ate and got the kids to bed, I followed Charli to her room and closed the door. Going directly to her dresser, she opened the top drawer and stared down into it. "Well, I'm pretty tired, so I think I'm going to go to bed," she said without turning around. Her voice was flat, and there was a quality to it that I couldn't quite define. Honestly, it scared the shit out of me.

Approaching her carefully, I stroked my hand down her ponytail. "Ok, precious girl. We can go to bed early. Are you feeling okay? Do you want me to give you a bath before bed to help you relax?"

"I'm not a child, Beau. I'm perfectly capable of taking a bath if I want one," she said coldly, still with her back to me.

Taken aback at her tone, I inhaled a trembling breath. *Something is wrong. Really wrong.* "I know you are, Peach. I was just trying to be nice." I reached around her to pull out her blue pajamas. "Here. Put these on and get in bed. I'll rub your back until you go to sleep."

She took the pajamas and stepped away from me as she headed toward the bathroom. "And I meant that I was going to bed alone. I really need to get some sleep, so..." She paused by the door and took a deep breath. "I guess I'll talk to you later."

I was on her in two steps, whirling her around to face me, but she didn't meet my eyes. "What do you mean you'll talk to me later? You don't want me to stay with you?"

She lifted her chin defiantly, but her gaze was stuck somewhere near my throat. *Why won't she look at me?*

"No. I don't," she said firmly. "I need some... time." Her eyes flashed to mine so quickly I almost missed it and then skittered off to the side.

"Time," I repeated, quite honestly dumbfounded, and she nodded. "How much time are we talking here, Charli?" I growled.

I saw her swallow roughly before finally meeting my eyes and saying the words that were like a white-hot knife to my heart. "You're smothering me, and I need some space."

I was having trouble finding enough oxygen to fill my lungs. "All I'm hearing here is *time* and *space*, and it sounds a lot like you're..." I could barely get the words out, "...breaking up with me." She didn't say anything, and I felt an icy chill snake down my body. "Charli?" I gripped her shoulders firmly, trying to resist the urge to shake an *I love you* from her mouth.

She stared at the floor and nodded. In a voice that was barely audible, she whispered, "Yes."

No, baby. Just... no.

I staggered backwards a few steps, unable to fully comprehend what she was saying. "Don't do this, Charli. I can... I can be different. Just tell me what you need."

"You're very nice, Beau, but..."

Fucking NICE?

"But you need space. And time," I snapped bitterly. She placed a trembling hand over her mouth, and the sight made my heart ache. She was hurting. I didn't know why, but I couldn't stand seeing her hurt. Softening my tone, I dipped my head to try and catch her downcast eyes. "Talk to me, Peach. What specifically did I do to make you feel this way? I thought we were... good."

"We're just too different." I waited for her to elaborate, but she didn't.

We're just too different. That's all I get?

I wanted to look at her all night but at the same time, the sight of her was like a million shards of glass piercing my corneas. I managed to tear my eyes away from her as I turned and grabbed two handfuls of my hair, my head falling to my chest. This hurt. Bad.

"I'm sorry, Beau," she said softly.

Unable to speak around the giant ball that was growing in my throat by the second, I walked toward the door leading outside. I moved slowly, like a man heading to his own execution. Because that was what this felt like. *I'll shrivel up and die without her.*

I turned to look back at her once more and was surprised to find that she had followed me. Picking up my jacket that I had left here so many weeks ago, she held it out to me. Through my incredulity, I found my voice. "You're giving it back?"

In my mind I could see her flirty eyes and hear her breathy voice. *"I still have your jacket. Would you like to come inside and get it?"* Our little running joke that we had used in the beginning as an excuse for me to come to her room. The reality of the situation slammed into me like an eighteen-wheeler. This felt so fucking... final.

At her short nod, my heart constricted. Back to the sad little walnut-sized organ it had been before her. "If you give this back, it means we're over, Charli. For good," I warned.

Her arm jerked the jacket to her chest for a moment before she tightened her jaw and pressed her lips into a thin line. Then she extended her arm, holding the jacket out to me and effectively crushing me in the process. I reached out slowly, willing her to change her mind, but she didn't. I took my jacket and turned away from her.

With my hand on the doorknob, I said shakily. "You are my world, Peach. I would have done anything for you." As I stepped outside, I ordered, "Lock the door."

As soon as I heard the lock click, I dropped to my haunches with my head between my knees and my hands wrapped over the back of my neck. I thought I heard a cry from inside, but it was hard to tell over the sounds of my own weeping.

BEAU

Dark, dreary clouds hung menacingly over the city, accurately reflecting my mood. Everyone had just thought I was a grumpy asshole before. Jesus fucking Christ, I couldn't even stand to be around myself right now.

Tonight would make eleven days since my life imploded, and I was not fucking okay. "Mr. Atwood," came Aspen's nasally voice through my intercom. *Fuck.* I wanted to strangle the life out of her for merely existing. But it wasn't just her. It was anyone who crossed my path in the past—I checked my watch—258 hours.

"Yes," I barked.

"Your sister is here to see you."

Great. Just super goddamn great. I tried to think of an excuse. "Tell her I'm in a—" I stopped when Blaire pushed the door open and pranced into my office. "Never mind," I said dryly.

My annoying little sister looked around the empty room and said, "Hope I'm not interrupting your very important meeting."

"Come on in and make yourself at home," I said as she flopped down on the couch and patted the seat beside her.

"Thanks, bro. I appreciate your hospitality."

"I was being sarcastic."

"So was I, assclown. Now sit." I rammed my ass down beside her and crossed my arms like an insolent child. "There. Now, isn't that better?" she cooed, patting my arm.

"Just fucking dandy," I muttered.

"That's the spirit!" She curled one leg up underneath her butt and turned to me, softening her voice. "How are you, Beau?" I opened my mouth to say *fine*, and she warned, "If you say, 'fine,' I'm going to throat punch you," so I clamped my lips shut. "The kids miss you." Yeah, my sister fights dirty.

"They okay?" I asked, feeling like shit that I hadn't seen my nieces and nephews since...

"Yeah, they're excited for Christmas." My sister reached over and took my hand. "She moved out last week and put in her two weeks' notice," Blaire said, not bothering to even say her name. We both knew who *she* was. "She moved in with her friend, Bristol."

"Wait. What? What's she going to do?"

"She got a job at a department store selling perfume. I think she said she starts in a month."

"That's, um... nice?" I finally met Blaire's skeptical gaze and said angrily, "Actually, that's fucking ridiculous. She needs to work with kids. That's what makes her happy."

"I know, Beau. I think she was just desperate to get away from anything that reminded her of you, so she took the first job she could find. She's been miserable."

"*She's* been miserable? *She* broke up with *me*, remember?" I said in a near-shout.

My sister grabbed me in a fierce hug, and I stiffened. "I'm so sorry, Beau. I know how this feels. Trust me." I had been there for her when she and Axel had broken up years ago, and now she was reversing the roles. I wrapped my arms around her and accepted her warm comfort.

Unable to hold them back, I let the tears run down my face. "I tried so hard, Blaire. I tried to be good enough for her. I would have given her anything." Even I could hear how broken I was.

"I know you would. And you're way more than good enough, big bro. You're the best man I've ever known."

Pulling away and resting my elbows on my knees, I swiped my hands down my face. "Then why?"

"I have no idea. I offered her my ear to talk about it once, but she just clammed up. What did she say to you?"

"Just a bunch of vague shit. She needs *time* and *space*. And we're *too different*. I genuinely have no idea why she broke up with me. I thought everything was fine. We had the best time at the wedding. I even danced with her," I added, one side of my mouth tipping up at the memory.

"Do you think maybe the wedding made her think about your future and she got scared?"

"I don't know, sis. She certainly didn't act like it afterward in our hotel room." Blaire rubbed my back encouragingly, so I continued my train of thought. "We made love. Like *really* made love. Not fucking. It was so goddamn special. We probably said *I love you* a hundred times in bed that night. And then two nights later, she dropped a fucking bomb on my head."

"And then what?" she pressed. "Did you argue on the way home?"

"No, she barely said a word on the way home." I thought back to that day. "In fact, she was quiet from the time she woke up that morning."

"Soooo, between the sex and waking up the next morning, something must have happened," she said thoughtfully. "Did you talk after the sexy times?"

I pressed the heels of my hands into my eye sockets as I thought. "Shit, Blaire. I don't... all I can remember is being so fucking happy."

"Walk me through it, step-by-step."

I stared at her for a long moment. "Well, I spread her legs and took my di—"

"No! No, no, no!" she said holding her hands palm out to me. "Start at the end, for shit's sake. I don't need to hear *those* details about my brother." The disgusted look on her face was amusing, and I heard a rough noise burst out of my mouth.

Oh my God. Was that a laugh? I hadn't heard that sound from myself in so long... eleven days to be exact. Damn my sister for making me laugh when I was trying to be miserable and wallow in self-pity. "Okay, so we finished..."

"Did you make sure she had a happy ending?"

I shot her a look. "Of course. Who do you think you're talking to here?"

Blaire raised her eyebrows in mild amusement. "So sorry to have insulted your abilities, Casanova. Please continue." She waved her hand in invitation.

"So, we finished together, *spectacularly* I might add, and I kissed her for a while before, um, sliding off and laying beside her. I think I told her I loved her again." Blaire nodded at me in encouragement. "Then I cuddled her up against me."

"Awww, you cuddled?"

Rolling my eyes, I said, "Yes, Blaire. Your big grouchy-ass brother is a fucking fantastic cuddler." I tried to concentrate on that night again. "Let's see... oh yeah. Allie and Lester told us they're having a baby."

"Allie and Lester were in the room with you? I didn't know you were into that weird shit, bro."

I cracked a grin. "No, they weren't in the room with us, jackass. They had told us before we went up to our room, and they asked us to be godparents. Anyway, I guess with that announcement and what we had just done, I was thinking about *us* being parents. So, I asked her how many kids she wanted." I rubbed my temples. "She said she wasn't sure and asked how many I wanted."

My sister frowned thoughtfully. "You had the baby talk, huh? You know with endometriosis, there are—"

"Fertility issues," I finished. "Yeah, I know." At her surprised look, I said, "The woman I love tells me she has a condition, and you didn't think I would learn everything I could about it? Of course, I researched it."

Blaire's eyes became unfocused as she stared into nothingness over my shoulder, her mouth mumbling near-incoherent words as she rambled through her thought process. I knew better than to interrupt this whole procedure. My sister was a fucking genius, and when her mind was clicking, it was best to just stand back and let her roll.

"So, if she... and then you... then Allie's pregnant and... fuck, she probably... but no, she wouldn't... who the fuck am I kidding? It's Charli... so damned sweet... thinking that... but she didn't know about... Christ on a cracker, Charli... you precious, stupid girl."

Blaire looked at me then, her eyes completely focused on mine. "You done?" I asked with a smirk, and she nodded, giving me a look somewhere between a smile and a grimace.

"In a noble act of self-sacrifice, Charli let you go because she thinks she can't give you the children you want," my sister announced smugly.

"What?" I practically yelled, startling Blaire so badly she almost fell off the couch. I reached out a hand to steady her and lowered my voice. "Sorry, but what the fuck are you talking about?"

"This is just my speculation, of course, but I think when you started talking about wanting kids, Charli freaked about it. If she's had doctors worth a damn, they've surely had discussions about potential problems with conceiving. She thinks you want kids, and she thinks she might not be able to get pregnant, so she broke up with you."

"That's the dumbest thing I've ever heard. I don't care about that. Jesus, why would she think..."

"Have you told her?" she asked pointedly.

"No, it's never come up, and you know I never think about that anyway." I rubbed my palm hard over my forehead. "Why wouldn't she have discussed it with me? Why did she dump me?"

"Many women that are faced with infertility feel like failures or like less of a woman." She held up a hand to stop me when I opened my mouth. "I know, bro. That's not what defines a woman, but some are very self-conscious about it."

"That's bullshit. Charli is all woman, no matter if she has forty kids or none." I said with a scowl.

My sister smiled gently at my words. "I love you, ya big lug."

"I love you, too, brat. Now get the hell out of my office so I can figure out how to get my stupid, wonderful woman back."

"You go, boy," she said, high fiving me and making me smile. I had honestly thought my face had forgotten how to smile, but after my visit with my persistent, intelligent little sister, my face—as well as the rest of me—finally had some hope.

With Blaire gone, I steeled my spine and dialed Charli's number. I knew hearing her sweet voice had the potential to bring me to my knees, and when it went to voicemail, I wasn't sure if I was disappointed or relieved. I almost groaned when I heard her chirpy little greeting. "Hi! This is Charli. Leave me a message, and I'll get back to you as soon as I can. Have a great day. Bye!"

My body's response was visceral, my upper body buckling forward until my forearms were resting on my desk and my heart pounding

Picking my phone back up, I decided that perhaps texting was better anyway. At least that wouldn't evoke memories of that exquisitely beautiful voice whispering my name, moaning my name, screaming my name.

Fuck! Not helping, Atwood.

> **Beau: Hi, Charli. I need to talk to you about something important. Can I come over tonight or maybe take you to dinner?**

I waited for a response, my body tensing with each passing second until I felt like I was going to explode.

"Mr. Atwood, I have Miss Songbird here."

Clenching my jaw, I pushed the intercom button and said, "Aspen, it's Miss *Birdsong*, and please send her in. Tell Journey and the other men to join us in my office in twenty minutes."

Tazanna Birdsong, or 'Taz' as she liked to be called, was a new security specialist I had hired. Since my business was growing by leaps and bounds, I thought it was time to bring an additional specialist into the fold. I had my five men, of course, and Journey was an excellent assistant, but she was more qualified for administrative duties than actual protection. My guys were stretched thin, and we needed some help. It was a bonus that Taz was a woman because we had been getting a lot of female clients, and many of them felt more comfortable with a female guard in their dressing rooms.

I took a couple deep breaths to calm my damn nerves down a bit. "Taz, come in," I said, going to the door to welcome her into my office. I gestured to the chairs in front of my desk and sat there beside her. She smiled as she sat, her brilliant white teeth a sharp contrast to her deep tan Native American skin. Her black hair was braided and wrapped around her head in a pretty but functional style.

Taz was about five-foot-six, and she was all muscle. A former Army soldier, she had lost her right leg below the knee, compliments of an ISIS bomb four years ago, but that hadn't slowed her down a bit. She was a motherfucking beast with firearms, probably rivaling Woody, who was a sharpshooter when we were in the navy.

"Are you settling in okay? Do you need anything?" Taz had relocated from Colorado last week, and she would be starting work Monday on an important assignment guarding an up-and-coming pop star named Ella Ervin. Miss Ervin was performing with several other artists in a televised Christmas concert in Dallas, and our agency had been contracted to provide security for her. Of course, the arena provided on-site security, but there was still the matter of transporting her to and from her hotel. That was where we came in.

"Yeah, I'm staying with a friend of my brother's until I can find a place to live."

"Excellent. Just let me know if there's anything I can do to help." I gave her a company cell phone and iPad and sent her to Sandra to complete some employment paperwork.

Journey and the guys filtered in, and I sat them down to have a little chat. "Okay, I've told you all that we have a new employee. Her name is Taz Birdsong, and I think she will be an excellent addition to our team. She's former army, and we're going to show her all the respect in the world, right?" I eyed each of my men meaningfully, and they nodded.

Taz knocked on the door, and I let her in and introduced her to the team. Our newest member sat on the couch between Tank and Journey, who was enthusiastic to have another woman on board. As Taz sat down, the leg of her jeans rode up, and six pairs of eyes went directly to the sliver of her prosthetic leg that was exposed.

"What? You've never seen a chick with a fake leg before?" the new girl asked cheerily. She glanced around at her new team members and said, "Jeez, everyone stop looking so tragic. I can't stand pity, so I expect to be treated just like anyone with two good legs."

The guys nodded approvingly, and Hawk asked, "Did you lose it in service?"

"Actually, I was mauled by Mike Tyson's tiger in a Walmart in Vegas," she said with a straight face.

"No shit?" Woody asked, and Taz grinned.

"Kidding. It was a roadside bomb from our friends in ISIS." There were grumbles from around the room, most of them of the *hate those fuckers* variety. "And that was my favorite foot, too," she said forlornly.

"You had a favorite foot?" Journey asked with amusement.

"Hell yes. Don't you? That was my ass-kicking foot." She grinned again, and I couldn't help but notice how attractive she was when she smiled, which was a lot. I loved her attitude, which was one of the reasons I hired her—besides the fact that she was skilled and a total badass.

"Taz is an excellent markswoman," I added and noticed that Woody narrowed his eyes at her. He was generally a fun, easygoing guy who was always picking on everyone else in the group, but he was very serious and quite competitive when it came to shooting. *This should be interesting,* I thought with an internal smile. "Okay, for Monday night's event, we will be protecting Ella Ervin. She's a rising star in the music industry, and most of us know her name, even if we don't listen to her music regularly. It seems that Miss Ervin has gotten herself some unwanted attention from an overzealous fan."

"A stalker?" Bode asked.

"Yup. So, we'll be providing security to and from her hotel. Her detail will consist of Me, Bode, Cam, Woody, and Taz. Cam, Bode, and Woody… I'll let you three go over the plan with Taz. I can assure you that she is top notch at what we do. Now, all of you get the hell out of my office and get back to work."

I picked up my phone to check my messages, and my stomach went on a little rollercoaster ride when I saw that Charli had answered my text.

Charli: *That's probably not a good idea.*

Well, fuck.

47

CHARLI

I stared at my phone, trying to ignore the beeps from the machines surrounding me. Beau wanted to see me. No, he said he *needed* to see me. This was the first time I'd heard from him since I had broken both of our hearts, and his message was both a curse and a blessing. A curse because it hurt so fucking much to hear from him and a blessing because I was selfish and cherished the thought that he was thinking of me.

I wanted to see him so bad I ached, but I knew it was a bad idea. What could he want to say to me? Maybe he wanted to rail at me for being such a callous bitch and dumping him with no warning. I think that might actually make me feel better. If he was mean to me, it might make it easier for me to fall out of love with him.

Oh, who the hell am I kidding? I would never stop loving Beau Atwood.

"How are we doing today?" Nurse Shanna entered my room with a smile. "Would you like some pain medication now?"

"I'm okay, and no. I'm fine."

Shanna patted my hand. "Okay, Charli. Just let me know if you change your mind. You have a visitor, by the way."

"Bristol or Allie?" They were the only two who knew I was here, and Allie just found out this morning. She called while I was in surgery, and Bristol answered my phone. Bris was trying to bluff her way through when Allie heard an announcement over the hospital PA system in the background and figured out that we were at a hospital. She threatened to call Beau immediately if Bristol didn't tell her what the hell was going on, so Bris filled her in.

"The strawberry blonde one. Is it okay to send her in?"

"Sure, that's fine. And thank you, Shanna."

Thirty seconds later my new friend burst through the door and wrapped me in a warm hug before yanking back in horror. "Oh, shit. Did I hurt you?"

I laughed and then abruptly stopped, holding my hand over my belly. "No, you didn't hurt me, but laughing doesn't feel so good right now, so if you could please refrain from being hilarious..."

"Oh, I am not feeling hilarious at all, Miss Charli Casper." Allie set her hands on her slim hips and glared at me. "Why the hell didn't you tell me you were having surgery? And what was it for? Your friend Bristol said it was some kind of female surgery."

"I have endometriosis, and they just went in laparoscopically to remove some adhesions that have been causing some pain. I didn't tell you because it was no big deal."

"*No big deal*, she says. "You just didn't tell me because you thought I would tell Lester, and he would tell Beau." Allie gave me her sassiest look, and my mouth dropped open at the mention of my former boyfriend. "I don't like keeping things from my husband, but I would never reveal your private information like that if you asked me not to, Charli."

I breathed a sigh of relief. "Thank you, Allie. I appreciate that. And thank you for coming by, but you really didn't need to."

"Don't be ridiculous! Of course I had to come. I would have been here earlier, but I was waiting on a call from Les. He's away at training, and I don't get to talk to him often."

"Where is he?" I asked.

"I'm not sure, but I do know he's being deployed overseas soon. I miss the snot out of him when he's gone." Catching the look on my face, she grabbed my hand. "Oh, damn. I'm so sorry. That was really insensitive of me because of what you're going through with, um, everything."

"It's okay, Al. You can talk about missing your husband without upsetting me. It's my fault I'm missing Beau anyway." I had to force his name from my lips, and even then, my voice cracked a little.

"I have some questions about that, but first things first... ta-dahhh!" She pulled a bag out of her huge purse, and the room filled with the most delicious aroma.

"Straight from Mason's Deli, I present to you their famous loaded baked potato soup." She gestured toward the bag like a Vanna White wannabe.

"You brought me food?"

"Hell yes, I did. Hospital food is shit and shouldn't be consumed by humans. And Bristol told me you could only have soft foods for now." She started pulling bowls and plasticware out of the bag and setting it up on the little table that slid over my bed. "I hope you don't mind, but I got some for me, too, so we can eat together. My little bumpkin craves it," she said, patting her barely visible baby bump.

"How are you and the little one doing, by the way?"

"Good for the most part. I've been having a lot of headaches, but I figure it's just hormonal or something. I'll see my OB in a few weeks and mention it to him. But if you happen to talk to, uh, *anyone*, please don't mention it. I don't want Les to find out because he worries so much when he has to leave me."

"I doubt I'll talk to *anyone*, but if I do, I'll keep your little secret." I took a bite of the soup and dropped my head back to the pillow. "Holy damn, that's good! I think my mouth just had an orgasm."

"I know, right? Les said he gets horny when I eat this soup because of all the moaning I do," she said with a giggle before her mouth dropped into a little O. "Well, hell. I did it again. I shouldn't be talking about sex when you're not getting any. Unless… you're not with someone else now, are you? Is that what happened with you and Beau… I mean, um, *him*? Shit, I'm fucking this up."

She was getting flustered, and I had to fight not to laugh. "It's okay, Allie. You don't have to tiptoe around me." Though it was hard to hear *his* name. I think about it in my head at least a thousand times a day, but hearing it out loud… yeah… not fun.

She took a bite of soup and did indeed let out a soft moan. We ate without speaking for a few minutes before my friend just couldn't take it anymore. "So, are you going to tell me what happened with you two, or are you just going to let me suffer?"

"It's complicated," I said, staring into my half-empty bowl before finally meeting her eyes. "There are fertility issues with endometriosis."

"Okay. And?"

"And *he* wants children." Allie stared at me blankly, so I tried to explain. "He wants children, and there's a chance I won't be able to give them to him, so…" I took a deep breath, "...so, I let him go so he could find someone who could give him the family he wants and deserves."

Allie's vehement outburst shocked the shit out of me. "Are you fucking kidding me? You let that man go because of *that*?"

"*That* is a very important thing, Allie. It's not like I broke up with him because I'm lactose intolerant and he loves milk. We're talking about children here. A family."

She put her bowl down and grabbed one of my hands. "Oh, Charli. You sweet, beautiful dumbass." A sharp laugh escaped, and I put my free hand over my abdomen to quell the bite of pain that shot through me. "Sorry, but this is hitting a little close to home for me," she said.

"What do you mean?"

She let go of my hand and stirred her soup around and around with her spoon. "Not many people know this, but Les and I have had fertility problems. We've been trying to get preggers for about three years now." She took a bite of her soup and looked up at me expectantly.

"Oh. I'm sorry." It was all I could think to say just then.

"I'm not, because it's only brought us closer, and now..." she placed her hand over her stomach and smiled in that way that only a pregnant mommy can achieve. All curved lips and soft, dreamy eyes.

"And now you have your little bumpkin to look forward to," I finished.

"Exactly. But by your way of thinking, Lester never should have married me."

I blinked hard. About a hundred times. "Wha— why, I mean, I never said that."

"You said Beau should go find someone who can give him what he wants. So, should Les have done the same thing when we started having problems conceiving? Was I selfish for not letting him go?" Her eyes were like angry little accusatory laser beams boring into my face.

"Oh, Allie, no! Of course not! You two belong together no matter what. And there are so many other options to start a family. If you love each other..."

My words and my thoughts trailed off. *Oh, dear God. She's right. I'm such a dumbass.* Tears streamed down my face, and a ragged sob escaped from my chest. "If you love each other, you can get through anything together," I whispered through my tears, and Allie's smile took up her entire face before she pulled me into a hug and let me cry my eyes out.

My sweet friend stayed with me for a couple hours that Friday evening before the nurses kicked her out. As soon as she left, I sent Beau a text telling him I wasn't around this weekend, but that we could meet next week. I wasn't sure if he still wanted me back after the heartbreak of the past eleven days, not that I was counting, but he deserved to hear the truth.

I loved Beau Atwood, and I would weather any storm with him—if he still wanted me after I told him the truth.

I was allowed to go home on Sunday, and as I packed up my toothbrush and other belongings, my cell phone rang. "Charli!" Bristol's panicked voice said through the phone. "I was on my way to get you, and I had a blowout."

"Oh shit, Bristol! Are you okay?"

"Yeah, I'm fine. The car service people are on the way, so I'm sending Aaron to come pick you up."

Hells bells. He's the last person I want to see. Swear to God, if he wanted to collect on our "just as friends" date, I would probably punch him.

"It's okay, Bris. I can just wait until you get your tire fixed."

"He's already on the way, and don't worry. I told him not to act douchey or hit on you. He's just giving you a ride, okay?"

Trying not to sigh heavily, I told her okay. Nurse Shanna came in to have me sign the discharge papers as I was hanging up. "You ready to go home, sweetie?"

"So ready," I told her as she ran through my instructions.

"No sports, running, moving furniture, carrying heavy weights, climbing stairs, jumping, or other strenuous activities for at least a week from your surgery date. Just initial right here that you understand these instructions."

I finished initialing and signing everything just as Aaron walked through the open door of my room. "Hey, Charli," he said shyly.

"Hey, Aaron." I said feeling extremely uncomfortable. Shanna wheeled me downstairs, despite my protests that I could walk, and loaded me into Aaron's SUV.

"Do you need anything to eat?" Aaron asked politely as we headed toward Bristol's apartment.

I was starving, but the awkwardness was hanging thickly in the air between us, so I declined, just ready to get home and away from him. I leaned my seat back and closed my eyes to discourage any more conversation between us and actually dozed off on the way home.

"Charli," Aaron said, placing a hand gently on my forearm. "We're here. I'll get your bag and walk you up."

Opening my eyes and readjusting my seat, I blinked to clear the blurriness away. "It's okay, Aaron. I can get it."

He frowned and said, "I'm pretty sure you're not supposed to be lifting anything. I'll just carry it up to the apartment for you." Remembering my discharge instructions, I relented. Aaron grabbed my bag from the back and held one of my hands as I stepped gingerly from the vehicle. Holding my arm as we walked up the five steps to the apartment building, he said, "I can stay with you until Bristol gets home, if you need me to."

I politely declined and was thankful when he dropped my bag inside the door and left without stepping foot inside.

Now, if I could just avoid the man for the rest of my life, things would be great.

BEAU

I PULLED THE HOOD of my sweatshirt off as soon as Cam and I entered the warmth of our house. We had just run six miles, and we were both covered in sweat, despite the chilly temperatures outside. It was finally starting to feel at least a little bit like December.

We headed straight to the mats in the dojo to do our post-run stretching. "You okay?" Cam asked as we stretched out our hamstrings and calves, and I knew he wasn't talking about the strenuous exercise we had just done.

"Better," I said, and my friend nodded. This was why we got along so well. I knew he was there for me if I wanted to talk, but he didn't force the issue. We continued stretching in silence and then I rose and muttered, "Hitting the shower."

I turned on my shower to let it warm up before stripping off my damp clothes and tossing them in the hamper. Stepping under the hot spray, I shampooed my hair and washed my body. I looked down at my rigid cock and clenched my hands at my side. I hadn't touched myself since Charli had left, subjecting myself to some kind of obscene self-denial punishment for whatever I had done to make her leave me. But *fuck*...

I closed my eyes and reached for myself, groaning as my fingers wrapped around my hardness. Damn, that felt good. Giving myself a long stroke from root to tip, I allowed myself to think about *her*. Her cornflower blue eyes. Her soft cheeks. Her pillowy lips. *Goddamn. Those lips.* Wrapped around my dick, sucking just the way she knew I liked it, hands behind her back and eyes looking up at me.

Widening my stance, I braced myself with a hand against the tile wall as my hand began to move. Up and down. Up and down. Steady, measured strokes. *Christ, Charli. Suck me harder, baby.* I tightened my grip, imagining the feel of her warm mouth surrounding me. *Fuck, I'm coming in your mouth, my sweet Peach.* I closed my eyes as I started to come, long spurts of heat that came from deep inside my balls. *I love you, Charli.*

I leaned my forehead against the wall, my legs trembling, not from the run, but from the long-awaited sexual release. I stood like that for a while until I was sure my legs would be able to perform their intended purpose, and then I rinsed off, got out of the shower, and toweled off.

Picking up my phone from where I had thrown it on the bed, I opened my text thread with Charli, re-reading and analyzing every word. She had messaged me a few hours after she turned down my proposal to talk on Friday, and suddenly I had a glimmer of hope.

> ***Charli: Actually, I think we do need to talk, if you still want to. But I'm away for the weekend.***

> ***Beau: Of course. Whenever you want.***

> ***Charli: Monday evening?***

> ***Beau: Oops. Except Monday. I'm on a job that night. How about Tuesday?***

> ***Charli: Okay.***

This was Sunday, and Tuesday seemed like a really long way away. Maybe she was home from wherever she'd been this weekend. And speaking of that, where did she go and with whom? Tank had told me that he'd tried to booty-call Bristol on Saturday, and she said she wasn't available. Was she just blowing him off, or was she somewhere with Charli?

Maybe I should call Tank and see if he would call Bristol and casually bring up Charli's name. Shaking my head, I gave myself a mental facepalm. Fuck, what next? Would I have him ask Bristol to ask Charli if she would go to prom with me?

Man the fuck up, Atwood. If you want to see Charli, do it the old-fashioned way—stalking.

Yeah, it's possible I'd been driving by Bristol's house ever since Blaire had told me Charli was living there. Not often. Just a couple times a day... or maybe five. Whatever. I threw on a sweatsuit and grabbed my keys.

I drove around the block, noticing that Charli's car was parked in the same place it had been all weekend. And all the lights were out in their apartment. I went to a local coffee shop and bought a cup of plain, black brew before heading back and parking across the street from the apartment.

Half an hour later, I noticed a silver SUV pull up and park on the street. I didn't pay much attention until I saw Aaron get out of the driver's side. *What the fuck is that asshole doing here?* His sister wasn't even at home. He went around to the back and took out an overnight bag. A blue flowery bag that I recognized since I had seen it several times on my bedroom floor.

Sitting forward in my seat, I watched as that prick opened the passenger-side door and held out his hand. And there she was. *My Peach. With him.* She had gone away with Aaron fucking Hopkins, and that was why she couldn't meet with me this weekend. He put his goddamn dirty hand on her as he carried her bag and led her to the door before they disappeared inside. Together.

Goddammit. Fuck. Shit. Sonofamotherfuckingbitch. How could she? I threw my coffee against the opposite door and jammed my truck into gear, peeling out like a fucking maniac before I marched inside and killed that sleezy twat Aaron.

If that's what she wanted, *fine*. She could have him.

Here I was thinking Charli had dumped me for some altruistic, selfless reason, but then I find out she actually left me for another man. And not just any man. She left me for that fuckfaced bastard.

Storming into the house, I slammed the door so hard it rattled the windows. "Whoa, Shark. What the fuck?" Cam asked, leaping up from the couch and running toward me.

"Charli," I said hoarsely.

"'Kay, man. I got you. Just sit down." He shoved me toward the couch and disappeared into the kitchen, returning a minute later with two glasses of vodka on the rocks in his hands and the bottle under his arm. "Here," he said, handing me one of the glasses, the contents of which I slammed down my throat before holding it out for a refill.

Cam poured me another and said, "Hit me with it, brother."

BEAU

WE HAD SAFELY GOTTEN Ella Ervin from the airport to the hotel this afternoon and then to the arena this evening. The concert had gone off without a hitch, and I had to admit that Miss Ervin was fantastic. Not only did she sing like an angel, but she was courteous and grateful to my staff.

Now we were on the way back to the hotel, Woody and I in the lead car, Cam and Bode in the follow car, and Taz riding in the armored limo with the singer.

"I'm telling you, Shark. I don't like that Taz woman one bit."

Sighing, I checked the rearview mirror to make sure the limousine was following us closely enough. "What's the problem, Wood?"

"She's just… inappropriate."

I glanced over at him with a frown on my face. Yes, the perpetual frown was back after what I had seen yesterday. "Did she hit on you or something?"

"Fuck no! She knows better. I wouldn't touch her with a ten-foot pole. Let me tell you what she did. When we were going over the game plan for tonight, she made a suggestion about the airport pickup. Then she said, 'If that won't work, just tell me I don't have a leg to stand on.' Then she stuck out her leg, her fucking *fake* leg and wiggled it. And she smiled!" Woody said, outraged. "Who does that? An amputee joke? She's a fucking psycho, Shark."

I shook my head. "Well, seeing as how she's an amputee, she can make jokes about it if she wants to. At least she has a sense of humor about it instead of bitching and whining."

"I don't like it," he said irritably, his eyes sweeping the area as we pulled up the driveway to the hotel.

"You don't have to like it. Just do your job," I said sullenly.

"I will do my job, you grouchy fucker. I always do my job," he retorted. "You just tell her to do *her* job."

"Was the suggestion she made any good?" I already knew the answer because Cam had filled me in, and we had implemented the change at the airport.

"Yeah," Woody grumbled, "but that's beside the point."

"All right. Enough about Taz. Let's just wrap this up, and we'll be done for the night." I put the vehicle in park, and Woody and I climbed out of the black SUV as Bode and Cam climbed out of the follow car. We took our positions, eyes roving and roaming constantly across the elegant front of the hotel and beautifully landscaped grounds. I tapped the top of the limo, a signal to Taz that they could exit the vehicle.

The door opened, and Miss Ervin stepped out with Taz as Cam and Bode automatically flanked them from behind. Woody and I took our positions in front and started leading the entourage toward the hotel. The revving of an engine caught my attention, and I spun to see a black Mercedes sedan bearing down on us from the left, and I quickly drew my weapon.

And Bode. Dear, crazy Bode. He shoved everyone in front of him out of the way and was struck by the sedan, his body outstretched and moving through the air like he was in the Matrix. He landed on the hood, rolled off the side, and crumpled to the ground. Then the entire scene spun like it was in very, very fast motion. I fired three shots in rapid succession, and the vehicle slowed.

"Cam! Woody!" I screamed, but they were already on it, scrambling to their feet without hesitation and approaching the vehicle. Taz was on the ground, using her body to shield Miss Ervin while I ran to Bode.

"Dead!" Cam called, and I panicked at first, thinking he was talking about Bode, who was lying lifeless on the ground in a heap.

"Cam, ambulance! Now! Woody, call the police and then Tank and Hawk! Taz, how is the client?" I was spitting out orders like machine gun fire.

"Fine. Scraped up, but okay."

With all that taken care of, I bent to Bode, and he rolled over onto his back and opened his eyes. "Don't move, buddy. You could have a spinal injury."

I was surprised when Ella Ervin knelt beside him, pulling off her white wrap and pressing it to Bode's bleeding shoulder. "He's right. Stay very still." She started calmly doing an assessment on him like a fucking pro before meeting my eyes. "Doesn't appear to have any spinal injuries, but I think this arm is broken, and he probably has a concussion." My questioning eyes held hers over Bode's body as Cam relayed the vital info to the hospital. "I wasn't always a singer, you know. I worked as an EMT before," she told me.

I nodded my gratitude. "Thank you," I said quietly before turning my attention to my employee, *my friend*, lying on the fucking ground. "How you doing, ace?"

"Been better, to be honest, Shark. Hurts like a motherfucker," he said coarsely. "What do you need me to do?" he asked, like I was actually going to give him a task to do.

"Just lie there and look pretty," I said, with a hint of a smile.

Bode grinned—actually fucking grinned, the crazy fucker—and said, "I can do that all day, err day, boss."

Ella wiped her bloody hands on what was previously a pristine white dress and pushed Bode's hair away from his face. "Thank you, Bode," she said softly and simply.

"'S'okay." He held her eyes for a moment. "You're really sexy," he uttered, which was totally unprofessional, but the man was bleeding on the ground after saving our client's life, so I cut him some damn slack.

Ella smiled at him, still stroking his face gently. "So are you, sweetie."

"Must be the injuries. I always look sexier after I've been hit by a car."

Jesus. Fucking Bode.

Grabbing one of his hands and holding it tightly between my own, I said, "Okay, not exactly the time for flirting, dude. Just be quiet until we get to the hospital. You're going to be okay, buddy."

"'Kay, Shark," he said, gripping my hand.

Please, God. Let him be okay.

50

CHARLI

I WAS GOING TO miss my job so damned much. I adored those precious little toots, but I would definitely miss their parents, as well. Blaire had accepted my "I had a minor procedure related to my endometriosis and can't pick anyone up" explanation without pause. Hell, she was a doctor. I'm sure she knew exactly what I'd had done, though she hadn't questioned me about it.

Carrie was out of school for the Christmas holidays, so I had spent most of the day working puzzles at the table with her while Blaire and my mom wrangled the triplets and Danica. I had finally told my mom about the surgery, and she spent the day glaring at me for not telling her before. She had insisted that I take a nap when the boys did, for which I was very grateful because, minor or not, the surgery had sapped my energy.

Not feeling like cooking, I stopped at my favorite deli on the way to my new home and got a cup of tomato basil soup. Settling into a padded chair, I ate my soup, forgoing the wonderful smelling focaccia bread because I was still supposed to be on a liquid/soft foods diet. When I was about halfway done, my phone rang.

"Hey, Bristol. I'll be home in a couple minutes. I just stopped at—"

She cut me off, her voice breathless and a little panicked. "Oh my God, Charli. Bode's been hit by a car."

"What? Bode... he's..." I remembered that Beau had told me he had a job tonight, and my breath seized in my lungs. "Is Beau... is he..."

"All I heard was that Bode was injured, so I'm sure Beau's fine. I'm headed to the hospital now."

"I'll come, too," I said, making a snap decision. My poor Beau. I needed to be there for him. Bristol gave me the hospital information, and I abandoned the rest of my meal, heading directly out to my car.

Walking down the second-floor corridor of the hospital twenty minutes later, I texted Bris. She said she and Tank had gone downstairs to get coffee for everyone and would meet me in the waiting area. I turned the corner and had to physically restrain myself from running. Beau and Cam were standing like sentinels outside a door at the end of the hallway. I hadn't seen Beau in two weeks, and God, I had almost forgotten what a beautiful man he was.

I approached, unable to stop the small smile that curled against my lips at the sight of him. He stared back at me, not smiling in the least. In fact, he looked downright angry. He was probably just scared about his friend. "How's Bode?" I asked, stopping about a foot away, even though I wanted to jump up and wrap myself around him. But his body language didn't seem conducive to that kind of display, his legs aggressively wide and his arms crossed tightly over his chest.

He didn't answer, so I reached out a comforting hand and laid it on his bulging bicep. "Is there anything you need?" He jerked away like I had shot electricity from my hand, and I took a step back.

"Yes. There is," he hissed, his words dripping with venom and his spittle dotting my face. "You can stay the fuck away from me." And then he was gone, leaving me staring blankly at the wall where he had just been standing. I finally blinked as hurt and confusion bubbled up inside me and turned my eyes to Cam, but his blue eyes looked just as stony.

Finding my voice around the lump in my throat, I rasped, "Cam, what was that?" I knew I had hurt Beau by leaving him, but he *had* asked to talk to me. Was this the reason? He just wanted to let out his anger on me?

"He knows," Cam said icily.

"Knows what?" I asked with genuine confusion.

"He knows what you did this weekend."

Beau found out I had surgery?

"But... why is he so mad about it?"

Cam looked at me incredulously, and I had the distinct feeling I was missing something. He shook his head and barked out an angry laugh. "You are something, you know that, Charli? Why the fuck do you think he's mad? That man is so goddamn in love with you, it's not even funny."

"He's upset I didn't tell him," I said almost to myself.

"He's upset you did it at all!" Cam said forcefully.

Now I was getting angry. "It's my body!" I retorted, and Cam's face twisted into an ugly mask. "It wasn't that big a deal. I'm just a little sore today."

His eyes went hard as steel and a livid smile crossed his lips. "Well, good for you, sweetheart. I hope he showed you a good time."

Okay, I was pretty sure we weren't on the same page. Hell, I wasn't sure we were even reading the same book. "Who?"

"Fucking Hopkins," he spat.

"Bristol?"

Cam rubbed his thumbs against his temples as if I were giving him a headache. "Her brother. The one you screwed this weekend."

What the actual fuck is he talking about?

"Aaron? I didn't... I would never..."

"He saw you, Charli. You told him you were away for the weekend, and then he saw you getting out of that asshat's car with an overnight bag on Sunday."

I felt pressure behind my eyes like they were about to pop out of my head. "He thought... that dumbass... how could he think I would do that?"

"So, you didn't sleep with Hopkins?" Cam asked skeptically, his arms crossing over his broad chest.

"Of course not, you fucking idiot. Shit! How could y'all be so stupid?" His eyes widened at my vehemence, but I wasn't worried about Cam right then. "I have to find him."

Desperate to talk to Beau, to explain, I turned and sprinted down the hallway, my mind so intent on finding him that I didn't see the nurse coming around the corner. She was pushing a wheelchair—empty, thank God—and it hit me right at the waist. The momentum from my running launched me over the wheelchair and I hit the ground, sprawled out on my belly. I felt a ripping pain in my abdomen and rolled over onto my back, my face a harsh grimace.

I heard a familiar voice scream my name, and within seconds, Bristol was kneeling beside me. "Oh my God, Char. Are you okay? You know you're not supposed to be running."

I felt something wet on the hand I had clenched to my stomach, and I pulled it away to find a blotch of red widening on my gray sweatshirt. "Oh, shit," I grunted, and Bris yanked my shirt up, exposing my bra to anyone who may have been walking by.

"Fuck. Fuck, fuck, fuck. You've had a blowout, Charli girl." I looked down to see that one of my small surgical scars had opened up. "Waylon!" she snapped, and I frowned.

"Who's Waylon?" I asked, trying to focus on anything except the blood seeping from my open wound.

"That's Tank's real name," she said as the big guy lumbered over and lifted me easily in his arms. The nurse had snapped out of her shocked stupor and pushed the wheelchair toward me as Tank lowered me into the seat.

"Ma'am, I didn't see you. I'm sooooo sorry. I'll get you down to the ER right away."

"No, no. I'm fine. Just get me a Band-Aid or something," I said, shaking my head and trying to get out of the chair. I didn't have time for this shit. I needed to find Beau.

"Charli, do what she says," Tank, er, *Waylon* growled, as authoritative as I'd ever heard him.

"Fine!" I snapped, realizing my shirt was still pulled up and tugging it down.

"I'll go with you," Bristol said before turning to *Waylon*—would I ever get used to that?—and nodding toward the two drink carriers filled with cups of coffee that were sitting on the floor. "Take those to the waiting room, hon. I'll get Charli taken care of."

"But what's wrong with her? Why's she bleeding like that?" I heard him ask in a low voice rimmed with genuine concern.

She pressed a quick kiss to his cheek. "I'll fill you in later, boo."

"Boo?" I asked as the nurse started pushing me toward the elevator with Bristol walking briskly beside us. "He lets you get away with calling him 'boo?'"

"He likes anything I call him, especially if it's while I'm using my—"

"Ah! Ah! Ah!" I said, holding my hand up and glancing at the nurse, who was blushing furiously and trying not to giggle. "You keep that mess to yourself."

"Why were you running down the hall like a goddamn maniac anyway?"

How could I tell her that Beau was pissed because he thought I was banging her brother all weekend? I certainly didn't want to spill those beans in front of a total stranger. "I was chasing after Beau. There was a... miscommunication, and I wanted to catch him and straighten it out." I shot her the *not now. I'll tell you later* look, and she nodded and dropped it.

We introduced ourselves and chatted with the nurse, who apologized no less than five more times on the way down to the ER. This was the same hospital where I'd had the surgery, so they already had my records, and I was placed in a room as soon as we arrived. Another nurse cleaned the open wound and covered it with gauze, telling us the doctor would be in shortly.

A young, dark-haired doctor came into the room just a few minutes later and gave me a gentle lopsided smile. "I'm Doctor Quinn. I hear you got into a fight with a wheelchair, Miss Casper?"

"Yep. Wheelchair: One, Charli: Zero," I quipped as he lifted the gauze and inspected the area.

"Hmmm, your surgery was on Friday?" he asked, and I nodded. "Well, it's gaping pretty good, Charli. I'm going to put a couple sutures in since you're apparently too rough for mere steri-strips." He gave me a flirty grin, and Bristol checked out his ass from behind, making a *panting like a dog* face. He mistook my *trying not to laugh* face as fear and placed a calming hand on my forearm. "Don't worry. I'll give you a numbing shot first, so you won't feel a thing." He patted my arm twice before leaving the small room.

"Oh my God. Doctor SexyQuinn is fuck-hot!" Bristol hissed as soon as he was gone. "And he's totally into you, girlfriend."

"Hush! He is not!" I hissed back.

"He is so. I can tell he wants to push your shirt the rest of the way up to check out your girls."

"Well, since you already flashed *my girls* to half of the second floor, what's the difference now?" I shot back with an eye roll.

Doctor SexyQuinn, er, Doctor Quinn returned with a suture kit and a syringe with a fierce-looking needle, all of which he laid out on a tray. I wasn't scared of needles, having been poked and prodded for most of my adult life, but he was going to poke that damned thing in my belly, for fuck's sake. I was a tad disconcerted. Luckily, Bristol chose to distract me while he poured some smelly orange liquid on the area and rubbed it around. She began with a fist to her mouth and her tongue in her cheek, miming a blow job, and finished up with a series of elaborate hip thrusts behind the admittedly handsome doctor's back.

"Bristol, since the doctor is about to jab me in the stomach with a needle, why don't you come hold my hand?" I said, biting my cheek and giving her a wide-eyed *cut the shit* look.

"It's okay, Charli. I'll be gentle," the doc said, his blue eyes twinkling as Bristol stopped her crazy antics and stood beside me to grip my hand.

I closed my eyes so I couldn't see it coming. "Okay. I'm ready," I breathed.

BEAU

Pacing back and forth along the sidewalk outside the hospital, I was tempted to gouge my fucking eyes out so I would never have to lay eyes on Charli Casper again. Because as soon as I had seen her, my body threatened to betray my broken soul. I wanted to scoop her up and kiss her when I realized she was actually walking down that hospital corridor toward me.

But instead, I'd lashed out as soon as she put her hand on my arm. Her soft smell and the warmth of her hand made me want to do things that weren't at all in line with my attempts at hating her, and that pissed me the fuck off.

I just couldn't be around her. I already felt like shit for the way I'd gotten right up in her face and let my vile words spew out, but I'd just been so damned wounded. I would have to stay away, and that way neither of us would get hurt any more.

I felt my phone buzz at my hip and pulled it out to find that Tank was calling. "Hey, man. What's up? Something new with Bode?" The doctors had informed us that our friend was going to be okay, but that he did indeed have a broken arm and a concussion. They were waiting on neuro to come do an assessment.

"No, nothing new. Uh, Shark. I wasn't sure if you wanted to know this, but, um, Charli is in the emergency room."

My fucking blood boiled at the mention of her name. "Yeah, I saw her upstairs. She must have come in through the ER entrance."

"No, I mean she's *in* the emergency room. As a patient. She was bleeding."

"Like her period?" She was probably cramping badly and needed to take a hot bath when she got home. I could—

No, you dumb shit! She's not your problem anymore.

"Ew. How the fuck would I know if Charli was on her period, Shark? No, it was from her stomach. I saw it when Bristol pushed her shirt up to see where the bleeding was coming from."

"Why the hell would her stomach be bleeding?" I felt a sliver of panic twisting up my spine.

"Well, I don't know. She was running and then this nurse came around the corner and Charli tripped over the wheelchair and fell and then she was just bleeding, man." His words came fast and without pause. "I picked her up and put her in the wheelchair, and the nurse took her to the ER. Bristol went with them."

I couldn't make sense of what I was hearing. How does a person just bleed from the abdomen? He said she tripped over a wheelchair. Did something on the chair cut her? Even though she was no longer my problem, I needed to know she was okay, and all thoughts of staying away were pushed to the back of my mind.

You're an idiot, Atwood. Yeah, I was well aware of that. Maybe I could just catch Bristol alone and ask her what was going on, and then I wouldn't actually have to see Charli. *Okay, that's the plan.*

"Thanks for letting me know, Tank. I'm on the way." I pushed through the front doors of the hospital and asked for directions to the ER. Taking off at a jog down the corridor to the right, I saw the red sign up ahead. Once in the ER, I glanced at the board listing patients by their initials for privacy and found CC beside the number twelve.

I walked briskly down the hallway, my eyes darting to each door until I found the one marked twelve. It was partly open, but a curtain had been drawn around the bed. I stepped silently around it and took in the scene. Charli was lying on the bed with her eyes closed as Bristol held her right hand. A doctor leaned over Charli's body with a fucking needle poking in her stomach.

Bristol looked up at me, a glimmer in her bright purple eyes, and I gestured for her to switch places with me. As I took Charli's hand from her, Bristol patted my bicep approvingly and winked before squeezing the hard muscle and wiggling her eyebrows.

I couldn't help but smile at that crazy girl as she walked out the door. It took Charli a moment to figure out that it wasn't Bristol's small, soft hand holding hers anymore, but my big, rough one. Her thumb swiped across my forefinger a few times before a tiny furrow formed between her eyebrows. She lifted her lids, her face softening as she exhaled my name. "Beau..."

"I'm here," I said simply. That's all I could promise right now. I glanced down at her stomach, noticing the gaping wound and two more incisions that were covered with steri-strips. "You had surgery." Stating the obvious. *Genius, Atwood.*

"Yeah, Friday. I was in the hospital over the weekend." I nodded, something tight and hard releasing inside me. She hadn't gone away with fuckface. But she had been with him on Sunday. "Bristol was supposed to pick me up to bring me home Sunday, but she had a flat. She sent—"

Getting the gist of what had happened, I placed a finger gently on her lips. "Shhh. Don't worry about that now." The rest of that tight, hard ball in my gut loosened into nothingness, and I finally felt free for the first time since yesterday when I had seen Charli with Aaron.

As the doctor started to slide the suture needle through her flesh, Charli looked down, her face paling and her lips rolling inward. I pressed my fingers against her cheek to turn her face toward me. "Just look at me, baby." Lifting our joined hands, I kissed the back of hers as my other hand swiped a rogue tear from her cheek. "It's okay, Peach. I'm here now."

"You're here now," she repeated, closing her eyes, the most serene look smoothing out her face as she leaned her cheek into my touch. *Jesus, this woman could set my heart on fire with just her eyelids.*

"Tell me about Bode," she said, and I sensed that she needed a distraction, so I filled her in.

"Now we're just waiting for neuro to get done with him. They should be done soon."

Her lids opened, and those fucking gorgeous eyes met mine with concern etched around each blue iris. "You should go back up there," she said. "I'll be fine."

"No," I said decisively, kissing her hand again and leaving no room for discussion.

"All done," the doctor said, pulling Charli's shirt back down. And thank God. I knew he was a doctor, but I didn't like seeing him with his hands on my Peach's sweet body, professional or not. "You can take showers, but no baths or hot tubs until the sutures come out in seven days. If you can't get in to see your regular doctor, just call me, and I'll meet you up here and remove them," he said, smiling at Charli in a way I didn't like one fucking little bit.

He pulled a card from his pocket, and I smoothly took it from him, flashing him a smile that showed all my teeth. Glancing at the name embroidered on his jacket, I said, "Thank you, Dr. Quinn, for taking care of my girl." *My girl, fucker. Mine.*

He nodded with a tight smile and left us alone in the room. *Alone. With Peach.* I didn't give a damn about anything else right then. After holding her hand and feeling her soft cheek against my palm, I was sucked right back into the magical realm of Charli.

I gave her a cocky grin while I crumbled Doctor Flirty Pants's card and tossed it in the trash, never looking away from her eyes.

"Nice shot," she said, returning my smirk. I sat on the edge of her bed and pulled her across my lap with her head tucked under my chin.

"Will you tell me about your surgery, baby?" I asked, wrapping my arms around her and soaking up everything I had missed for the past two weeks. Her sounds. Her smell. Her softness.

"It was no big deal. I just had some adhesions removed."

"To help with the pain," I stated. "Were there any on your bladder or intestines?"

I felt her body stiffen in surprise. "One on my bladder, but my intestines were clear." She paused for a moment. "You've done your research."

"Yep."

She turned her face up to mine, apprehension radiating from her eyes. "About everything?"

"Yes, Peach. About everything." *Including infertility, and it's okay*, I told her with my eyes as my hand pushed a stray strand of hair from her face. I didn't want to get into that whole discussion right now, when a nurse would be coming in to clear the room at any minute.

Her eyes darted back and forth between mine several times before she nodded. "I talked to Cam when you ran off. He told me what you saw, and nothing happened with Aaron. I really didn't want to be around him, but Bristol sent him when she had a flat."

"You can call me next time. And I would like to know if you're having surgery. I would have come and stayed with you."

She snuggled her forehead into the crook of my neck. "But we were..." She sighed, searching for the right words.

"I don't care what labels you decide to put on our relationship. I still care about you, and I want to be here for you. No matter what."

"You should get back upstairs," she murmured, and I nodded.

"Come with me."

She straightened, holding her bloody shirt away from her body. "I look like an extra in a horror movie. I need to go home and change, but keep me updated, if you don't mind."

I tried not to pout like a twelve-year-old girl who didn't get tickets to a Justin Bieber concert.

"Will you come over when I get home? I really want to talk to you." She hesitated, and I unashamedly resorted to begging. "Please, Charli? I've been going insane without you."

"I'm sorry," she said, and my heart sped up, thinking she was going to flat-out refuse. But then she pressed her lips softly to mine. "I'll come over."

I tried really hard to play it cool, but I couldn't hold back the gigantic smile that stretched across my face. That kiss may have been chaste and brief, but it gave me all the tingles. And a small slice of hope.

52

CHARLI

Beau called shortly after I got out of the shower. Bode was going to be okay, but they were keeping him overnight. They even got to talk to him for a while before they were kicked out of his room so he could rest. Beau offered to come get me, but I wanted my own ride in case our talk went badly.

He swung open the door a few seconds after I knocked and pulled me into the house by my hand. Cam was sitting on the couch watching TV, and he greeted me with a smile and a wave when I walked in. He was slightly friendlier than when I had seen him earlier, and I assumed Beau had told him the truth about this weekend.

"We can talk in my room," Beau said, leading me down the hall and closing the door. He had obviously showered while I was on my way over because the room had that lingering clean, damp smell. Plus, his hair was still slightly wet and sexily disheveled like he had just rubbed a towel through it. I had the sudden urge to bury my face in his damp hair and sniff him like a weirdo, but that would probably lead to me climbing him like he was a building and I was Spiderwoman.

Is there even a Spiderwoman superhero? If not, there really should be.

I sat cross-legged on the bed, and Beau propped up pillows against the headboard, fussing over me until I assured him I was comfortable and not hurting. Then he sat facing me, wrapping his long legs around mine with his feet at my hips, so that I was sitting in the circle of his limbs. "You go first," we said at the same time and then laughed awkwardly.

Beau held both of my hands and kissed them one-by-one. "Baby, you're the one who ended things, so why don't you start. I feel like maybe you were leaving out part of the reason you broke up with me, and I would appreciate it if you could talk to me about it."

I sucked in a shaky breath. "Okay. Since I just found out you've been doing research into my... condition, I'm thinking you've probably come across some of the fertility statistics." He nodded but didn't say anything, so I continued. "There's about a 30 to 50 percent chance that I can't conceive."

"So that means there's a 50 to 70 percent chance that you can," he said smugly.

"Oh. Well, yeah. I guess that's true." He threw me off a little with that fact. I had never thought about it quite like that. "I've seen how you are with your nieces and nephews, so I know you love kids. I just... I want you to be able to have kids of your own, so I left so you could find a woman who could give that to you."

"But I'm not in love with any other woman, so that would pretty much suck ass," he said definitively.

This was not going how I expected. At all. "But you deserve the chance to raise a family," I argued. "I don't want you to miss out on anything."

Beau gave me a placid smile. "Baby, I won't be missing out on a thing. I've been with Carrie since she was a baby. In fact, I was in the room when she was born. I took care of her when Blaire was in med school and Evan was working. I've done diaper changes, late night illnesses, bath time, bed time, play time; pretty much anything you can think of, I've done it. And you know how close I am with the other kids, too. I have five wonderful little people in my life, and I'm happy with that. All I need is the woman I love." In a conspiratorial whisper, he said, "That's you, sweetheart."

"But I want you to have children of your own."

"Good. Then we'll adopt. How ever many you want."

"But you can't really want that. It's not the same." Why wasn't he getting what I was saying?

"How do you know what I want? You've never talked about it with me. And for the record, I'm a huge fan of adoption."

I was getting exasperated. "You're just going by your feelings right now because we're newly in love. I'm afraid later on you're going to be disappointed in me if I can't get pregnant, and adoption is our only choice."

"Number one, I could never be disappointed in you. And number two, if adoption is our only choice, I will still be the happiest man in the world. I would love to raise children with you because you would be a fantastic mother, Charli. And I don't care where the kids come from."

"I don't either. Though I would love to experience pregnancy for myself, I've always been drawn to adopting a child that needed a good home and loving parents. I'm just not sure if you've thought this all the way through, Beau."

"Oh, I've thought about it a lot more than you probably realize, sweetheart." He gave me a self-satisfied smile and whispered, "Why don't you ask me why I'm a fan of adoption?"

I rolled my eyes. "Okaaaay, why are you a fan of adoption, Beau?"

His grin widened across his face. "Because I was adopted," he said proudly.

I felt like one of those cartoon characters whose eyes pop comically out of their head. I stared at him as he lifted his eyebrows at me. Finally finding my voice, I rasped, "You and Blaire?"

Beau shook his head. "Nope. Just me. So technically, her kids aren't biologically related to me, but I couldn't love them any more if I had birthed them myself."

"So…" I was so stunned, I couldn't think of any intelligent thing to say.

"So, when I tell you it doesn't matter to me, I'm not just blowing smoke up your ass to get you to stay with me, Charli. I would love nothing more than to adopt a whole slew of kids and love the shit out of them like Madeline and James Atwood loved me."

Cue the ugly cry. "Why didn't you ever tell me?" I sobbed as he pulled me into his lap with my legs wrapped around his waist and my arms around his neck.

"Because I don't really ever think about it. My parents were my parents, and Blaire is my sister. I don't give a damn what any DNA test says. Family isn't about blood, Charli. It's about love. Just like us. I couldn't love anyone as much as I love you, and we're definitely not related."

"Oh God, Beau Atwood. I love you, too."

"Then stop crying all over me and kiss me," he demanded. Our lips touched, but it was hard for us to kiss properly at first because we couldn't stop smiling long enough. We finally got it right, and our lips melded together like they were made for each other. When our tongues touched, they danced happily around each other as Beau laid me back and hovered over me, being cautious not to squish my stomach.

Breaking the kiss, he trailed his lips down my jaw and to my ear. "Does this mean we're not broken up anymore?" he asked, nipping at my earlobe.

"Do you want to be?"

"Fuck no," he said working his mouth down my neck, his lips and tongue teasing my sensitive skin. "How do you expect us to spend the rest of our lives together if we're broken up?"

"That would make things difficult," I said, my heart soaring as he pulled the neck of my shirt to the side and nibbled on my collarbone.

Lifting his head, he looked down at me with a heavy-lidded gaze. "I've missed you so fucking much, Charli."

A tear slipped down my face and into my hair. "I've missed you, baby. I'm so sorry."

"No apologies, my sweet girl. You were doing what you thought was right, even though it was a little misguided." He smiled down at me, his molten green eyes filled with so much love and understanding. "Don't ever hesitate to talk to me, Charli. I will work through anything with you. I would walk through fire for you."

Gripping his face in my hands, I pulled him down to kiss him hard. "I love you so much."

My beautiful man tugged my shirt off, murmuring the sweetest words as his lips moved down the skin of my chest with feather-light brushes of his mouth. He wasn't just kissing me. He was adoring me, and it hit me then how much I had hurt him. All he had done was love me like I had never been loved before, and I had callously left him. As I watched him taking his time kissing each of my ribs, the emotions built and built until they finally bubbled over like a volcano.

When the first sob escaped my chest, Beau looked up from where he was softly worshiping my abdomen. "Hey," he said, sliding up my body until we were face-to-face. "What's wrong, baby?"

I shook my head as tears streamed from my eyes, and my mind and body tried to rid themselves of my dark thoughts and fears. "I... almost... lost you. I... hurt you," I managed to force out through my sobs.

His face was one of concern and sympathy, which only made me cry harder. I didn't deserve this man. "Shhhhh, we're not going to think about that now. We're together, Peach." Each tear he swept away was replaced by two more until I was bordering on hysterical. Every thought and feeling and worry from the past two weeks was now simmering right at the surface, threatening to pull me under.

"Charli, look at me." Beau's voice was somehow gentle and commanding at the same time, and I looked up into his eyes, seeing only love shining back at me. "I'm right here. We're together now, my Peach."

My tears and fears began waning as our eyes stayed locked together. "Forever," I whispered.

"Forever," he agreed before lowering his mouth to mine and kissing me with all the love and tenderness in the world. Our hands clutched at each other as we made love to each other with our mouths, reconnecting and forging a bond that would never be broken.

Finally ending the kiss, Beau pulled back and cupped my chin, his fingers tracing tenderly along my jaw. "I don't want to sound like a perv here, but I really need you naked right now." At my lifted eyebrow, he grinned. "Not for sex. I need to be able to touch all of you. To feel your soft skin against me."

"We can make love if you want to," I offered. "As long as we go easy."

His grin turned into a frown. "You just had surgery, Peach," he said sternly, putting a finger over my lips when I tried to interrupt. "No. I always want you like that, but tonight I just want to hold you."

We undressed each other slowly, taking all the time in the world to kiss and touch each other, until we were bare and pressed together beneath the covers.

Cupping his face between my hands, I spilled my heart. "I love you, Beau. I don't know how in the hell I thought I could ever live without you, because I can't."

"Charli..." His gorgeous eyes were shiny with emotion.

"Let me finish. I need to tell you how perfect you are for me." Beau pressed his forehead against mine as I continued. "You're protective and sweet. Loyal and beautiful. You love me bigger and better than I could have ever imagined."

"I love you exactly like you deserve to be loved, baby."

I rubbed my nose up and down his. "Though I love your body and the things you can do with it, I love your heart even more." I lowered my head and pressed my lips over the left side of his chest, inhaling his perfect, masculine smell. "I even like when you get all stubborn and possessive because that means that I belong to you. And you belong to me."

"I do," he confirmed.

"I promise I'll never leave you again, and I'll talk to you if I'm worried about something. And I swear I'll be the best girlfriend I can be."

His eyes searched my face with an intensity that made my cheeks warm. "And if I wanted you to be more than my girlfriend?" His deep, smooth voice and his penetrating gaze quickened my heart rate.

Was he asking me...

"Yes," I whispered without hesitation, and his heartbeat thumped hard against my chest, as if that little three-letter word had a direct connection to his heart.

Nipping my lips with his own, he growled, "Kiss me, baby. Let's seal the deal."

And seal the deal we did.

BEAU

I WIPED MY SWEATY palms on my jeans as the Zoom call connected, and I saw their faces. All four of them.

"Atwood," Justin greeted as his brothers and Elizabeth looked on.

"Hey, guys," I said, trying to regulate my breathing so I didn't puke. "How's everyone doing?"

"Cut the chit chat," Ethan growled. "Why did you need to talk to us? Is Charli okay?"

"She's fine. Really good. Great, in fact," I babbled like a fucking idiot. They just stared at me impassively. "I, um, I wanted to talk to you all about something important." I reached for the small box on my desk and opened it, revealing the ring I had bought weeks ago. A large pear-shaped diamond with smaller diamonds surrounding it, set in a delicate platinum band with a pretty scrollwork pattern.

Elizabeth let out a long, low whistle, and Henry elbowed Ethan. "You owe me ten bucks, dude," he said with a grin.

Ethan shook his head and, in a rare display of humor, said, "While I appreciate the sentiment, you're not my type, Atwood."

I huffed out a little laugh, and my nerves calmed to a low simmer. "I hate to hear that, Ethan, so maybe instead, I could ask your little sister to marry me."

"And you want our permission?" Justin asked with a small frown.

I straightened my shoulders and lifted my chin. "Seeing as how Charli and I are both adults, I don't need your permission." Three pairs of eyebrows lowered, but

Lizzy's lifted in impressed amusement, as did the corners of her lips. "But I would like your *blessing*."

"Run down your case for us," Ethan said curtly, and though they knew pretty much everything they needed to know about me from their previous interrogation, I played along.

Ticking them off on my fingers, I began speaking. "Well, I'm a successful business owner with a steady income. I've already started looking at houses for us. I would protect your sister with my fucking life. I'm not a crackhead or a serial killer." Henry and Lizzy laughed out loud, and even Justin and Ethan cracked a smile. Turning dead serious, I leaned forward on my forearms, my face filling the screen. "And most importantly, I love Charli with everything I am, and it would be my greatest honor to love and support her for the rest of my life."

After a long staredown and then a few glances exchanged between the siblings, Ethan nodded his head and said, "Okay."

My eyebrows nearly hit my hairline. "That's it? Okay?" I expected much more resistance. Kicking. Screaming. Threats.

Matching my pose, Ethan leaned forward on his forearms. "All we care about is Charli's happiness and that she's with a good and decent man." He pointed a thick finger at me. "That's you, Atwood. I know we've given you a hard time, but we just wanted to make sure you were worthy. Charli is the sweetest, kindest person I know, but she's also strong, and she needs a man that can handle that and nurture that, not hold her back."

"She's damn sure strong enough to keep my ass in line. I would do anything to make her life better because she makes mine better just by being in it."

"Welcome to the family, Beau," Elizabeth said, her eyes filled with tears. "When are you planning to ask her?"

"I was thinking Christmas Eve, in front of both of our families."

"You want us to be there when you do it?" Henry asked, pleased. Blaire and Axel had invited Charli's family to their Christmas Eve celebration. That's when we exchanged gifts with each other and the kids.

"I think it would make Charli happy," I said with a shrug. That's all that mattered to me. "Now, if you'll excuse me, I need to go pick up my prospective fiancée and take her shopping." Neither of us had felt much like Christmas shopping while we were apart, and with just a few days left until Christmas, we had a lot of catching up to do.

CHARLI

It was Christmas Eve, and my family had joined the Broxton clan in their living room to open gifts.

Beau and I grinned when we gave my brothers and Axel their gifts, which were wrapped with many layers of duct tape. "What the, uh, heck," Justin said, catching himself before he got fined by Carrie. They all peeled and cut away at the tape to reveal their Man Crates. "What is this?" he asked with a grin.

I pointed at the small laser-etched crowbar attached to the top of the sealed crate. "You have to use the crowbar to get into it." The guys started popping their crates open to discover what was inside. Ethan and Justin got the Whiskey Appreciation Crate, while Axel and Henry received the Exotic Meats Crate, which was filled with strange jerkies like elk, pheasant, and wild boar. Beau had assured me they would love the unique gifts, and they all did.

Blaire was pelting her brother in the head with crumpled up wrapping paper, and he was swatting it away and laughing. The triplets had turned their blow-up punching dolls into tackling dummies while the adults watched with amusement. The room was filled with noise and chaos and so much joy.

Blaire looked around the living room. "Where did Axel go? I wanted to show him..." Just then Axel and Henry came into the room carrying a very large, wrapped gift.

"Special delivery for Miss Charli Casper," Axel said as they set the giant present down in front of me. He grinned as I read the tag and saw that it was from Beau.

Looking at Beau with narrowed eyes, I asked, "Did you buy me a refrigerator for my room?"

"Maybeeee," he hedged. "Open it and see." I tore off the wrapping paper to discover that it was indeed a refrigerator box. *What the hell? This is way too big for my room.* "Here, let me help you," Beau said, taking out his pocket knife and cutting open the box to reveal... another wrapped box, this one about half the size of the first one.

"Oh, ha ha. Very funny, mister," I said, ripping off the paper and opening the box to find—you guessed it—another smaller box. By the time I got to the sixth box, it was quite small. In fact, it was the size of a...

Dear God. It was a blue velvet ring box. I glanced over at Beau, and he swallowed and nodded nervously. *Holy shit, is this really happening?*

My fingers shook as I opened the ring box and saw... nothing? The box was empty. There was the little cushion thing where a ring was supposed to fit, but...

"Looking for this?" Beau asked, and I looked over to see him on one knee with the most gorgeous diamond ring I had ever seen on the end of his pinky finger. I heard gasps and murmurs from around us, but my gaze shifted from the ring to his grinning face, and everything else faded away. It was just the two of us. Inhaling a deep breath, he said, "Charli, I... God, I had a whole thing I was going to say, but I can't remember a word of it." His embarrassed chuckle brushed across my face.

I bit my bottom lip as he took my left hand in both of his. "It's okay. Just stick with the basics," I said quietly, a huge smile taking over my face. *This* is *really happening.*

"Charli, ever since you've come into my life, you've changed me. With your light. With your sweetness. You took a grumpy, unemotional man and turned me into someone who lives for loving you." He pressed a kiss to my ring finger. "I want to put my ring right here to remind you every day how much I love you. To remind you that I belong to you. Will you wear my ring, Peach? Will you be my wife?"

I touched his handsome face with my free hand, my breaths coming faster. "Yes, Beau. Nothing would make me happier than marrying you." I vaguely heard the cheers rising up around us as Beau slid the ring onto my finger and pulled me tightly to him, my legs going around his waist.

We hugged for a long time before he pulled back to look at me. "I'm the happy one, baby." He kissed me then, our lips crushing as our tongues rubbed against each other until someone cleared their throat.

I pulled back and whispered against his lips, "More later." Then I pressed my mouth against his ear. "A lot more."

In one swift move, he sat on the couch, turning me so that I was sitting on his lap with my back pulled against his chest. "Stay right there so I don't embarrass myself," he said in a low voice, flexing his sudden erection against my ass.

Afterward... after all of the hugs and congratulations and champagne that Beau had bought and slipped into the refrigerator, we were finally alone together in my room. I had moved back into my downstairs suite in the Broxton house after asking for my job back earlier this week, to which Blaire and Axel had readily agreed.

Beau and I tugged at each other's clothes, desperate to be skin-to-skin as an engaged couple for the first time. "My brothers were surprisingly happy for us," I said.

"I don't want to talk about your brothers right now," he growled against my neck as his hands shoved down my pants and panties.

"Mmmm," I said as he pushed me back onto the bed while simultaneously yanking my leggings and underwear over my feet and immediately burying his face between my legs. "Apparently, getting engaged makes you horny."

Kneeling beside the bed and giving me a long swipe with his tongue, he grinned up at me, his lips coated with my arousal. "Yeah. Who knew?" He sucked on my clit before mumbling against me, "All I could think of was eating my fiancée's sweet little pussy and then filling her with my cock." His mouth devoured me with hungry licks and nibbles until I was ready to blow.

He pushed his long tongue inside of me, fucking me with it while his nose nuzzled my clit. "Oh, God. Beau. Yes, baby." I grabbed two handfuls of his hair, grinding myself against his mouth as all the emotions of the night exploded from me in a giant, powerful climax. "Soooo good," I moaned as he licked me through it.

"Fuck, you're tasty, sweetheart," he said, licking up the rest of my desire before standing and removing his jeans and underwear. I pulled off my bra and threw it to the side as Beau stood gloriously naked before me, stroking himself slowly.

"Lie on your back," I told him, my voice husky.

"And so it begins. We've only been engaged a few hours, and the little woman is nagging me already."

"Nagging, huh?" I said, crawling toward him with a pout on my lips. "I was so going to make it worth your while, big boy." I traced a finger up his shaft, gathering the thick bead of liquid at the tip onto my fingertip and sucking it off. I released my finger with a loud pop. "But I certainly don't want to be a nag."

"You want me on my back, Peach?"

"Uh-huh," I said, sinking my teeth into my bottom lip.

He pushed me down and covered my body with his. "What if I want to be on top?" The tip of his hot tongue tantalized the pulse point under my jaw.

"Then you won't get to watch me ride your cock," I said, nonchalantly, reaching between us and wrapping my hand around him.

"Fuck, baby. When you put it that way…" He rolled us over, placing his hands behind his head and grinning playfully as I straddled his hips. I loved him like this. "Get on it, Peach."

I leaned down and kissed him, my hair forming a curtain around us. "First, I want to make sure you're ready for me," I teased.

He looked wryly down at his very eager-looking dick. "Seriously? I could drive a goddamn hole through the wall with that thing right now. I'm ready."

I swiveled my hips, sliding my wetness over him as my hair swung over my shoulders. "Better safe than sorry," I said, continuing to circle and roll myself against him. "And it feels so good," I groaned, tipping my head back.

"God, you're beautiful," he breathed, reaching up and rubbing my hair over my breasts. "Especially when you're turned on and your cheeks get all flushed. Take me inside you, Peach. Let me feel how tight and warm you feel around my cock. I want to see you lose yourself on me and feel you flood me with your sweet cum."

Damn, he knew just what to say to get what he wanted. I lifted up, and he gave me a satisfied smile as he reached down and held his erection up for me. I notched my opening over the thick head before sliding slowly down onto him. It was such a snug fit that I had to rock my hips back and forth to get him inside. "That's it, baby. Work that hot little pussy on me. Ahhhh, fuck yeah." Beau pressed his head back into the pillow as his hands gripped my hips and guided my movements.

I moved sensually on top of him, feeling him penetrate me so deeply I could barely breathe. "Beau, ohhhh. I love riding your big, hard cock."

His hands roamed my body, up and down my ribcage, cupping my breasts, sliding over my shoulders and down my arms. I loved the way he treasured me with his touches. "Shit, baby. If you keep talking like that, you're going to make me come too soon."

Throwing his words back to him with a flirty look, I said, "We've only been engaged a few hours, and you're already losing your touch?"

Giving me a devilish grin, he said, "Them's fighting words, baby. Hang on tight and I'll show you my touch." He lifted me and slammed me down onto him, forcefully pushing a moan from my lungs. He did it again and again, thrusting up into me as he pulled me down. The bed was squeaking rhythmically as we hit our stride, moving together as one, the pleasure almost unbearable.

"Coming," I gasped, pressing my hands against his tight abdomen, the muscles there tightening under my fingers with each deep pump. I started to cry out, but he sat up and covered my mouth with his, swallowing the sounds of my orgasm as he moaned his own release into my mouth.

He lowered us to the mattress, turning us on our sides without breaking the connection between our legs. Stroking his hand from my hip to my neck and back down again, he kissed me deeply. "Love you, baby. I can't wait for you to be my wife."

I cupped his scruffy jaw with my palm, letting my fingers rub softly against his cheek. "I love you, future husband. I think I really like engaged sex," I said against his lips, drawing a smile from him.

"Me too, but I'm sick of never being totally alone with you. I've started looking at houses for us, but you need to tell me what you like."

"Houses? Really?" He nodded emphatically. "Hmmm, let's see. I think I would like a master bedroom with a big ole bed, so I can fuck my sexy husband all over it."

"Noted," he said, nuzzling our noses together. "What else?"

"A nice yard so our kids can play outside."

At the mention of children, his eyes went soft, and he kissed my forehead. "I like that, Peach," he whispered. "Any other requests?"

"I'm not picky. As long as we're together, I'll be happy."

"Me too, sweetheart. Ecstatically."

55

CHARLI

THREE MONTHS LATER

Snuggling up beside Beau on his bed, I kissed his neck. "I got some really nice stuff at my lingerie shower today."

His hand stopped its soft stroking up and down my back, ending on my butt cheek. "You gonna show me?" he asked gruffly.

"Not till the honeymoon," I teased, earning me a growl from my fiancé. "Don't you want to be surprised?"

"No," he deadpanned. "I hate surprises."

Rolling on top of him, I kissed the sexy little dimple in his chin before sitting up and straddling him. "I think you'll like these surprises. Just think... every night you can be waiting on the bed in our hotel room, and I'll come out from the bathroom dressed in lingerie that you get to take off me."

The corners of his lips crested up into a smug smile as his hands slid up my sides to cup my breasts. "That sounds like something I might like. I do enjoy getting my beautiful Peach naked."

I spoke with false hesitancy, teasing him in an effort to rile him up. "And there were... well... there were toys and, um, accessories, too."

Beau's eyes widened, and his green eyes searched my face. His voice was a mere croak as his fingers and thumbs tightened around my nipples. "Toys and accessories?"

"Uh-huh." I tapped my bottom lip thoughtfully with the tip of my finger. "Do you know how much liquid we can take in our carry-on luggage?" My fiancé's brow creased in confusion. "Never mind. It's probably best to put the bottles of lube in the checked bag, don't you think?"

His cock hardened beneath me before I was suddenly on my back with a hot, horny male on top of me. "Bottles of lu—what the hell kind of party was this, Charli?"

"Just some naughty, fun times with the girls," I told him airily. "They wanted to make sure I would have some naughty, fun times with my husband."

Firm lips crushed my own, and his tongue pressed into my mouth, seeking and finding mine. Mutual groans filled our mouths as he rocked his steely length against my core, and I melted, letting him take control of my body. "Say it again," he murmured. "Say the part I like."

"My husband," I whispered against his lips.

"My wife," he whispered back, growing even firmer between the cradle of my thighs. This marriage thing really turned him on. His big hand slid down my bare thigh and cupped the back of my knee, curling my leg around his hip and opening me up as he continued his slow grind against me. "You're the sexiest thing on two legs, Peach, and you're all mine."

"One-hundred percent yours," I confirmed, sliding my fingers into his hair as he dipped his mouth to my neck, peppering me with open-mouthed kisses. "Baby?"

"Mmhmm?"

I smiled at the ceiling as I readied myself for his response. "If any of the stuff I got today is too... kinky for you, just let me know."

His mouth stilled on my neck before he lifted his head in almost slow-motion. The look on his face was fucking priceless. "What the fuck is that supposed to mean? Too kinky for *me*?"

I'd wiped the smile from my face, my expression one of pure innocence. "You know. The girls may have gone a little wild. I just don't want you to think you have to—"

My words were halted when he pressed a finger against my lips. "Whatever the hell it is, fucking bring it, Peach. I'm down for it all." I grinned, and he rolled us so that I was on top again. "You're trying to kill me, aren't you?"

"Of course not. Not until you put me on your life insurance policy." He chuckled and slapped my ass. It was a playful gesture, but a trickle of wetness dripped from between my legs. Beau's eyes narrowed, and his nostrils flared, as if he could sense my arousal. The raw, lustful heat in his pine-colored eyes sent a shiver through me. "Wait," I said, my hand pressing against his chest, "I did bring you something from the shower."

His brows lifted in excitement as I reached for my purse and pulled out a cookie wrapped in a napkin. He unwrapped it and laughed at the pink, panty-shaped snack. "Thank you, Peach, but I'd rather eat what's inside *your* panties." He devoured the cookie in two bites and then grinned lasciviously.

"We'll get to that, but first, I need to call and make sure Allie and her mom got home safely. I think this pregnancy is harder on her than she's letting on. She didn't seem quite herself today."

Beau bit back a groan but nodded as I climbed off him and sat against the headboard beside him. I dialed my friend and chatted for a few minutes, swatting my fiancé's hand every time he slipped it underneath my flirty, white skirt.

Allie asked me again to thank Beau for doing the heavy lifting last weekend after her baby shower. He'd gone with me to set up the nursery stuff since Les was deployed.

"Girl, you know I love seeing my man putting those muscles to work. At least he's good for something."

Beau was suddenly between my legs, yanking me down the bed. "I'll show you what I'm good for, woman," he growled, and I squealed in surprise.

"Beau, cut it out! I'm—" My skirt was around my waist, and he pulled my panties to the side a split second before his warm, firm tongue swiped through my sex and flicked rapidly against my clit. "Ohhh, that's—shit! I'm on the phone, baby. Can you just—"

"No."

He plunged his tongue inside me, and my eyes rolled back in my head.

"Allie, gotta go," I said hastily, hanging up with her laughter in my ear as I tossed my phone to the side. Curling my fingers into my fiancé's thick, brown hair, I moaned, "Beau, that was—"

My words were cut off when he pushed two fingers roughly inside of me as his lips closed around my little nub of nerves. He sucked. Hard. I cried out and came around his plunging fingers, gushing against his skilled mouth.

"Fuck. Yeah," he grunted around long, slow licks as my orgasm subsided. I was on my back with my legs trembling uncontrollably, and he lifted his head and grinned with shiny lips before rising up to his knees. "What were you saying?"

My mind wasn't working quite right after that brain-melting orgasm, so I replied with, "Huh?"

"Before I sucked that orgasm from your perfect little pussy, you said, 'Beau, that was—' What were you going to say?"

Oh. That's right. Giving him my best pouty frown, I replied, "I was going to say that sticking your tongue inside me while I was on the phone was rude."

A lifted eyebrow. Two strong thighs bracketing my hips as he straddled and towered above me. I heard the rattle of metal and then the sharp snap of leather as he unbuckled and whipped his belt off.

Though I knew Beau Atwood would never strike me with a belt, the sound was oddly arousing. Or maybe it was the lustful burn in his eyes that had my sex throbbing for him as he unfastened his pants.

"Peach, you haven't even begun to imagine how rude I can be." His voice was low and gravelly. And fucking intense.

Gulp.

"I look forward to it, future husband," I said, my voice soft and sweet.

At that last word, his eyes softened as another part of him—a very large part—visibly hardened.

If you were wondering about rude sex with Beau Atwood... yeah... definitely a five star rating.

CHARLI

THREE MONTHS LATER

"Okay, now put your leg over here."

"I can't, Beau. It doesn't bend that way."

"Shit, hold on, let me move over a little. Okay, now try it."

I got the giggles, and my husband mock-glared at me. "I never thought I would be in the back of your truck with you trying to put clothes *on* me."

"Just stick your leg in here, goofball." He maneuvered us around in the tight space before changing tactics. "Let's try putting it over your head."

"I'm all twisted up. Why are we doing this again?" I asked from beneath the thousand layers of tulle that were surrounding my head.

"I told you. I want to carry you over the threshold in your wedding dress."

"Shouldn't you be wearing your tuxedo then?"

"Cam took it to the cleaners. Please, baby. Just do this one little thing for me."

I pulled and tugged at the dress until I could finally see him. "Yeah, that's what you said on the second night of our honeymoon, and I'm still walking funny."

Beau grinned at me as he pulled me across his lap, letting me feel his erection against my behind. "It was fun though, right?"

"Uh-uh, I know that look, and we are *not* having sex in this truck tonight. Now get your jackhammer away from my ass."

"That's not what you said on the fifth night of our honeymoon," he said, biting me on the neck.

"Beau, I'm serious. Let's just go in the house."

"Okay, party pooper," he said with a sigh, pulling my poofy white dress down over my waist. "Just put your arms in, and I'll zip you up."

"This dress doesn't have a zipper. It has buttons," I said, slipping my arms through the holes and shifting around so that my back was facing him.

He flicked on the overhead light in the truck and groaned. "Fucking hell, how many goddamn buttons are on this thing? Couldn't you have just gotten one with Velcro or something?"

"Vera Wang would be outraged and would slap you upside the head if she heard you say that," I said, as I felt his fingers fumbling over the tiny satin buttons.

"Speaking of wangs..." he said, dropping his voice to a sultry level as he kissed the bare skin over the top of my spine, "...mine is ready to be back inside my gorgeous wife."

I laughed, despite the heat forming between my legs. "I wasn't speaking of *that* wang, though I do love yours. I was talking about Vera Wang, the dress designer."

"What's she got against Velcro?" he grumbled, still working on the buttons. "Fuck it, I'm just doing a few of them."

"Well, hurry up before the neighbors call the cops. This is a nice neighborhood." We were parked in the driveway of our new house. We had started moving our stuff in a week before the wedding, but we had decided that we wanted our first night in the house to be spent as a married couple.

Our house was in the same gated community as Blaire and Axel's, but it was a couple streets over from theirs. And quite a bit smaller, though I thought it was still too big for the two of us. Beau insisted that it gave us room to grow our family over the years, and I had to agree that made sense. It was, after all, our dream home, and we didn't want to outgrow it and have to move.

One of the best parts of the property we had bought was the guesthouse to the right of the house. Beau and his buddies had spent every weekend the past few months renovating it to make a small preschool for me. The first three students that were enrolled were the Broxton triplets, and thanks to Blaire singing my praises, I was at capacity before I even opened the doors. It would still be a couple months before we opened because I had to interview and hire staff, as well as buy supplies, set up bank accounts, have a sign made, and about a million other little things.

"Okay, that's good enough," Beau said. "Now, where's the little head dealie?"

"The veil?" I asked dryly, praying that the Wedding Gods didn't decide to strike my husband down with lightning due to his Velcro and "head dealie" comments.

"Yeah. That," he said, turning my face to meet his so I could see his soft smile. "You looked so pretty with that on." He was so fucking sweet that I couldn't bear to tell him that my messy bun wasn't exactly the proper hairdo for the veil I had worn on our wedding day. And he really didn't care about my makeup-less face and disheveled hair. He had it in his mind that he wanted to carry his bride over the threshold in her wedding finery, so I would plop the "head dealie" on and let him have his little fantasy.

After all, he had made all of my fantasies come true. Our wedding had been a peach and white dream, and the ten-day honeymoon in Hawaii had been nothing short of spectacular.

Unhooking the veil from the dress bag, I worked the little combs into my messy hair as Beau got out of the truck and came around to my side. As soon as he opened the door, his eyes filled with tears, just like they had when I walked down the aisle toward him eleven days ago. "Peach," he said on an exhale, "you take my breath away." We had been traveling all day, and I knew I looked a hot mess, but my new husband made me feel like the most gorgeous woman in the world.

Suddenly, all the fumbling and fussing in the backseat was totally worth it. I would do anything he asked if he promised to never stop looking at me like he was just then. He helped me out of the truck and gathered me in his arms to carry me to the front door.

Beau managed to unlock the door without looking because his eyes were trained on my face. "Welcome home, Mrs. Atwood," he said softly as he stepped into our living room and kicked the door closed behind us. Leaning down, he took my lips in the sweetest kiss I could have ever imagined. He pulled back long enough for me to look around the living room, which had a trail of candles and deep red rose petals leading to the stairs.

"Beau, what is all this?" I asked delightedly.

"A little surprise for my bride. Cam helped." He kissed me again. And he kept kissing me as he followed the roses and candles all the way up the stairs and into our bedroom. He finally set me on my feet so I could take in the candles grouped on every hard surface, giving the room a soft, romantic glow. More rose petals covered the bed, and I walked over to run my hands through them.

"What's this?" I asked, squinting in the dim light to try and see what was lying on the center of the bed. I picked up a large pink dildo and turned to look inquisitively at Beau, who was frowning.

"That's *not* supposed to be there."

"There's a note taped to it," I said, peeling it off and unfolding it. "Dear Mrs. Atwood, This is for you, just in case you wore the old man out in Hawaii. Enjoy! Love, Cam."

"That asshole," Beau said with a laugh, taking the pink toy from me and tossing it over his shoulder as he grabbed me around the waist. "We won't be needing that. This old man doesn't need any help pleasuring his bride."

"Based on the evidence presented over the past ten days, I would say you are correct, dear husband."

"Though I do feel the need to prove myself."

"Ah! A quest! What did you have in mind?"

"Well, first I would like to remove this Vera Bang dress from your luscious body."

I giggled. "Vera *Wang*," I corrected.

"Wang. Bang. What-the-fuck-ever," he muttered, gripping my ass through the dress. "As I was saying, I want to remove this dress and then fuck my wife on a bed of rose petals."

"Mmmm, that sounds perfect," I said as he deftly unbuttoned my dress and slid it from my body.

He laid the dress carefully over a chair. "Let's leave the head dealie on," he said, lifting me and placing me on the bed. "Have I told you how much I appreciate all the lingerie you've been wearing for me?"

"You can thank Allie, Blaire, and Bristol for that. I racked up on sexy and naughty things to turn on my new hubby from them at my lingerie shower."

"It fucking worked. My dick hasn't settled down in over a week. I really liked that black one with the straps."

"I could tell. I plan to work that into the rotation at least once a week."

"Dear God, give me strength," he groaned.

"It gave my mom the giggles when she saw it."

Beau's eyes widened. "Ms. Casper saw all that stuff you wore? Holy shit, I'm not sure I'll ever be able to look her in the eye again."

"Who do you think bought me the crotchless red one?" I asked, lifting an eyebrow.

"The slutty one?" he asked, his eyes almost bugging out of his head. "*Your mom* bought you that?" I nodded. "I'm buying that woman an extra Christmas present this year just for that. I almost broke my dick trying to get it inside you while you were wearing it."

"You were rather, um, eager," I commented.

Beau pulled down the cups of my ivory demi bra and circled my nipples with his tongue. "I do like this one, though. It's sweet and sexy at the same time, just like you." He took turns loving my breasts with his lips and teeth until I couldn't take it anymore.

"That feels so good, baby, but I want your clothes off. Now," I demanded.

"Okay, my greedy little Peach," he said before standing and removing his clothes while I got rid of the sexy bra and panty set I was wearing. Crawling back onto the bed with me, he said, "First time in the new bed in the new house. Let's make it a good one."

And oh, did we ever.

I woke up the next morning with Beau's lips pecking across my shoulder. "Good morning, Mrs. Atwood. How did you sleep?"

"Good," I slurred sleepily, "but I think I've got rose petals stuck in my butt crack."

"That sounds like something I should investigate," Beau said, disappearing beneath the covers.

"Beau, stop it," I said with a laugh as he nipped my ass cheek with his teeth.

He rolled me over onto my back and lifted my legs in the air. "Just trying to be thorough, baby." He lowered his mouth to me just as his phone rang on the nightstand. "Fuuuuck. Noooo," he complained, shoving the covers off, revealing his mussed hair and scowling face. "Already? Couldn't they give us a few hours to sleep in? Swear to God, if it's Cam, I'm cutting his nuts off with a butter knife."

"It's Allie," I said, glancing at the display on his phone. "You should probably get it in case it's about the baby." Lester had been deployed months ago, so Beau had promised him that we would be there if the baby was born before he got back. Allie wasn't due for another couple weeks, and Les was due back any day now.

Beau answered the phone, putting on a more cheerful tone. "Hey, Allie Cat! How's our godson do—" He paused and frowned, swinging his legs over to sit up on the edge of the bed. "Slow down, sweetheart. Just... tell me what... fuck, and how long has he been MIA?" That caught my attention. *Lester is missing in action?* I immediately sprang out of bed and started tossing clothes into a small duffle bag.

I glanced over at Beau who was rubbing the top of his head with one palm. "No... Allie, no... Jesus, that can't be right. You're sure that's what they said?" His tone was alarmed, and then his breathing hitched as he listened. "Shit. I'm so sorry, honey... yeah, I'm on the way... is, um, is the baby okay?" He nodded, murmuring, "We love you, too, Allie Cat," before hanging up and dropping his phone to the bed.

"Beau," I said softly, walking toward him. His elbows were on his knees, his head hanging low.

I placed my hand on his shoulder, and without looking up, he uttered the words that stopped my heart. "He's dead. Les is dead."

"No, Beau. Oh my God!" I cried. Standing between his knees, I wrapped my arms around his head and pressed it into my stomach. I bent and kissed the top of his head as tears flowed from my eyes. "I'm so sorry, baby." Beau hesitated before wrapping his arms around my thighs and releasing a deep sob. "I'm sorry," I whispered over and over, stroking his hair and neck.

Beau was always the strong one, but today he was letting me in, letting me hold and kiss him while he mourned his friend. For a couple minutes anyway, and then he lifted his eyes to me, wiping his wet face roughly with his palms. "I need to go," he said gruffly.

"I've got us a bag started," I sniffed as Beau stood.

"You don't have to go, baby. I know you're probably—"

"They're my friends, too," I said softly but firmly, and he leaned down to kiss me, cupping my face and taking back his role as comforter-in-chief.

"I know, sweetheart." He kissed me tenderly, sharing his grief with me through soft pecks against my lips. "Will you get my dress uniform out of the closet while I call the guys? I'll need it for the... funeral." His voice broke on that last word, and I wrapped my arms tightly around his middle as another wave of tears hit me. Beau rocked us slowly from side to side for a few minutes before whispering, "We need to go."

I nodded and went to the closet, pulling out his uniform and a black dress for me. Beau was just hanging up the phone from talking to Cam when I emerged from the closet. "We need to shower before we leave," I told him, laying our clothes on the bed. "We smell like, um, newlyweds."

He gave me a half smile. "Yeah, good call," he said, leading me to the bathroom and turning on the shower. "I'm sorry, Peach. This isn't how I wanted our first day back to be."

"That's not important at all," I said, stepping under the spray and pulling him with me. "Let me take care of you for just a few minutes." I washed his big, muscular body while he pressed his hands against the tile wall and squeezed his eyes closed.

Twenty minutes later, we had our bags packed and were heading west to Fort Worth. Other than a few brief comments like "where's my toothbrush?" or "it's time to go," Beau hadn't spoken at all. I placed my hand face-up on the console, and he pressed his warm palm to mine and linked our fingers, his face a mask of grief and determination.

"Do you think you could tell me what happened before we get there?" I asked quietly, not wanting to push him, but also not wanting Allie to have to retell the story of her husband's death once we arrived. I felt tears seeping down my face as I thought of poor, sweet Allie, a young widow with a baby on the way.

"Seven days ago, Les's chopper went down in an undisclosed location. Everyone else died, but his body wasn't recovered, so he was considered MIA, probably captured. Two days ago, his remains were discovered during a raid of a house. He's... he's on his way home now."

So many questions. Was he tortured? Did he die quickly? If this was killing me, I could only imagine how Allie was feeling.

It was another thirty minutes before he spoke again. "He loved Allie so fucking much. He was like an inspiration to me, seeing how he loved and treated her. Being around them made me think that I could possibly have that one day. But I never thought it would actually happen for me." He squeezed my hand and glanced over at me. "Until I met you."

"They were a beautiful couple," I said, kissing the back of his hand.

As we pulled up to the house, Beau said, "If she needs us to stay with her, we will. Otherwise, we'll get a hotel room nearby."

"Whatever Allie needs," I agreed.

As we approached the house, it appeared unoccupied, no lights showing through the windows. "Do you think she's here?" I asked.

Beau shrugged as he knocked lightly on the door. A short gray-haired woman in scrubs answered the door. "Hi," she said in a near whisper. "You must be Charli and Beau. Allie said to be expecting you." She motioned us inside the dark house.

Beau and I glanced at each other, both wondering what the hell was going on. All the windows were covered with black paper, and there was a single light burning in the living room to the right. A small lamp behind a bed.

A hospital bed.

"Allie?" I asked, approaching the bed. I found it necessary to verify because I barely recognized my friend. Her face was gaunt, and I could have wrapped my small hand around her wrist. I searched my mind, trying to remember the last time I had seen her in person. It had been at my lingerie shower about three months ago. We texted several times a week, but with the wedding plans and the new house and work...

How could she have changed so much in such a short time, and better yet, what was wrong with her that had caused this drastic change? It couldn't have been Lester's capture and death. That had been less than a week. I glanced back at Beau, but he was frozen in the archway leading to the living room, taking in the scene, his mind obviously working through the details like mine was.

I sat on the edge of the bed and took Allie's bony hand. "Allie, sweetie. What's going on? What's all... this?" I indicated the machines flashing her vital signs silently from beside her bed.

She smiled, one hand resting on her swollen belly. "Hey, Charli. I'm sorry to have interrupted your first day back from your honeymoon. Did you have fun?"

"It was great, but I need you to tell me about *you*. Is something wrong with the baby?"

Her smile faltered as her hollowed-out eyes found mine. "Little Les is fine. It's... it's me. I'm sick."

Beau finally found his legs and strode over to sit in a chair on the other side of her bed, his hand looking huge where it rested on her thin arm. "What's wrong, Allie Cat? We can get you to a doctor or a hospital or whatever you need."

Her lips twisted into a harsh grimace. "No, no more doctors or hospitals. I've seen what seems like a million of them in the past couple of months." She glanced slowly back and forth between us. "I have a brain tumor."

Oh, dear God. No.

"Your headaches," I murmured, thinking back to something she'd said about six months ago. "Didn't you get that checked out?"

"Yeah, at first we thought it was just hormones or something. I treated it with Tylenol for a couple of months, but then they just started getting worse."

"What are they doing for it?" Beau asked, frowning as his hand rubbed gently up and down her arm.

Allie smiled sadly. "Nothing."

"Nothing? What do you mean nothing?" Beau asked loudly, and our friend winced.

"Loud noises and bright lights bother me. That's the reason for all this," she said, her eyes darting to the covered windows.

"I'm sorry, honey," Beau said, lowering his voice. "I'm so sorry, but why aren't you getting treatment?"

"Because the baby… Lester's baby," she said on a sob, "wouldn't survive it."

Beau's eyes met mine over the frail body on the bed between us, and we communicated our shared thought. *She's sacrificing herself for her baby.* My tears came with a vengeance.

"Oh God. Allie." It was all I could come up with to say.

Beau's voice trembled when he spoke. "What did Les say about this, sweetheart? About you not getting treatment? I can't imagine he would have been okay with it."

Her big, teary eyes went to him. "I didn't tell him. I didn't get the diagnosis until after he was deployed, and I didn't want him to worry and get distracted while he was over *there*. I was going to tell him when he got home, which was supposed to be three days ago, but…"

Now he's gone. She didn't have to say it. We were all thinking it.

"But… but you can get treatment after the baby is born, right?" I asked tremulously.

Allie gave me a sympathetic smile. "No, Charli. I can't. Look at me. It's already too late." She took a long, shaky breath. "I've just been trying to hang on long enough to see Les again and to get our baby strong enough to make it."

Beau averted his eyes, focusing on the machine flashing Allie's heart rate and blood pressure. "How long do you have?" he asked quietly.

"Not long. The tumor is growing *exponentially*. That's the word the neurologists use. Which in layman's terms means that I'm pretty much fucked." She gave us a weak smile that we didn't return. "I can't stand noise or light, and I throw up everything I eat now. I'm on hospice care, and I have a feeding tube to keep the baby healthy." She rubbed her belly absently. "I love him so much. I just want him to grow up and have a happy life, even though I can't be here to see it."

Beau stood and leaned over Allie, gathering her gently in his arms as his hand stroked through her lank hair. "I'm sorry, Al. This is so fucked up. Losing Les and now this." He released her and kissed her forehead. "I'll go meet Lester's plane, of course, and then Charli and I will handle the funeral arrangements. What else can we do to help you?"

"There is one thing. That's why I called you first. You see, this was going to be Les's last deployment. He was leaving the navy."

"Yeah, he told me," Beau said.

"So, I thought he would be around to love and raise our son, even though I wouldn't. But now..."

"You want us to keep an eye on him?" Beau asked, with a smile. "You can count on it."

"Actually, it's a little bigger than that." Allie's eyes moved slowly between me and Beau. "I would like you two to raise little Lester as your own." At our combined gasp, she held up her hand. "I know it's a lot to ask, but I'm also aware that you two are considering adopting in the future. This is probably a lot faster than you intended, since you've only been married for about five minutes."

Allie's eyes met mine, pleading woman-to-woman for me to understand. I tried to cover my shock. "But Allie, don't you want someone in your family or Lester's family to take him?"

"Les's mom is dead, and his dad doesn't know anything about raising babies. He's an older man, and I don't think he's even ever changed a diaper. My father has dementia, so my mother has her hands full with him. There's no way she could take a baby, too."

"Don't you have a sister?" Beau asked.

Allie wheezed out a laugh. "Dana has been in and out of rehab for over ten years. She can't stay off the meth long enough to take care of herself, much less raise a child." She squeezed both of our hands. "You two are the best people I know, and my baby deserves to have parents who will love him like he's their own." She took in a shuddery breath. "Beau, you're so much like Les. Hardworking, loyal, protective. Someone who can teach this baby how to be a man and who would be a wonderful role model just like Les would have been." Her eyes filled with tears as she mentioned her husband, and then she turned to me. "And Charli, you have the biggest heart and the most maternal instincts of anyone I know. Not to mention that you're friggin' brilliant."

"Hey, I want to be brilliant, too," Beau teased gently.

"I know you do, dear," she said, patting his hand indulgently and making us all smile. Our smartass Allie was still there underneath all of the tubes and grief. "Look, I know this is sudden, and I know you'll need to discuss this. I'm so sorry to burden you with it, and I totally understand if it's too much to ask. I just can't stand the thought of my baby going into foster care. I want him to be with someone we know and love."

Beau's eyes met mine again before he spoke. "Are you sure this is what you want, Allie?"

"It's what I want, and I know it's what Les would want." Her voice cracked on her dead husband's name.

I patted her hand, my voice thick with emotion. "We'll talk about it, okay? But why didn't you tell me you were sick? We talk on the phone or text all the time."

"I didn't want to burden you when you were planning a wedding, not to mention buying a house and starting a business. This is all supposed to be such a happy time for you."

"Oh, Allie. Don't say that. You're one of my best friends." I kissed the back of her hand and then held it to my cheek. "I would have done anything to help you."

She sighed. "I'm sorry, Charli. I just wanted to tell Lester first, but then the tumor grew a lot faster than I or the doctors thought it would. I thought I would have more time. I figured I would have a few months after Les got home and the baby was born, and we could break the news to our friends together."

Allie's voice started drifting off, and her eyelids fluttered shut. I looked at Beau, and he jerked his head toward the other room.

57

BEAU

My heart was goddamn broken. First Lester's death, and now the news about his sweet Allie. And that poor baby having to grow up without his parents. *My God! Could this story get any more tragic?* Well, there was no fucking way I could allow that boy to go into the system. I prayed my wife would go along with this. I knew it was a lot to ask of a brand-new bride, to take on the responsibility of a child when we hadn't even had time to be newlyweds.

We walked quietly into the kitchen where Charli fell into my arms, clutching onto my shirt like her life depended on it. "Beau," she wept against my chest, "I just can't take this. It kills my soul that she's been going through this by herself. And now she's lost Les."

I wrapped my arms tightly around my wife, resting my cheek against the top of her head. "I know, baby. It's killing me, too. They're such good people." I stroked a hand soothingly up and down her back. "Sweetheart, we should probably talk about the baby," I said tentatively.

Please, God. Let her say yes.

Before I could take a breath, Charli's head popped up, her blue eyes fierce through her tears. "Beau, we *have to* take this baby. I know you're probably reluctant since we haven't even been married for two weeks, but we can't let Lester and Allie's baby go to strangers."

"I know, babe, but ar—"

Her bossy little ass didn't let me get another word in. "No. No *buts*. We can do this. I *want* to do it. Do you have any idea how long the adoption process is?

It could be years and years before we could get a child. And this baby *needs* us, Beau." Her face was pleading and determined. "I swear, I will be the best wife ever. I'll give you sex whenever you want it, even if I'm tired from being up with the baby all night. Just please don't say no. Please, Beau. I know it will be hard, but—"

I cut off her diatribe by taking her mouth in a crushing kiss. I had never loved this woman as much as I did right at that moment. She had the biggest, sweetest heart of any human I had ever met, and I was so fucking lucky that she was mine. I cupped her beautiful tear-stained face with my hands as I plunged my tongue into her mouth, licking and sucking at her until we were both breathless.

When I pulled back, her eyes were foggy, and her mouth was slack. "I wasn't going to say no, Peach, though I would like to hear more about this *sex any time I want it* thing."

Her eyes looked up at me with so much gratitude, I thought my heart might burst. She could literally ask me for the moon right now, and I would find a way to give it to her. "You mean it, baby?"

"Of course, Peach. If it's what you want."

Her bottom lip trembled. "What I really want is for Lester and Allie to be able to raise their little boy themselves."

"I know, honey. Me too." I turned away from her as anger took over. "God-dammit, I fucking hate this. Why them? Why does bad shit happen to such good people?" I wanted to put my fist through the wall.

I felt Charli's hands wrap around my waist and her cheek rest against my back, and a bit of my anger seeped away. I put my hands over hers and linked our fingers. "I know this is what we've talked about... adopting a baby, but this is the last way I ever wanted it to happen," I said miserably.

"Yeah, me too, but we have to make the best of a shitty situation. Little Les needs a good home and two loving parents. Our timeline may have been bumped up a notch or two, but we can be that for him. And we will always have a little piece of our friends to keep close to us."

I turned in her arms so that her head was against my chest. "I like that." We held each other for a while before I pulled back to look at her. "I need to call the guys and give them a heads up about Allie. Otherwise, they will pile in here like a herd of buffalo, and she needs it quiet."

Charli nodded. "Maybe we can see if the funeral home can do an evening graveside service so that the sunlight won't be uncomfortable for Allie."

I kissed her softly. "That's a good idea. I'll talk to them and also make sure Les gets a full military burial. Can you arrange hotel rooms for us and the guys?"

"Of course. You go do what you need to do, and I'll stay here with Allie. I know she has her nurse to take care of her, but she needs a friend with her, too."

"You're an amazing woman, Charli Atwood."

"And you're the best man I know, Beau Atwood."

58

CHARLI

ALLIE'S EYES FLUTTERED OPEN and then closed again. I held her hand patiently as she struggled to fully awaken. "Charli?" she croaked.

"I'm here, Allie." I held a straw to her lips so she could drink some water.

Her hands went automatically to her stomach, and she smiled contentedly before her face fell. "Oh God. Les," she cried. I pushed her hair back from her face as she fell apart. "I keep thinking it's a nightmare, and then I wake up, and he's really gone."

I sat crying with her, not knowing what else to do. Her pain was raw and immense as she sobbed for her husband and for the loss of her future with her son. I couldn't even imagine what she was going through, but my heart ached deeply.

When Allie's weeping finally ebbed away, I cleaned her face with a damp cloth. "Can I get you anything?"

Her hand reached for her throat. "My necklace. In the bathroom," she said weakly. "I forgot to put it back on after my shower." I retrieved a long golden chain with two rings on it, Allie's engagement and wedding rings. As I slipped it over her head, she explained. "They fall off my finger now, so I wear them around my neck." She stared down at the rings and then looked back to me. "Do you think they will return Lester's wedding ring to me?" Her voice was so full of hope for that band of gold, that small token of love between her and her mate.

"I'm sure if it was still with him when they... uh, found him, they will make sure you get it."

"Do you think he suffered?"

Oh God, the pain she must be going through right now. Wondering. Not knowing. I answered as honestly as I could. "I have no idea, but I hope not. Lester was so strong, Allie, and I know his last thoughts were of you and the baby, no matter what he went through."

She nodded and gave me a small smile. "I'm sure you're right." Her eyes seemed to clear as she leveled her gaze at me. "Not to pressure you, but we don't have a lot of time. Did you and Beau talk?"

We don't have a lot of time. Those words pierced me like a sword.

I took her hand. "Yes, and we would be honored to raise your son. I swear, we will love little Lester so damned much, Allie."

"Thank you," she said with tears in her eyes. "And you don't have to name him Lester. That was just what his daddy and I started calling him ever since we found out he was a boy."

"I love the name, and that's already how I think of him. Did you have a middle name picked out?"

"No, not really, but I do want him to have your last name since he will be your son now. I'll put that on the birth certificate."

"*Our* son," I corrected gently. "He will always be your son as well as ours. We will make sure he knows you and Les." She pressed her lips together and nodded. "What if we gave him your last name as a middle name? Lester James Atwood."

Her beautiful smile shone through the gauntness of her face, and I saw a sliver of the old Allie. "I really like that, but of course, you should discuss it with Beau."

"Discuss what with Beau?" my husband said, entering the living room, having just returned from meeting the plane carrying Lester's body. "Are you two lovely ladies gossiping about me?"

I smiled up at him as he dropped a kiss on my forehead before sitting beside Allie on the soft blue sheet. "We were talking about the baby's name. Do you like Lester James Atwood?"

Beau's hand went to his chest, rubbing absently over his heart. "I love that," he said, his voice thick with emotion.

Allie's eyes went back and forth between my face and Beau's. "Not to get too sappy, but I just wanted to thank you both for taking little Les. I couldn't imagine a better home or better parents for him. I know it's a lifetime commitment, and it just seems too much to ask of you."

Beau held her hand and kissed the back of it affectionately. "We should be thanking you, Allie Cat. You are giving us a gift. A true blessing. It means so much to us that you have the faith in us to trust us with the one thing that means the most to you."

"Can you hand me that folder over there?" Allie asked, pointing to the coffee table. I retrieved it for her, and she opened it up. "Here are our wills. We both had new ones written after I got pregnant, and we asked you to be godparents." She flipped a few pages. "We both stated that everything goes to the surviving spouse unless we both die at the same time. We were worried about what would happen if we both died in a car crash or something, so we named you two as our child's legal guardians in case of that. We thought we would have all the time in the world, so we were going to discuss it with you when Les got back to make sure you were okay with it. He knew his job was dangerous, so he wanted to have the wills done before he left, but we had no clue we would also be dealing with all... *this*." She waved her hand up and down her body.

"I'm certainly not a lawyer, so I'm not sure how this works," I said. "Would we have to go to court?"

"Our attorney made sure we signed guardianship papers, as well as putting it in our wills. Beau, you will be named what's known as temporary or emergency guardian as soon as I, um, when I'm no longer here." *When she dies. Oh, God.* "Our parents are aware and won't contest it, so there shouldn't be a problem. You will just have to go before the judge. Our attorney knows most of the family court judges in this county, and he doesn't anticipate any issues. They usually follow the wishes of the parents. The whole process should take weeks, possibly months."

"Thank you for being so thorough, Al," Beau said. "Is there anything else we need to know?"

She pulled a small notebook out of the folder. "You shouldn't have to buy anything right away. Here's a list of everything we have already. Stuff we bought and gifts we received at the baby shower." She smiled over at me. "You probably won't have to buy diapers until he's two. Everything is in the nursery."

"Okay, don't worry about a thing. If there's anything he needs, we will make sure he has it."

"There's a... a letter I wrote to little Lester in an envelope in the back of the notebook. And a few that his daddy wrote to him while he was away. Would you give those to him when you think he's old enough?"

Beau nodded. "And he will know what wonderful, brave people his parents were because we will tell him." He hesitated before speaking again. "Allie, I have Les's things. Would you like to see them, or do you just want me to hold onto them for a while?"

Her hollow eyes widened. "Is his wedding ring in there?"

"I'm not sure, sweetheart. Do you want me to check for you?"

"Yes, please."

Beau left the room and returned a minute later with the golden band pinched between his fingers. Allie gasped as her face melted into a mask of combined sadness and relief. I removed her necklace and added Lester's larger ring to rest beside her smaller ones before putting the chain back around her neck.

"Thank you," she whispered to us both as she turned on her side away from us and clasped the rings in one fist. "But can I please be alone now?"

59

BEAU

Two nights later, our group stood beside our old friend Lester's coffin. Alllie's mother and Charli stood on either side of her, holding her hands, while I stood behind her wheelchair with my hands on her shoulders. I was trying to remain strong, but this fucking hurt.

I had been to military funerals before, but never for someone I was so close to. Add that to the fact that Allie would be joining him soon... *Shit! This is just too much.* I rubbed my hands soothingly across her shoulders when she held her head up high as the folded flag was presented to her.

I slipped noise-canceling headphones on her ears before Taps and the twenty-one gun salute so the noise didn't hurt her head, and then I came around the wheelchair and helped her to her feet so she could approach her husband's coffin. I supported her with an arm around her waist as she laid her hand on the smooth mahogany surface and said her goodbyes to the love of her life. I said my own in my head, directly to my brother.

I've got her, Les. I'll take care of her until it's her time. And I'll take care of your boy. I will love him with my whole heart, brother. I swear to you... our son will never want for anything. I love you, bro. Rest easy.

As they lowered Lester James into the ground, I saluted sharply, clenching my jaw and drawing on every bit of strength I had in my body. Allie looked up at me, the haggard planes of her face in sharp relief in the moonlight, and whispered a simple, "Thank you." I gathered her in my arms, taking most of the weight of her emaciated body as she clung to me.

Settling Allie back into the wheelchair, I stood beside her like a sentinel as the others knelt in front of her, kissing her cheek and whispering what comfort they could muster for the dying widow. Cam. Tank. Hawk. Woody. Bode. And so many others. One-by-one they paid their respects to the widow of one of the finest men I had ever known.

When the crowd finally dispersed, I squatted down beside Allie. "You ready, sweetheart? Or do you need another minute?"

"I'm ready. Thank you for everything, Beau. I know Les would appreciate everything you're doing for me and this little one." She rubbed her hand over her belly. "And your sweet Charli has been such a comfort to me. You did good with that one."

I had walked in on many of their conversations over the past few days, mostly about the baby. Charli told her about how she would read to little Les every night and discussed what adventures we might take him on. Allie filled in the conversation with her hopes and desires for her unborn baby and his future. The warmth and genuine friendship between these two mothers did weird and wonderful things to my heart.

"Yeah, I don't know what I did to get so lucky," I sighed, looking over at my wife, who was standing nearby chatting with my friends. Feeling my stare, she met my eyes and smiled. That sweet, perfect, gentle smile that was all for me.

"It wasn't luck. You were smart enough to open that big ole heart of yours at just the right time and let her in," Allie said, tapping my chest with her thin fingers.

I chuckled. "She just swooped in and stole the damn thing," I said, standing as Lester's father approached, his eyes rimmed in red.

He bent to hug his daughter-in-law. "Allie dear," he said as she clung to his neck, "I am so sorry. I had no idea you were sick until you called me a couple days ago. If you'd told me sooner, I would have helped you in any way I could."

Despite the fact that they had never been close, Allie kindly said, "That's very sweet, Merritt, but I've been doing okay. I have excellent nurses, and my mom helps when she can. Thank you, though."

The older man's chin trembled as he stood. "I'm so sorry about Les." He focused off in the distance with his hands in his pocket before turning back to her. "I'm sorry about a lot of things. I should have been around more. I should have..." His voice broke and trailed off.

Allie patted his arm. "It's okay. You're a busy man, and Les and I understood that. You loved him, Merritt, and you didn't have to be around every day for him to know that."

"Thank you, hon, and please call me if you need anything," he said before turning to me. "Beau, could I speak with you for a minute?"

"Sure. Give me a second." I pushed Allie's wheelchair over to Charli and the guys, assuring my wife I would be right back.

Standing on tiptoe, she kissed my cheek, smoothing her hands across my uniformed shoulders.

I gripped her waist and kissed my way across her soft cheek. "Les's dad wants to talk to me, and then we can get Allie home. And after that, I'm going to take my beautiful wife back to the hotel room for the night."

"Sounds good," she said, a pretty blush rising up her cheeks.

"How are you doing, sir?" I asked Merritt when I returned to him.

He rubbed a hand across his mouth as his eyes stared at the hole in the ground. "My son is dead. I spent all my fucking life traveling and working instead of spending time with my family and now it's too late. My wife's gone. My son's gone. What was it all for?"

"May I speak freely, Mr. James?"

"Of course, and call me Merritt."

"Okay, Merritt. I served with Lester for many years. He and I had very similar temperaments, which meant we argued like brothers, but I also loved him like a brother. After I got out of the service, I may not have seen Les every day or every week, but we had a bond. I feel like I knew him as well as anyone, except for his wife, of course. He was by far the hardest working man I ever knew." His dad nodded in acknowledgement. "He got that work ethic from you, Merritt. He spoke of you often, and not once did he ever question your love for him. He knew you loved him because you worked so hard to provide for your family. I know it was hard to sacrifice time with your kid so none of his needs ever went unmet, but you did that for your family."

"I did, but it all seems so worthless now. I just wish... fuck! I don't even know what I wish." Changing the subject, he said, "I understand you're going to be raising my grandson?"

"Yes, with my wife," I said, glancing over at her.

Merritt smiled. "I spoke with her earlier. She's a special lady."

"She is," I agreed, my heart swelling with love.

He put his hand on my shoulder. "If I could give you a word of advice, Beau... work hard, but don't sacrifice the most important thing in the name of the almighty dollar. Time. Time with your wife and time with your son. Don't make the same mistakes I did, because I guarantee you will regret it one day." He turned and walked away, his shoulders sagging heavily.

"Merritt?" I called, jogging toward him when he stopped and turned back to me. "Charli and I would love it if you would come visit your grandson any time. We want you to be a part of his life."

The older man's chin trembled slightly before he uttered an emotional, "Thank you, Beau." I watched him as he slowly trudged toward his car, his drooping shoulders straightening slightly.

I heard Charli call my name and turned to see her frantically waving me over. "What is it?" I asked, walking quickly to her as she squatted in front of Allie.

"I think she's in labor." I looked down at Allie who was covering her protruding stomach, her body curling forward.

"The baby..." she grunted.

I sprang into action, lifting Allie into the car. I tossed my hotel room key to Cam and asked him to bring Charli and me some clothes.

Climbing into the limo and settling with Allie's head in her lap, my wife took charge, calling out the name of the hospital to the driver. "You're okay, little mama," she cooed at the pregnant woman as she slid her fingers through her hair. "Just breathe."

Allie's mother, Rachel, sat at her feet, reaching for her daughter's hand and speaking softly to her. Charli handed me her phone, asking me to call Allie's OB/GYN and let him know we were on the way to the hospital. My wife was fucking amazing.

The limo driver kept shooting looks into the back seat as he dropped his foot on the accelerator, obviously not wanting a baby born in the back of his vehicle. We made it in record time, and Allie was whisked away to a room while Charli, Rachel, and I were shown to a waiting room.

I paced back and forth, practically wearing a hole in the gray industrial carpet while Charli and Rachel sat calmly in forest-green cushioned chairs. "Beau, why don't you come sit down?" my wife asked softly.

"Because I'm freaking out here, Charli," I said sharply as the two women shared an indulgent smile.

"It's okay. They're just checking her, and then they'll let us see her." I sat beside Charli, my leg jiggling nervously until she put her small hand on my knee. I covered it with my own hand, and the feel of her soft skin soothed me. No one could calm me like my wife.

Twenty minutes later, my entire crew arrived, and Cam handed me a bag of clothing. They had all changed into casual clothes, so Charli and I headed for the large restroom and swapped out our funeral attire for some simple shorts and t-shirts. "You alright, baby?" she asked me, wrapping her arms around my middle.

"I am when you're in my arms like this," I said, burying my face in her hair. "I'm just worried about Allie and the baby. Do you think they'll be okay?"

"I honestly don't know. She's so weak, but she said the baby has been fine at all the doctor's visits."

When we emerged from the restroom, we found a doctor talking to Allie's mother. Rachel introduced us, and Dr. Lopez asked us to step into the hall. "I've examined Allie, and she's definitely in labor. She's not strong enough to give birth, so we've decided to do a c-section." He gestured to me and Charli. "She filled me in on the situation, and she would like you two in the room with her, but first she wants to spend a few private minutes with her mother."

As Rachel went in to see her daughter, I asked the doctor, "How is she? And the baby?"

"The baby is doing well. His heartbeat is strong." I stared at him, waiting for his response regarding the mother. "Allie is weak. To be honest, I'm not sure if she will make it through the surgery, so you need to be prepared for that."

"What?" Charli asked, her hand going to her throat. "But... isn't there something you can do? Can we put off the birth until she's stronger or... or something?"

Dr. Lopez smiled sadly. "She's not going to get any stronger, Charli. I'm sorry." My wife let out a deep sob and buried her head in my chest as I hugged her and tried my best to control my own emotions. *We just buried Les a couple hours ago, and now this?* "Allie knows, and she's at peace with it. All she's worried about now is her baby. She's a very brave and selfless woman. She could have ended the pregnancy months ago and gotten treatment for the tumor, but this is what she has chosen, so all you can do is support her."

"We will," I assured him. "Whatever she needs."

"You're already doing exactly what she needs by giving her the peace of mind that her child will be okay. Now come on, and let's get you two scrubbed up and dressed. You'll be meeting your son soon." Despite the circumstances, that gave me a little thrill.

Twenty minutes later we were in the operating room wearing surgical clothing and standing beside Allie. "How you feeling, sweetheart?" I asked, holding one of her hands.

"I'm good. It was hard saying goodbye to my mother. She has so much to deal with anyway with taking care of my father, and now she's going to lose me."

"You don't know that for sure," Charli said as she took her other hand.

"Yeah, I do. But don't be sad for me, okay? Promise me."

"No, I'm certainly not going to promise not to be sad, you lunatic," Charli said. "I'll be sad if I want to."

"Stubborn ass," Allie said, giving my wife a genuine smile. "Thank you for being here with me. You always cheer me up, Charli." She turned to me. "And I guess you do too, Mr. Grumpy Pants."

"He is grumpy, but at least he's nice to look at," Charli said teasingly.

Allie winked at me. "You just sit over there and look handsome, big fella. I'll do all the work here."

"Stop flirting with my husband, you floozy."

"Y'all are making me feel really cheap here," I said with a mock pout. "I have feelings, you know."

"Charli's told me all about your, um, *feelings*," Allie said, and both women giggled.

"Hush, woman," Charli hissed playfully. "That was supposed to be private girl talk." The women shared a smile, and I was amazed once again at my wife. She brought joy wherever she went; hell, she could even make a dying woman smile.

Dr. Lopez came into the room with a smile. "Well, it looks like you two have our patient in high spirits. Happy mommies make happy babies," he sang. "Allie has already had an epidural, so she won't feel any pain. We're about to get started here," he said as the rest of the surgical team entered the room.

"Will you two pray with me?" Allie asked us, grabbing our hands, and we readily agreed. The busy room went instantly silent as we closed our eyes and listened to Allie's sweet words. She told God she was prepared and that she was ready to see her husband. She prayed for me and Charli. I'm not ashamed to admit that I cried when she spoke about her unborn baby, asking God to watch over him for the rest of his life.

When she was done, Charli and I both kissed her cheek and told her we loved her. Dr. Lopez gave us a moment before asking quietly, "Are we ready?"

"Definitely," Allie said confidently with a serene smile on her face.

Less than fifteen minutes later, Lester James Atwood made his appearance into this world. Allie asked me to cut the umbilical cord, which honestly freaked me the fuck out, but I did it. The doctor handed the squirming baby to a nurse, who quickly wiped him down before laying him gently on Allie's chest. We released her hands so that she could touch his little body, but we each kept our hands on her shoulders.

"Oh God," she rasped, her fingers lightly touching his precious face. "He's beautiful. So perfect." She tried to raise her head, but she was too weak, so I put my hand behind her neck and lifted gently so that she could kiss his tiny head. "I love you, Lester James," she cooed, cradling him with both hands a second before her eyes went glassy.

An alarm sounded, but a nurse quickly silenced it as Allie stared at the ceiling. "Les," she whispered, a beatific smile forming on her face as the life left her body.

I had witnessed men dying in battle, but this was totally different. This was peaceful and, while tragic, it was the most beautiful thing I had ever witnessed. Tears were streaming down my cheeks as I looked at her lovely face that was finally free of worry and pain.

After a moment, we heard the doctor quietly say, "She's gone." A tiny cry pierced the room just then, as if the baby knew his mother had left this Earth, and I instinctively placed my hand on his tiny back to comfort him. The still and silent room suddenly seemed to jump right back into action as a nurse removed the baby and took him to a little glass bed thing in the corner. There were soft murmurs and the sound of the doctor giving orders as he began closing Allie's abdomen.

I was overwhelmed by... everything. Watching life come into this world at the same minute that life left this world. I finally remembered to look up at Charli, whose face was wet as she cried silently, looking down at our friend's now-slack body. I quickly rounded the bed, ignoring what was going on behind that drape, and lifted my wife in my arms.

"I've got you, sweet girl," I murmured, holding my gorgeous wife tightly to me as the room buzzed with activity around us..

After a few minutes, a nurse approached and led us to a private room where we removed our surgical gear and stuffed it into the proffered bin. Her face was stoic, but I could read the raw emotion in her eyes as I sank onto a cushy couch, settling Charli on my lap. "We will bring your, um, the baby in here in just a minute. I'm sorry, I'm not sure what to call him. I know you're going to take him, but... crap, this is awkward."

"He's our son," I said gently. "He will always be Allie and Lester's son, but he's also ours."

The nurse smiled in weak relief. "Okay. I'll go get your son." She was back a minute later carrying a bundle in a blue blanket. "Babies like skin-to-skin contact, so if you would like to remove your shirts, he can lie on your chest. I'll give you some privacy." She set a bottle on the small table beside the couch.

When she was gone, Charli and I removed our shirts, and she unwrapped and cuddled little Lester James Atwood to her chest. Mother and baby sighed simultaneously as if they had been waiting their entire lives to meet each other, and tears pricked the backs of my eyelids. I leaned closer to Charli, my head resting on her shoulder as we looked down at our new baby.

My wife held his little diapered bottom with one hand, using the other to explore his soft baby skin and hair. "He's so perfect and sweet," she said, kissing his downy blonde hair.

I reached out a finger to stroke his hand. "Look at his tiny fingers," I said, tracing each teeny digit. Les opened his lids and peered at me with bright, curious light-colored eyes. "Hey, little man," I purred, drawing a finger down his chubby cheek.

"How is it that I can feel so happy when I'm so sad?" Charli asked, her voice not much more than a whisper.

Placing a finger under her chin, I tilted my wife's face toward mine. "I was thinking about this earlier. We witnessed something incredibly wonderful and something incredibly sad in the span of about a minute. It's okay to have mixed feelings, sweetheart. I feel the same." I kissed her lips tenderly.

"Okay," she said, smiling at me. "So, I think we should mourn our friends when we're alone, but when we're with this little guy, we should focus only on the joy. He deserves to feel how happy we are to have him." She sifted her fingers through his hair. "Do you want to hold him now?"

"Yeah," I breathed, "I do." I reached for our son and nestled him against my bare chest. *Oh. God.* I had never felt anything as blissful as this. His faint little puffs of breath against my chest. His soft cheek against my skin. I pressed my lips against his tiny head and found it easy to focus on the joy.

My son. A warm wave of love and protectiveness spread throughout my body, and I knew I would burn down the world before I ever let any harm come to my baby boy.

"I love you," Charli said. "Both of you."

"We love you, too," I said, my heart so full I thought it would burst. "Hey, come sit on me so he can feel both of us at the same time."

Straddling my knees, she leaned forward so that her chest was lightly pressed against Lester's back. "Like this?"

"Just like that," I said, looking down at the baby resting between us. I wrapped one hand around the back of Charli's head while holding Lester's fat little arm to my chest with the other. I pulled her face against mine and whispered against her cheek. "I never knew how perfect it would feel to hold my family in my arms."

My family... damn, that feels good to say.

Beau

Three days later we arrived back at our new home with our new baby.

Pulling Charli toward me by her hips, I kissed the tip of her nose. "Have I told you how much I love you, wife?"

"You might have mentioned it, husband, but you can tell me again."

"I love you." *Kiss.* "I love you." *Kiss.* "I love you." *Kiss.* Our son let out a little whimper, and I bent to kiss his head. "Didn't mean to leave you out, buddy. I love you, too."

Charli insisted on giving Lester a tour of the house. I tried not to laugh as she introduced the infant to the kitchen where his bottles would be prepared and to the living room where he could sit and watch Uncle Axel play football on TV. She was talking to him like he could understand every word she said, but he didn't seem to mind. He loved to hear his mommy's voice.

Carrying him up the stairs to our room, she said, "This is Mommy and Daddy's room."

Leaning over, I faux-whispered, "This is where all the action takes place, son."

Charli swatted my arm and giggled. "Stop it, Beau! His delicate little ears don't need to hear about your depravity."

"*I'm* depraved? Need I remind you of night eight of our honeymoon?" I asked with a raised eyebrow.

"Hmmm, I could use a little 'night eight' tonight," she said, reaching around me and grabbing my ass.

"Aw, hell. I'm going to need to do some warm-up exercises if we're going to do that again. I'm pretty sure I pulled a groin muscle last time."

"I'm sure I could come up with something a little less strenuous, if you're going to complain about it like an old man," she said cheekily.

"Bring it on, woman. I can handle whatever you've got for me."

"Later, baby. Right now, let's show this little guy his soon-to-be nursery. I like the blue room, but it's two doors down from ours. Do you think that's too far away?" Her brow creased with worry.

"I think it's fine, sweetheart. We have the baby monitors, so it doesn't matter if he's ten rooms away." We'd had this conversation no less than six times in the past couple days, but she was still fretting about it. "We can repaint the room right next to ours, if that would make you feel better, but if you're worried about his delicate ears, we might want a bit of a buffer."

"What do you mean?" she asked with a grin, knowing exactly what I meant.

"I mean that we're still newlyweds, and I'm going to be fucking his mother seven ways from Sunday every night," I said in a low voice directly in her ear. I flicked her lobe with my tongue before sucking it into my mouth. "Do you really want him hearing how I make Mommy scream my name when I hit that perfect spot inside her? Or how Mommy makes Daddy groan when she's swallowing his cock?"

"Beau," she moaned, "don't start with the dirty talk. We can't right now."

"Oh yes, I will. And yes, we can," I said seductively, running my open mouth up and down her neck, teasing her with my tongue and lips. "Someone seems to have grown bored with his tour," I said, taking the now sleeping Les from her arms and placing him gently on our bed. I surrounded him with pillows even though he was only a few days old and couldn't roll over yet. It was the only way Charli would be able to relax enough for what I had planned.

Walking back toward her, I let my hungry eyes rake up and down her slim, luscious body, giving her *that* look. She bit her bottom lip and gave me a shy smile as I took her hand and led her to the unfurnished room all the way at the other end of the hall. Closing the door behind us, I backed her up against the nearest wall, pressing my body against hers until she was pinned there. Letting my lips hover a mere half-inch from hers, I murmured darkly, "I need a bit of privacy for the things I like to do to you." I swiped my tongue thickly over her slightly parted lips before pushing it into her mouth, exploring and tasting every inch of the hot cavern. "I need to hear your noises. The sounds you make when I'm arousing you, making you come."

As if on cue, a deep moan emanated from her throat. "Are we about to re-enact night eight?"

"No, baby. We need a bed, a towel, and at least six strategically placed pillows for that. I promise we'll get to that later, but for now, turn around and put your hands on the wall," I ordered.

When she was in place, I knelt behind her, snaking my hands around her front to unfasten her shorts before pulling them and her underwear down her legs. "Spread your legs and show me that ass, sweet girl." She stepped out of her pants and spread her legs, arching her back so that her backside was presented gloriously in front of me. "You are perfection, Peach," I groaned just before my hands gripped her ass cheeks and spread them as I slid my tongue through her seam.

My dick was instantly hard at the first taste of her, and I lost a bit of control as I licked her, pushing my tongue deeply into her sex. Repeatedly, until she was bending farther forward, her hands high on the wall as I loved her with my lips, my teeth, my tongue. I locked my mouth over her pussy lips, sucking viciously as the tip of my tongue circled her hole.

"Oh God, Beau. I love your mouth on my pussy." Hearing her dirty words drew me in like a moth to the flame, and I plunged into her, maintaining my hard suction as I tongue-fucked her to a fast, intense orgasm. I felt her sweetness flood my mouth, and I licked and swallowed every drop of her as she braced her hands against the wall, grinding her perfect cunt in my face and moaning my name.

Smacking her firmly on the ass, I stood and took off her shirt and bra before removing my own clothes. Pulling her against me so that my erection was sandwiched between us, I took her mouth in a hard, longing kiss. "I need to fuck you, baby. Hard and dirty. That okay?"

"Do I have a choice?" she asked with a smirk, and I just lifted an eyebrow in answer. "Hands and knees?"

"Hands and knees," I confirmed, and she turned and lowered herself into position on the floor, looking over her shoulder as I towered over her, just appreciating the view for a moment before I knelt behind her. I gripped the base of my penis and rubbed the swollen head through the wetness. Her clit throbbed in rhythm with my own pulsing, and I slid my hand up and down her back, drawing out the anticipation for both of us.

"Please, Beau," she begged, pumping her hips until I wrapped my hands around her waist and pulled her back onto my waiting cock. "Yeah, baby. Like that," she moaned. "I love the way my *husband* fucks me."

God, this woman... she knew exactly what got my juices flowing. Would I ever get tired of hearing her say 'husband?' "I'm only halfway in, *sweet wife*." Her pussy clenched around my shaft, and I smiled. She liked it, too. I leaned down and licked obscenely up her spine. "You want all your husband's cock, baby?"

"Yes," she breathed. "Every hard inch."

Fuck me.

I pulled back and pushed back in, only managing about another inch. "You're too fucking tight, Peach. Soften up for me," I groaned. I reached around and feathered my fingers over her clit until a gush of wetness flooded her channel. "Fuck, yeah. Let me in, Charli."

I surged forward, taking all of her at once as she cried out with a long, "Ohhhhhh." I spread my knees, widening her legs as I began to fuck her with sharp snaps of my hips.

"Take. Every. Fucking. Hard. Inch." I punctuated every word with a harsh thrust as Charli's hands clutched at the carpet underneath her hands. "I love bottoming out in you. Making all of you mine."

"I am yours," she gasped.

I curled over her back, pressing my chest to her. Skin-to-skin. Nibbling her neck, I rode her wet heat with long, smooth strokes as one hand slid up and underneath to cup her breast and roll her firm, sensitive nipple between my finger and thumb. Angling my hips slightly, I found just... that... perfect... spot. A low, guttural groan dripped from my wife's mouth with every deep thrust. *Yeah, that's it, baby.*

"Show me you're mine, Peach. Come for me. Come *with* me."

She tightened around me until the pressure on my dick was almost intolerable, and I started to come inside her, filling her with my seed. I loved that part the most. Not just because of the delicious release, but because I was marking her from the inside out. Claiming her as mine forever. It was fucking heady.

Before Charli, I had never had emotions while fucking. It was just... well... fucking. But I *loved* loving her, and every climax with her was a million times more intense because of it.

Every one of her exhales was a soft sob, and I rested on one hand, using my other to gently tug her hair to the side so that I had access to her gorgeous face. I tilted my head down, kissing and licking her mouth tenderly, whispering my love to her.

I pulled out and collapsed on my back, pulling her down so that she was draped halfway over my body with one of her legs between mine. I could feel my cum seeping out of her and pooling on my thigh, and God help me, that gave me the deepest sense of satisfaction.

"We're getting messy," she murmured against my chest.

"I like it," I admitted, kissing the top of her head as my hand caressed her from ribs to thigh. "Mine," I whispered.

"Which part is yours?" she replied, and I could feel her smile against my chest. We had played this little game before.

I stroked a finger across her hip. "This part." A finger in her belly button, making her giggle. "This one." I kissed her pert nose. "Definitely this."

I wiggled my big toe against hers and she looked up at me. "My toe?"

"Mmhmm. You have sexy toes." I circled her nipple with the tip of my finger. "Here. One of my favorite places to kiss."

"Mine too," she said, scraping her teeth across my nipple.

I drew a heart on the curve of her shoulder because I was a big fucking sap. "Here too." Cupped her pussy. "Another fan favorite." She grinned up at me, and I reached behind her knee to pull her leg up to my waist before laying my palm on her knee. "This is also mine." Noticing her wince, I looked down at her knee and felt my heart drop when I saw a large red abrasion. "Shit, Charli. What's wrong with your knee?" I rolled her and inspected the other one. "Fuck!"

Glancing down she said, "I think it's carpet burns. From... you know..." She was smiling.

Why the fuck is she smiling?

"Christ, baby. Why didn't you tell me?"

"I didn't even realize. In case you weren't paying attention, I was otherwise occupied with other parts of my anatomy." She lifted a sardonic eyebrow at me.

Pulling her on top of me, I cupped her face with my hands. "Honey, you have to tell me if I'm hurting you. Always. Promise me." I frantically kissed every inch of her perfect, pretty face.

"Beau, calm down. It's no big deal. I like when we lose ourselves in each other."

She's telling me to calm down? After I fucked her so hard I made her knees bleed?

"I might like it rough, but I never want to hurt you, Peach."

"I know, baby." She pecked me on the lips. "I'll bet a nice bath with my sexy husband would make me feel all better." She blessed me with more of her sweet little kisses until my heart migrated back to somewhere near the vicinity of my chest. Then I gathered her in my arms and carried her to our bathroom.

CHARLI

Four hours later, after a sensual bath where Beau had gently washed my knees and kissed the perimeter of each of the carpet burns, we were sitting in our living room with all his buddies, Bristol, Blaire, and Axel. We had just polished off eight pizzas, and now we were relaxing and having a few beers as everyone passed Lester around.

The whole crew had come over to help us move all the baby's stuff up to his nursery. Allie hadn't been joking when she said they had everything little Lester James would need, including a baby bed, a glider rocker, a changing table that doubled as a dresser, and a matching armoire. We'd had to rent a U-Haul to get it all home.

Tank was holding our baby in one gigantic hand and cooing at him. It was freaking adorable. "L.J. is a cool baby," Bode proclaimed, sitting beside Tank on the couch and nursing a beer as he lightly squeezed the baby's chubby foot.

"He's a big dude," Woody added. "How much did he weigh?"

"Ten pounds and one ounce," Beau answered before I could. "Friggin' Les made a big ole baby."

"Hell yeah, he did," Hawk said, lifting his beer in a salute. "To Les and Allie."

"To Les and Allie," we all repeated, raising our own beers before drinking.

Pulling his bottle away from his lips, Cam tilted it toward my legs. "What happened to your knees, Charli?"

Trying not to blush, I said, "Oh, um, I fell earlier. Going into the, uh, the... up the stairs."

Grinning wickedly, Cam said, "You're a terrible liar, Charles. And you're blushing. What are they? Carpet burns?" He waggled his eyebrows at Beau, who was practically glaring his face off. "Fucking beast mode, Shark."

Through gritted teeth, Beau said, "Shut up, asswipe. If I wanted any shit out of you, I would squeeze your head."

"As long as you don't make me get on my knees while you do it, you brutal bastard. Poor little Charli," he crooned, knowing he was getting under Beau's skin. "Couldn't you at least have gotten her some knee pads?"

While Beau seethed, Blaire chimed in. "I can't tell you how many times I've had rug burns. Knees. Elbows. Back. It's usually from when we have to hide in the closet to screw."

"Who are you hiding from?" Woody asked with a laugh as Beau choked on his beer.

"Our kids," Axel said, shaking his head. "It's like the little shits have some kind of radar that tells them Daddy is trying to get his wiener wet."

"Yeah, we tell them there's a mouse loose in the closet, so they don't try to come in. That also explains any thumping or smacking they may hear," Blaire explained, and we all burst out laughing.

Everyone except for my husband. "Jesus fucking Christ," he groaned, closing his eyes and rubbing his forehead like he was getting a headache. He was obviously not as amused as the rest of us at the revelation of his sister's sneaky sexcapades with her husband.

Axel pointed a long finger at him and nodded sagely. "Just wait, dude. In a couple years when L.J. is older, you and Charli will be doing your own mouse hunt in the closet."

The baby let out a little whimper, and Beau was on his feet in an instant, taking him gently from Tank and kissing Les on his fat cheek. "What's wrong, son? Is my little man hungry?"

Blaire's face melted into a gushy smile at her brother's obvious infatuation with his new son. "Let me feed my handsome nephew," she said, holding out her hands and wiggling her fingers impatiently. "The guys have been hogging him, and I need me some baby snuggles. Dani is crawling everywhere now and will barely let me hold her unless she's sleepy."

"She's a friggin' nosy butt, like her mama," Axel said with a proud grin. "That kid is into everything."

I handed her the bottle I had prepared a little while ago, anticipating Lester's hungry little tummy. Seriously, the boy's appetite was like clockwork. Blaire popped the bottle into his mouth like the pro that she was and sighed, "Between Danica being mobile and the triplets being the wildest humans on the planet, I'm not sure we will survive the next couple of years. Charli, when will you have the pre-school up and running?"

"Within the next month or two, I hope. I've gotten some excellent applications, so as soon as I get my staff interviewed, hired, and trained, we should be good."

"And there's a room near Charli's office that will be a perfect little nursery for L.J., so he will be close to Mommy all the time," Beau said, putting an arm around my waist and pulling me onto his lap. "Within a couple months she's become a wife, a mother, and a business owner. And she's gonna fucking kill every bit of it." I bent to kiss him softly, loving that he had so much faith in me, but he grabbed the back of my head to press his mouth firmly against mine, sneaking a little tongue against my lips.

"Aw, hell. Here they go," Cam said with a chuckle. "I think that's our cue."

"Yeah, get the fuck out," Beau said, nuzzling my neck.

"Beau! Don't be rude! They've spent the last couple of hours helping us move an entire baby store into our house."

"You're right, Peachy." He turned to his friends with a fake grin and said, "Thanks. Now get the fuck out."

I sighed as I rose to my feet. "Please excuse my husband. We're really grateful for all your help." I went around the room, giving each of them a hug and a thank you. I got to Blaire and Bristol last, pulling them into a group hug. "And thank you for all your help setting up the nursery." They had spent over an hour helping me organize, fold, and hang little Les's clothes.

"It was fun," Blaire said. "Let's go shopping this weekend and we can buy some decorations. Then you and my cranky brother can come over for dinner. Carrie's itching to meet her new little cousin. The boys are a little confused still. We'd told them you were going to Hawaii, and the next thing they know, you have a baby. Max is now convinced that Hawaii is where babies come from."

"I tried to set him straight, but Blaire smacked me in the head," Ax said, scowling at his wife.

"Yeah, you big doofus. Because you said the word *vagina* to a two-year-old."

"He's almost three," Axel shot back.

"Lord, give me strength to deal with this man," Blaire said, rolling her eyes before kissing my sleeping son and handing him to me. She hugged me and said quietly, "He's absolutely precious, Charli. I'm so happy for you and Beau. And I'm really sorry about your friends. I didn't know Lester well, but I liked Allie a lot. I hate the circumstances, but I'm glad this little one has you two for parents now. He's a very lucky little boy."

"We're the lucky ones," I said, feeling Beau come up behind me and wrap his arms protectively around me and the baby. He did that a lot. If I was holding Lester, Beau wanted to be holding both of us.

When our guests were gone, Beau pressed tightly against my back while kissing up my neck to my ear. "You ready for bed, sweetheart?"

I twisted my head to offer him my lips for a kiss. "I'm ready," I said after he gave me a long smooch.

He took our boy from my arms. "Let me carry this chunky monkey up the stairs for you. I'll put him in bed, and you get the pillows set up." He grinned. "Then I'll get busy proving to you that night eight wasn't a fluke."

"If you can reproduce those results again, I'll be very impressed," I teased, leading him up the stairs.

"O' ye of little faith," he sang, patting my bottom when we reached the second floor. Once in our room, I put on a sexy little nightgown and was startled to hear Beau's voice before I realized it was coming from the baby monitor. He was whispering to our son, and I sat on the bed and shamelessly eavesdropped.

"Good night, my sweet boy. Daddy loves you. And Mommy does, too." I heard a soft rustling as he laid the baby in the crib. "She's the best, you know. She's sweet and smart and so beautiful, and you're a lucky kid to have a mommy like her."

Tears filled my eyes and dripped down my face until I heard the nursery door quietly close through the monitor. I swiped the tears away and started arranging the pillows on the bed. When I turned around, my husband was leaning against the door jamb watching me with his burning green eyes. *Lord, he is yummy.* I crooked a finger at him, and he stalked toward me, pulling his shirt over his head as those eyes devoured me.

My heart clenched with the realization that all my dreams had come true. I had a beautiful son sleeping down the hall, and I was married to the sweetest, grumpiest, sexiest man alive, who was also madly in love with me.

My. Heart. Was. Full.

Epilogue

TWO YEARS LATER

CHARLI

I spun the platform and held the icing smoother vertically along the side of the cake. *Almost perfect. Almost...*

A tiny finger inserted itself into the bright blue buttercream frosting, forming a deep groove in my almost perfect decorating efforts. I stopped the spinning and cut my exasperated eyes to the face beside me, which now had the tiny blue finger stuffed in his tiny mouth.

"Das good, Mommy."

I put on my best maternal glare and leaned down nose-to-nose with my son, but he wasn't fooled even a little bit. In the face of my scariest look, he just giggled and stuck his soggy finger in my mouth. *Okay, toddler slobber aside, that tasted pretty damned good.* Lester James Atwood's birthday cake was probably going to look like shit, but at least the flavor was going to kick ass.

"L.J.," I said sternly, "what did Mommy say about keeping your fingers off the cake?"

From his perch on the counter beside me, he looked up at me with innocent green eyes. "I sowwy, Mommy." He looked down contritely before looking back up at me from under mile-long lashes. I had seen that expression many times before. It was my son's *sorry, not sorry* look, and I couldn't resist it.

Sucker!

Aiming for a patient tone, I said, "I'm trying to make you a Spiderman cake for your birthday party like you asked for, sweetheart. Don't you want a Spiderman cake?"

"No! Superman!" he shrieked with a big grin.

Well, shit. At least he didn't request a Hulk cake, so the blue frosting would still work.

"Then keep your grubby little paws off the cake," I said, kissing his adorable button nose. "Understood?"

"'Kay, Mommy."

I turned to the mixing bowl and scooped up some more frosting to cover the part Lester had ruined. When I turned back, there was another deep divot in the cake, and I looked suspiciously at the two-year-old little boy who now had blue frosting around his mouth, on his nose, and somehow a dab on his left eyebrow. "Lester Jaaaames," I scolded, receiving only a guileless stare in return.

I heard keys hit the table beside the front door, and L.J.'s wide eyes went to mine, reflecting my own excitement at what that meant. *Daddy's home!*

"Peach?"

"In the kitchen," I said, trying to wipe our son's face, but he wasn't having it. He was trying to squirm his way off the counter, so I picked him up and set him safely on the floor. The kid was off like a shot, meeting my husband just as he walked into our bright, modern kitchen.

"There's my boy!" Beau yelled over L.J.'s scream of delight, lifting our son over his head before pulling him down to rest on his hip. It was the same thing every time Daddy walked in the door. L.J. acted like his father had done a three-year stint in a Siberian prison, rather than having been at the office for a couple hours. "Where are my kisses?" my husband asked, ignoring the blue frosting all over our toddler's face as they smooshed their lips together.

"I misted you, Daddy."

"I missed you, too, little buddy." He turned and looked me up and down with a heated gaze that made me squeeze my thighs together, his voice low and smooth when he said, "I missed Mommy, too." I pursed my lips, throwing him a kiss, and he threw me a suggestive wink before turning back to L.J. "Hey, I'm just curious, but did you happen to get into the frosting today?"

"I wuuuuuv fwosting," he said in response, happily scrunching his little shoulders up around his ears.

"Uh-huh," his dad said good-naturedly. "I'm going to take that as an admission of guilt. As if I needed more evidence." He swiped his finger through the frosting on L.J.'s eyebrow and wiped it on a dish towel. I smirked at my husband, whose face was smeared with blue from kissing our son. "What?" he asked, and I just shook my head.

"Just glad you're home."

Holding L.J. on his hip with one arm, he sneaked the other one around my waist and said seductively against my ear, "I'm glad I'm home, too, gorgeous."

Oh. He's in that *kind of mood.*

I swiped the magnetic kitchen timer from the refrigerator and set it for fifteen minutes. "L.J., don't you need to finish your Lego building you made for Daddy?"

My husband knew the drill, widening his eyes at our little boy. "Did you build something for me? I was hoping I would come home and get to see one of your buildings. Would you go finish that for Daddy?"

"Okay," he said excitedly, wiggling until Beau put him down as I pushed the start button on the timer and handed it to him.

"Hurry! Go to your playroom and finish," I said, and L.J. took off.

As he scampered from the room, Beau wrapped his arms around me from behind. "Do you ever get tired of outsmarting our son?"

I pointed to the jacked-up frosting on the cake. "The cute little fart messed up twenty minutes of hard work, so I don't feel one bit sorry for him. And he manipulates me all the time with that little angel face and those dadgum eyes."

Beau and the older Les could have passed for brothers, and L.J. was the spitting image of his biological father. He had green eyes that were a shade lighter than Beau's, but they were close enough that he looked like he could have sprung directly from my husband's loins. And I was a total sucker for both of my men and their green eyes.

"Well, I would like to manipulate *you*, especially in this apron. It's very June Cleaver. Just add some pearls, and I'd have you bent over this counter before you could say 'Beaver.'" He yanked me toward him.

"Good to know you have a 1950s housewife fetish," I said, wrapping my arms around his neck.

"I have a Charli fetish," he said, lowering his mouth, his lips sucking at mine before pressing his tongue into my mouth. As always, I melted against him as he kissed me deeply, his fingers in my hair and his palms against my cheek. "Seriously though, this fucking apron is doing things to me, baby," he mumbled against my lips before sliding his hands down to cup my ass and grind his hard-on against me.

"Maybe I'll wear it to bed tonight," I said.

"Mmmm, *just* the apron, right?"

"I might be able to dig up a pearl necklace and earrings."

"Fuck yeah," he said pulling back and looking at me before he started chuckling. "You have blue all over your face."

"That's because you have blue all over *your* face, compliments of our little frosting monger."

"Do I really?" he asked, swiping a hand over his mouth and rolling his eyes at the blue smear there.

I pulled out of his arms and grabbed the dish towel on the counter, wetting a corner of it under the faucet. When I turned back, I realized there was a new flaw in the cake frosting, this one definitely *not* from a toddler-sized finger. Looking at the guilty face of my husband, I scowled at him. "Beau Atwood! You're as bad as your son!"

I wiped his hand and face with the towel as he grinned unapologetically. "What can I say? I'm a scoundrel," he said, palming my breasts.

"Oh, I know you're a scoundrel. That's why I married you."

He took the towel from me and wiped the telltale frosting from my face. "Your frosting is really delicious, by the way. You're so amazing at everything you do."

"Are you trying to sweet talk your way out of trouble?"

"Is it working?" he asked with a roguish grin. I gave him a wry look, even though his smile was sexy as fuck. Peering into the mixing bowl, he said, "It looks like you might have some left over. Maybe we could smear it all over each other later and play Sexy Smurfs. You could be Slutty Smurfette, and I could be Horny Smurf."

I laughed at my husband. "I don't think those are actual Smurfs. And I thought we were playing June and Ward tonight."

"We can be the Cleavers tomorrow night. I would hate to let this frosting go to waste."

"Always keeping things spicy while also maintaining efficiency," I said, kissing him on the nose before turning to one of the kitchen drawers and pulling out a small, wrapped gift. "I have a present for you," I said as I handed it to my husband.

"It's L.J.'s birthday, not mine," Beau said, but he was grinning.

"That doesn't mean I can't surprise my fine-ass husband. Just open it." I chewed my bottom lip as he turned the package over in his hands.

"Why do you look so nervous, Peach?" He leaned toward me and whispered, "Is it a butt plug or something?"

"No, you perv," I said, exasperated, "it is not a butt plug." I chewed anxiously on my thumbnail. "Would you just open it, please?"

"Okay, Peach. Calm your tits. I'll open it." He leveled an amused look at me before sliding his finger under the paper and tearing it off. He was still smiling when he lifted the lid off the box, but when he looked inside, his smile slowly faded.

Oh. Shit.

He stared at the little stick for what seemed like a half an hour without speaking. "Beau?" I said quietly. "You're making me really nervous here."

His eyes finally lifted from the stick to me, and I saw the sheen of tears in his eyes. "Is this for real? You're... are you..."

I gnawed on my bottom lip and nodded. "I'm pregnant." Beau's broad chest was heaving like he couldn't quite catch his breath. "Are you mad?"

"Mad? Hell no, I'm not mad. I'm fucking ecstatic, Peach!" He wrapped his arms around my waist, lifting me and spinning me in a circle. "We're having another baby!" Then he dropped me to my feet, his eyes wide. "Shit! Did I hurt you? Or the baby?"

"No, you didn't hurt us," I said with a laugh. "You're really happy? I know you said you wanted to wait another year before we tried to adopt again, but then... well, *this* happened..."

"Of course, I'm happy. I freaking love being a Dad." He looked down at me with so much excitement and tenderness in his eyes that I was finding it hard to swallow. "The only thing equal to it is being your husband." He ran his knuckles down my cheek before kissing me thoroughly, and that was about all I could take. The tears were dripping steadily down my face, causing Beau to pull back and look at me quizzically.

"What's wrong, baby? What did I say?" he asked, gently swiping my tears away.

"Nuh-nuh-nothing," I weeped. "Just pregnancy hormones, I think."

"Awww, sweetheart. Is that why you cried like a baby when I accidentally hit that squirrel with my truck yesterday?"

A fresh round of tears started as Beau held my cheek to his chest. "Oh gawwwwd, that was so sad," I wailed. "He looked so young. Not a baby, but I'll bet he was like a teenaged squirrel. He was probably out gathering nuts for the winter for his family because the daddy squirrel was trying to teach him some responsibility. And now their whole squirrel family might starve to death. We should find where they live and take them some extra acorns or something."

I knew I sounded utterly ridiculous, but my heart was broken for the squirrel family, and I couldn't help the squirrel-related word vomit coming from my mouth. "And can you just imagine when little Sammy didn't come home last night? His parents were probably worried sick. Probably thought he was dead in a ditch. Ohhhh, his poor mother! What if she went out looking for him and found him all flat and squished in the street? No mother should ever have to go through that."

Beau's entire body was shaking when he choked out, "Who is Sammy?"

"Sammy the Squirrel. The one you murdered," I said lifting my head and glaring at him, instantly going from sad to angry. "Are you laughing at me, Beau Atwood?"

He rolled his lips inward and shook his head rapidly back and forth. "Of course not. And I'm very sorry about... uh..."

"Sammy."

"Yeah, Sammy. It was an accident, baby, and I should have been more careful," my husband said solicitously. "Tell you what, I don't have Sammy's family's address, so I'll just leave a can of Planters outside in the yard for them. They can drop by when they have time. Okay, angel?"

I snuggled back into my husband's strong chest and sighed, "I think that would be nice. Thank you, Beau."

He stroked his hands up and down my back and kissed the top of my head. "Do you think we should send a flower arrangement to Sammy's funeral?"

I jerked my head up and frowned. "Well, now you're just being ridiculous, Beau. Squirrels don't—" That's when he lost it, covering his mouth with his hand to try and hide his laughter. I tried to get mad, but his laughter was contagious, and then we were both practically hysterical. "I'm sorry," I gasped. "Damn stupid hormones have got me talking crazy."

He kissed my lips through his smile over and over. "It's okay, my sweet girl. I love you so much, even when you're acting a wee bit crazy." Then his face turned serious as his hands dropped to my belly. "Are you okay? Have you been sick? Does anything hurt?"

"Yes, kind of, and no. I'm perfectly okay. I've been a little nauseous, but so far, I haven't thrown up. Eating a piece of toast as soon as I wake up helps. And nothing hurts."

"Well, I'm going to rub your feet tonight even if they don't hurt. And I'll bring you toast every morning before you get out of bed." He kept one hand on my stomach, but the other one was gently cupping my face. "I'm so happy, Charli."

"Me too," I whispered. We heard L.J.'s timer go off, and I stood on my tiptoes and kissed his lips. "Time's up. Go see your son's Lego masterpiece."

Beau grinned as he backed away from me. "I'll bet he's going to be an architect one day."

"Or possibly a cake thief," I said with a laugh. "Will you keep him entertained so I can finish this cake?"

"I sure will, little mama." He winked before turning to go marvel at our little boy's creation. He was such a good daddy, always spending time with L.J. when he got home from work because he knew I had him all day at the preschool.

Ten minutes later, I was finally getting the frosting situation straightened out when Beau came back in the kitchen, pushing a stool under me and forcing me to sit while I finished working on the cake. Five minutes after that, he brought me a glass of iced water because he said I needed to stay hydrated for the baby. A half hour later he caught me carrying a small cooler of ice out to the patio and almost lost his damn mind, snatching it away from me and scolding me like he had caught me trying to lift a Buick.

This man is so freaking sweet, but he's going to drive me insane, I thought with a grin.

Beau

L.J.'s second birthday party was in full swing. He was having a blast running around the back yard with his cousins, which was good, because the little dude was all hyped up on sugar and excitement. He would sleep well tonight when he finally crashed.

I was washing food platters at the sink when Blaire wandered in and leaned up against the cabinet, swiping a carrot from a vegetable tray. "So, when is she due?" she asked, biting the carrot in half with a loud snap.

I turned around so quickly, I slopped suds all over the floor. Bending over to wipe up my mess, I asked, "Who's doing what?"

"Charli. When is the baby due?"

"What... I mean... did she... huh?" *Just play dumb, Atwood.*

"Don't fuck with me, Beau. I know she's pregnant." At my consciously blank look, she rolled her eyes. "Number one, she's been drinking water all evening instead of having beer or wine." I started to interrupt, but she held up a hand to silence me. "Number two, you've been strutting around like a fucking peacock the entire party. And number three, you haven't let her stand up for more than two seconds at a time."

I couldn't help the grin that curled my lips upward. I was just so goddamn happy, and I was bursting to tell someone. "Well, she has an appointment on Monday, so we'll find out more then. Were there anymore clues, because we're trying to keep this a secret at least until then?"

Blaire tilted her head to the side and said, "Only that she cried at practically every single present that L.J. opened." She pointed the remains of her carrot stick at me. "Pregnancy hormones are a bitch, am I right?"

"Oh, my God, yes. There was a squirrel incident, and I thought I was going to have to medicate her."

My sister pushed off from the counter and wrapped her arms around me. "I have no idea what that means, but congratulations, big bro. I'm so happy for y'all."

"Me too," I said, holding my sister and trying not to let my emotions get the best of me. "I'm just worried about making sure L.J. doesn't get jealous. He's been the baby of the family for two years now."

"Yeah, I had to worry about that with Carrie when the boys were born because having triplet infants takes up a shitload of time. I just tried to make her a part of everything. She's a little mother hen anyway, so she loved helping with everything, especially bath time. And we always made sure she had a job, like putting on their socks or holding one of their bottles at feeding time."

"L.J.'s getting older now, so I can take him fishing and stuff like Dad used to do with me when you were a baby. It made me feel special that he spent time with just me."

"Until I got old enough to tag along and annoy the shit out of you."

I laughed at the memories of my dad and I taking Blaire fishing. "You were just so goddamn loud. We never caught a thing when you went with us."

"But we had fun anyway," she said.

"Yeah right," I teased, kissing her on the forehead. "I guess you were a pretty good little sister."

"I still am, mister. I'm the best freaking sister in the world. Look at all the practice you got with my heathens. That's why you're a total rockstar dad with L.J., and I know you will be with this new baby, too."

"Thanks, Blaire," I said, squeezing her a little tighter.

"Hey, is everything okay?" Charli asked, walking into the kitchen and finding me hugging my sister.

"Blaire guessed our little secret," I said, and my wife's mouth popped into a little O. "Apparently, you cry too much, and I'm some kind of peacock-slash-mother hen hybrid."

Charli's face broke into a grin as Blaire crossed to her and embraced her. "I'm so excited for both of you! Now you make sure to call and let me know what the doctor says on Monday."

"We will," Charli said. "I'm excited, too."

She and Blaire hugged and jumped up and down happily in place until I barked, "Charli, no jumping!"

"See what I mean?" Blaire said, shooting me a look before looking back at my wife. "Mother freaking hen." In an act of supreme maturity, I stuck my tongue out at my sister.

That night after everyone left, Charli and I tag-teamed getting L.J. to bed, me giving him a bath and her reading his bedtime story. I stood in the doorway of our son's room, watching my wife read to him as my heart thumped every single beat for the two of them. *Well, I guess for the three of them now*, I thought happily.

When she was done with the third reading of *Goodnight Moon*, she kissed his soft little cheek before saying, "Okay, sweetie. That's it for tonight."

"One more kiss, Mommy?" he asked, and she willingly obliged. "Gimme Mallie and Popples," he said, reaching out his tiny hand for the picture on his nightstand. We had kept a picture of Allie and Les in his nursery since we brought him home, and he had recently started asking who they were. We explained that they were

Mama Allie and Poppa Les, which he promptly garbled into *Mallie* and *Popples*. It was so cute that the nicknames had stuck.

Because L.J. was so young, he didn't understand DNA and brain tumors and war and sacrifice, so we had simply told him that the people in the picture were his guardian angels and that they loved him very much. We would tell him the whole story when he was old enough to comprehend it, but for now he was happy to say goodnight to his Mallie and Popples when we tucked him in.

"Night-night. Wub you," he said, kissing the picture before handing it back to Charli, who arranged it carefully beside his bed so that Les and Allie were facing their son as he snuggled down under the covers. Logically, she knew that it was just a picture, and the people in it couldn't really see L.J., but she went through the same ritual every night, usually accompanied by a stream of silent tears as soon as our little boy closed his eyes.

I watched as my wife stroked L.J.'s blonde curls and spoke soft words that I couldn't quite make out to him. She reached up and swiped the telltale wetness from her face, and my heart constricted. Charli had the sweetest, most tender heart of anyone I knew, and my constricted heart began to swell with the love I had for my woman.

When L.J.'s breathing evened and deepened, she stood quietly and turned to find me still leaning with my shoulder against the door jamb. Her gaze swept me from the bottom up, from my bare feet, over my lounge pants, up my bare torso, and straight into my eyes. Then she gave me a look that melted my underwear as she walked slowly toward me, her hips swaying enticingly as she approached.

"Did you bring my apron upstairs?"

"I did. Did you find some pearls?"

"Mmhmm," she said, nodding as my hands dropped to circle her still-slim waist and pull her toward me. It hit me then that very soon, this flat stomach would be swollen with my child, and my cock instantly responded, lengthening and thickening against her tummy.

She looked between us at my very obvious erection and then smiled up at me. "If I had known pearls turned you on that much, I would have been wearing them every day."

"It wasn't the pearls, Peach," I said, walking her backward into the hallway and quietly closing our son's door. "I was thinking about how you're going to look in a few months with our baby growing inside you."

"You mean fat," she said dryly.

"No, I mean full and glowing and so goddamn beautiful I will have to force myself to go to work every day instead of staying home and sticking my dick in you every time I look at you."

"Well, that would be kinda hard since I'll be at work during the week," she said. I could feel a frown furrowing my forehead, and she tugged my head down so that she could press her lips against the creases there. "I can see your mind spinning, Atwood, and don't start any of your macho shit with me. I'm going to continue working. Pregnant women do it every day."

"I'm not worried about those other women. Just you. But you're right about working." Her eyebrows raised at my admission, and I grinned. *See? I can be reasonable.* "You won't be happy unless you're surrounded by children all day, and the only thing that matters to me as much as your safety is your happiness." And just so she wouldn't think I was a total pushover, I gave her my half-strength glare. Not the pissed off one, but the one that said, *I mean business, woman.* "But I do expect you to do everything the doctor says and not be stubborn. If she says at any time during your pregnancy that you should be on bedrest, then your pretty little feet will not touch the floor until the baby is born. Understood?"

"Understood. Now, are you going to stand out here in the hallway being bossy or are we going to have a little fun?"

"I'm not bossy," I argued, knowing damn well that I was bossy as hell.

"Yeah, right," she said, taking my hand and leading me down the hall to our room. "You already nixed our sexy Smurf game."

I gave her a chagrined smirk. I had Googled the effects of artificial dyes on fetal development earlier and told her there was no way in hell I was smearing frosting with blue food coloring all over my pregnant wife. I had even asked her *very nicely* to please try and avoid foods with artificial dyes while she was pregnant.

"We still have the Dirty Cleavers game," I said with a grin as I shamelessly checked out her ass swiveling in front of me. She led me into our room, and I went directly to the closet, pulling on a charcoal gray suit with a white shirt. Sliding my thumb across the line of ties, I stopped at a red silk one, slipping it from the tie hanger and looping it around my neck. I quickly tied it into a perfect knot in the mirror on the back of the closet door and straightened it before buttoning my jacket.

"I'm readyyyy," Charli called out from the bedroom, and the sound of her voice had my dick pressing hard against the zipper of my trousers.

"June, you get your sexy, pregnant ass in the kitchen where you belong, and wait for your husband to get home and fuck you," I called back, unable to stop smiling.

"Okay, Ward," she said with a giggle just before I heard our bedroom door click softly shut. I gave her two minutes before I headed downstairs and fucked my apron-and-pearl-wearing wife all over the damn kitchen.

An hour later, we were back in our bed, our arms around each other as we kissed. Slowly. Languidly. Just tasting and feeling each other. "You know I love you, right?"

"I know, baby," she said, her lips softly kissing the hollow just below my bottom lip.

"I know I'm sometimes grumpy and bossy."

"Don't forget overbearing and overprotective," she said, and I could feel her smile against my skin.

"Yeah, that too." I lifted her chin with my knuckle so that I could see her eyes shining in the darkness. "I'm only like that because I love you so much. You and L.J. and our little Peach Pit are the most important things in my life."

"Peach Pit?" she asked amusedly.

"Uh-huh," I said, rolling her onto her back as I hovered over her and splayed my hand across her belly.

Charli smoothed her hand up my face and sifted it through my hair. "I know your secret, Atwood. You're not nearly as grumpy as you let on. In fact, I think you're a big softy."

"Guilty as charged," I said, smiling against her lips. "But let's keep that our little secret."

"Beau?"

"Yes, Peach?" I asked, rubbing my nose against hers.

"Can you go get L.J.? I want us all to be together tonight."

"Sure, baby." I turned on the lamp beside the bed and got Charli some pajamas from her drawer before getting myself a pair of underwear. Turning the lamp back off, I went to our son's room and picked him up.

"Daddy?" he mumbled sleepily as I held him against my chest.

"I've got you, baby boy. I'm taking you to Mommy and Daddy's bed." I carried him into our room and nestled him next to Charli. She curled her body around him, and I did the same to her, wrapping my arm around both of them as I sighed with contentment.

I had everything I needed right here in my arms.
And I wasn't feeling the least bit grumpy.

Also By Jade

Thank you for reading **Dauntless Protector**. Did you know that one of the most important ways you can support indie authors is by leaving them a nice review? So, if you would be so kind, please leave me a review on Amazon. Here is the link to my Amazon author page: https://amazon.com/author/jadedollston

Did you enjoy reading about Axel and Blaire in this book? Well, they have their very own book, my debut novel, **Delay of Game**? You can read it here: https://mybook.to/delayofgameJD It's free to read on Kindle Unlimited!

Dauntless Protector was the first book in the **Fierce Protectors Series**. The rest of Beau's buddies will be getting their own books, starting with Tank in **Devoted Protector**. His release is scheduled for January 31, 2023, but you can pre-order it on Amazon now by clicking this link: https://mybook.to/devotedprotector

Feel free to message me on Facebook or Insta and let me know which of these hotties you're most excited about.

Meet the Men of the Fierce Protectors Series
Beau "Shark" Atwood
Waylon "Tank" Hanford
Camden "Cam" Fitz
Mario "Woody" Diaz
Bode
Tate "Hawk" Gentry

Check out my website or hit me up on my socials by clicking the links below.

You can also check out my author's page on facebook by searching for Jade's Kiss & Tell.

DEVOTED PROTECTOR
Coming January 31, 2023

Three years ago, **Bristol Hopkins** swore to her fiancé on his deathbed that she would never give her heart away to another man. She even had rules to ensure that she would never fall in love again.

Rule One – No feelings.
Rule Two – No staying the night.
Rule Three – No receiving oral.
Rule Four – One-night stands only.

Then she met former Navy SEAL, **Waylon "Tank" Hanford**, a six-foot-eight mountain of muscles, and they spent a glorious night together in her bed. Waylon was a sweet and generous lover—thank God because the man was massive *everywhere.*

Rule Two flew right out of the window because they couldn't stay off each other long enough for him to leave.

The next morning, the guilt and regrets creeped in. Even though Waylon would be any woman's dream man, she couldn't break any more rules by seeing him again.

Despite her best efforts, she found it impossible to push him away because the biggest thing about Waylon Hanford was his heart. One-by-one, the rules were broken until only Rule One remained.

No. Feelings.

Oops. Too late.

Playlist

Heaven by Warrant
   Naughty Girl by Beyoncé
   Bad Girls by Donna Summer
   Super Freak by Rick James
   Shivers by Ed Sheeran
   Hot in Herre by Nelly
   I Can Love You Like That by John Michael Montgomery
   Waiting for a Girl Like You by Foreigner
   Candy Shop by 50 Cent
   Milkshake by Kelis
   Grenade by Bruno Mars
   With Arms Wide Open by Creed
   Taps Bugle Call

Acknowledgments

First of all, thank you so much to my **readers** (hopefully, I'm not being overconfident by making that plural). It means so much that you took a chance on a newbie author, and I appreciate the time you took to read **Dauntless Protector.** I love when readers reach out to me while they're reading, so feel free to do so on my social media platforms that are listed on the "Also by Jade" page.

My undying gratitude goes out to the lovely **TL Swan**, who has encouraged so many of us to become authors. I've never felt anything except love, support, and encouragement from you, and it gives me the strength to get through the hard times that inevitably come while writing, editing, formatting, and the million other behind-the-scenes things we do to get a book out. Lady, you are one amazing author and a damn good person.

To my fellow **Cygnets,** our group is absolutely the best, most supportive group in the world, and I'll fight anyone who disagrees with me. I always know that I can ask a (dumb) question and receive some excellent and honest replies. Anything from blurb help to formatting... you ladies have helped me from start to finish on both of my books.

Lizzie and Lakshmi, you two have been amazing beta readers and an insightful source of opinions and knowledge. Lizzie, you've been with me from the beginning, and I treasure your friendship and the confidence you give me almost every day. You are AMAZING! Lakshmi, I'm so glad I found you. You're funny and smart, and I love the links you send me (wink wink), even though you distract me from editing.

To my ARC readers and street team: God, I don't even have words to say what you mean to me. Thank you for taking a chance on an unknown author and for pimping my book to the masses. I truly treasure each and every one of you and love our conversations in the facebook groups.

To Chrisandra of Chrisandra's Corrections: First of all, you should win some type of award for putting up with me. I was looking for an editor, and I found a friend, a human sounding-board, and a partner in crime. When I was down on myself, you kicked my ass into believing I was enough. I don't think you can even comprehend what you've done for me since I've met you. {Cue *Wind Beneath My Wings*.} Thank you for sharing my passion for these books and for our late-night chats that I hope never become public. Eek! And thank you for talking me down when I get neurotic. You have the patience of a saint.

To Katie Evans, PA extraordinaire: You've taken a nervous, slightly insane person and turned her into a nervous, slightly insane AUTHOR. You made me believe in myself again, and I can never thank you enough. Having you in my corner gives me a confidence boost and makes me want to be a better writer. Thank you for always checking on me and for being so much more than a PA. {Cue the theme from *The Golden Girls*}

AK Landow and **Carolina Jax**, I'm not sure how I would survive this journey without you two and our daily group messages. Carolina, what started out as chatting about football romance has turned into a beautiful friendship. You are such a positive person, and you make me smile every single day with your humor and constant encouragement. AK, my sistah from another mistah... you just get me. I'm so happy to have found someone with the same sense of humor as me. (Okay, I'll admit that's a little scary.) I love your "girl power" spirit and the way you lift other women up and make us stronger. I'm considering buying you a cheerleader suit and pompoms so you can make little videos for me and Carolina. I promise we won't share them with anyone except your husband. (You can thank me later.)

To BJ Alpha: Holy hell, woman, I never would have made it through this without you. You are so kind, positive, and willing to share your knowledge with others. You are truly one of my favorite people in the world. Thank you for being there to answer questions from the annoying noob and for always making me smile.

About Author

Jade Dollston is a Texas author who loves reading, Doritos, and rum. She is married to her high school sweetheart, and they have one amazing daughter.

Her love of reading all things smutty has turned into a love of writing all things smutty. She enjoys a diverse selection of romance, and this is reflected in her writing style. Be prepared to laugh, cry, cringe, and fan your face, possibly all in a single chapter.

Jade is so excited to share her work with the world and hopes that you enjoy reading the words from her heart... and other parts of her anatomy.

Made in the USA
Monee, IL
03 January 2023